CAPTAIN ANTIFER

BY
JULES VERNE

Fredonia Books
Amsterdam. The Netherlands

Captain Antifer

by
Jules Verne

ISBN: 1-58963-322-9

Copyright © 2001 by Fredonia Books

Reprinted from the 1895 edition

Fredonia Books
Amsterdam, The Netherlands
http://www.fredoniabooks.com

In order to make original editions of historical works
available to scholars at an economical price, this
facsimile of the original edition of 1895 is
reproduced from the best available copy and has
been digitally enhanced to improve legibility, but the
text remains unaltered to retain historical
authenticity.

CAPTAIN ANTIFER.

CHAPTER I.

IT is September 9th, 1831. The captain left his cabin at six o'clock. The sun is rising, or to speak more exactly, its light is illuminating the lower clouds in the east, for its disk is still below the horizon. A long luminous effluence plays over the surface of the sea, which is broken into gentle waves by the morning breeze.

After a calm night there is every promise of a fine day—one of those September days in which the temperate zone occasionally rejoices at the decline of the hot season.

The captain rests against the skylight on the poop, places the telescope to his right eye, and sweeps the horizon.

Lowering the telescope he approaches the man at the wheel—a grey-bearded, keen-sighted old man—who blinks as he looks at him.

"When did you come on duty?"

"At four o'clock, sir."

The two men speak a language that no European would understand unless he had sailed in the Levant. It is a dialect of Turkish and Syriac.

"Nothing new?"

B

" Nothing, sir."

" And you have sighted no ship since the morning ? "

" Only one—a large three-master, which would have crossed us on the opposite tack, and I luffed a point so as to leave her as far off as possible."

" You did well. And now ? "

The captain looked searchingly round the horizon.

" Ready about," he shouted loudly.

The men on watch ran to their stations. The helm was put down, the sheets were shortened in, the ship came up in the wind and went off on the opposite tack towards the north-west.

She was a brigantine of four hundred tons, a merchant vessel used as a yacht. The captain had under his orders a mate and fifteen men, whose jacket and cap and wide trousers and sea-boots were those of the mariners of Eastern Europe.

There was no name on the brigantine, either under the counter or at the bow. There was no flag. To avoid any salute the brigantine changed her course whenever the look-out reported a sail in sight.

Was she then a pirate—for pirates were not unknown in those days in these parts—which feared pursuit ? No. A search for arms on board would have been in vain. And it was not with so small a crew that a vessel would run the risk of so dangerous a trade.

Was she a smuggler working along the coast or from one island to another ? By no means. The keenest custom-house officer might have gone down into her hold, over-hauled her cargo, dived into her packages, ransacked her cases, without discovering any dutiable merchandise. To tell the truth she had no cargo at all. She carried provisions for several years in her hold, and in the lazarette there were three oak casks, strongly hooped with iron ; the rest was mere ballast, heavy ballast to enable her to carry so large a spread of canvas.

Perhaps you may think that these three barrels contained powder or some other explosive ?

Evidently not, for none of the indispensable precautions were taken in entering the store-room in which they were kept.

Besides, not one of the sailors could have given you any information on the subject—neither on the brigantine's destination, nor on the motives which made her change her course whenever a ship appeared in sight, nor on the goings to and fro during the fifteen months she had been at sea, nor even on her position at the present moment, sometimes under full sail, sometimes under hardly any at all, sometimes on an inland sea, sometimes on a boundless ocean. During this inexplicable voyage what high lands had been sighted which the captain had immediately steered away from! What islands had been discovered, which the helm had at once been shifted to avoid! Looking at the log-book, you would have found the strangest changes of course which neither the caprices of the wind nor the appearances of the sky could possibly explain. That was a secret between the captain—a grizzly man of forty-six—and a personage of lofty mien, who at the moment appeared at the companion—

" Nothing ? " he asked.

" Nothing, your Excellency," was the reply.

A shrug of the shoulders betraying some annoyance terminated this conversation of four words. Then the personage went down the steps and regained his cabin. There he stretched himself on a couch and abandoned himself to a kind of torpor. He could not have been more motionless if sleep had taken possession of him, and yet he was not asleep. He seemed to be under the influence of some fixed idea.

He might be fifty years old. His tall stature, his powerful head, his abundant hair, with the grey showing in it, his large beard spreading over his chest, his black eyes with their keen glances, his proud but evidently gloomy physiognomy, the dignity of his bearing, indicated a man of noble birth. A large burnous braided at the sleeves fringed with many-coloured scales, enveloped him from shoulders to feet, and on his head he wore a greenish cap with a black tassel.

Two hours later his breakfast was brought in to him by a boy; it was laid on a rolling table fixed to the floor of the cabin, which was covered with a thick carpet diapered with raised flowers. He scarcely touched the dainty dishes, but devoted his chief attention to the hot and perfumed coffee, served in two small finely chased silver cups. Then a narghili was placed before him crowned with scented fumes, and with the amber mouthpiece between his lips he resumed his reverie amid the fragrant vapours of latakia.

Part of the day was thus passed, while the brigantine, gently cradled on the billows, continued her uncertain course over the sea.

About four o'clock his Excellency arose, took a few turns backwards and forwards, stopped before the light ports open to the breeze, looked away to the horizon, and stood before a sort of trap-door which was covered by a piece of carpet. This door swung open by pressing the foot on one of the angles, and disclosed the way down into the store-room beneath the cabin-floor.

There lay side by side the three casks we have spoken of. The distinguished personage stooped over the trap and remained in that attitude for some seconds, as if the sight of the casks had hypnotized him. Then he stood upright.

"No," he murmured, "no hesitation! If I cannot find an unknown island where I can bury them in secret, it would be better to throw them into the sea!"

He shut down the trap-door and replaced the carpet; then he went to the companion stairs and mounted to the poop.

It was five o'clock in the afternoon. There was no change in the weather. The sky was dappled with white clouds. Barely heeling to the gentle breeze, the vessel glided along on the port tack, leaving a light lacework of foam to vanish in her wake.

His Excellency slowly looked round the clear horizon. Afar off, at a distance of from fourteen to fifteen miles, he could see moderately high land ; but there was no sharp ridge to break the line of sea and sky.

The captain walking towards him was received by the inevitable—

"Nothing ? "

Which provoked the inevitable reply,—

" Nothing, your Excellency."

The personage remained silent for a few minutes. Then he went off and sat down on one of the seats, while the captain walked to windward; and in an excited way he worked about with the telescope.

" Captain ? " he said at last.

" What does your Excellency desire ? "

" To know where we are exactly."

The captain took a large scale chart and opened it out on the deck.

" Here," he answered, pointing with his pencil to where a line of latitude crossed a meridian.

"At what distance from that island to the east ? "

" Twenty-two miles."

" And from that land ? "

" About twenty-six."

" No one on board knows where we are just now ? "

" No one, save you and I, your Excellency."

"Not even on what sea we are ? "

" We have been sailing so many different courses for so long that the best of seamen could not tell you."

" Ah ! Why has ill-fortune prevented us from reaching some island that has escaped the search of other navigators, or if not an island, an islet, or even a rock of which I alone should know the position ? There would I bury this treasure, and in a voyage of a few days I could recover it, if ever the time came for me to return ! "

And so saying he lapsed into silence. With a long look down over the taffrail into the water, which was so transparent that he could see quite eighty feet beneath him, he returned to the captain, and with a certain vehemence exclaimed,—

"I will throw my riches into the sea."

"It will never give them up again, your Excellency."

"Let them perish rather than fall into the hands of my enemies or those who are unworthy of them."

"As you please."

"If before to-night we have not discovered some unknown island, those three casks shall be thrown into the sea."

"Ay, ay, your Excellency!" replied the captain, who at once gave orders to haul a little closer to windward.

His Excellency returned to the stern and, sitting down on the deck, resumed the dreamy state which was habitual to him.

The sun was sinking rapidly. At this time of year, a fortnight before the equinox, it would set but a few degrees from the west. That is to say in exactly the direction the captain was looking. Was there in this direction any high promontory on the shore of the continent or on some island? Impossible, for the chart showed no island within a radius of from fifteen to twenty miles, and this on a sea well known to navigators. Was this then a solitary rock, a reef rising but a few yards above the surface of the waves, which would serve as the spot which up to then his Excellency had sought in vain as a deposit for his treasure. There was nothing answering to it on the very careful charts of this portion of the sea. An island with the breakers around it, girdled with mist and spray, was not likely to have escaped a sailor's notice. The charts should have shown its true position ; and according to the chart he had, the captain could declare that there was not even a reef marked anywhere within sight.

"It is an illusion!" he thought, when he had again brought his telescope to bear on the suspected spot, although he picked it up immediately.

In fact there was nothing so indistinct within the telescope's field of view.

At this moment—a few minutes after six—the solar disk was just on the horizon, and "hissing at the touch of the sea," if we believe what the Iberians used to say. At his setting, as at his rising, refraction still showed his position when he was below the horizon. The luminous rays obliquely projected on the surface of the waves extended as in a long diameter fiom west to east. The last ripples like rays of fire gleamed beneath the dying breeze. This light suddenly went out as the upper edge of the disk touched the line of water, and shot forth its green ray. The hull of the brigantine became dark while the upper canvas shone purple in the last of the light.

As the shades of twilight began to fall a voice was heard from the bows,—

"Ho, there!"

"What is the matter?" asked the captain.

"Land on the starboard bow!"

Land, and in the direction the captain had been watching the misty outline a few minutes before. He had not been mistaken then.

At the shout of the look-out the men on watch had rushed to the bulwarks and were looking away to the west. The captain, with his telescope slung behind him, grasped the main shrouds, and slowly mounted the ratlines to reach the crosstrees and there sit astride on them ; with his glass at his eye he looked at the land in sight.

The look-out was not mistaken. Six or seven miles away was a small island, its lineaments standing out black against the sky. You would have said it was a reef of moderate height, crowned with a cloud of sulphurous vapour. Fifty years later a sailor would have said it was the smoke of a large steamer passing in the offing ; but in 1831 no one imagined that the ocean would one day be ploughed by these monsters of navigation.

The captain had little time to look at it or think about it. The island was almost immediately hidden behind the evening mist. No matter, he had seen it, and seen it well. There was no doubt of that.

The captain descended to the poop, and the distinguished personage, whom this incident had awakened from his reverie, made a sign for him to approach.

" Well ? "

"Yes, your Excellency."

" Land in sight ? "

"An islet at least."

" At what distance ? "

" About six miles to the westward."

" And the chart shows nothing in that direction ? "

" Nothing."

" You are sure about that ? "

" Sure."

" It must be an unknown island, then ? "

" I think so."

" Is that possible ? "

"Yes, your Excellency, if the islet be of recent formation."

" Recent ? "

" I am inclined to think so, for it appeared to me to be wrapped in vapour. In these parts the plutonic forces are often in action, and manifest themselves by submarine upheavals."

" I hope what you say is true. I could not wish for anything better than that one of these masses should suddenly rise from the sea ! It does not belong to anybody—"

"Or rather, your Excellency, it belongs to the first occupant."

" That would be to me, then ? "

" Yes, to you."

" Steer straight for that island."

" Straight, but carefully," replied the captain. " Our brigantine would be in danger of being dashed to pieces if the reefs extend far out. I propose to wait for daylight, to make out the position, and then land on the islet."

" Wait, then.

This was only acting like a seaman. It would never do to risk a ship in shoals that were unknown. In approaching an unknown coast, the night must be avoided and the lead used.

His Excellency went back to his cabin; if he slept at all the cabin-boy would have no occasion to call him at dawn; he would be on deck before sunrise.

The captain would not leave his post, but preferred to watch through the night, which slowly passed. The horizon became more and more obscure. Overhead the clouds became invisible as the diffused light left them. About one o'clock the breeze increased slightly. Only sufficient sail was set to keep the vessel under the control of her helm.

The firmament became lighted by the early constellations. In the north Polaris gazed gently with a motionless eye, while Arcturus shone brightly to continue the curve of the Great Bear. On the other side of the pole Cassiopeia traced her sparkling W. Below, Capella appeared where she had appeared the day before and would appear on the morrow, allowing for the four minutes of advance with which her sidereal day begins. On the surface of the sea reigned that inexplicable torpor due to the fall of the night.

The captain, resting on his elbow in the bow, never moved from the windlass against which he leant. Motionless, he thought only of the spot he could see through the gloom. He doubted still, and the darkness made the doubts more serious. Was he the sport of an illusion? Was this really a new islet risen from the sea? Yes, certainly. He knew these parts; he had been here a hundred times before. He had fixed his position within a mile, and eight or ten leagues were between him and the nearest land. But if he was not mistaken, if in this spot an island had risen from the sea, would it not be already taken possession of? Had not some navigator hoisted his flag on it? Was there no gleam of a fire indicating that the place was inhabited? It was possible that this

mass of rocks had been here for some weeks; and how
could it have escaped a sailor's notice?

Hence the captain's uneasiness and his impatience for the
daylight. He saw nothing to indicate the islet's position,
not even the reflection of the vapours which seemed to
envelop it, and which might have thrown a fuliginous hue
on the darkness. Everywhere the air and the water were
mingled in the same obscurity.

The hours rolled by. The circumpolar constellations
had described a quarter circle around the axis of the
firmament. About four o'clock the sky began to brighten
in the east-north-east, and a few clouds came into view
overhead. Two hours and more were still to run before
the sun rose, but in such a light an experienced mariner
could find the reported island, if it existed.

At this moment the distinguished personage came on
deck and approached the captain.

"Well, this islet?" he asked.

"There it is, your Excellency," replied the captain,
pointing to a heap of rocks less than two miles away.

"Let us land there."

' As you wish."

CHAPTER II.

THE reader will hardly be astonished at Mehemet Ali entering on the scene at the beginning of this chapter. Whatever may have been the importance of the illustrious Pasha in the history of the Levant, he must inevitably have appeared in this story on account of the unpleasant experiences the owner of the brigantine had had with the founder of modern Egypt.

At this epoch Mehemet Ali had not begun, with the army of his son Ibrahim, the conquest of Palestine and Syria, which belonged to Sultan Mahmoud, the sovereign of Turkey in Europe and Turkey in Asia. On the contrary, the Sultan and the Pasha were good friends, the Pasha having helped the Sultan successfully to reduce the Morea and overcome the attempt at independence of the little kingdom of Greece.

For some years Mehemet Ali and Ibrahim remained quietly in their pachalik. But undoubtedly this state of vassalage, which made them mere subjects of the Porte, lay heavy on their ambition, and they were only waiting an opportunity for breaking the bonds which had existed for centuries.

There then lived in Egypt a personage whose fortune, accumulated for many generations, made him one of the most important men in the country. He lived at Cairo, his name was Kamylk Pasha, and he it was whom the captain of the brigantine addressed as Excellency.

He was an educated man, well versed in the mathematical sciences, and in their practical or even fanciful application. But above all things, he was steeped deep

in Orientalism, and an Ottoman at heart although an
Egyptian by birth.   Having persuaded himself that the
resistance to the attempts of Western Europe to reduce
the people of the Levant to subjection would be more
stubborn under Sultan Mahmoud than under Mehemet Ali,
he had thrown himself heart and soul into the contest.
Born in 1780 of a family of soldiers, he was scarcely
twenty years of age when he had joined the army of Djezzar,
where he soon attained by his courage the title and rank
of Pasha.   In 1799 he many times risked his liberty, his
fortune, and his life in fighting against the French under
Bonaparte.   At the battle of El-Arish he was made
prisoner with the Turks, and would have been set at liberty
if he had signed an undertaking not to bear arms again
against the French.   But resolved to struggle to the end,
and reckoning on an unlikely change of fortune, obstinate
in his deeds as he was in his ideas, he refused to give his
parole.   He succeeded in escaping, and became more
energetic than ever in the various encounters which distinguished the conflict of the two races.

At the surrender of Jaffa on the 6th of March, he was
among those given up under the capitulation on condition
that their lives were saved.   When these prisoners—to the
number of four thousand, for the most part Albanians or
Arnauts—were brought before Bonaparte, the conqueror
was much disturbed at the capture, fearing that these
redoubtable soldiers would go to reinforce the Pasha's
garrison at Acre.   And even in those days showing that
he was one of those conquerors who stick at nothing, he
gave orders that the prisoners should be shot.

This time there was no offer as to the prisoners of El-
Arish, to set them at liberty on condition of their not serving again.   No, they were condemned to die.   They fell
on the beach, and those whom the bullets had not struck,
believing that mercy had been shown them, were shot
down as they ran along the shore.

It was not in this place nor in this way that Kamylk
Pasha was to perish.   He met with some men—French-

men be it said to their honour—who were disgusted
at this frightful massacre, necessitated perhaps by the
exigencies of war.   These brave fellows managed to save
several of the prisoners.   One of them, a merchant seaman,
was prowling at night round the reefs on which several
of the victims were lying, when he found Kamylk, seriously
wounded.   He carried him away to a place of safety, took
care of him and restored him to health.   Would Kamylk
ever forget such a service ?   No.   How he rewarded it, it
is the object of this curious story to tell.

Briefly then, Kamylk Pasha was on his feet again in
three months.

Bonaparte's campaign had ended in the failure before
Acre.   Under the command of Abdallah, Pasha of
Damascus, the Turkish army had crossed the Jordan on
the 4th of April, and the British fleet under Sidney Smith
was cruising off the coast of Syria.   Bonaparte had hurried
up Kleber's division with Junot, and had himself taken
the command, and routed the Turks at the battle of
Mount Tabor, but he was too late when he returned to
threaten Acre.   A reinforcement had arrived, the plague
appeared, and on the 20th of May he decided to raise the
siege.

Kamylk thought he might venture to return to Syria.
To return to Egypt, which was much disturbed at the
time, would have been the height of imprudence.   It was
better to wait, and Kamylk waited for five years.   Thanks
to his wealth, he was able to live in easy circumstances in
the provinces beyond the reach of Egyptian covetousness.
These years were marked by the entry on the scene of a
mere son of an aga, whose bravery had been remarkable
at the battle of Aboukir in 1799.   Mehemet Ali already
enjoyed such influence that he was able to persuade the
Mamelukes to revolt against the governor Khosrew Pasha,
to excite them against their chief, to depose Khourschid,
Khosrew's successor, and finally in 1806 to proclaim himself Viceroy, with the consent of the Sublime Porte.

Two years before, Djezzar the protector of Kamylk

Pasha had died. Finding himself alone, he thought there would be no danger in his returning to Cairo.

He was then twenty-seven, and new inheritances had made him one of the richest men in Egypt. Having no wish to marry, being of a very uncommunicative nature, preferring a retired life, he had retained a strong liking for the profession of arms; and until an opportunity came for him to exercise his skill, he would find an outlet for the activity so natural to his age in long and distant voyages.

But if Kamylk Pasha was not to have any direct heir for his enormous fortune, were there not collaterals ready to receive it ?

A certain Mourad, born in 1786, six years younger than he was, was his cousin. Differing in their political opinions, they never saw each other, although they both lived at Cairo. Kamylk was devoted to the Turkish interest, and as we have seen had proved his devotion to the cause. Mourad opposed the Ottoman influence by his words and actions, and became the most ardent adviser of Mehemet Ali in his enterprizes against Sultan Mahmoud.

This Mourad, the only relative of Kamylk Pasha, as poor as the other was rich, could not depend on his cousin's fortune unless a reconciliation took place. This was not likely. On the contrary, animosity, violent hate even, had made the abyss deeper between the only two members of this family.

Eighteen years elapsed, from 1806 to 1824, during which the reign of Mehemet Ali was untroubled by foreign war. He had however to struggle against the increasing influence and formidable agitation of the Mamelukes, his accomplices, to whom he owed his throne. A general massacre throughout Egypt in 1811 delivered him from this troublesome militia. Thenceforth long years of tranquillity were assured to the subjects of the Viceroy, whose relations with the Divan continued excellent—in appearance at least, for the Sultan distrusted his vassal, and not without reason.

Kamylk was often the mark of Mourad's ill-will.
Mourad, taking advantage of the testimonies of sympathy
he received from the Viceroy, was continually inciting his
master against the rich Egyptian. He reminded him that
he was a partisan of Mahmoud, a friend of the Turks, and
that he had shed his blood for them. According to his
account he was a dangerous personage, a man to be
watched—perhaps a spy. This enormous fortune in one
man's hand was a danger. In short he said all he could
to awaken the greed of a potentate without principle and
without scruple.

Kamylk would have taken no notice of this. At Cairo
he lived alone, and it would have been difficult to devise a
plot to catch him. When he left Egypt it was on a long
voyage. Then, on a ship that belonged to him, commanded by Captain Zo—five years his junior, and entirely
devoted to him—he cruised on the seas of Asia, Africa and
Europe, his life without an object, and marked by a
haughty indifference to humanity.

We may even ask if he had forgotten the sailor to whom
he owed his escape from the fusillades of Bonaparte?
Certainly not. Such services he did not forget. But had
these services received their reward? That was not likely.
Would it enter the thoughts of Kamylk Pasha to recognize
them later on, waiting an opportunity of doing so until one
of his maritime expeditions took him into French waters?
Who could tell?

In process of time the rich Egyptian could not hide
from himself that he was narrowly watched during his
stay in Cairo. Several journeys he wished to undertake
were forbidden by order of the Viceroy. Owing to the
incessant suggestions of his cousin, his liberty was in
danger.

In 1823, Mourad, at the age of thirty-seven, married, in a
way that did not promise to improve his position in the
world. He had espoused a young fellah, almost a slave.
There is no room for astonishment then that he continued
the tortuous proceedings by which he hoped to ruin

Kamylk, by means of the influence he possessed with Mehemet Ali and his son Ibrahim.

Egypt, however, was about to begin a period of military activity in which its arms were to have brilliant success. In 1824, Greece was against Mahmoud, who called on his vassal to aid him in putting down the rebellion. Ibrahim, at the head of a hundred and twenty sail, started for the Morea, and landed there.

The opportunity had come for Kamylk to have an object in life ; to venture in the perilous enterprizes which for twenty years he had abandoned, and with all the more ardour as it was to maintain the rights of the Porte, menaced by the rising in the Peloponnesus. He would have joined Ibrahim's army ; he was refused. He would have served as an officer in the Sultan's troops ; he was again refused. Was this not in consequence of the ill-omened influence of those whose interest it was not to lose sight of their millionaire relative ?

The struggle of the Greeks for independence was to end in the victory of that heroic nation. After three years, during which they were inhumanly treated by Ibrahim's troops, the combined action of the allied fleets destroyed the Ottoman navy at the battle of Navarino in 1827, and obliged the Viceroy to recall his vessels and army to Egypt. Ibrahim then returned to Cairo, followed by Mourad, who had been through the Peloponnesian campaign.

From that day Kamylk's position grew worse. Mourad's hatred became all the more violent in 1829 owing to his having a son born of his marriage with the young fellah. His family was increasing and not his fortune. Evidently his cousin's fortune must find its way into his hands. The Viceroy would not refuse to sanction this spoliation. Such readiness to oblige is not unknown in Egypt nor in other less oriental civilized countries.

Saouk, it may be as well to remember, was the name of Mourad's child.

Under these circumstances, Kamylk saw that there was

only one thing to do ; to get his fortune together, the
greater part of it being in diamonds and precious stones,
and depart with it out of Egypt. This he did with as
much prudence as ability, thanks to the assistance of some
foreigners at Alexandria, in whom the Egyptian did not
hesitate to trust. His confidence was well placed, and the
operation was accomplished in the utmost secrecy. Who
were these foreigners, to what nation did they belong ?
Kamylk Pasha alone knew.

Three casks of double staves hooped with iron, similar
to those in which Spanish wines are put, sufficed to contain all his wealth. They were secretly placed on board a
Neapolitan speronare, and their owner, accompanied by
Captain Zo, went with them as a passenger, not without
escaping many dangers, for he had been followed from
Cairo to Alexandria, and kept under observation all the
time he was in that town.

Five days afterwards the speronare landed him at
Latakia, and thence he gained Aleppo, which he had
chosen for his new residence. Now he was in Syria, what
had he to fear from Mourad under the protection of his old
general, Abdallah, now Pasha of Acre ? Would Mehemet
Ali, however daring he might be, venture to seize him in
a province over which the Sublime Porte extended its all-
powerful jurisdiction ?

And yet this was possible.

In fact, this very year, 1830, Mehemet Ali broke off his
relations with the Sultan. To break the bond of vassalage
which attached him to Mahmoud, to add Syria to his
Egyptian possessions, perhaps to become sovereign of the
Ottoman empire, were ideas not too high for the Viceroy's
ambition. The pretext was not difficult to find

Fellahs, ill-treated by the agents of Mehemet Ali, had
sought refuge in Syria, under Abdallah's protection. The
Viceroy demanded the extradition of these peasants. The
Pasha of Acre refused. Mehemet Ali requested the Sul-
tan's permission to reduce Abdallah by force of arms.
Mahmoud replied at first that the fellahs being Turkish

c

subjects he had no intention of handing them over to the Viceroy of Egypt. But a little time after, desirous of securing the aid of Mehemet Ali, or at least his neutrality, at the outbreak of the revolt of the Pasha of Scutari, he gave the required permission.

Several events—among others, the appearance of the cholera in the ports of the Levant—delayed the departure of Ibrahim at the head of thirty-two thousand men and twenty-two ships of war. Kamylk had time to think of the danger to him of a landing of Egyptians in Syria.

He was then fifty-one, and fifty-one years of a life troubled as his had been brings a man almost to the threshold of old age. Wearied, discouraged, his illusions dispelled, longing only for the rest he had hoped to find in this quiet town of Aleppo, here had events again turned against him.

Was it prudent for him to remain at Aleppo, while Ibrahim was preparing to invade Syria? Admittedly his business was only with the Pasha of Acre, but after he had turned out Abdallah, would the Viceroy halt his victorious army? Would his ambition be satisfied with a mere chastisement of the guilty? Would he not take advantage of the opportunity to attempt the conquest of this Syria, which had been the constant object of his desires? And after Acre, would not Damascus, and Sidon, and Aleppo, be threatened by the soldiers of Ibrahim? It was at least to be feared so.

Kamylk Pasha took a final resolution this time. They did not want him, but the fortune coveted by Mourad, and of this his relative would deprive him at the cost of handing over the greater part to the Viceroy. Well, he would make away with this fortune, and hide it in some secret place where no one would discover it. Then he would see how matters turned out. Later on, if Kamylk decided to leave these oriental countries, to which he was so much attached, or if Syria became safe enough for him to live there in security, he could bring back his treasure from its hiding-place.

Captain Zo approved Kamylk's plans, and offered to carry them out in such a way that the secret would never be discovered. A brigantine was bought. A crew was formed of sailors having no bond between them, not even the bond of nationality. The casks were put on board without anyone suspecting what they contained. On the 13th April, the vessel on which Kamylk embarked as a passenger at the port of Latakia, put to sea.

His object, as we know, was to discover an island, the position of which should only be known to himself and the captain. It was therefore necessary for the crew to be so mystified, that they could not guess the direction followed by the brigantine. For fifteen months Captain Zo acted with this object in view, and changed his course in every possible way. Did he come out of the Mediterranean, and if he did, did he go back into it? Did he not cross the other seas of the old continent? Was he even in Europe when he sighted this unknown island? Certain it is that the brigantine had been in very different climates one after the other, in very different zones, and that the best sailor on board could not say where they actually were. Provisioned for several years, they had never touched land but when they wanted water, and the watering places were only known to Captain Zo.

The voyage was long. Kamylk had grown so hopeless of discovering his island, that he was about to throw his diamonds into the sea, when the unexpected at last appeared.

Such were the events relating to the history of Egypt and Syria, which it was necessary to mention. They will not trouble us again. Our story will have a more romantic voyage than this grave beginning might lead the reader to expect. But it had to rest on a solid basis, and this the Author has given it, or at least he has attempted to do so.

CHAPTER III.

CAPTAIN ZO gave his orders to the man at the helm, and reduced the canvas till it was but just enough to keep steerage way on the vessel. A gentle morning breeze was blowing from the north-east. The brigantine neared the island under jib, fore-topsail and mainsail, the other sails being furled. If the sea rose she would find shelter at the very foot of the island.

While Kamylk rested on his elbows on the poop, the captain took up his position forward, and acted as a prudent mariner does when approaching a coast of whose bearings his charts give no indications.

There was the danger in fact. Under these calm waters it is difficult to recognize where the rocks may be almost at the water level. There was nothing to show the channel to be followed. The vicinity was apparently very open. There was no appearance of a reef. The boatswain who was working the lead found no sudden shoaling of the sea.

The islet was seen from about a mile off at this hour. The sun was lighting it up obliquely from east to west after clearing it of the mists with which it had been bathed at daybreak.

It was an islet, and nothing but an islet, which no State would have claimed as a possession, for it would not have been worth while. Speaking generally, it was a plateau measuring some six hundred yards round an irregular oval, about three hundred yards in length, and from a hundred and twenty to a hundred and sixty wide. It was not an agglomeration of rocks, heaped up in disorder one on the other in seeming defiance of the laws of equilibrium, but was evidently caused by a quiet and slow uprising of the earth's crust. The edges were not cut up into creeks or indentations. It did not resemble one of those shells in which capricious Nature revels in a thousand fancies, but rather had the regularity of the upper valve of an oyster or the carapace of a turtle. This carapace rose towards the centre in such a way that its highest point was a hundred and fifty feet above the level of the sea.

Were there any trees on its surface? Not one. Any traces of vegetation? None. Any vestiges of exploration? Nowhere. The islet then had never been inhabited —there was no doubt about that—and it could not be. Considering that its bearings had never been noted, and its utter barrenness, his Excellency could not have wished for a better as a secret deposit for the treasure he was about to confide to the interior of the earth.

" It would seem as though Nature had made it expressly," said Captain Zo.

Slowly the brigantine approached it, gradually reducing sail as she did so. When she was within a cable's length of the shore, the order was given to let go the anchor. The anchor dropped from the cathead, and dragging the chain after it through the hawse-hole, struck ground at twenty-eight fathoms.

The slope of the shore was thus very sudden, on this side at all events. A ship could come close up without risk of grounding, although it would be safer for her to remain at a distance.

As the brigantine swung to her anchor, the boatswain furled the last sail, and Captain Zo mounted the poop.

" Shall I man the large boat, your Excellency ? "

" No, the yawl. I would rather we two went alone."

A minute afterwards the captain, with two light oars in his hands, was seated in the bow of the yawl, the Pasha being in the stern. In a few moments the boat had reached the shore, where landing was easy. The grapnel was firmly fixed in a crack of the rock, and his Excellency took possession of the islet.

No flag was run up; no gun was fired.

It was not a State taking possession of it, but an individual, who landed with the intention of leaving it in a few hours.

Kamylk and Captain Zo remarked, to begin with, that the flanks of the island had no sandy base to rest on, but rose direct from the sea at an inclination of from fifty to sixty degrees. Hence, doubtless, its formation was due to an elevation of the bed of the sea.

They commenced their explorations by going round the islet, walking over a sort of crystallized quartz, bare of all footprints. Nowhere did the shore appear to be worn by the action of the waves. On the dry and crystallized surface the only liquid was water, left in crevices and depressions here and there by the last rains. There was not a trace of vegetation, not even a lichen or a marine moss, or any of those hardy plants sturdy enough to thrive among the rocks, where the wind may have scattered their germs. There were no mollusks, either living or dead, an anomaly truly inexplicable. Here and there were a few traces of birds, which could be accounted for by the presence of a few gulls, the sole representatives of animal life in its vicinity.

When the circuit of the islet was completed, Kamylk and the captain walked towards the rounded elevation in the centre. Nowhere was there a trace of a recent visitor otherwise; everywhere there was the same crystalline freedom from spot or stain.

When his Excellency and the captain reached the centre of the carapace they were about a hundred and fifty feet above the sea. Sitting down, they carefully looked round the horizon.

Over the vast surface of waves reflecting the solar rays, there was no sign of land. The islet thus belonged to no group of cyclades, no archipelago, however small. Captain Zo, telescope in hand, searched in vain for a sail

in sight. The sea was deserted, and the brigantine ran
no risk of being seen during the few hours she would
remain at her moorings.

"You are certain of our position on this 9th of September ?" asked the Pasha.

"I am certain, your Excellency, and to leave no doubt
I will take the position again."

"That is important. But how do you account for this
islet not appearing on the chart ?"

"Because in my opinion it is of very recent formation.
In any case it ought to be all the better for you that it is
not on the chart, and that we are sure of finding it when
you wish to return—"

"Yes ; when these troublous times are over. What does
it matter if these millions remain buried among these rocks
for long, long years. Will they not be safer here than in
my house at Aleppo ? It is not here that the Viceroy or
his son Ibrahim, or that rascally Mourad, would come
to steal them ! Leave this fortune to Mourad ? I would
rather leave it at the bottom of the sea !"

"That would be a pity," said Captain Zo ; "the sea never
gives back what you entrust to its depths. It is lucky that
we found this islet. It at least will guard your riches,
and faithfully restore them."

"Come," said Kamylk Pasha, rising, "we must be quick
at what we are about ; and it would be better if our ship
were not seen."

"I am ready."

"No one on board knows where we are ?"

"No one, your Excellency."

"Not even in what sea of the Old or New World ! We
have been sailing the ocean for fifteen months, and in fifteen
months a ship can travel great distances between the continents without her whereabouts being known."

The Pasha and the captain returned to the yawl.

As they embarked the captain said—"When we have
finished our work here, is it the intention of your
Excellency to steer straight for Syria ?"

" That is not my intention. Before I return to Aleppo, I will wait until the soldiers of Ibrahim have evacuated the province, and the country recovered its tranquillity under Mahmoud."

" You do not think that it will ever form part of the possessions of the Viceroy ? "

" No ! by the Prophet, no ! " exclaimed Kamylk, firing up at the suggestion. " For a period, of which I hope to see the end, Syria may possibly be annexed to the domains of Mehcmet Ali, for the ways of Allah are inscrutable. But that it should not return eventually to the rule of the Sultan, Allah would never permit ! "

" Where is your Excellency going to reside when you leave these seas ? "

" Nowhere. When my riches are safe among the rocks of this island, there they will remain. We will continue to cruise about the world as we have done during the many years we have been together."

" As you please "

And a few minutes afterwards the Pasha and his companion had returned on board.

About nine o'clock the captain took a first observation of the sun with a view of obtaining his longitude, that is to say the time of the place, an observation which would be completed at noon when the sun passed the meridian, and when he would obtain his latitude. He brought out his sextant and took the altitude, and, as he had promised the Pasha, he fixed the position as accurately as possible.

Meanwhile he had given orders for the boat to be prepared. His men had to take with them the three casks from the lazarette, as well as the tools, picks and shovels, and the cement necessary for the burial of the treasure.

Before ten o'clock everything was ready. Six sailors under the boatswain's orders occupied the boat. They had no suspicions of what the casks contained, nor why they were going to bury them. It was none of their business, and they did not trouble about it in the least.

They were sailors, accustomed to obey, mere machines as it were, working without asking the why and the wherefore.

Kamylk and the captain took their seats in the stern, and reached the island in a few strokes of the oars.

The first thing to be done was to choose a suitable spot for the excavation ; not too near the shore, within reach of the waves on stormy days, nor too high up to be subject to the risks of a landslip. A suitable place was found at the base of a steep rock on one of the south-eastern capes of the islet.

At the captain's orders, the men landed the casks and tools, and began the attack on the ground at this spot.

It was heavy work. As the pieces of crystallized quartz were chipped out they were carefully put into position, so as to be used for filling in the hole where the casks were buried. No less than two hours were spent in digging a hole some five or six feet wide and long.

Kamylk remained at a distance, pensive and sad. Perhaps he was pondering if it would be better for him to sleep for ever by the side of his treasure ? And where else could he have found a safer shelter from the injustice and perfidy of man ?

When the casks were lowered into the excavation, the Pasha took a last look at them. Then it was that the captain imagined from the Pasha's behaviour that he was about to countermand the order, renounce his intentions, and return to sea with his wealth. But no ! With a gesture the command was given to continue the work. The captain steadied the casks together with lumps of quartz, and covered them with hydraulic cement, so that they became one solid mass, as compact as the rock of the islet itself. Then the outer pieces were put back in their places, and cemented, so as to fill up the cavity to the level of the soil. When the rain and storm had swept the surface for a little it would be impossible to discover the place where the treasure was buried.

It was necessary, however, that some mark should be

made—an ineffaceable mark—in order that some day the seeker might find it. On the vertical face of the rock which rose behind the excavation the boatswain carved out with a chisel a monogram of the two K's of the name of Kamylk, placed back to back, which was the Egyptian's usual signature.

There was no need to prolong the stay on the islet. The treasure was safe in its grave. Who would discover it here ? who would carry it off from its unknown resting-place ? Here it was secure, and if Kamylk and the captain took the secret to their graves with them, the end of the world might come without anybody finding where the millions were hid.

The boatswain ordered the men into the boat, while his Excellency and the captain remained on a rock by the shore. A few minutes afterwards the boat came to fetch them, and brought them on board the brigantine, which had remained at anchor.

It was a quarter to twelve. The weather was magnificent. There was not a cloud in the sky. In a quarter of an hour the sun would have reached the meridian. The captain went in search of his sextant, and prepared to take his meridian altitude. When he had taken it, he found from it the latitude, and then with the longitude, obtained by calculating the horary angle after the nine o'clock observation, he obtained the position of the islet within half a mile or less.

He had finished this, and was preparing to go on deck, when his cabin door opened.

Kamylk appeared.

" Have you got your position ? " he asked.

"Yes, your Excellency."

" Give it to me."

The captain held out the sheet of paper on which was the working.

Kamylk looked it through attentively, as if he would fix the position of the islet in his memory.

" You will keep this paper," he said. " And as to the

log-book you have been keeping for the last fifteen months
in which you have recorded our course—"

" No one will ever have that, your Excellency."

" To be quite certain of that, destroy it at once."

" As you please."

The captain took the book in which were registered the
directions taken by the brigantine during her lengthy
cruise on so many different seas; and he tore out the
leaves and burnt them in the flame of a lantern.

Some hours were spent at anchor. About five o'clock
clouds began to appear on the western horizon; and
through their narrow intervals the setting sun shot his
streams of rays, which strewed the sea with scales of gold.

The captain shook his head, like a sailor whom the
appearance of the weather did not please.

" Your Excellency," he said, " there is a strong breeze
in those heavy clouds, perhaps a storm to-night! This
islet affords no shelter, and before it is too dark, I should
like to get a dozen miles to windward."

" And there is nothing to keep us here!" said the
Pasha.

" We will go, then."

" For the last time there is no need for you to verify
your observations for latitude or longitude ? "

" No, your Excellency; I am as sure of my position as
I am of being my mother's child."

" Get under way, then."

The preparations did not take long. The anchor left
the ground, and was hauled up to the cathead; the sails
were set, and the vessel headed north-west.

Kamylk watched the unknown islet as they left it until
it disappeared in the shades of the night. But the rich
Egyptian could find it again when he pleased, and with it
the treasure he had buried in it, a treasure worth four
millions sterling in gold, and diamonds, and precious
stones.

CHAPTER IV.

EVERY Saturday about eight o'clock in the evening Captain Antifer would smoke his pipe—a regular furnace, very short in the stem—and plunge into a blue rage, from which he would emerge quite red, an hour afterwards, when he had relieved himself at the expense of his neighbour and friend Gildas Tregomain. And what caused this rage? Simply his not being able to find what he wanted on one of the maps in an old atlas!

"Confound this latitude!" he would exclaim. "If it even ran through the furnace of Bœlzebub, I should have to follow it from one end to the other!"

And until he put this plan into execution Captain Antifer dug his nails into the said latitude, and punctured it with pencil-points and compass-prods, until it was as full of holes as a coffee-strainer.

The latitude which brought down Antifer's objurgations was written at the end of a piece of parchment which was almost as yellow as an old Spanish flag :

Twenty-four degrees fifty-nine minutes north.

Above this, in a corner of the parchment, were these words in red ink—" Let my boy never forget this."

And Captain Antifer would exclaim :

" Never fear, my good old father, I have not forgotten it, nor will I ever forget it. But may the three patron saints of my baptism bless me if I know what use it can ever be!"

It is the 23rd of February 1862, and this evening Captain Antifer is behaving himself as usual. He is in a howling rage ; he is swearing like a topman when a rope slips through his hands ; he is grinding away at the pebble

which he has in his mouth. He is pulling away
at his pipe, which has gone out twenty times, and which he
has lighted again and again from a box of matches; he
has thrown his atlas into one corner, his chair into another ;
he has smashed a big shell on the mantelpiece ; he has
stamped so as to shake down flakes of whitewash from the
ceiling ; and in a voice accustomed to be heard above a
roaring gale he shouts :

"Nanon ! Enogate !" making a speaking-trumpet out of
a roll of cardboard.

Enogate and Nanon, the one busy knitting, the other in
front of the kitchen stove, judged it time to put a stop to
their troubled domestic elements.

One of the good old houses of St. Malo, built of granite,
facing the Rue des Hautes Salles; a ground-floor and two
storeys, each containing two rooms, and the upper one,
at the back, overlooking the road round the ramparts.
There you could see its walls of granite, thick enough to
defy the projectiles of the olden days, the narrow windows
with the iron bars, the massive gate of heart of oak,
ornamented with iron fastenings, and furnished with a
knocker you could hear at Saint Servan when Captain
Antifer had it in hand: its slate roof pierced with dormer
windows, from which the old sailor's telescope was
occasionally visible. This house—half a casemate, half a
fortress—adjoining an angle of the ramparts which
surround the town, has a superb view ; to the right, Grand-
Bé, a corner of Cézembre, the Pointe du Decollé, and Cape
Frehel ; to the left, the jetty and the mole, the mouth of the
Rance, the beach of Prieuré, near Dinard, and the grey
dome of Saint Servan.

Formerly St. Malo was an island, and perhaps
Captain Antifer regretted the time when he would have
been called an islander. But the ancient Aaron has become
a peninsula, and he has to make the best of it. Besides,
one has a right to be proud at being a child of this
Breton city which has given so many great men to France
—among others, Duguay-Trouin, whose statue our worthy

mariner saluted every time he crossed the square, Lamen-
nais, although this writer in no way interested him, and
Chateaubriand, whose best work he did not know, and
whose proud and modest tomb on the little island of Grand-
Bé we cannot pass without mention.

Captain Antifer (Pierre Servan Malo) was then forty-
six years old. Eighteen months before, he had retired
from the sea with a certain independence which sufficed
for himself and his people. A few thousand francs in the
funds had resulted from his service on the two or three
ships he had commanded, which had always hailed from
St. Malo. These ships belonged to Le Baillif and Co.,
and traded in the Channel, in the North Sea, in the
Baltic, and even in the Mediterranean. Before attaining
this lofty position, Captain Antifer had been about the
world a good deal. A good seaman, very enterprising,
hard master to himself and others, never sparing himself,
his courage beyond reproach, his obstinacy unyielding,
the obstinacy of a true Breton. Did he regret the sea ?
No, for he had left it in the prime of life. Had his health
anything to do with this resolve ? No, for he was built of
the pure granite of the Breton Coast.

It was quite enough to look at him, to hear him, to
receive one of the grips of his hand, of which he was not
sparing. Figure a sturdy man of medium height and
thickish neck. Here is his description in detail—a woollen
cap ; hair bristling like the quills of a porcupine ; face
tanned, cooked and re-cooked by sea water, and bronzed
by the sun of southern latitudes ; beard like a lichen on
the rocks, with the grey hairs bristling all round it ; bright
eyes, veritable carbuncles beneath the arched eyebrows,
with the pupils black as jet and gleaming like a cat's ;
nose big at the end, and long enough to carry the spectacles,
and with two wrinkles at the base near the eyes ; teeth
complete, sound and healthy, clicking with the convulsions
of the jaw, particularly as their owner always had a pebble
in his mouth ; ears hairy, tip erect, lobe pendent, one of
them with a copper ring, on which an anchor was engraved ;

body rather thin, set on nervous legs firm enough on their strong supports, and straddling at the most appropriate angle for dealing with the rolling and pitching of a ship at sea. Evidently a man of unusual strength, due to the muscles massed together like the rods in a Roman lictor's bundle ; a man, drinking well and eating well, who would have a clean bill of health for many a long day. But of what irritability, nervousness and impetuosity was the individual capable who forty-six years before had been entered in the parish register under the name of Pierre Servan Malo Antifer !

And this evening, he stormed and raved, and the house shook, so that you would think that there was beating round its foundations one of those equinoctial tides which rise for fifty feet and cover half the town with spray.

Nanon, the widow of La Goât, forty-eight years of age, was the sister of this noisy sailor. Her husband, a clerk in Le Baillif's, had died young, leaving her a daughter, Enogate, who had been brought up by Uncle Antifer, who fulfilled his functions as a guardian with conscientiousness and discipline. Nanon was a worthy woman, loving her brother, trembling before him, and bending when he stormed. Enogate, charming with her golden hair, her blue eyes, her fresh carnation colour, her intelligent face, her natural grace, more resolute than her mother, and sometimes standing up to her terrible guardian, who adored her and did his best to make her the happiest of the girls of Saint Malo, as she was one of the prettiest. But perhaps his idea of happiness was not quite the same as that of his niece and ward.

The two women appeared at the door of his room, the one with her long knitting-needles, the other with the flat-iron she had just taken from the front of the fire.

"What is the matter ? " asked Nanon.

" Only my latitude ; my confounded latitude ! " answered Captain Antifer ; and he gave himself a knock on the head which would have cracked any other crown than that which Nature had fortunately given him.

"Uncle," said Enogate, "the latitude that troubles you is no reason for you putting your room into disorder."

And she picked up the atlas, while Nanon gathered together the pieces of shell that had been scattered about as if it had gone off like a bomb.

"Did you break that ?"

"Yes, I did, and if anyone else had done it, he would have had a bad quarter of an hour—"

"Why did you throw it down?"

"Because my hand itched."

"This shell was a present from our brother," said Nanon, "and you are to blame—"

"Well ? If you were to keep on repeating until to-morrow that I am to blame, will that put it back again ?"

"What will my cousin Juhel say ?" asked Enogate.

"He will say nothing, and he had better say nothing !" replied Antifer, regretting that he had only got the two women before him, on whom he could not reasonably gratify his anger.

"And by-the-bye," he added, "where is Juhel ?"

"You know, uncle, that he has gone to Nantes," replied Enogate.

"Nantes ! that is something new ! What is he going to do at Nantes ?"

"Uncle, you yourself sent him there—you know, his examination for his certificate as long-voyage captain—"

"Long voyage captain—long-voyage captain !" growled Antifer; "why could not he be content to be a coasting-captain like me ?"

"Brother," said Nanon, timidly, "he only took your advice—you wished—"

"Well—because I wished it—that is a fine reason ! And if I had not wished it, would he not have gone all the same ! Besides, he will fail."

"No, uncle."

"But he will ! and if he does I will give him a reception—a regular whirlwind !"

You see there was no way of reasoning with this man.

On the one hand he did not want Juhel to go up for the examination, and on the other, if he failed, the said pupil would catch it, as would " those asses of examiners, those pedlars in hydrography."

But Enogate had evidently a presentiment that the young man would not be rejected, first of all because he was her cousin, then because he was an intelligent, studious young man, and then because he loved her and she loved him, and they were engaged to be married. And can you imagine three better reasons than those?

We may add that Juhel was a nephew of Captain Antifer, who had acted as guardian to him until he became of age. He had been left an orphan at an early age by the death of his mother, who had died at his birth, and by the death of his father, a naval lieutenant, whose death took place a few years afterwards. We need not be astonished that it was written above that he should be a sailor. That he would obtain his captain's certificate Enogate did not doubt, nor did his uncle, for that matter, although he was too bad-tempered to say so.

And this was of all the more importance to the girl as her marriage was to take place when he passed his examination. The two young people really loved each other, and would probably be happy for the rest of their lives. Nanon was delighted to see the day coming of this wedding, which was approved of by all the family. What obstacle could there be if the all-powerful head gave his consent— or rather, refrained from giving it until Juhel had won his captaincy? Juhel had served a complete apprenticeship to his trade, first on vessels belonging to Le Baillifs, then in government vessels, and then as mate for three years in the mercantile marine. He knew his trade in practice and theory. And Captain Antifer was really proud of his nephew. But perhaps he had dreamt of a richer alliance for him, because he was a lad of real merit; perhaps he had even wished for a better husband for his niece, than whom there was no better-looking girl in the whole district. And if a million had fallen into his hands—and he was

D

as happy with his five thousand pounds in the funds—it is not impossible that he would have lost his head and indulged in some such senseless dream.

Enogate and Nanon soon introduced a little order into the room of this terrible man, if not into his brain. Antifer strode about rubbing his eyes, in which the lightning still lurked—a sign that the storm was not yet over and a flash might come at any minute. And when he looked at his barometer hung on the wall, his anger awoke again because the scrupulous and faithful instrument remained at fine weather.

"And so Juhel has not come back?" he asked, turning towards Enogate.

"No, uncle."

"And it is ten o'clock!"

"No, uncle."

"You will see he will miss the train."

"No, uncle."

"Ah! Are you going to do nothing but contradict me?"

"No, uncle."

Nanon might gesticulate in vain, for evidently the young Breton was resolved to defend her cousin against the unjust accusation of her boisterous uncle.

Evidently the thunder-clap was not far off. But was there not a lightning-conductor to take off the whole of the electricity accumulated in Captain Antifer's reservoirs?

Perhaps so. That was why Nanon and her daughter hastened to obey him when he yelled in the voice of a stentor, "Send Tregomain here!"

They rushed from the room, opened the street door and ran out in search of Tregomain.

"It is to be hoped he is at home!" they said to each other.

He was, and five minutes afterwards he was in the presence of Captain Antifer.

Gildas Tregomain, fifty-one. Points of resemblance

with his neighbour—a bachelor as he was, had navigated as he had, no longer navigated as he no longer navigated, had retired as he had, was a native of Saint Malo as he was. There the resemblance ended. Gildas Tregomain was as calm as Antifer was stormy, as philosophical as Antifer was the reverse, as accommodating as Antifer was difficult to get on with. Physically the friends were even more unlike if possible. They were close friends, but the friendship of Antifer for Tregomain was far more intelligible than that of Tregomain for Antifer. To be the friend of such a man was not without its drawbacks.

We have said that Tregomain had "navigated," but there are navigators and navigators. Antifer had visited the principal seas of the globe, not so his neighbour. Tregomain, being the son of a widow, had been exempt from serving the State, and he had never been on the sea.

Never! He had seen the Channel from the heights of Cancale and even from Cape Frehel, but he had never ventured on it. He had been born in the painted cabin of a canal barge, and in a barge he had spent his life. First as a "hand," then as "captain" of the *Charmante Amélie*, he had been up and down the Rance from Dinar I to Dinan, from Dinan to Plumaugat, to return with a load of wood, of wine, of coal, according to the trade. He hardly knew of any other river. He was a fresh-water sailor no more and no less, while Antifer was the saltest of salts—a mere boatman by the side of a coaster captain ; and so he lowered his flag in the presence of his neighbour and friend, who had no difficulty in keeping him at a distance.

Tregomain lived in a pretty little house, about a hundred yards away from Antifer's, at the end of the Rue de Toulouse, near the ramparts. One view looked out to sea, the other over the mouth of the Rance. He was a powerful man, of extraordinary breadth of shoulder—nearly a yard—five feet six inches high, a body like a box, invariably wearing a huge waistcoat with two rows of bone buttons, a brown jacket, always very clean, with great folds in the back and at the armholes. From this trunk came two huge arms big enough for the thighs of an ordinary man, terminated by enormous hands, big enough for the feet of a grenadier of the Old Guard. With such limbs and muscles, Tregomain could not be otherwise than of enormous strength. But he was a gentle Hercules. Never had he abused his strength, and never did he shake hands but with his thumb and index finger, for fear of smashing your fingers. Strength was latent in him. It never ent was far as blows, but manifested itself without effort.

To compare him with machines, he was less of the sledge-hammer than of the hydraulic press. That came from the circulation of his blood, great and generous, slow and insensible.

From his shoulders rose a big head, wearing a high hat with a broad brim. His hair was flat, his whiskers mutton-chop, his nose curved, his mouth smiling, his lower lip projecting, his chin double and even treble, his teeth white, one incisor in the top row missing—teeth which had never been stained with the smoke of a pipe—eyes limpid and kind, under thick brows, colour brick-red, due to the breezes of the Rance, and not to the stormy gales of the ocean.

Such was Gildas Tregomain, one of those obliging men to whom you can say, Come at twelve o'clock, come at two o'clock, and they will always be there.

He was also a sort of unshakable rock, against which the surges of Captain Antifer beat in vain. When his neighbour was in one of his whirlwind moods he was sent for, and he came to placidly take all the buffetings of this tumultuous personage.

And so the ex-captain of the *Charmante Amélie* was adored in the house—by Nanon to whom he served as a rampart, by Juhel who had vowed, eternal friendship for him, by Enogate who did not hesitate to kiss his rounded cheeks and his wrinkleless forehead, that incontestable sign of a calm and conciliating temperament, according to the physiognomists.

As the boatman mounted the wooden staircase that led to the first floor, the steps groaned under the heavy weight. Pushing open the door, he found himself in the presence of Captain Antifer.

CHAPTER V.

" So you have come at last ? "

" I came as soon as you sent for me, my friend."

" Not without taking your time ! '

" The time to come here—"

" Indeed ! One would think you had taken your passage on the *Charmante Amélie !* "

Tregomain took no notice of this allusion to the slow progress of canal-boats compared with that of sea-going ships. He saw that his neighbour was in a bad temper, in which there was nothing astonishing, and he made up his mind to put up with it, as was his custom.

Antifer stretched out a finger, which he gently squeezed between his thumb and index of his large hand.

" Eh ! Not so strong ! You always squeeze too tight ! "

" Excuse me. I took particular care—"

" Well, you could not have made a worse mess of it."

And with a gesture Captain Antifer invited Tregomain to sit down at the table in the middle of the room.

The boatman obeyed, and sat himself in a chair, his legs wide apart, his feet placed firmly in shoes without heels, his huge handkerchief spread on his knees—a cotton handkerchief with blue and red flowers, ornamented with an anchor at each corner.

This handkerchief always made Antifer shrug his shoulders. An anchor for a bargeman ! Why not a fore-mast or a mainmast or a mizen on a barge !

" You will take some brandy," said he, bringing out two glasses and a bottle.

" You know, my friend, that I never take anything."

This did not prevent Antifer from filling two glasses.
According to a custom now ten years old, he first drank
his own brandy, and then drank Tregomain's.

"And now let us talk."

"Of what?" asked the bargeman, who knew exactly
what was coming.

"Of what? Of what would you like us to talk, if not of—?"

"That is true. Have you found the spot that interests
you on this famous latitude?"

"Found it? And how would you like me to find it?
By listening to the chatter of the two females who were
here just now?"

"The good Nanon and my pretty Enogate!"

"Oh! I know—you are always ready to take their part
against me. But that has nothing to do with it. Here
has my father been dead for eight years, and for eight
years this latitude question has not advanced a step. It is
time it should finish."

"I," said the bargeman, winking, "would soon finish it,
by not bothering any more about it."

"Indeed. And my father's command on his death-bed,
what would you do with that? That sort of thing is
sacred I believe."

"It is a pity," said Tregomain, "that the worthy man
did not say a little more."

"If he did not say a little more it was because he
did not know a little more! Am I, too, to see my last day
without knowing any more?"

Tregomain was about to answer that it was very
likely—and even desirable. He refrained, however, so as
not to excite his excitable friend.

What had happened a few days before Antifer died was
as follows :—

It was in the year 1854—a year which the old sailor was
not to see out in this world. Feeling himself very ill, he
thought he would tell his son a story, the mystery of which
he had been unable to penetrate.

Fifty-five years before—in 1799—while he was trading

in the Levant, Thomas Antifer was cruising off the coast
of Palestine, the very day that Bonaparte was massacring
the prisoners of Jaffa. One of these unfortunates, who
had taken refuge on a rock, where he was awaiting
inevitable death, had been taken away by the French
sailor during the night, embarked on his ship, had his
wounds dressed, and finally recovered, after two months of
good treatment.

This prisoner told his rescuer who he was. He said he
was Kamylk Pasha, a native of Egypt, and when he took
his leave, he assured the gallant sailor that he would not
forget him. When the time came he would receive a
proof of his gratitude.

Thomas Antifer pursued his voyages, thinking more
or less of the promises that had been made to him, and
made up his mind to think no more of them, as it did not
seem that they would ever be realized.

In his old age he retired to Saint Malo, devoting himself
to the maritime education of his son, and he was seventy-
seven years old when a letter reached him, in June, 1842.

Whence came this letter, written in French? From
Egypt evidently, from the postmark. What did it contain?
Simply this :—

"Captain Thomas Antifer is requested to note in his
pocket-book this latitude, 24 degrees 59 minutes north,
which will be completed by a longitude that will eventually
be communicated to him. He will do well not to forget
this, and to keep it secret. It is of considerable importance to him. The enormous sum in gold, diamonds and
precious stones that this latitude and longitude will one
day be worth to him, will only be the just recompense
for the services he formerly rendered to the prisoner of
Jaffa."

And this letter was signed with a double K, in the form
of a monogram.

This is what it was that fired the imagination of the
worthy man—the worthy father of his son. And so after
forty-three years Kamylk Pasha had remembered him !

He had taken his time about it! But probably obstacles of all kinds had delayed him, in this country of Syria, the political position of which was only definitely settled in 1840 by the treaty of London, signed on the 15th of July, and to the advantage of the Sultan.

Now Thomas Antifer was the possessor of a latitude which passed through a certain point of the earth where Kamylk Pasha had buried a fortune. And what fortune? In his opinion nothing less than millions. In any case he had been required to keep the matter secret, until the arrival of a messenger, who would some day bring him the promised longitude. And so he spoke to no one about it —not even to his son.

He waited. He waited for twelve years, and if he had had a sister Anne on a tower, sister Anne would have seen nothing. But was it reasonable that he should carry the secret to the tomb with him, that he should reach the end of his life without having to open his door to the envoy of the Pasha? No! he could not believe it. He said to himself that this secret ought to be entrusted to him who would stand in his place, his son Pierre. And in 1854 the old sailor, then aged eighty-one, thinking that he had only a few days to live, told his son and heir of Kamylk's intentions. He made him promise—as he himself had done—never to forget the figures of this latitude, to carefully preserve the letter signed with the double K, and to await in all confidence the appearance of the messenger.

Then the worthy man, wept for by his family, lamented by all those who knew him, was buried in the family grave.

We know Captain Antifer, and we can easily imagine with what intensity such a revelation worked on his mind, and on his inflammable imagination : the millions his father had imagined, he multiplied by ten. Of Kamylk Pasha he made a sort of nabob of the Arabian Nights. He dreamt only of gold and precious stones buried in an Ali Baba's cave. But with his natural impatience, his characteristic nervousness, it was impossible for him to show the same reserve as his father. To remain a dozen years without saying a word, without confiding to anybody, without doing anything to discover what had become of the signatory of the letter with the double K—the father might be able to do this, but not the son. And so in 1855, during one of his voyages in the Mediterranean, having put in at Alexandria, he judiciously obtained as much information as he could concerning Kamylk Pacha.

Had he existed? There was no doubt as to this, for the old sailor possessed a letter in his handwriting. Did he still exist? This was a serious question, to which Captain Antifer attached particular importance. The information was disconcerting. Kamylk Pasha had disappeared for twenty years, and no one knew what had become of him.

Here was an obstacle for Captain Antifer to run into ; but he did not sink, all the same. He might be without news of Kamylk, but there was no doubt Kamylk was living in 1842, the famous letter proved it. Probably he had had to leave the country, for reasons he was not obliged to reveal. When the time came, his messenger, the bearer of the interesting longitude, would present himself, and as the father was no longer in the world, it would be his son who would receive him, and give him a warm welcome, you may be sure.

Captain Antifer returned then to St. Malo, and said nothing to anybody, much as it might cost him. He continued at sea until his retirement in 1857, and since then he had lived in the midst of his family.

But what an enervating existence ! Occupationless, unemployed, always possessed with one fixed idea ! These twenty-four degrees and these fifty-nine minutes flew about his brain like so many tormenting flies. He could keep his tongue still no longer ; he confided his secret to his sister, to his niece, to his nephew, to Gildas Tregomain. And soon the secret—in part at least—was known all over the town, and even beyond Saint Servan and Dinard. It was known that an enormous fortune was to fall some day into the hands of Captain Antifer, and that it could not fail to come to him. And there never came a knock at his door without his expecting to be greeted with the words,—

"Here is the longitude you have been waiting for."

Years went by. The messenger of Kamylk gave no sign of life. No stranger had crossed the threshold of the house. Hence continual excitement on the part of Captain Antifer. His family had given up believing in the fortune, and the letter seemed to them merely a mystification. Tregomain, without letting it appear, looked upon his friend as a simpleton of the first water. But Antifer never faltered. Nothing could shake his conviction. This fortune was as surely his as if he had received it ; and those who would say otherwise did so at the peril of a storm.

And so the bargeman, when he found himself in his presence seated before the table, was firmly resolved not to provoke an explosion.

"Look here," said Captain Antifer, looking him in the face, "answer me without prevarication, for you always appear as though you did not understand me After all the skipper of the *Charmante Amélie* never had occasion to fix his position. It is not between the banks of Rance—a mere rivulet—that it is necessary to take altitudes, observe the sun, the moon, the stars—"

And in this pleasant way we may be sure it was Antifer's intention to show the immense difference between a coaster-skipper and a bargee.

The excellent Tregomain smiled, and looked at the many-coloured rays of the handkerchief on his knee.

"Are you listening ?"

"Yes, my friend."

"Well, once for all, do you know exactly what a latitude is?"

"Very nearly."

"Do you know that it is a circle parallel to the Equator

that it is divided into three hundred and sixty degrees, which means 2160 minutes, or 129,600 seconds?"

"Why should I not know it?" replied the smiling Tregomain.

"And do you know that an arc of fifteen degrees corresponds to an hour of time, and an arc of fifteen minutes to a minute of time, and an arc of fifteen seconds to a second of time?"

"Would you like me to repeat it?"

"No, that would be useless. Well, I have this latitude of 24 degrees 59 minutes north of the Equator. Well, in this parallel, which contains three hundred and sixty degrees—three hundred and sixty, you understand—there are three hundred and fifty-nine which are of no more use to me than an anchor without flukes. But there is one, and only one, which I do not know, and never shall know until I have been told the longitude that crosses it, and there, at that very spot, there are millions—Don't smile—"

"I am not smiling, my friend."

"Yes, millions which are mine, which I have the right to dig up, the day I find the place where they are buried—"

"Well," replied the bargeman sweetly, "you must wait patiently until the messenger comes with the good news."

"Patiently—patiently. What is there that flows in your veins?"

"Syrup, I imagine—nothing but syrup!" replied Tregomain.

"And in mine it is quicksilver; there is saltpetre dissolved in my blood—I cannot rest—I eat myself, I devour myself—"

"Really you should take it calmly."

"Calmly! Do you forget that we are in '62; that my father died in '54; that he had possessed this secret ever since '42; and that for twenty years we have been waiting for the word of this confounded charade—"

"Twenty years!" murmured Tregomain, "how the time passes! Twenty years ago I was still in command of the *Charmante Amélie.*"

" Who is talking about the *Charmante Amélie?* " asked Antifer. " Are we talking about the *Charmante Amélie* or the latitude in this letter ? "

And beneath the bargeman's blinking eyes he tossed the famous letter, all old and yellow, on which figured the monogram of Kamylk Pasha. " Yes, this letter, this confounded letter," he continued, " this diabolical letter, which I have sometimes been tempted to tear up, to reduce to cinders—"

" And that might perhaps be wise ! " ventured the bargeman.

" See here, Tregomain," said Antifer, his eyes flashing, his voice ringing, " mind you never answer me like that again."

" Never."

" And if ever, in a moment of madness, I wish to destroy this letter, which is as good as a title-deed to me—if ever I am unreasonable enough to forget what I owe to myself and mine, and you do not prevent me—"

" I will prevent you, my friend ; I will prevent you," Tregomain hastened to reply.

Antifer in great excitement seized his glass of brandy, chinked it against that of the bargeman and said,—

" To your health, Captain ! "

" To yours ! " replied Tregomain, lifting his glass up to his eyes, and then setting it back again on the table.

Antifer became thoughtful, running his feverish hand through his hair, muttering to himself, and grinding the pebble between his teeth. Suddenly he crossed his arms and looked at his friend.

" Do you know where this wretched latitude goes ? "

" How could I not do so ? " asked the bargeman, who had submitted a hundred times to this lesson in geography.

" Never mind ! There are some things we cannot know too well." And, opening the atlas at the map of the world,— " Look ! " he said in a tone that admitted of neither hesitation nor reply.

Tregomain looked.

"You see St. Malo, don't you?"

"Yes, and there is the Rance."

"Never mind the Rance! You will make me curse the Rance! Get on to the meridian of Paris, and run down to the twenty-fourth parallel."

"I run down."

"Traverse France, Spain. Enter Africa; cross Algeria; reach the Tropic of Cancer. There, above Timbuctoo—"

"I am there."

"Well now, we are on this famous latitude."

"Yes, here we are."

"Now run along to the east. Cross Africa, walk over the Red Sea, stride through Arabia. Take your hat off to the Sultan of Muscat, jump into India, leaving Bombay and Calcutta to starboard, skirt the base of China, run across Formosa, the Pacific, the Sandwich Islands—do you follow me?"

"I am following you," replied Tregomain, wiping his head with his huge handkerchief.

"Well, here we are in America, in Mexico, then in the Gulf, then near Cuba. You jump the Straits of Florida, cross the Atlantic, skirt the Canaries, reach Africa, come up the Paris meridian and return to St. Malo after having made the tour of the globe on the twenty-fourth parallel."

"Yes!" said the complaisant bargeman.

"And now," continued Antifer, "we have traversed the two continents, the Atlantic, the Pacific, the Indian oceans, in which islands and islets are in thousands, and can you tell me where my millions are hidden?"

"That is what we do not know."

"That is what we shall know."

"Yes—that is what we shall know when the messenger—"

Antifer took the second glass of brandy, which had not been sipped by his friend.

"To your health!" he said.

"To yours!" said Tregomain, clinking the empty glass against the full one which was once his.

Ten o'clock struck. A loud knock shook the street door.

"If that is the man with the longitude!" exclaimed Antifer.

"Oh!" said his friend, who could not restrain this gentle exclamation of doubt

"And why not?" said Antifer, his cheeks flushing purple.

"Just so! Why not?" replied the conciliating barge-man, thinking of the beginning of a salute for the bearer of good news.

Suddenly shouts were heard on the ground-floor—shouts of joy, it is true, which, coming from Nanon and Enogate. could not be addressed to an envoy of Kamylk Pasha.

"It is he! It is he!" repeated the two women.

"He? he?" said Captain Antifer, and he was walking towards the stairs when the door of his room opened.

"Good evening, uncle, good evening!"

This was said in a cheery, satisfied voice, which had the effect of exasperating the uncle in question.

"He!" was Juhel. He had just arrived. He had not failed in catching the train from Nantes, nor in passing his examination, for he shouted,—

"Passed, uncle, passed!"

"Passed!" repeated the woman and the girl.

"Passed—what?" replied Captain Antifer.

"Passed as long-voyage captain, with the maximum of marks!"

And as his uncle did not open his arms to him he fell into those of Tregomain, who hugged him to his heart in a way that nearly squeezed the breath out of him.

"You are suffocating him, Gildas!" said Nanon.

"I only just touched him!" replied the smiling barge-man.

Juhel panted a little, and recovered himself, and then turning to Antifer, who was walking about feverishly, said,—

"And now, uncle, when shall the wedding be?"

"What wedding?"

"My wedding with my dear Enogate," replied Juhel; "was it not agreed upon?"

"Yes, agreed upon," said Nanon.

"At least, unless Enogate does not care for me now I am a captain."

"Oh! Juhel!" answered the girl, holding out a hand in which the worthy Tregomain—so he pretended—thought he saw her put her heart.

Antifer did not reply, but seemed to be trying to find out which way the wind blew.

"Come, uncle," said the young man, and he stood there, his face radiant, his eyes bright with happiness.

"Uncle," said he, "did you not say that the wedding should take place when I passed, and that we would fix the day as soon as I came back?"

"I believe you did say so, my friend," ventured the bargeman.

"Well, I have passed," said Juhel; "and here I have come back, and if it is not inconvenient, uncle, we will fix it for the first week in April—"

Antifer started.

"In eight weeks? Why not in eight days, in eight hours, in eight minutes?"

"Well, I should not object, uncle."

"Oh! we must have a little time," said Nanon, "there are preparations, purchases to make—"

"Yes, I have to get a new coat built," said Tregomain, the future best man.

"Then—shall we say the 5th of April?" asked Juhel.

"Be it so," said Antifer, who found himself driven behind his last entrenchments.

"Ah! my good uncle," said the girl, leaping on to his neck.

"Ah! my dear uncle," said the young man.

And as he embraced him on one side, while Enogate embraced him on the other, it is not impossible that their cheeks met.

"That is agreed," continued the uncle; "the 5th of April, but on one condition."

"Oh, no condition!"

"A condition?" exclaimed Tregomain, who feared some further device on the part of his friend.

"Yes, one condition."

"And what is that?" asked Juhel, beginning to frown.

"If my longitude does not reach me before then."

They all breathed again.

"Yes! yes!" they replied with one voice.

And really it would have been cruel to refuse this satisfaction to Captain Antifer. Besides, what likelihood was there that the messenger of Kamylk Pasha, whom they had been expecting for twenty years, would make his appearance before the date fixed for the wedding of Juhel and Enogate?

CHAPTER VI.

A WEEK went by. Of a messenger there was not even a shadow. Gildas Tregomain said he would be just as much astonished to see the prophet Elijah return from the sky. But he took care not to express his opinion in this biblical form before Captain Antifer.

As to Enogate and Juhel, they hardly gave a thought to the messenger of Kamylk Pasha, who, as far as they were concerned, was a purely imaginary being. No! They were busy with their preparations for that charming land of matrimony, of which the young man knew the longitude, and the girl the latitude, and which it would be easy to reach by combining these two geographical elements. They might rest assured that the combination would take place on the 5th of April, the date fixed.

As to Captain Antifer he had become more unsociable, more unapproachable than ever. The date of the ceremony was a day nearer every twenty-four hours. A few weeks only, and the young couple would be united. A fine result, truly! In his heart their uncle had been dreaming of superb alliances for them when he became a rich man. And if he made so much of these millions, these undiscoverable millions which belonged to him, it was not with the idea of enjoying them himself, of living a grand life, of dwelling in a palace, riding in a carriage, dining off gold plates, wearing diamond studs—No! He was thinking of wedding Juhel to a princess, and Enogate to a prince! That was his whim, his monomania. And here was his heart's desire in jeopardy owing to a messenger not arriving at a proper time ; and for want of a few figures which, combined with others he already possessed, Kamylk's hiding-place would not yield up its treasures until too late !

Antifer stormed no more. He could not remain inside the house, and it was all the better for the peace of the household that he was outside. They saw him only at mealtimes, and his meals he got through at double the usual rate. Whenever there was an opportunity, Tregomain offered his cheek to the smiter in the hope of provoking an explosion, which would relieve his friend who sent him to Jericho. In short it was to be feared that he was going to be ill. His only occupation was to stride about the railway station, watching the arrival of the trains, and about the Sillon quays, watching the arrival of the boats, endeavouring to discover among the passengers some exotic figure which might belong to the envoy of Kamylk, an Egyptian, without doubt, perhaps an Armenian, certainly a foreign personage recognizable by his appearance, his accent, his clothes, and who would ask for the address of Pierre Servan Malo Antifer.

And there was nobody of this sort ! Normans, Bretons, English, Scandinavians, there were many, but travellers from Eastern Europe, Maltese, or Levantines, there were none.

On the 9th of February, after a breakfast, at which he had not opened his lips—except to eat and drink—Captain Antifer went forth for his usual walk, like another Diogenes in search of a man.

He went along the narrow streets of the town, bordered by their tall granite houses, and paved with pebbles. He descended the Rue du Bey towards Duguay-Trouin Square, looked at the time on the dial at the Sous-Prefecture, hurried towards the Place Chateaubriand, turned round by the kiosk under its canopy of leafless planes, passed through the gate in the curtain of the rampart, and found himself on the quay.

He looked to the right, to the left, in front of him, behind him, puffing jerkingly and furiously at his pipe.

Every now and then he had to return a salute, for he was one of the notables of St. Malo, a man of consideration. But many were the salutes he did not return, owing to his not noticing that they were addressed to him.

In the harbour were a number of ships, sailing-vessels, and steamers, brigs, schooners, luggers, chasse-marées. The tide was then low, two or three hours having to elapse before the ships reported by the semaphore to be in the offing, could enter.

Antifer thought it would be wisest to go off to the railway-station, and await the arrival of the express. Would he be more fortunate on this occasion, than he had been during so many weeks ?

How easily the human machine can go wrong ! Antifer, occupied in watching the passers-by, did not notice that for twenty minutes he had been followed by somebody well worth his attention.

Here was a foreigner—a foreigner with a red fez and a black tassel, wearing a long, loose coat, fastened with a long single row of buttons right up to the neck, with a pair of baggy trousers, below which was a pair of big shoes like Turkish slippers. He was anything but young, perhaps sixty, perhaps sixty-five, stooping rather, and holding his long, bony fingers spread across his chest. If this good man were not the expected Levantine, there could be no doubt that he came from some land bordered by the Eastern Mediterranean—an Egyptian, an Armenian, a Syrian, an Ottoman.

In short, the stranger followed Captain Antifer in a hesitating way, sometimes on the point of accosting him, sometimes stopping for fear of making a mistake. At length at the corner of the quay he quickened his step, caught up Antifer, and then turned so suddenly as to run against him.

"Confound you, you clumsy brute!" exclaimed the captain, shaken by the collision.

Then, rubbing his eyes, and holding his hand to his eyebrows to shade his sight, he exclaimed,—

"Eh! Ah! Oh! He! Can it be? This must be the messenger of the double K."

If it were the said envoy he certainly did not look promising, with his smooth face, his fat cheeks, his pointed nose, his big ears, his thin lips, his huge chin, his furtive eyes—anything but a physiognomy that inspired confidence.

"Have I not the honour of addressing Captain Antifer, as an obliging sailor has just told me?" said the stranger, in a most deplorable accent.

"Antifer, Pierre Servan Malo!" was the reply; "and you?"

"Ben Omar."

"An Egyptian?"

"Notary at Alexandria, just come from the Hôtel de l'Union, Rue de la Poissonneau."

A notary with a red hat! Evidently notaries in Oriental countries were not of the French type, with white cravat, black clothes, and gold spectacles; and it was just as astonishing to find that there were notaries at all in the country of the Pharaohs.

Antifer no longer doubted that he had before him the mysterious messenger, the bearer of the famous longitude announced twenty years before in Kamylk's letter. But instead of giving himself away, as might be supposed, instead of asking Omar questions, he had sufficient control over himself to await events, for the duplicity betrayed on the visage of the living mummy warned him to be circumspect. Never would Tregomain have believed his excitable friend capable of such prudence.

"Well, what do you want with me, Mr. Ben Omar?" he asked, noticing that the Egyptian looked embarrassed.

"A few minutes' conversation, Mr. Antifer."

"Do you mean at my house?"

"No—and it would be better to be somewhere where no one can overhear us."

"It is a secret then?"

"Yes and no—or rather a bargain."

Antifer started at this.   Evidently if this individual
had brought the longitude he had no intention of deliver-
ing it gratis, and yet the letter signed with the double
K said nothing about a bargain.

"Take care of the helm," he said to himself, "and keep
an eye on the way the wind blows!"

Then addressing himself to his interviewer, and pointing to a lonely corner at the end of the harbour, he said,—

"Come there! we shall be quite enough alone to talk
of secret matters.   But let us make haste, for it is cold
enough to cut you through."

They had not more than twenty yards to go.   No one
was on the vessels moored to the quay.   The custom-house
officer on duty was half a cable-length away.

In a minute or so they were at the spot, and seated on
the end of a spar.

"Will this place suit you, Mr. Ben Omar?" asked
Antifer.

"Oh, very well."

"Then speak out, and speak clearly, and not like your
sphinx, which amuses itself by offering conundrums to the
poor world."

"There will be no concealment, and I will speak
frankly," replied Ben Omar, in a tone which had little
appearance of frankness.

He coughed two or three times, and said,—

"You had a father?"

"Yes, as is customary in our country.   Well?"

"I hear that he is dead?"

"Eight years ago.   Well?"

"He had made several voyages?"

"I believe so, considering that he was a sailor.   Well?"

"In several seas?"

"In all.   Well?"

"He once happened to go into the Levant?"

"Yes.   Well?"

"During these voyages," continued the notary, to
whom these brief replies gave no loophole, "during these

voyages, he was about sixty years ago on the coast of Syria."

"Perhaps so; perhaps not. Well?"

These "wells" were as so many digs in the ribs to Ben Omar.

"You will have to try another tack, my good man," said Antifer to himself, "if you want me to pilot you."

The notary saw that he would have to attack him more straight-forwardly.

"Have you any knowledge," said he, "that your father had occasion to render a service, an immense service—to some one—on the coast of Syria?"

"I cannot say that I have. Well?"

"Ah!" said Ben Omar, much astonished at the reply. "And you do not know that he received a letter from a certain Kamylk Pasha?"

"A Pasha?"

"Yes."

"Of how many tails?"

"It does not matter, Mr. Antifer. The point is, Did your father receive a letter containing information of great value?"

"I know nothing of it. Well?"

"Have you not looked over his papers? It is not possible that such a letter would have been destroyed. It contained, I repeat, information of extreme importance."

"To you, Mr. Ben Omar?"

"To you also, Mr. Antifer, for—in short, it is that letter I am commissioned to get back again, and which might be the object of our bargain."

In an instant it became clear to Antifer that the people who had sent Ben Omar wanted to get hold of the longitude, to find the place where the millions were concealed.

"The rascals!" he muttered to himself, "they want to get my secret, to buy my letter, and then go and unearth my cash-box!"

And perhaps he was not far out.

At this stage of their interview they heard the steps of a man who was coming round the corner in the direction of the railway-station. The notary stopped in the middle of a sentence. It seemed as though the man gave Omar a side look as he passed, or made a sign of denial, at which the Egyptian appeared much disconcerted. The man passed on, and disappeared.

He was a stranger, about thirty years old, in Egyptian costume, of sallow complexion, black gleaming eyes, stature above the medium height, strongly built, determined looking, with anything but a pleasant expression about him. Did he and the notary know one another? Possibly. Were they not anxious that this should not be known just then? There was no doubt about that.

Anyhow, Antifer did not notice this little bit of bye-play—a look, a gesture, nothing more—and he continued the interview.

"Now, Mr. Ben Omar," said he, "will you kindly explain why you want so much to get this letter, to know what it contains, so much so that you are willing to buy it from me if I happen to have it?"

"Mr. Antifer," replied the notary, with some embarrassment, "I have had a certain Kamylk Pasha among my clients. On his behalf—"

"You have had, did you say?"

"Yes, and as the representative of his heirs—"

"His heirs!" exclaimed Antifer, with a movement of surprise that could not but astonish the notary. "He is dead, then?"

"He is dead."

"Steady!" muttered Antifer, grinding the pebble within his teeth. "Kamylk is dead. That is worth remembering, and if they are up to any games—"

"And so, Mr. Antifer," asked Ben Omar, giving him a side look, "you have not got this letter?"

"No."

"That is a pity, for the heirs of Kamylk Pasha, who

wish to collect everything that can recall the remembrance
of their beloved relative—"

"Ah! a matter of remembrance only. Dear, kind
hearts!"

"Simply so, Mr. Antifer, and these dear, kind hearts, as
you say, would not have hesitated to have offered you a
considerable sum to obtain possession of this letter."

"How much would they have given?"

"What does that matter if you have not got it?"

"You might as well say."

"Oh! a few hundred francs."

"Pheugh!" said Captain Antifer.

"Perhaps even a few thousand."

"Ha!" said Captain Antifer, whose patience was
exhausted. And he gripped Ben Omar by the throat,
dragged him towards him, and rolled out these words
into his ear, with a shake between each: "I have your
letter!"

"You have it!"

"Your letter with the double K!"

"Yes, the double K—that was my client's signature."

"I have it. I have read it and read it again. And I
know, or rather I guess, why you want to possess it!"

"Sir?"

"And you are not going to get it!"

"Do you refuse?"

"Yes, I do. Unless you buy it from me?"

"How much?" asked the notary, digging his hand into
his pocket to pick out his purse.

"How much? Fifty millions of francs!"

What a jump Ben Omar gave as Antifer, with his
mouth open, his lips up, his teeth showing, looked at him
as he had never been looked at before.

And then he drily added,—

"You can have it or leave it, as you please."

"Fifty millions!" repeated the gasping notary.

"There is no bargaining, Mr. Ben Omar. You will get
no discount out of me."

"Fifty millions?"

"That is the price, and they can be in cash or in notes or in a cheque on the Bank of France."

The notary, abashed for an instant, gradually recovered his coolness. Evidently this confounded sailor knew of what importance this letter was to the heirs of Kamylk. In fact, did it not contain the information necessary in the search for the treasure? The scheme for getting possession of it had failed. Antifer was on his guard. The letter must be bought, or rather the latitude which would omplete the longitude, which Ben Omar knew.

But, it may be asked, how did Ben Omar know that Antifer had the letter? Was he the former notary of the rich Egyptian? Was he the messenger instructed by the last wishes of Kamylk to bring Antifer the longitude in question? That we shall soon see.

In any case, whether Ben Omar was or was not acting under the orders of the Pasha's heirs, he clearly understood that the letter would not be handed over without its price in gold.

But fifty millions!

Assuming a sly, coaxing air, he said, "I think you said fifty millions?"

"I did."

"That is one of the funniest things I ever neard in all my life."

"Mr. Ben Omar, would you like to hear a funnier?"

"Gladly."

"Ah! Well then, you are an old thief, an old scoundrel from Egypt, an old crocodile of the Nile—"

"Sir!"

"There, I will stop. You are an old fisher in troubled waters, wanting to get at my secret instead of telling me yours, which is the only mission you were entrusted with—"

"You suppose so."

"I suppose what is."

"No. What it pleases you to imagine."

"Enough, you consummate fool!"

"Sir!"

"I withdraw the consummate—out of deference. And shall I tell you what you really want to know about the letter?"

Did the notary imagine that Antifer was going to commit himself? Anyhow, his two little eyes glowed like carbuncles as he waited.

"What you want to know, Ben Omar, is not what the letter says regarding the services rendered by my father. No! You want the four figures—you understand me well enough, the four figures—"

"The four figures?" murmured Ben Omar.

"Yes, the four figures it contains, and which I shall not hand over for less than twelve and a half millions each! That is all. We have said enough! Good morning!"

And sticking his hands into his pockets, Captain Antifer strode off, whistling a favourite air, of which nobody, not even himself, knew the origin, and which was more like the howling of a dog than any of the melodies of Auber.

Ben Omar, petrified, seemed to have taken root on the spot, as if he were a bollard or a mile-post. He who had reckoned twirling this sailor round his finger as if he were a fellah—and Mahomet knows how he had dealt with the unfortunate peasants whose ill-fortune had led them to his office, one of the best in Alexandria!

He saw, with haggard eye, the sailor going farther and farther away from him, swinging his hips, hoisting his shoulders, first one and then the other, and gesticulating as if his friend Tregomain was with him under the usual fire.

Suddenly Antifer stopped. Had he encountered an obstacle? Yes! This obstacle was an idea that had just occurred to him. He had forgotten something.

He returned to the notary, who still was as motionless as Daphne when she was turned into a laurel-bush, to the great disappointment of Apollo.

"Mr. Ben Omar?" he said.

" What is it you want ? "

" There is one thing I forgot to shout in your ear."

" What ? "

" The number—'

" Ah !   The number ? "

" Yes !   The number of my house—3, Rue des Hautes Salles.   You may as well have my address, and know that you will have a friendly reception when you come—'

" When I come ? "

" With the fifty millions in your pocket ! "

And Antifer went off again, while the notary sank and called on Allah and his Prophet.

CHAPTER VII.

DURING the night of the 9th of February the travellers at the Hôtel de l'Union would have run some risk of being troubled in their sleep if the door of Room No. 17 had not been shut, and draped with a heavy curtain, which prevented any noise from being heard outside.

In fact two men, or rather one of the two therein, spent the night in recriminations and menaces that bore witness to extreme irritation, while the other tried in vain to calm him, with supplications engendered by fear.

It is not likely that anybody would have understood what this stormy conversation was about, for it was held in Turkish, which is not a familiar language to the natives of the West.

A large wood fire blazed in the grate, and a candle on the table threw its light on to certain papers half-hidden within the pockets of a portfolio much worn by use.

One of these men was Ben Omar, who, in a helpless way, looked at the flames in the fire-place, which were far less ardent than those that blazed in the eyes of his companion.

This companion was the unprepossessing foreigner, to whom the notary had given the almost imperceptible signal, while he and Antifer were talking at the end of the harbour.

For the twentieth time this personage remarked,—

"And so you have failed ?"

"Yes, Excellency, and Allah is my witness—"

"I have nothing to do with the evidence of Allah or of anybody else ! There is the fact—you failed."

" To my great regret."

" This Antifer refused to give up the letter ? "

" He did."

" And he refused to sell it ? "

" To sell it ! He consented—"

" And you did not buy it, you dunderhead ! Is it not in your possession ? You came here without bringing it ? "

" Do you know what he asked ? "

" What does that matter ? "

" Fifty millions of francs ! "

" Fifty millions—"

And there was a volley of oaths.

".And so, you imbecile, this sailor knows of what importance this might be to him ? "

" There is no doubt of it."

" May Mahomet strangle me—and you, too ! " exclaimed the irascible personage, striding about the room ; " or, rather, that is my business as far as you are concerned, for I hold you responsible for all the misfortunes that may happen—"

" But it is not my fault, Excellency ! I was not in the secrets of Kamylk Pasha."

" You ought to have been, then ; you ought to have found them out when he was alive ; you were his notary ! "

And then came another broadside of oaths.

This terrible man was Saouk, the son of Mourad, the cousin of Kamylk. He was then thirty-one. His father being dead, he found himself the direct heir of his rich uncle, and would have inherited an immense fortune if this fortune had not been put out of reach of his covetousness in the way we know.

What had happened after Kamylk had left Aleppo, taking his treasure with him, to bury it on some unknown island, was briefly this :—

In October, 1831, Ibrahim, with twenty-two ships of war and thirty thousand men, had captured Gazza, Jaffa, Caiffa, and Acre had fallen into his hands the year following, on the 27th of March, 1832.

It seemed as though the territories of Palestine and Syria were to be finally severed from the Sublime Porte, when the intervention of the European powers stopped the son of Mehemet Ali in his career of conquest. In 1833 the treaty of Kataya was imposed on the Sultan and the Viceroy, and things remained as they had been.

Fortunately for his safety during this much-troubled period, Kamylk had placed his riches in the cavity sealed by the double K, and had continued his voyages. Whither went the brigantine under the command of Captain Zo? In what parts, far or near, did he plough the seas? Did he visit farthest Asia or farthest Europe? No one knew save his captain and himself, for none of the crew were allowed to land, and none of them knew whether they were in the west or the east, the north or the south, for such was their master's whim.

But after their many peregrinations Kamylk was imprudent enough to return to the Levant. The treaty of Kataya having stopped the ambitious march of Ibrahim, the northern part of Syria having submitted to the Sultan, the rich Egyptian had good reason to suppose that there was no danger in his returning to Aleppo.

As ill-luck would have it, however, in the middle of the year 1834 his vessel was driven by bad weather into Acre. Ibrahim's fleet was then cruising off the coast, and Mourad, invested with official functions by Mehemet Ali, was on board one of the ships of war.

The brigantine was flying Turkish colours. Was it known that she belonged to Kamylk Pasha! It matters little. She was chased, caught, carried by boarding, after a stout defence, which meant the massacre of the crew, the destruction of the ship and the capture of her owner and captain.

Kamylk was at once recognized by Mourad. A few weeks later he and Captain Zo were secretly carried to Egypt, and imprisoned in the fortress of Cairo.

But even if Kamylk had returned to his house at Aleppo it is probable that he would not have found the safety on which he reckoned. That part of Syria under Egyptian administration groaned under an odious yoke. This lasted until 1839, when the excesses of Ibrahim's agents were such that the Sultan withdrew the concessions to which he had been forced to yield. The result of this was a new campaign on the part of Mehemet Ali, whose troops gained the victory of Nezib; whereupon Mahmoud began to fear for the safety of the capital of Turkey in Europe; and England, Russia and Austria had to intervene to stay the march of the conqueror, and assure him hereditary possession of Egypt, and the governorship for life of Palestine west of the Jordan.

It is true that the Viceroy, intoxicated with victory, and encouraged by French diplomacy, refused the offer of the Allied Powers. But their fleets were sent against him. Sir Charles Napier captured Beyrouth and then Sidon, and then bombarded and captured Acre, so that Mehemet Ali had to yield, and recall his son to Egypt, leaving Syria entirely to Sultan Mahmoud.

Kamylk Pasha had been too hasty in his endeavour to return to the country of his choice, where he thought of peacefully ending his troubled life. There he intended to remove his treasure, and with some portion of it pay his debts of gratitude—debts perhaps forgotten by those who had helped him. And instead of Aleppo it was Cairo that he found, thrown into a prison, where he was at the mercy of his pitiless enemies.

Kamylk understood that he was lost. The idea of regaining his liberty at the cost of his fortune did not occur to him—or rather such was the force of his character, and his indomitable determination never to abandon his wealth to the Viceroy or Mourad, that he contented himself with an obstinacy that can only be ascribed to Ottoman fatalism.

The years he passed in solitary confinement, separated from Captain Zo, whose discretion he never doubted, were anything but pleasant to him. In 1842, in the eighth year of his imprisonment, he managed, through the connivance of a gaoler, to send away a few letters, one of them to Captain Thomas Antifer of St. Malo. An envelope containing his will also reached the hands of Ben Omar, who had formerly been his notary at Alexandria.

Three years afterwards Captain Zo died, and Kamylk remained the only one who knew where the treasure had been buried. But his health declined visibly, and the severity of his imprisonment could not but shorten a life which would have lasted for years beyond the walls of his cell. At length in 1852 he died, forgotten by those who had known him, without either menaces or ill-treatment forcing him to reveal his secret.

Next year his unworthy cousin followed him to the grave, without having enjoyed the immense riches he coveted, and which had led him to such criminal devices.

But Mourad left a son, Saouk, who inherited all his father's evil instincts. Although he was then but twenty-three, he had lived a violent, unscrupulous life among the political and other bandits who then swarmed in Egypt. As the only heir of Kamylk Pasha, it was to him that the inheritance would have come had it not been put beyond his reach, and consequently his anger knew no bounds when— as he thought—the secret of the whereabouts of this immense fortune disappeared with the death of the Pasha.

Ten years went by, and Saouk had given up all hopes of ever ascertaining what had become of the lost treasure.

Judge then of the effect on him of a letter received early in 1862, inviting him to visit the office of the notary Ben Omar on important business.

Saouk knew this notary : timid to excess, an arrant poltroon, with whom a determined man like himself could do anything he pleased. So he went to Alexandria, and unceremoniously asked Ben Omar for what reason he wished to see him.

Ben Omar was most obsequious in his reception of this client whom he believed capable of everything, even of

F

strangling him straightaway. He apologized for having put him to inconvenience, and said to him in his sweetest tone,—

" But is it not the sole heir of Kamylk Pasha that I have the honour of addressing ? "

" Just so, the sole heir," said Saouk, "for I am the son of Mourad, who was his cousin."

" Are you sure that there is no other relative in the line of succession than you ? "

" None. Kamylk Pasha has no heir but me. Only, where is the inheritance ? "

" Here—at your Excellency's disposal."

Saouk grasped at the envelope handed him by the notary.

"What is in this envelope ? " he asked.

" The will of Kamylk Pasha."

" And how did it get into your hands ? "

" It reached me a few years after he was imprisoned in the fortress at Cairo."

" How long ago ? "

" Twenty years."

" Twenty years ! " exclaimed Saouk. " And he has been dead ten years now—and you have waited—"

" Read, Excellency."

Saouk read the writing on the envelope. It said that this will was not to be opened until ten years after the testator's death.

" Kamylk Pasha died in 1852," said the notary. " It is now 1862, and that is why I sent for your Excellency."

" Cursed formalist ! " exclaimed Saouk. " For ten years I ought to have been in possession."

" If the will is in your favour ? " suggested the notary.

" In my favour. Who else can there be ? I will soon know—"

And he was about to break the seal when Ben Omar stopped him.

" In your own interest, Excellency, it had better be done in the proper form, in the presence of witnesses."

And opening the door Ben Omar introduced two merchants of the neighbourhood, whom he had asked to attend. These were to testify that the envelope was intact, and that it had been opened in their presence.

The will was not very long, it was in French and as follows :—

"I appoint as my executor Ben Omar, notary of Alexandria, to whom I leave a commission of one per centum on my fortune in gold, diamonds and precious stones, of the estimated value of four million pounds sterling. In the month of September, 1831, three casks containing this treasure were buried in a hole dug at the southern point of a certain islet. Of this islet it will be easy to discover the position by combining the longitude of fifty-four degrees fifty-seven minutes east, with a latitude secretly sent in 1842 to Thomas Antifer, of St. Malo, in France. Ben Omar in person is to take this longitude of fifty-four degrees fifty-seven minutes east to the said Thomas Antifer, or his nearest heir. But he is to accompany the said heir in the search for the discovery of the treasure, which is buried at the base of a rock marked with the double K of my name. To the exclusion of my unworthy cousin Mourad, and his still more unworthy son Saouk, Ben Omar will hasten to put himself in communication with Thomas Antifer, or his direct heirs, and with him follow the formal instructions that will be found in the course of the said search. Such is my last will, and I desire that it shall be respected in all its bearings and consequences.

"Written this 9th of February, 1842, in the prison at Cairo, by my own hand.

"KAMYLK PASHA."

We need not dwell on the reception given by Saouk to this curious will, nor to the agreeable surprise manifested by Ben Omar at the one per cent. on four millions which was to come to him on handing over the treasure. But the treasure had to be found, and the only way to discover the position of the islet was by combining the longitude given in the will with the latitude known only to Thomas Antifer.

Saouk immediately devised a scheme, and Ben Omar, under terrible threats, became his accomplice in it. They soon discovered that Thomas Antifer had died in 1854, leaving an only son. To this son they would go, and by skilful management obtain from him the secret of the latitude and then they would take possession of the fortune, and Ben Omar should have his commission.

This scheme Saouk and the notary set about without delay. They left Alexandria, landed at Marseilles, took the Paris express, and then went on to St. Malo, where they had arrived that morning.

Neither Saouk nor Ben Omar expected that there would be any difficulty in obtaining from Antifer the letter, of which they knew the value, and which contained the precious latitude—and they were prepared to buy it if necessary. We know how the attempt had failed. We shall not be astonished, therefore, at the irritation which his Excellency displayed, at his endeavouring to hold Ben Omar responsible for his ill-success, and at the noisy scene in the hotel, from which the unfortunate notary feared he would never emerge alive.

"Yes," said Saouk, "it is your bungling that has caused it all! You did not know what you were about! You let yourself be played with by this sailor, you, a notary! But do not forget what I told you! Woe to you if Kamylk's millions escape me!"

"I swear to you, Excellency—"

"And I swear to you, that if I do not attain my object you shall pay for it, and pay well!"

And Ben Omar knew only too well that Saouk was the man to keep his word.

"You must remember, Excellency, that this sailor is not one of those miserable fellahs, easily deceived and easily frightened"

"No matter."

"No! He is a violent man, who will listen to nothing—"

He might have added, "a man like you," but he took care not to complete the sentence in that fashion.

"I think," he continued, "we shall have to give up—"

"Give up!" exclaimed Saouk, slapping the table, "give up four millions?"

"No, your Excellency; give up—let the Breton know —the longitude the will orders us to give him."

"For him to take advantage of it, imbecile; for him to unearth the millions!"

Anger is a bad councillor, and this Saouk, who was not destitute of intelligence or astuteness, finally came to think. He calmed down as much as he could, and thought of the proposal submitted by Ben Omar. It was certain that nothing would be got from Antifer by stratagem, and that some other scheme must be thought of.

The plan agreed upon was this. His Excellency and his very humble servant would call in the morning on Captain Antifer, give him the longitude and learn from him in exchange what was the latitude. When the information was obtained Saouk would endeavour to forestall the sailor, and if he could not do this he would accompany Antifer during the search and endeavour to carry off the treasure. If, as was probable, the islet was situated in some distant part of the world, the plan had many chances of success, and the affair would end to Saouk's advantage.

When this plan had been definitely agreed upon Saouk added,—

"I rely on you, Ben Omar, to be straightforward; if not—"

"You can rely on me, your Excellency; but you promised me my commission."

"Yes, for according to the will the commission is due to you—on the express condition that you do not leave Antifer for an instant during the journey."

"I will not leave him!"

"Nor will I ! I will accompany him !"

"In what capacity ?   Under what name ?"

"As the chief clerk of Ben Omar, and under the name
of Nazim !"

"You ?"

And this "you" was said in a tone of despair that
indicated only too clearly what violence and misery Ben
Omar anticipated.

CHAPTER VIII.

WHEN Captain Antifer reached the door of his house he opened it, entered the dining-room, and sitting down at the corner of the fireplace, began to warm his feet, without saying a word.

Enogate and Juhel were talking near the window, but he took no notice of their presence. Nanon was busy cooking in the kitchen, and he did not worry as usual by asking a dozen times, "if it would soon be ready?"

Evidently Antifer was deep in thought; but it would not do to tell his sister, and his nephew and niece, what had happened at his interview with Ben Omar, the notary of Kamylk Pasha. During the meal he said nothing. He even refrained from any second helpings, and contented himself with prolonging his dessert by mechanically disposing of several dozen periwinkles, which he extracted from their greenish shells by means of a long copper-headed pin.

Several times Juhel spoke to him; but he answered not a word.

Enogate asked him what was the matter, as he did not seem to hear.

"Brother, what ails you?" asked Nanon, as he rose to retire to his room.

"I have got a wisdom tooth coming through!" he replied.

And each of them thought that it would not be too late if it could make him wise in his old age.

Then, without lighting his pipe, which he was so fond of smoking night and morning on the rampart, he went upstairs without saying good-night to anybody.

"Uncle is troubling about something," remarked Enogate.

"Has he had any news?" said Nanon, as she cleared the table.

"Perhaps we had better send for Tregomain?" replied Juhel.

The truth is that Captain Antifer was more uneasy and anxious than he had ever been since he had been expecting the indispensable messenger. Had he not failed in presence of mind, in acuteness, during his interview with Ben Omar? Had he done right in being so categorical and reserved with this fellow, instead of winning him over, of discussing the main points of the business, of trying to bargain with him? Had he done wisely in calling him a rascal, a crocodile, and so on? Would it not have been better, without showing so much caution as to his own interests to have temporized, to have appeared disposed to hand over the letter, to have pretended to have been ignorant of its importance, instead of asking fifty million francs for it? Of course, it was worth it; there was no doubt about that, but it would have been wise to have acted more circumspectly. And if the notary declined to submit to a similar reception? If he strapped up his portmanteau, left St. Malo and returned to Alexandria, how would the problem be solved? Would Captain Antifer have to go to Egypt after his longitude?

And so when he went to bed, he administered to himself quite a shower of hard knocks. He did not close his eyes during the night. The next morning he had firmly resolved to go in search of Ben Omar, to apologize for his rudeness, to enter into an arrangement at the expense of a few slight concessions.

But as he was reflecting on all this, and dressing himself, about eight o'clock, the bargeman gently pushed open the door of his room.

Nanon had sent for him, and he had come, the excellent man, to offer himself to his neighbour's blows.

"What brings you here?"

"The flood, friend," said Tregomain, hoping that this maritime locution would provoke a smile.

"The flood !" replied Antifer, sternly. "Well, the ebb is just taking me out."

"You are getting ready to go out ?"

"Yes, with or without your permission."

"Where are you going ?"

"Where it suits me to go."

"Nowhere else, of course, but you do not wish me to know what you are going to do ?"

"I am going to repair a mistake."

"And to make it worse, perhaps ?"

This reply, although given as a general observation, made Antifer uneasy. And so he decided to let his friend know what had happened. Continuing his dressing, he told him of his meeting with Ben Omar, of the notary's attempts to gain possession of the latitude, and his offer to sell the letter for fifty millions of francs.

"He should have made you an offer," observed Tregomain.

"He had no time, for I turned my back on him—in which I was wrong."

"That is my opinion. And so this notary came expressly to St. Malo to try and get this letter from you ?"

"Instead of giving me the communication he ought to have done. This Ben Omar is the messenger spoken of by Kamylk Pasha, and expected for the last twenty years—"

"Ah, then this matter is serious after all," Tregomain could not help saying.

The remark brought him such a terrible look and such a contemptuous epithet from Antifer, that he lowered his eyes and twiddled his thumbs after crossing his hands over the vast rotundity of his corporation.

A moment afterwards Antifer had finished dressing, and was picking up his hat when the door opened.

Nanon appeared.

"What is the matter now ?" asked her brother.

" There is a stranger downstairs. He wants to speak to you."

" His name ? "

" Here it is."

And she produced a card on which were these words : *Ben Omar, Notary, Alexandria.*

" The man ! " exclaimed Antifer.

" Who ? " asked Tregomain.

" The Omar in question. Ah ! I like that ! That he has come back is a good sign ! Show him up, Nanon."

" But he is not alone—"

" Not alone ? " exclaimed Antifer. " And who then is with him ? "

" A younger man whom I don't know, and who looks like a foreigner."

" Ah ! There are two of them ? Well, we shall be two to receive them ! Stop here, Tregomain."

" Do you wish it ? "

An imperious gesture kept the worthy neighbour in his place. Another gesture indicated to Nanon that she was to show the visitors upstairs.

A minute afterwards they had been ushered into the room, the door of which was carefully shut. If the secrets that were to be revealed were to escape it would have to be through the keyhole.

" Ah ! It is you, Mr. Ben Omar ! " said Antifer, in a careless and haughty tone, very different to what he would have adopted had he gone to make the first advances at the hotel.

" Myself, Mr. Antifer."

" And the person who accompanies you ? "

" My head clerk."

Antifer and Saouk, who was introduced under the name of Nazim, exchanged a look of indifference.

" Your clerk is acquainted with this business ? " asked Antifer.

" He is, and his assistance is indispensable to me throughout this matter."

" Be it so, Mr. Ben Omar. May I ask to what I owe the honour of this visit ? "

" Another interview I wish to have with you, Mr. Antifer, with you alone," he added, casting a side look at Tregomain, whose thumbs continued their twiddling.

" Gildas Tregomain, my friend," replied Antifer, " late captain of the barge *Charmante Amélie*, who is also acquainted with this business, and whose assistance is no less indispensable than that of your clerk Nazim."

It was impossible for Ben Omar to object. Immediately the four sat down round the table, on which the notary placed his portfolio. Then a certain silence reigned in the room until it pleased one or the other to speak.

Antifer broke the silence by addressing Ben Omar :

" Your clerk speaks French, I suppose ? "

" No," replied the notary.

" But he understands it ? "

" Not much."

This had been agreed between Saouk and Ben Omar, in the hope that Antifer, having no fear of being understood by the false Nazim, might let fall a few words of which dvantage might be taken.

" And now, proceed, Mr. Ben Omar," said Antifer, carelessly. " Your intention is to resume the conversation that ended abruptly yesterday ? "

" Certainly."

" Then you have brought me the fifty millions ? "

" Let us be serious, sir—"

" Yes, let us be serious, Mr. Ben Omar; my friend Tregomain is not one of those who will consent to lose time in useless pleasantries. That is so, Tregomain ? "

Never had the bargeman a more serious countenance, a more composed demeanour ; and when he enveloped his nasal appendage in the folds of his flag—we mean handkerchief—never had he produced more magisterial trumpetings.

" Mr. Ben Omar, I am afraid there has been some misunderstanding between us. It is better it should end,

or no good will come of this.   You know who I am, and 1
know who you are—"

" A notary."

" A notary, who is also the messenger of the deceased
Kamylk Pasha, whom my family have been expecting for
the last twenty years."

" You will excuse me, Mr. Antifer, but in admitting that
that is so I may say that I was not allowed to come sooner."

" And why ? "

" Because it is only a fortnight ago, that by the opening
of the will, I ascertained under what conditions your father
had received this letter."

" Ah, the letter with the double K !   We return to that,
Mr. Ben Omar ? "

" Yes, and my only idea in coming to St. Malo was to
put myself in communication with you."

" That is the only object of your journey ? "

" The only one."

During this exchange of question and answer Saouk
remained impassible, and did not seem to understand a
word that was said.   He played his game so naturally
that Tregomain, who was quietly watching him, saw
nothing suspicious in his behaviour.

" Then, Mr. Ben Omar," said Antifer.   " I have for you
the most profound respect, and as you know, I would not
say an unkind word to you—"

Really this was sublime—what about " rascal,"
" mummy," " crocodile," etc. etc ?

" But," he continued, " I cannot help observing that you
just lied—"

" Sir ! "

" Yes, lied like a steward's mate, when you asserted that
your journey had no other object than to know what was
in my letter ! "

" I swear—" said the notary, lifting his hand.

" Keep your hand down, old Omar ! " said Antifer,
waking up in spite of his good resolutions.   " I know perfectly well why you have come—"

" Believe me—"

" And on whose behalf you have come—"

" Nobody, I assure you—"

" So—on behalf of the deceased Kamylk Pasha—"

" He died ten years ago."

" Never mind. It is in execution of his last wishes that you are here to-day with Pierre Servan Malo, son of Thomas Antifer, and your orders are not to demand the letter in question but to give him certain figures—"

" Certain figures?"

" Yes, the figures of a longitude he requires for the completion of a latitude Kamylk Pasha gave twenty years ago to his good father."

" Well hit!" said Tregomain, tranquilly shaking his handkerchief as if he were signalling to the semaphores on the coast.

But the so-called clerk remained impassible, although he knew now that Antifer quite understood the position.

" And you, Mr. Ben Omar, have changed your errand, and have been trying to steal my latitude."

" Steal?"

" Yes, steal! And probably to make use of it in a way that only I ought to do—"

" Mr. Antifer," replied Omar, much disconcerted, " believe me, as soon as you give me this letter I will give you the figures—"

" Then you admit that you have them?"

The notary was fairly caught. Practised as he was at evasion, he saw that his adversary had him at his mercy, and that the best thing for him to do was to submit, as had been agreed the night before between him and Saouk. And now Antifer said—

" Come, play fairly, Mr. Ben Omar! You have been long enough on that tack—try another."

" I will," he replied.

He opened his portfolio, and drew from it a sheet of parchment streaked with lines of large handwriting.

This was Kamylk Pasha's will, and he handed it to Antifer, who, as it was written in French, readily understood it. He read it through in a loud voice, so that Tregomain did not lose a word of what the will contained, and then drew his note-book from his pocket, so as to inscribe therein the figures indicating the longitude of the islet— those four figures for each of which he would have given one of the fingers of his right hand, and Tregomain also brought out a note-book and wrote down the figures— 54° 57″ east.

The will was then returned to the notary, who put it into his portfolio, which was passed under the arm of Nazim, who remained seemingly indifferent to all that was going on, although the interview had now reached a point of considerable interest for him and Ben Omar. Antifer, knowing both the meridian and the parallel of the island, had only to cross these two lines to find the position. And this he was very naturally somewhat eager to do.

But as he rose, there could be no mistake as to the meaning of the bow he made his visitors, and the gesture with which he indicated the stairs. Evidently Saouk and Ben Omar were invited to depart.

The bargeman quietly watched the proceedings with considerable amusement. Nevertheless, neither the notary nor Nazim seemed disposed to rise. It was clear that their host would put them out, but either they did not understand or did not wish to understand. Ben Omar, who was much embarrassed, felt that Saouk was, by a look, giving him express orders to ask a final question.

He obeyed, and said,—

"Now that I have fulfilled the mission entrusted to me by the will of Kamylk Pasha—"

"We have only to take leave of each other politely," said Antifer, "and the first train being at 10.37 —"

"10.23, since yesterday," corrected Tregomain.

"Yes, 10.23, and I would not, my dear Mr. Ben Omar, make you or your clerk Nazim miss this express."

Saouk's feet began to beat a double shuffle on the floor,

and as he looked at his watch, it seemed as though he was anxious to be off.

"If you have any luggage to register," continued Antifer, "there is barely time."

"All the more so," added the bargeman, "as there is no end of it at this station."

Ben Omar saw that he must say something further, and half rising, he remarked, lowering his eyes,—

"Pardon me, but it seems to me that we have not said all we have to say."

"Quite the contrary, Mr. Ben Omar; as far as I am concerned I have nothing more to ask you."

"But I have a question to ask, Mr. Antifer."

"I am surprised, Mr. Ben Omar; but if you think so, what is it?"

"I have given you the figures of the longitude indicated in the will of Kamylk Pasha—"

"You have, and my friend Tregomain and I have entered them in our note-books."

"And now you have to give me those of the latitude indicated in the letter."

"The letter addressed to my father?"

"The same."

"Pardon, Mr. Ben Omar!" replied Antifer, frowning. "Did you not have orders to bring me the longitude in question?"

"Yes, and those orders I have fulfilled."

"With as much kindness as zeal, I admit. But, as far as I am concerned, I have nowhere seen either in the will or in the letter that I should reveal to you the figures of the latitude sent to my father."

"However—"

"However, if you have any orders concerning this, we might perhaps discuss them."

"It seems to me," replied the notary, "that between gentlemen who esteem each other—"

"It seems wrong then, Mr. Ben Omar. Esteem has nothing to do with it, however much we may have for each other."

Evidently the irritation which was taking the place of impatience with Captain Antifer would not be long in showing itself. And so, in his anxiety to avoid an explosion, Tregomain went to open the door so as to facilitate the departure of the visitors. Saouk never budged. It was, however, not his business as clerk and a foreigner ignorant of the language, to move before his master gave him the order.

Ben Omar quitted his chair, rubbed his head, adjusted his spectacles upon his nose, and, in the tone of a man who does the best with what he cannot prevent, remarked,—

"Excuse me, Mr. Antifer, you have made up your mind not to trust me."

"The more so, Mr. Ben Omar, because Kamylk Pasha's letter required my father to keep it a profound secret, and that this secret my father also required me to keep."

"Well, Mr. Antifer," said Ben Omar, "will you accept good advice?"

"What is it?"

"To take no further steps in this matter."

"And why?"

"Because you may meet on the way a certain person who may make you repent it."

"And who is that?"

"Saouk, the son of Kamylk Pasha's cousin, disinherited to your advantage, and who is not at all the man—"

"Do you know this son, Mr. Ben Omar?"

"No," replied the notary, "but I know that he is a formidable adversary—"

"Well, if you ever meet this Saouk, tell him I don't care a snap for him, nor for all the Saoukery of Egypt!"

Nazim did not move a muscle. And then Antifer went out on the landing.

"Nanon!" he shouted.

The notary moved towards the door, and this time Saouk, clumsily upsetting his chair, followed him, not without a furious desire to kick him downstairs.

But as he was at the door, Ben Omar suddenly stopped, and said to Antifer, "you have not forgotten one of the clauses in Kamylk Pasha's will ? "

" Which is that, Mr. Ben Omar ? "

" That which compels me to accompany you until you have taken possession of your legacy, of being present when the three casks are exhumed."

" Well, you shall accompany me, Mr. Ben Omar."

" Then I must know where you are going."

" You will know when we are there."

" But if it is at the other end of the world ? "

" It will be at the other end of the world."

" But remember that I cannot do without my head clerk."

" That is as you please, and I shall be no less honoured by his presence than by yours."

Leaning over the balusters, he shouted in a voice that showed he considered the interview at an end—

" Nanon ! "

Nanon appeared.

" Show these gentlemen a light ! "

" Good ! " said Nanon ; " it is broad daylight.

" Show them a light all the same."

And thus it was that Saouk and Ben Omar were shown out of this inhospitable house, the door of which was slammed behind them.

Then Captain Antifer was seized with such an attack of delirious delight as had seldom come to him before. But if he was not joyful on that occasion, when should he have been ?

He had it, this famous longitude so impatiently expected He had the power to change into reality what had hitherto been but a dream. The possession of this immense fortune depended only on the haste with which he went in search of the islet where it awaited him.

" Four millions—four millions ! " he repeated.

" That is to say a thousand times a hundred thousand francs ! " added the bargeman.

G

And then Antifer hopped on one leg, then on the other, then stooped and rose, and swung his hips and spun round like a gyroscope, and finally completed his performance with a furious hornpipe. Then he seized Tregomain, and setting that massive form in motion, he worked up the dance to such impetuosity, that the house shook to its foundations as he broke out in a voice that made the windows rattle,—

"I have my lon—lon—gi—
I have my gi—gi—tude ;
My lon, my gi, my tude—I have my longitude."

CHAPTER IX.

WHILE Antifer was performing in this quartette party Enogate and Juhel had gone off to the mairie and the church. At the mairie the clerk of the marriage department—a leather-faced old fellow, engaged in the manufacture of honeymoons—had shown them the notice of their banns stuck up among the other notices. At the Cathedral the vicar promised them a choral service, address, organ and bells complete.

How happy they were? With what impatience—ill-disguised on the part of Juhel, more reserved on the part of Enogate—did they wait for the 5th of April, the date that had been won from their uncle's hesitations! How busy they were with their preparations, their wardrobe, their furniture for the pretty room on the first floor, which the generous Tregomain embellished every day with odds and ends that during many years he had collected among the shorefolk of the Rance. Was he not their confidant, and could they have found a better, a safer depository of their hopes and future projects? And twenty times a day would the old bargeman repeat,—

"I would give a lot for the marriage to be over."

"And why, my good Gildas?" the girl would ask, a little uneasy.

"Friend Antifer is so singular when he gets astride of his hobby, and goes prancing among his millions!"

That, too, was Juhel's opinion. When you depend on an uncle, an excellent man but somewhat unsettled, you are sure of nothing until the "Yes" has been uttered before the maire.

And as is usual among sailor families there was no time to lose. Either they would have to remain unmarried, or be married as soon as possible. Juhel was under orders to sail as first mate of one of Le Baillif's largest ships. And then for what months, for what years even, he might be on the seas, thousands of miles from his wife and children, if God blessed their union. As a sailor's daughter Enogate had reconciled herself to long voyages taking her husband away from her, never imagining it could be otherwise ; and therefore all the more reason for not losing a day, as their lives would consist of so many during which they would be separated.

It was of their future that they were talking when they returned from their walk. To their surprise they saw two strangers come out of the house in the Rue des Hautes Salles, and move off, gesticulating furiously. Had these people been to call on Captain Antifer ? Juhel had a presentiment that something unusual had occurred.

And any doubt as to this was removed when he and Enogate heard the noise overhead and the improvised song, the last line of which could be heard at the further end of the ramparts.

Had their uncle gone out of his mind ?

"What is the matter, aunt ? " asked Juhel.

"Your uncle is dancing, my children," said Nanon.

"But he could not shake the house like this ? "

"No, that is Tregomain."

"What ! Is Tregomain dancing too ? "

"Probably not to annoy uncle ! " said Enogate.

The three went upstairs, and very naturally supposed that Antifer had gone mad, when they saw him capering about and yelling at the top of his voice,—

> "I have my lon—lon—gi—
> I have my gi—gi—tude."

And then Tregomain, joining in, puffing as if he were in danger of a stroke of apoplexy,—

"Oh yes, his gi, his longitude !"

A revelation suddenly enlightened Juhel.   Those two strangers who had just left the house !   Was this the untoward messenger of Kamylk Pasha who had arrived at last ?

The young man turned pale, and stopping Antifer in the middle of a step,—

"What, uncle," he said, " have you got it ? "

"I have it."

"He has it !" murmured Tregomain.   And he sank on to a chair, which being unable to oppose an impossible resistance, broke to pieces beneath him.

As soon as their uncle had recovered his breath, Enogate and Juhel were told what had happened the day before,—the arrival of Ben Omar and his clerk, the attempt at extortion relative to Kamylk's letter, the contents of the will, the exact longitude of the island where the treasure was buried—Captain Antifer had only to stoop to pick it up !

"Well, uncle, now that these two individuals know where the nest is, they can get it before you can ! "

"Wait a minute !" exclaimed Antifer, shrugging up his shoulders.   "Do you think I was fool enough to give them the key of the strong-box ? "

And Tregomain emphasized the question by solemnly shaking his head.

"A strong-box which holds four millions !"

And the word millions appeared to swell in Antifer's mouth as if it would choke him.

If he expected that this declaration would be welcomed with shouts of enthusiasm, he was promptly undeceived. What ! a shower of gold of which Danae would have been jealous, a torrent of diamonds and precious stones pouring on to this humble house, and not a hand held out for them, not one to tear off the roof so as not to lose a drop of the rain of wealth.

Yet so it was. A glacial silence received the phrase stuffed with millions so triumphantly declaimed by the author.

"Ah, that is it!" he said, looking at one after the other his sister, his nephew, his niece, his friend. "I tell you I am as rich as Crœsus, that I return from Eldorado laden with gold enough to sink me, and you do not even fall on my neck and wish me joy!"

There was no reply. Nothing but eyes cast down and faces turned away.

"Well, Nanon?"

"Yes, brother," replied Nanon, "it is a nice little fortune."

"A nice little fortune! More than three hundred thousand francs to eat every day of the year! And you, Enogate, do you also think it is a nice little fortune?"

"Uncle!" said the girl, "it is not necessary to be as rich as that—"

"Yes. I know. I know the rest! Money does not make happiness! Is that your opinion, Mr. Captain?" asked the uncle of his nephew.

"My opinion," replied Juhel, "is that this Egyptian ought to have thrown the title of Pasha into the bargain, for so much money and no title—"

"Ha, ha! Antifer Pasha!" said the bargeman with a chuckle.

"Steady there!" in a tone of command! "Steady there, ex-captain of the *Charmante Amélie*, are you trying to make fun of me?"

"I, my worthy friend!" replied Tregomain—"certainly not. And if you are so pleased with your millions, I offer you a hundred million compliments."

But why was it that the family received the exultations of its chief so coldly? He might perhaps think no more of his plan of superb alliances for his niece and nephew; perhaps he would give up his idea of breaking off or at least delaying the marriage of Juhel and Enogate, although his longitude had arrived before the 6th of April. But

there was a doubt as to this, and hence the anxiety of
Enogate and Juhel, Nanon, and Gildas Tregomain.

Tregomain resolved to give his friend an opportunity of
explaining. Better to know at once what was going to
happen. At least they could discuss the matter, and let
this terrible uncle hear reason.

"Look here, my friend," said Tregomain, rounding his
back, "suppose you have these millions—"

"Suppose? Why suppose?"

"Well, let us say you have them—a good fellow like you
accustomed to live in a humble way, what are you going
to do?"

"What I please," replied Antifer, drily.

"You are not going to buy all St. Malo, I imagine—"

"All St. Malo, all St. Servan, and all Dinard, if it suits
me, and even that ridiculous brook the Rance, which has
no other water than what the tide chooses to bring it."

He knew that in insulting the Rance he was stinging to
the quick one who had been up and down this charming
river for twenty years of his life.

"That may be," said Tregomain, biting his lip; "but you
cannot eat a morsel more, or drink a glass more, unless
you buy a supplementary stomach—"

"I will buy what I like, Mr. Freshwater Sailor, and if
any one says no to me, if I find any opposition among my
own people—"

This was addressed to the lovers.

"I will eat my millions. I will dissipate them, I will
turn them into smoke, into dust, and Juhel and Enogate
shall have none of the two each I intend one day to leave
them—"

"Better say the four to both, my friend."

"Why?"

"Because they are going to get married."

This touched the burning question.

"Hold there, bargeman," said Antifer, in the voice of a
stentor. "Up you go to the main-royal, and take a look
around."

This was his way of sending Tregomain about his business—figuratively be it understood, for to hoist such a mass to the top of any mast whatever would have been impossible without the aid of a capstan.

Neither Nanon, nor Juhel, nor Enogate, dare interfere in the conversation. The young captain got so white that he was evidently hardly able to master his indignation.

But the bargeman was not one to desert anybody in the open sea. Approaching his friend he said,—

" However, you made a promise—"

" What promise ? "

" To consent to their marriage."

" Yes—if the longitude did not come, and as the longitude has come—"

" All the more reason for assuring their happiness—"

" Exactly. And therefore Enogate shall marry a prince—"

" If she can find one."

" And Juhel a princess."

" There are none to marry ! " replied Tregomain, who could argue no more.

" You can always find one when you have a dowry of two millions to offer."

" Then you had better search—"

" I will seaich and I will find—and in the *Almanach de Gothon* too."

He meant to say the *Almanach de Gotha*, this obstinate intractable coaster, possessed with the idea of mingling the blood of potentates with the blood of the Antifers.

But not wishing to prolong a conversation which might end badly, resolved to yield in no respect on this marriage question, he let it be understood—very clearly—that he wished to be left alone in his room, and not to be disturbed by anybody before dinner.

Tregomain judged it prudent not to withstand him, and all four went downstairs. They were all in despair, and the girl was crying. This was almost more than Tregomain could bear.

"I don't like people to cry," he said, "not even when sorrow comes to them, my little one."

"But," said she, "all is lost. Uncle will never give in. This enormous fortune has turned his head."

"Yes," said Nanon; "and when my brother gets an idea into his head—"

Juhel did not speak. He strode about the room cross-ing and uncrossing his arms, opening and shutting his hands. Suddenly he exclaimed,—

"After all he is not master! I have no need of his permission to marry. I am of age—"

"But Enogate is not," said the bargeman. "And as her guardian he can object."

"Yes, and we are all dependent on him," added Nanon, bowing her head.

"My advice," said Tregomain, "is not to oppose him directly. It is not impossible that this mania will pass away, particularly if we seem to give in to him."

"You ought to be right," said Enogate. "We shall gain more by gentleness than violence, at least I hope so."

"Besides," said the bargeman, "he has not got the millions yet."

"No," said Juhel; "and in spite of his latitude and his longitude, he may come to grief before he lays his hands on them. It will take a good deal of time."

"A good deal!" murmured the girl.

"Yes, dear Enogate, and there may be delays! Ah! the confounded uncle."

"And the confounded brutes who have come from the confounded Pasha!" growled Nanon. "I should have welcomed them with the bróomstick."

"They would have managed to see him, all the same," said Juhel, "and this Ben Omar, who has a commission on the business, would never have left him alone."

"Then uncle is going away?" asked Enogate.

"Probably," said Tregomain, "now he knows where the island is."

"I will accompany him," said Juhel.

"You, Juhel?" exclaimed the girl.

"Yes, it must be so; I should like to be there to prevent his committing some stupidity, to bring him back if he stays away too long."

"Well thought of, my boy," said the bargeman.

"Who knows where he may be dragged, running after this treasure, and to what dangers he may be exposed."

Enogate felt as sad as ever, but she understood him. Juhel's resolve was dictated by good sense; perhaps the length of the voyage might be shortened by it.

The young captain did his best to console her. He would write to her often; he would tell her all that happened; Nanon would not leave her, nor would Tregomain, who would see her every day, who would teach her resignation.

"Depend on me, my girl," said the bargeman, much moved. "I will teach you not to dwell on it too much. You don't know the adventures of the *Charmante Amélie!*"

No, Enogate did not know them, for he had not yet dared to recount them for fear of Captain Antifer.

"Well. I will tell you them. They are very interesting. The time will pass. Some day we shall see our friend return with his millions under his arm—or the bag empty—and our brave Juhel, who will take but one jump from the house to the Cathedral. I will not stop you. If you like, I will have my new coat made while they are away, and wear it every morning."

"Below there! Bargeman!"

The well-known voice made the whole company start.

"He calls me," said Tregomain.

"What does he want with you?" asked Nanon.

"That is not the way he speaks when he is angry," suggested Enogate.

"No," said Juhel. "There is more impatience than anger in the tone."

"Tregomain—will you come?"

"I am coming," said Tregomain. And the stairs began to groan as the bargeman went up them.

A minute afterwards Antifer had pushed him across the room, and locked the door.   Then drawing him before the table on which the atlas was open, he held a pair of compasses out to him.

" Take this ! " he said.

" These compasses ? "

" Yes," said Antifer sharply ; " this island—this island with the millions in it—I have been trying to find its place on the map—"

" And it is not there ? " exclaimed Tregomain, in a tone that betrayed less surprise than satisfaction.

" Who says so ? " replied Antifer.   " And why is this island not on the map ? "

" Then it is ? "

" If it is.   I believe that it is ; but I am so nervous, my hand shakes, the compasses burn my fingers, I cannot touch the map with them."

" And you want me to do it ? "

" If you are able to."

" Oh ! " said Tregomain.

" Well, try and we shall see.   Hold the compasses and run the point along the fifty-fourth meridian, or rather the fifty-fifth, for the islet is fifty-four degrees, fifty-seven minutes—"

The figures began to trouble the worthy man's head.

" Fifty-seven degrees, fifty-four minutes ? " he repeated, blinking his eyes.

" No—animal ! " exclaimed Antifer.   ' It is the contrary.   Go on."

Tregomain put the compasses on the western side of the map.

" No ! " roared his friend.   " Not west !   East, understand, you duffer !   East, east, east ! "

Tregomain, deafened by these recriminations and objurgations, was incapable of doing the work properly.   His eyes became veiled in a mist, drops of perspiration rolled down his forehead, and the compasses shook like the clapper of an electric bell.

"Touch the fifty-fifth meridian," vociferated **Antifer**
"Begin at the top of the map, and move down till you cut
the twenty-fourth parallel!"

"The twenty-fourth parallel!" stammered Tregomain.

"Yes! the idiot! Yes, and the point where they
cross is the position of the island."

"The position—"

"Well. Go on down"

"I am going down!"

"Oh! the noodle! You are going up!" The
truth is that the bargeman did not know where he was,
and was no fitter than his friend to solve the problem.

Both of them were greatly agitated, and their nerves
were vibrating like the strings of a double bass in the
finale of an overture.

Captain Antifer thought he was going mad. And so
doing the only thing he could, he shouted for Juhel in a
voice that sounded as if it came through a speaking-
trumpet.

The young captain appeared almost immediately.

"What do you want, uncle?"

"Juhel—where is Kamylk Pasha's island?"

"Where the longitude crosses the latitude."

"Well, look for it."

That was enough for Juhel. His uncle's agitation told
him what had happened. Taking the compasses in a hand
which did not tremble, he placed the point where the
fifty fifth meridian started from the north of the map and
followed it down.

"Tell me where it passes!" commanded Captain
Antifer.

"Yes, uncle," said Juhel.

And thus it was he continued,—

"Franz Josef Land, in the Arctic Sea."

"Good."

"Barents Sea."

"Well."

" Novaia Zemlia."

" After ? "

" Kara Sea."

" And then ? "

" The north of Asiatic Russia."

" What towns does it run through ? "

" First, Ekaterinburg."

" Then ? "

" Sea of Aral."

" Go on."

" Khiva in Turkestan."

" Are we getting near ? "

" Very soon !   Herat in Persia."

" Is that it ? "

" Muscat, at the south-east end of Arabia."

" Muscat ! " exclaimed Antifer, leaning over the map.

In fact the fifty-fifth meridian and the twenty-fourth parallel crossed on the territory of the Sultan of Muscat, in that part of the Gulf of Oman above the Persian Gulf, separating Arabia from Persia.

" Muscat ! " repeated Captain Antifer.

" Mascotte ? " asked Tregomain.

" Not Mascotte, but Muscat, you bargee ! " roared his friend, shrugging his shoulders up to his ears.

But this was only approximate, for they had as yet taken no account of the minutes.

" You are sure it is Muscat ? "

" Yes, uncle, within seventy miles of it."

" Can you get any nearer ? "

" Yes."

" Then go on, go on—don't you see I am bursting with impatience."

And a boiler worked up as he was, would have been on the point of explosion.

Juhel picked up the compasses again, and taking account of the minutes in the longitude and latitude, he obtained the position so exactly that he could only be a mile or two out.

" Well ? " asked Antifer.

" Well, uncle, it is not on the territory of the Sultan of Muscat, but a little to the east of it, in the Gulf of Oman."

" To be sure ! "

" Why to be sure ? " asked Tregomain.

" Because if it is an island, it could not be on a continent, you bargeman ! "

This was said in a tone impossible to describe.

" To-morrow," added Antifer, " we will begin our preparations for departure."

" You are right ! " said Juhel, resolved not to withstand his uncle.

" We will see if there is a ship in the harbour bound for Port Said."

" That will be the best, for we have not a day to lose."

" No ! They shall not steal my island from me."

" Oh, it will take a famous thief to do it ! " answered Tregomain. And Antifer shrugged his shoulders again.

" You will accompany me, Juhel."

" Yes, uncle," said Juhel.

" And you too. Mr. Bargeman."

" Me ! "

" Yes. You ! "

These two words were uttered in such a commanding tone, that the worthy man's head could do nothing but bow in sign of consent.

And yet he had reckoned on Antifer's absence to be able to console Enogate, by recounting the adventures of the *Charmante Amélie* on the fresh waters of the Rance !

CHAPTER X.

On the 21st of February the steamer *Steersman* left St. Malo at the morning tide. She was a collier of 900 tons, running direct between Newcastle and Port Said, but on this occasion a slight accident to her engine had made it necessary for her to put into port. Instead of going to Cherbourg, her captain had brought her on to St. Malo in the hope that he might see an old friend. Two days afterwards the steamer was at sea again, and had put Cape Frehel thirty miles behind when we call the reader's attention to her.

And why should we call attention to this collier more than to another, considering that hundreds of colliers pass down channel, and that the United Kingdom sends its coal to every part of the world? Why? Because Captain Antifer was on board, and with him his nephew Juhel, and with them their friend Tregomain. And why were they on an English steamer instead of in a railway carriage? When a man is interested in four millions, surely he would take his ease and think nothing of the expense! And this Antifer would have done had not an opportunity offered of travelling under pleasant conditions.

Captain Chip, who commanded the *Steersman*, was an old acquaintance of Antifer's. When the Englishman put in at St. Malo he did not fail to look up his old friend, and was warmly welcomed. When he learnt that Antifer was about to start for Port Said, he offered him a passage on the *Steersman* on reasonable terms. She was a good ship, capable of nine knots an hour in a calm sea, and

taking a fortnight or thereabouts on the voyage to the far
end of the Mediterranean. The *Steersman*, it is true, was
not designed for passengers ; but sailors are not very
difficult to please. There was at least a comfortable
cabin for them, and they would not have to change
vessels on the voyage—which was not without its advan-
tages.

And it is easy to understand why Antifer had preferred
it. To be shut up in a railway carriage for so long a
journey was not to his taste. Far better in his opinion to
spend two weeks on a good ship amid the fresh sea
breezes, than six days in a rolling box breathing smoke and
dust. This was also the opinion of Juhel, if not that of
the bargeman, whose field of navigation had been bordered
by the banks of the Rance. He had hoped to accomplish
most of the journey by railway, but his friend had decided
otherwise. They were in no hurry for a day or so. If
they arrived in a month or two the island would still be
where it had been, and where it was no one knew but
Antifer, Juhel, and Tregomain. The treasure which had
been buried for thirty-one years under the seal of the double
K was in no danger for a few weeks more. Consequently
Antifer, eager as he might be, had accepted Captain Chip's
proposal, and that is why the reader's attention has been
called to the *Steersman*.

Captain Antifer, his nephew, his friend Tregomain—
provided with a good sum in gold, which the bargeman
wore in his belt, and taking with them an excellent
chronometer, a sextant, a nautical almanac, besides a spade
and pickaxe—took their passage on the collier. The
bargeman had to overcome his repugnance at venturing on
a sea voyage, to brave the anger of Neptune, although he
had hitherto only replied to the enchanting smiles of the
river nymphs ; and when Antifer ordered him to pack his
portmanteau and deposit himself on board the *Steersman*,
he obeyed without a murmur. Touching farewells were
exchanged, Enogate was tenderly pressed to Juhel's heart.
Nanon shared her embraces between her brother and her

nephew, and Tregomain took particular care not to squeeze too tight those who had the courage to come to his arms.

Promises were made that they would not be long away, and that in six weeks they would be back again at St. Malo ; and then, millionaire or not, Antifer would be persuaded to approve of the marriage so unluckily interrupted. And then the steamer went to the westward, and the girl followed it with her eyes until its masts disappeared below the horizon.

But had the *Steersman* forgotten the two personages —who are not of minor importance—whose duty it was to follow the legatee of Kamylk Pasha ? Ben Omar and Saouk were not on board ; had they missed the boat ?

By no means. The fact is that it had been found impossible to persuade the Egyptian notary to embark on the steamer. On the voyage between Alexandria and Marseilles he had been as ill as even a notary could be ; and now that he was doomed to go to Suez—and he knew not where—he had resolved to journey on land so long as he could avoid the sea. Saouk had not the least objection to this. Antifer was anything but eager to secure them as travelling companions, and had made an appointment to meet them at the end of the month at Suez, without saying that thence they would have to go on to Muscat, when the notary would have to brave the horrors of the perfidious element.

Antifer had even added :

" As your client has ordered you to be present at the digging up of the legacy, you shall be there. But if circumstances oblige us to travel together, let us keep to ourselves, for I have no desire to be on intimate terms with either you or your clerk."

In consequence of this, Ben Omar and Saouk had left St. Malo before the departure of the *Steersman,* and no one regretted them. The notary was not likely to miss the appointment ! On the one hand he was urged by the fear of losing his commission, and on the other he was domi-

H

nated by Saouk's implacable will. He would be at Suez
first, and there he would await Antifer's arrival with
impatience.

The *Steersman* ran down along the French coast,
sheltered by it from the southerly winds. Tregomain
could but congratulate himself. He had resolved to make
the best of the voyage by studying the manners and
customs of the different countries he would be obliged to
visit. But as it was the first time in his life that he had
been on the sea, he was afraid of being sick; and it was
with a curious and anxious eye that he gazed at the
horizon where the sea met the sky. He did not try to play
at being a sailor, the worthy man, nor at braving the
movement of the vessel by walking about the deck. In
fact his feet, accustomed to the level deck of his barge,
seemed to fail him, and he sat in the stern on a bench
grasping one of the stanchions, and submitting with
resignation to the pitiless pleasantries of Captain
Antifer.

"Well, bargeman, how are you?"

"Up to the present I have had nothing much the
matter with me."

"Ah! This is only fresh-water sailing as yet; we are
coasting the land, and you might suppose you were on
your barge on the Rance. But we shall get a northerly
wind soon, and then the sea will shake its fleas, and give
you no time to scratch for yours."

"Friend, I have no fleas."

"It is a way of speaking. Wait till we get out of the
channel."

"You think I shall be sick?"

"Badly; I am sure you will."

Antifer's way of consoling his friends was peculiar.
Juhel tried to remove the depressing effect of his prognos-
tics by observing,—

"My uncle exaggerates. You will be no more sick
than—"

"Than a porpoise? That is all I wish!" replied the

bargeman, pointing to two or three of those clowns of the sea tumbling in the vessel's wake.

In the evening the steamer rounded the furthest points of Brittany. As she was in the Straits of Four under shelter of the heights of Ouessant, the sea was not rough although there was a head wind. The passengers went to bed between eight and nine o'clock, leaving the vessel to pass Cape St. Matthieu, the Gulf of Brest, Douarnenez Bay, the race of the Sein, and head south-westwards across the Iroise.

The bargeman dreamed that he was sick unto death ; but fortunately it was only a dream. When the morning came, although the ship was rolling from side to side, diving into the hollows of the waves, and rising on their crests to dive again, he did not hesitate to go on deck. If destiny intended to close his career as a mariner by a sea voyage, the least he could do was to fix the various events in his memory.

Behold him appearing on the deck. What does he see, extended on a grating, pale as death, and rolling from side to side like an empty barrel? Antifer himself, as much upset as any gentle lady crossing from Folkestone to Boulogne.

And what a string of oaths, terrestrial and maritime ! And how the captain swore high and low when he beheld the tranquil, fresh-coloured face of his companion, betraying not the least sign of discomfort !

"A thousand thunders!" he exclaimed, "Would you believe it. Here am I, a coasting captain, yet not having set foot on a boat for ten years, much more sick than a bargeman."

"But I am not sick at all," said Tregomain, favouring him with one of his sweetest smiles.

"You are not ? And why are you not ? "

"I am surprised at it."

"But the Rance is not like this Iroise."

"Not at all."

"And you do not seem to be in the least upset."

"I am sorry for it, if it annoys you," said Tregomain.

But this illness of Captain Antifer did not last long. Before the *Steersman* had sighted Cape Ortegal, at the north-west corner of Spain, while she was still in the Gulf of Gascony, so terribly lashed by the Atlantic surges, Antifer had regained both his sea-legs and his sailor's stomach. What had happened to him happens to many others—even to the most experienced sailors, when they have been away from the sea for a time. His mortification was none the less extreme, and his self-conceit considerably cooled, at finding that this mere fresh-water sailor had remained unaffected while he had been almost turned inside out.

It was a rough night, during which the *Steersman* passed off Ferrol, and Captain Chip would have lain to, had not Antifer persuaded him to drive ahead. Long delays would cause anxiety as to catching the mail-boat at Suez, which only starts once a month for the Persian Gulf. The equinox was near, and there was always a chance of bad weather; so it was better to drive on as long as there was no obvious danger in continuing the voyage.

The *Steersman* gave a wide berth to the reefs along the coast of Spain. Vigo Bay and the three sugar-loaves at its entrance were left on the port hand, as was also the coast of Portugal. The day afterwards, the Berlings were left to starboard, those islands formed by Providence for the site of the lighthouses which mark the proximity of the Continent for ships coming from seaward.

You may easily imagine that during these long hours, our friends were talking about this extraordinary voyage and its certain results. Antifer had recovered completely With his legs wide apart, he looked defiantly at the horizon, striding about the deck, and watching the cheery face of the bargeman for some symptom of the sickness which obstinately refused to appear.

"What do you think of the ocean?"

"There is a good deal of water in it."

" Yes, rather more than in the Rance ? "

" Undoubtedly, but we need not scoff at a river which has its charm."

" I do not scoff at it, I despise it, bargeman."

" Uncle," said Juhel, " you should not despise anyone ; a river may have its value—"

" As well as an island ! " added Tregomain.　And at the word, Antifer raised his ear, for he was hit in a sensitive place.

" Certainly," he said, " there are islands worth putting in the first class—mine, for example ! "

The pronoun showed what had been working in the Breton's brain.　This island in the Gulf of Oman belonged to him by inheritance.

" With regard to this island, Juhel.　Are you verifying your chronometer every day ? "

" Certainly, and I have seldom seen a more perfect instrument."

" And your sextant ? "

" It is as good as the chronometer."

" Thank goodness ; they cost enough."

" If they are going to bring us four millions," judiciously insinuated Tregomain, " we can hardly look at their price."

" Quite so, Mr. Bargeman."

But if Captain Antifer and his two companions had reason to place implicit confidence in their instruments, they mistrusted—and very justly mistrusted—Ben Omar. They were often talking about this, and one day the uncle said to his nephew,—

" I do not like the looks of this Ben Omar at all ; and I shall keep a very close watch on him."

" Who knows if we shall meet him at Suez ? " asked the bargeman, in a dubious tone.

"'Oh ! " said Antifer, " he will wait for us for weeks if need be.　Did not the scoundrel come to St. Malo solely to steal my latitude ? "

" I think, uncle," said Juhel, " that you will not be far wrong in keeping an eye on these Egyptians. I don't think much of the notary, and I think still less of his clerk."

"I agree with you, Juhel," added the bargeman. "This Nazim is no more like a clerk than I am."

"It is a pity he does not speak French," said Antifer. "We might pump him."

"Pump him!" said Juhel. "If you have not got much out of the master, you are not likely to get more out of the clerk. I fancy you had much better give a thought to this Saouk—"

"What Saouk?"

"The son of Mourad, the cousin of Kamylk Pasha, the man who was disinherited in favour of you."

"I will know how to deal with him when I come across him. Was not the will in proper form? What can he do then, this descendant of pashas, whose tails I may have to cut?"

"However, uncle—"

"I care no more for him than I do for Ben Omar—and if this manufacturer of contracts does not walk straight—"

"Take care, my friend," said Tregomain. "You cannot get rid of the notary. It is his right and his duty to accompany you, to follow you to the island—"

"My island."

"Yes, your island! The will expressly says so; and he has a commission of one per cent., that is forty thousand pounds—"

"Forty thousand kicks!" said Antifer, whose irascibility was increasing at the thought of the enormous amount to which Ben Omar was entitled.

During the night the *Steersman* sighted the lights of Cadiz and passed the Bay of Trafalgar, and during the morning she entered the Straits of Gibraltar.

It was delightful travelling, and the passengers could not be insensible to its inexpressible charm, when the ship that carried them passed in sight of the African coast. Nothing could be more picturesque, nothing more varied than this panorama, with its mountains in the background, the many indentations of the coast, the seaside towns rising unexpectedly from around the lofty cliffs in their frame of verdure. Did the bargeman appreciate these natural beauties as he should have done, and did he compare them with those of his dearly loved Rance, between Dinard and Dinan? What did he think when he saw Oran, dominated by the cone with the fort clinging to it, Algiers terraced on its casbah; Stora, lost amid the mighty rocks; Bougie, Philippeville, Bone, half modern, half antique, hiding at the end of its bay? In a word, what was in the mind of Tregomain in the presence of this superb coast unrolling before his eyes?

The weather continued favourable. A squall occasionally, and then a calm, leaving a wide horizon clear. Under such conditions Pantellaria showed its slender summit—an old volcano, now asleep, which will some day awake. The bed of the sea hereabouts from Cape Bon to the Greek Archipelago is all volcanic. Islands appeared, such as Santorin and others, which may one day form a new archipelago.

Juhel had therefore some justification for saying to his uncle,—

"It is fortunate that Kamylk Pasha did not choose an island in these parts to bury his fortune in.'

"It is fortunate—very fortunate," said Antifer.

And his face grew quite pale at the thought that his islet might have emerged from a sea incessantly troubled by subterranean forces. Fortunately, the Gulf of Oman is guaranteed against eventualities of this sort; such commotions were unknown to it; and whatever the islet might be, it would be found in its place.

Passing Gozo and Malta, the *Steersman* headed straight for the Egyptian coast. Captain Chip made the land at Alexandria, and coasting along the network of mouths of the Nile, spreading out like a fan between Rosetta and Damietta, he was signalled off Port Said in the morning of the 7th of March.

The Suez Canal was then under construction; it was

not opened until 1869; the steamer had consequently to stop at Port Said. Antifer and his companions left Captain Chip, with many expressions of gratitude for the way in which they had been treated on board, and next day started by train to Suez.

It was a pity that the Canal was not finished, as a trip along it would have much interested Juhel, and Tregomain night have fancied himself between the banks of the Rance; although the aspect of the Bitter Lakes and Ismailia is not as western as Dinan, and certainly more oriental than that of Dinard.

Would Antifer have taken much notice of these marvels? No; neither of those due to nature nor of those dlue to the genius of man. For him there existed in the whole world but one point, the island in the Gulf of Oman, his island, which like a bright metal button hypnotized his whole being.

And he would have taken as little notice of Suez, a town occupying so important a position in geographical nomenclature, had he not seen as he came out of the railway station a group of two men, one of whom greeted him with excessive salutes, while the other departed not from his oriental gravity. They were Ben Omar and Nazim.

CHAPTER XI.

BEN OMAR and his clerk had kept the appointment. They had taken very good care not to miss it. For some days they had been at Suez, and the impatience with which they had expected Antifer may be guessed.

At a sign from Antifer, neither Juhel nor Tregomain took the slightest notice of them. The three continued their conversation as if nothing could distract their attention.

Ben Omar came forward in the obsequious attitude which was customary with him.

They seemed to be unconscious of his presence.

"At last, sir—" he ventured to say, in the most amiable tone he could manage.

Captain Antifer turned his head, looked at him, and positively did not seem to recognize him.

"Sir—it is I—it is I—" the notary repeated, as he bowed.

"Who—you?"

And this as much as to say, "Whatever can this escape from a mummy-box want with me?"

"But—it is I—Ben Omar—notary of Alexandria—do you not recollect?"

"Do we know this gentleman?" asked Antifer, winking at his companions, as he shifted the pebble from his right cheek to his left.

"I think I do," said Tregomain, taking pity on the notary's embarrassment. "It is Mr. Ben Omar, we once had the pleasure of meeting."

"So it is—so it is—" replied Antifer, as if he had a distant recollection of him, a very distant recollection. "I remember, Ben Omar—Ben Omar!"

"That is it."

"Ah! Well, what are you doing here?"

"What am I doing here? But I have been waiting for you, Mr. Antifer."

"Waiting for me?"

"Certainly. Have you forgotten? The appointment for us to meet at Suez?"

"Appointment?—and what for?" asked Antifer, in such a tone of surprise that the notary was completely taken aback.

"What for? Why, the will of Kamylk Pasha—the millions he left you—the island—"

"You meant to say my island, I believe!"

"Yes, your island. I see you are beginning to remember—and as the will imposed on me the obligation of—"

"I understand, Mr. Ben Omar. Good morning—good morning!"

And without another word, he shrugged his shoulders as an intimation for Juhel and the bargeman to follow him.

But as they were going away from the station the notary stopped them.

"Where are you going to stay at Suez?" he asked.

"In some hotel, I suppose," replied Antifer.

"Will the hotel suit you where my clerk and I have put up?"

"Either that one or another: it does not matter! For the forty-eight hours we have to stay here—"

"Forty-eight hours?" asked Ben Omar, in a tone of evident uneasiness. "Have you not reached the end of your voyage?"

"Not the least in the world!" replied Antifer. "We have got another sea passage—"

"A sea passage!" exclaimed the notary, turning as pale as if a ship's deck were oscillating beneath his feet.

" A sea passage, which, if you please, we will take on
board the *Oxus*, which runs to Bombay—"

" Bombay ! "

"And which starts from Suez the day after to-morrow.
I advise you to take your passage in her, as your company is forced upon us—"

" Where then is this island ? " asked the notary, with a
gesture of despair.

" It is where it is, Mr. Ben Omar."

And thereupon Antifer, followed by Juhel and Tregomain, walked into the nearest hotel, where their luggage—
which was not extensive—was soon brought to them.

A minute afterwards, Ben Omar had rejoined Nazim,
and an observer could not fail to have noticed that the
so-called clerk gave him anything but a respectful
welcome. Ah! If it had not been for that one per cent.
on those millions, and for the fear with which Saouk
inspired him, how gladly he would have been quit of this
legatee, and this will, and this island, in search of which he
was to be trotted over land and sea.

Antifer was told that Suez was formerly called Soueys
by the Arabs and Cleopatris by the Egyptians, but his
only reply was, " As far as I am concerned, it makes no
difference."

It hardly occurred to this impatient personage to visit
a few mosques—old buildings without anything special
about them—two or three places, the most curious of which
is the grain market, or to look at the house facing the
sea where General Bonaparte lodged. But Juhel thought
that the two days could not be better spent than in exploring this town of fifteen thousand inhabitants, the irregular
wall of which is so miserably kept up. He and Tregomain
spent their time in wandering about the streets and lanes,
and exploring the roadstead, where five hundred ships can
find good anchorage in from eight to ten fathoms, well
sheltered from the north-north-west winds, which prevail
all the year round.

Suez had a certain amount of oversea trade, even before

the Canal was projected, thanks to the railway running to Cairo and Alexandria. By its position at the end of the Gulf which bears its name, it commands the Red Sea ; and although its growth may be slow, its future is assured.

But this did not trouble Captain Antifer. While his two companions went cruising about the town he hardly left the superb beach, which has been transformed into a promenade. He knew he was watched, it is true. Sometimes it was Nazim, sometimes it was Ben Omar, who never lost sight of him, while keeping at a distance. He pretended to take no notice of this. Taking his ease on a seat, absorbed, meditative, he gazed at the horizon out in the Red Sea. And occasionally, so much was he possessed with the one fixed idea, he would fancy he saw the island, his island, emerge from the mists of the south— by an effect of mirage which is frequently produced on the extremities of these sandy beaches, a marvellous phenomenon by which the eye is always deceived.

On the morning of the 11th of March, the mail-steamer *Oxus* had finished its preparations for departure, and taken in the coal necessary for the voyage across the Indian Ocean, and the stoppages at the regulation ports. We need not be surprised to find that Antifer, Tregomain and Juhel were on board at daybreak, and that Ben Omar and Saouk had taken passage with them. The large steamer was really a cargo-boat, but she had accommodation for a few passengers, most of them bound to Bombay, some of them to Aden and Muscat.

The *Oxus* was under way at eleven o'clock. A fresh breeze was blowing from the north-north-west with a tendency to work round to the westward. As the voyage would last a fortnight, owing to the numerous stoppages, Juhel had secured a cabin with three berths, which could be arranged either for the day's siesta or the night's repose. Saouk and Ben Omar occupied another cabin, from which the notary would probably make but few and short appearances. Antifer, determined to have as little intercourse as possible with them, had begun by saying to the unfortunate notary, with the delicacy of a sea-bear which characterized him,—

"Mr. Ben Omar, we have to travel together it is true, but let us keep our places. I will go my way, you will go yours. It will be enough for you to be present to witness my taking possession, and when that matter is over, I hope we shall have the pleasure of never meeting again either in this world or the next."

As long as the *Oxus* was running down the Gulf, sheltered by the heights of the Isthmus, the navigation was as tranquil as if on the surface of a lake. But when they got out into the Red Sea, the fresh breezes from the plains of Arabia gave her a roughish reception. The consequence was a good deal of heavy rolling, which many of the passengers found discomforting. Nazim did not mind it much—neither did Antifer, nor his nephew, nor Tregomain, freshwater sailor though he might be. But the notary's condition it is impossible to describe. He never appeared either on deck or in the saloon, or in the diningroom. In the depths of his cabin his groans were heard throughout the voyage. Better for him if he could have travelled as a mummy! The worthy bargeman, taking pity on the poor fellow, visited him several times, as might be expected from his good nature; but when he tried to get Antifer to sympathize with him, all he received was a shrug of the shoulders. Antifer could never forgive Ben Omar for having attempted to steal his latitude.

"Well, bargeman," he would say, "Mr. Omar is empty? eh?"

"Almost."

"My compliments."

"My friend, will you not go and see him, if it were only once?"

"Yes, bargeman, yes! I will go, when there is nothing left of him but his skin."

What could be said to a man who answered like that, with a burst of laughter at his own wit?

But if Antifer suffered no annoyance from the notary

during the voyage, his clerk Nazim was several times the
cause of his almost justifiable irritation.   It was not that
Nazim thrust his presence on him.   No!   Besides, what
could he do, for as they did not speak the same language,
conversation was impossible.   But the so-called clerk
was always there, keeping close watch on Antifer, as if he
had received orders to do so from his master.   Great
would have been Antifer's delight at pitching him overboard, supposing that the Egyptian had been the man to
submit to such treatment.

The descent of the Red Sea was anything but pleasant,
although it was not made during the intolerable heat of
summer.   Then it is that the care of the boilers can only
be entrusted to Arab stokers, for they alone will not cook
where eggs will cook in a few minutes.

On the 15th of March, the *Oxus* was running through
the narrowest portion of the Straits of Bab-el-Mandeb.
Leaving Perim on the left, and Obock, on the African coast,
on the right, the steamer entered the Gulf of Aden, and
headed for the port of that name, where several of her
passengers were to be landed.

Aden, yet another key of the Red Sea, hanging from
the belt of Great Britain—that good housekeeper, always at
work!   With the Isle of Perim, of which she has made
another Gibraltar, she holds the entrance of this corridor,
eighteen hundred miles long, opening out into the Indian
Ocean.   The port of Aden may be partially silted up,
but it at least possesses a vast and commodious anchorage
to the east, and in the west a harbour where quite a fleet
might find shelter.   The English have been installed
there since 1823.   The town itself, which was a flourishing
one in the eleventh and twelfth centuries, was evidently designed as the emporium of commerce with the furthest east.

Captain Antifer did not think it worth while to go
ashore, but spent the time railing at the delay, one of
the most serious inconveniences of which was to permit
the notary to appear on deck.   But in what a state!   He
had hardly strength enough to drag himself along.

"Eh! Mr. Ben Omar, is that you," asked Antifer ironically. "Really I should never have recognized you! You will never get to the end of the voyage! If I were in your place, I should remain at Aden."

"I should like to," replied the notary, in a voice that was hardly above a whisper. "A few days might pull me round, and if you could manage to wait for the next steamer—"

"I am sorry, Mr. Ben Omar. I am in such a hurry to pour into your hands the splendid commission that is to come to you, that I cannot possibly stop on the way!"

"Is it much farther?"

"More than farther!" answered Antifer, sweeping his hand round so as to indicate a curve of enormous diameter. And thereupon Ben Omar regained his cabin, dragging himself along like a lobster, and having derived but little comfort from this brief conversation.

The following afternoon the *Oxus* was off again, and found the Indian Amphitrite anything but kind. The goddess was ill-tempered, capricious, nervous, as those on board could testify. Better not seek to know what happened in Ben Omar's cabin. He might have been brought up on deck in a cloth and dropped into the bosom of the above-mentioned goddess with a round shot at his feet, and he would not have had strength to protest against the funeral ceremony.

The bad weather lasted until the third day, when the wind hauled to the north-eastward, so as to bring the steamer under the shelter of the coast of Hadramaut.

Saouk might stand the ups and downs of the voyage without being inconvenienced; but if his body did not suffer, his mind could not help doing so. To be at the mercy of this abominable Frenchman, to be unable to get out of him the mystery of this island, to be compelled to follow him to—to where? to Muscat, to Surat, to Bombay, at all of which the *Oxus* was to call. Would they have to land at Muscat and cross the Straits of Ormuz? Was it on one of the hundreds of islands in the Persian Gulf that Kamylk had buried his treasure?

This ignorance, this uncertainty, kept Saouk in a state of perpetual exasperation. He would have dragged the secret from Antifer's very vitals—if he could. Often would he catch a few words exchanged between Antifer and his companions! As he was supposed not to know French, there was no reason for their being careful when he was by. But it had all ended in nothing. The pretended clerk was justly regarded with suspicion, even with aversion. It was with repulsion that he inspired them; and the instinctive, unreasonable sentiment was felt as much by his companions as by Antifer himself. When Saouk came near them they moved away, and this he noticed only too well.

On the 19th of March the *Oxus* stopped for twelve hours at Birbat, on the Arab coast. From this point she continued along the coast of Oman so as to get up to Muscat. Two days afterwards she had doubled Cape Raz-el-Had. Twenty-four hours later she had reached the capital of the sultanate. Captain Antifer seemed to be nearing the end of his voyage.

And it was time. The nearer he drew towards his goal the more nervous, the more unsociable he became. All his life was centred in this island, this mine of gold and diamonds which belonged to him. To him it was an Ali Baba's cave which had been transferred to him by law in the very country of the Arabian Nights, whither Kamylk Pasha's fancy had led him.

"Do you know," said he one day to his companions, "that if the fortune of this worthy Egyptian had been in ingots of gold, I should have had a good deal of trouble in getting it to St. Malo?"

"So I should think," said Juhel.

"But," returned Tregomain, "if we filled our bags, our pockets, and our hat-case—"

"There's a bargeman's notion for you. He fancies he can put a million into his pocket!"

" I fancy, my friend—"

" But you have never seen a million in gold ? "

" Never. Not even in a dream ! "

" Do you know what it weighs ? "

" I know nothing about it."

" Well, I do, for I have had the curiosity to calculate ! "

" Tell us."

" An ingot of gold worth a million would weigh about seventeen thousand seven hundred and seventy-five pounds avoirdupois ; and four millions would consequently weigh over seventy-one thousand pounds."

" Ah ! " said the bargeman, " you must have made it too much ! "

" Do you know how many men it would take to carry those four millions ? "

" How many ? "

" Why, three hundred and twenty-three, and as we are but three, you can see what our embarrassment would be when we reached my island ? Fortunately my treasure is chiefly composed of diamonds and precious stones—"

" Uncle is right," said Juhel.

" And I may add," said Tregomain, " that this excellent Pasha could not have arranged matters more conveniently."

" Oh ! these diamonds ! " exclaimed Antifer—" these diamonds are easily sold among the Paris and London jewellers. What a sale, my friends, what a sale ! Not all, though, not all—"

" You will only sell a part of them ? "

" Yes, bargeman, yes ! " replied Antifer, his face convulsed, his eyes glowing like fire. " Yes ; and first, I will keep one for myself, a diamond worth forty or fifty thousand pounds say, and I will wear it in my shirt."

" In your shirt, friend ? " said Tregomain. " You will be simply dazzling ! No one will be able to look you in the face—"

I

"And Enogate shall have another," added Antifer; "that is a little gem to make her pretty—"

"No prettier than she is now!" Juhel hastened to remark.

"Quite so, quite so. And there shall be a third diamond for my sister!"

"Ah! Good Nanon!" said Tregomain. "Do you want somebody to come and propose for her?"

Antifer shrugged his shoulders.

"And there shall be a fourth diamond for you, Juhel, a fine stone you can wear as a pin—"

"Thank you, uncle."

"And you shall have a fifth, old man."

"Me? If it had been to put on the figurehead of the *Charmante Amélie*—"

"No, bargeman, on your finger—a ring—a signet ring—"

"A diamond—on my great red hands—that would suit me as well as socks would a Franciscan!" replied the bargeman, extending an enormous hand much more suited to haul a hawser than to display diamond rings.

"Never mind. It is not impossible that you might find some woman who would—"

"Whom would you suggest? There is a fine fat widow who keeps a grocer's shop at Saint Servan—"

"Grocer—grocer!" exclaimed Antifer. "What a figure your grocer would make in our family when Enogate has married her prince and Juhel his princess!"

There the conversation ended, and the young captain could not stifle a sigh at the thought that his uncle still encouraged these absurd dreams. What would bring him back to sanity, if misfortune—yes, misfortune—willed it that he should become possessed of these millions of the island!

"Positively he will go out of his mind if this lasts much longer!" said Tregomain to Juhel, when they were alone.

" I am afraid so ! " said Juhel, looking at his uncle, who was talking to himself.

Two days afterwards the *Oxus* arrived at Muscat, and three sailors extracted Ben Omar from the depths of his cabin. But in what a state! He was reduced to a skeleton, or rather to a mummy, for the skin still hung on the bones of the unfortunate notary.

CHAPTER XII.

WHEN Tregomain asked Juhel to point out on the map the precise point where Muscat was situated, he could not believe his eyes. The ex-captain of the Rance barge transported to this place, so far, so very far, to the seas of the Asiatic continent!

" And so, Juhel, we are at the end of Arabia ? " he asked, adjusting his eye-glasses.

" Yes, at the south-east extremity."

" And what is that gulf there finishing like a funnel ? "

" That is the Gulf of Oman."

" And this other which looks like the leg of a salt marsh ? "

" That is the Persian Gulf."

" And the strait that unites them ? "

" Those are the Straits of Ormuz."

" And our friend's island ? "

" Ought to be somewhere in the Gulf of Oman."

" If it is there! " replied the bargeman, taking care that Antifer was not within earshot.

The Sultanate of Muscat, lying between the fifty-third and fifty-seventh meridians, and the twenty-second and twenty-seventh parallels, extends to about 350 miles in length, and 180 in breadth. To this should be added a stretch of the Persian coast from Laristan to Moghistan, another stretch of coast from Ormuz to Kistrim, and certain settlements on the coast of Africa. With the addition of these its area is about the same as that of France, and it has ten millions of inhabitants, Arabs, Persians,

Hindoos, Jews, and a large number of negroes. The Sultan is consequently a sovereign of a certain amount of importance.

In ascending the Gulf of Oman, the *Oxus* had coasted a desolate, sterile shore, bordered with high perpendicular cliffs. Behind them rose a few hills about fifteen hundred feet high, the outlying spurs of the range of Ghebel Achdan, which runs up to three thousand feet. It is not to be wondered at that the country is barren, for it is watered by no river of real importance; although the environs of the capital yield enough to support a population of sixteen thousand. There is plenty of fruit, grapes, mangoes, peaches, figs, pomegranates, water-melons, citrons and lemons, and dates are in profusion. The date-tree is the chief tree of the district. By it the value of property is estimated, and people talk of an estate of three or four thousand date-trees, as we do of one of two or three hundred acres. There is all the more trade in the Sultanate owing to the Sultan being not only the chief of the state and the high-priest of religion, but the chief merchant of the district. Under his flag are two thousand ships, whose total tonnage exceeds thirty seven thousand; and he has a navy of a hundred vessels armed with several hundred guns. His army consists of twenty-five thousand men, and his revenue almost amounts to a million pounds.

His power is absolute in the country which was conquered by Albuquerque in 1507 and afterwards threw off the Portuguese yoke. Having recovered its independence a century ago, it has been supported by the English, who probably hope after the Gibraltar of Spain, the Gibraltar of Aden, the Gibraltar of Perim, to form the Gibraltar of the Persian Gulf, and finish by Gibraltarizing all the straits of the globe.

Had Captain Antifer and his companions any political object in coming to Muscat?

Not the least.

Were they interested in the country?

Not at all, for their attention was concentrated on one of the islands in the gulf.

But had they no opportunity of studying the state of affairs in the Sultanate?

Yes, for their intention was to enter into communication with the representative of France in this corner of Arabia.

Antifer thought it advisable to call on the agent at once. The police of the country, who are well organized, would probably have their suspicions regarding the arrival of three strangers at Muscat, unless some plausible reason could be given for the voyage. But it would never do to give the real reason.

The *Oxus* was due to start for Bombay within forty-eight hours. Antifer, Tregomain and Juhel landed immediately. They did not trouble themselves about Ben Omar and Nazim, but left them to find out their movements, and accompany them when they began their search in the gulf.

Our three friends followed a guide to an English hotel across the squares and streets of this modern Babylon. Their luggage followed. How carefully they carried the sextant and the chronometer bought at St. Malo— particularly the chronometer, which Antifer would entrust to no one but himself. By its aid the longitude of the famous island was to be determined. With what punctuality he had wound it up every day ! What precautions he had taken to save it from the shocks that might interfere with its regularity !

When the travellers had taken their rooms they went off to interview the consular agent, who was much surprised to see three Frenchmen appear at his door.

He was a Provençal, of some fifty years of age, his name being Joseph Bard. His business was in white and manufactured cottons, in Indian shawls, in Chinese silks, in gold and silver embroideries, all of them articles in much request among the wealthy Orientals.

Among Frenchmen, particularly when one of them is a native of Provençe, acquaintance is soon made. Antifer introduced himself and his companions. After shaking hands and offering refreshments, the agent asked his visitors the object of their voyage.

"I do not often receive a visit from my countrymen," he said, "and it is a pleasure to welcome you. Anything I can do for you I will."

"We are much obliged to you," answered Antifer, "for you can be very useful to us in giving us some information regarding the country."

"Is this merely a pleasure trip?"

"Yes and no. We are all of us sailors, my nephew, long-voyage captain, Gildas Tregomain, an old commander of the *Charmante Amélie*—" And this time, to his friend's extreme satisfaction, he spoke of the barge as if it were a frigate—"and I am a coasting captain," he added; "we have been sent out by an important house at St. Malo to open a branch establishment either at Muscat or at one of the ports in the Gulf of Oman, or in the Persian Gulf."

"Sir," said Bard, only too glad to have something to say about a matter which would certainly add to his profits, "I can but approve of your plans, and offer you my services towards making them successful."

"In that case," said Juhel, "we would ask if our branch had better be opened at Muscat, or at some other town on the coast."

"At Muscat, by preference," said Bard. "The place is daily increasing in importance by its communications with Persia, India, Mauritius, Reunion, Zanzibar, and the coast of Africa."

"And what are its exports?" asked Tregomain.

"Dates, raisins, sulphur, fish, copal, gum arabic, shells, rhinoceros horn, oil, cocoanuts, rice, millet, coffee, and sweets."

"Sweets?" asked the bargeman, licking his lips with the tip of his tongue.

"Yes, sir," replied Bard. "Sweets they call *hulwah* in this country, which are made of honey, sugar, gluten, and almonds."

"We will taste them."

"As much as you like," said Antifer, "but let us return to the question. It was not to eat sweets that we came to Muscat. Monsieur Bard has kindly told us the chief articles of commerce."

"To which I should add the pearl fishery in the Persian Gulf," said the agent, "which fishery is of the annual value of £320,000."

You should have seen the disdainful pout with which Antifer greeted this. Pearls to the value of £320,000 was but a trifle to a man who possessed £4,000,000 in precious stones.

"True," said Bard, "the pearl trade is in the hands of Hindoo merchants, who will admit of no competition."

"Not even from Muscat?" asked Juhel.

"Not even from Muscat, where the merchants are not particularly pleased at seeing strangers establish themselves."

Juhel took advantage of this remark to give the conversation another turn.

As Muscat is in 50° 20′ east, and 23° 28′ north, it followed that the island they were in search of was beyond it. Evidently they must leave Muscat on pretence of d s-covering a favourable place for this imaginary branch establishment, and what Juhel did was to remark that it would be wise to visit the other towns in the Sultanate before settling on Muscat, and he then asked what those towns were.

"There is Oman," said Bard.

"To the north of Muscat?"

"No, to the south-east."

"And in the north or north-east?"

"The most considerable town is Rostak."

"On the gulf?"

"No, in the interior."

"And on the gulf?"

"There is Sohar."

"How far is that from here?"

" About a hundred and twenty-five miles."

A wink from Juhel made his uncle understand the importance of this reply.

" Is there much trade at Sohar ? "

" A good deal. The Sultan often resides there when such is the fancy of his Highness—"

" His Highness ! " exclaimed Tregomain. Evidently the title sounded agreeably in the bargeman's ears. Perhaps it ought properly to be reserved for the Grand Turk, but Bard thought otherwise.

" His Highness is at Muscat," he added, " and when you have decided on a town for your offices, you will have to apply for his permission."

" Which his Highness will not, I hope, refuse us ? " asked Antifer.

" On the contrary," replied the agent, " he will be most happy, provided you pay the fees."

Antifer indicated by a gesture that he was prepared to pay for the privilege right royally.

" And how do you get to Sohar ? " asked Juhel.

" By caravan."

" By caravan ! " ejaculated the bargeman, evidently uneasy.

" Well," said Bard, " we have no railways or tramways in the Sultanate. You can go in a cart or on a mule, unless you prefer to walk—"

" These caravans only start at long intervals, I suppose ? " said Juhel.

" Pardon," said the agent, " there is a very active trade between Muscat and Sohar. One starts to-morrow—"

" To-morrow ? " said Antifer, " that will suit us splendidly : to-morrow we will caravan it ! "

The prospect of having to " caravan " it was evidently not pleasant to Tregomain to judge by the grimace he made. But he had not come to Muscat for the purpose of throwing obstacles in the way, and he had to resign himself to travelling under such painful conditions.

" But I do not see," said the bargeman, "why we cannot

go by water to Sohar. A hundred and twenty miles in a boat—"

"Why not ?" said Antifer, "Tregomain is right. We should gain time—"

"Undoubtedly," said Bard; "and I should be the first to advise you to go by sea if there were not certain dangers."

"What dangers ?" asked Juhel.

"The Gulf of Oman, gentlemen, is not safe. As a trading vessel with a large crew there might not be much to fear—"

"Fear ?" said Antifer. "Fear a few squalls ?"

"No—pirates, who are rather plentiful in the Straits of Ormuz."

"Confound it ! " said Antifer.

But to do him justice, he was only thinking of what he should do on his return with the treasure.

In short our travellers resolved not to return by sea, and thought it useless to go to Sohar by sea under the circumstances. They would go with one caravan, and return with another, and thus travel in safety.

Here the interview ended, the travellers promising to call on their return, and report the results of their inquiries, in the hope of profiting by his advice ; Antifer even having the audacity to remark that the establishment of their branch would bring in important business by which the agency would profit. Before they went away Bard renewed his offer to introduce them to his Highness, and undertook to obtain an audience for such distinguished foreigners. And then the said distinguished foreigners departed for their hotel.

Meantime in a room of the same hotel Ben Omar and Nazim were conferring together. They had arrived at Muscat, but they were still unaware if Muscat were the end of the voyage.

Was Antifer going farther ? It was for Ben Omar to know this, he had a right to know it, but he knew no more about it than Saouk.

" That is the consequence of having been so beastly ill ! "
said he ; " why could you not have been well ? "

" May your Excellency be calm," said Ben Omar.   " This
very day I will see Mr. Antifer—and I will learn—providing he is not going on board again."

Surely Antifer would not refuse to give a direct answer
as to the whereabouts of this island, for the will distinctly
stated that the executor must be present when the legacy
was dug up.   But when the island was reached and the
three precious barrels handed over, how was Saouk to
obtain possession of them ?   Several times the notary had
asked this without receiving an answer, for the very good
reason that Saouk did not know what to say.   It was clear
enough that he would stick at nothing in seizing on a
fortune which he looked upon as his, and of which Kamylk
had deprived him to a stranger's advantage.   And this
was what frightened the inoffensive, conciliatory notary,
who hated nothing so much as force, knowing that his
Excellency thought no more of a man's life than of a dry
fig.   In any case, it was essential to follow the three
Frenchmen, keep them in sight during their investigations,
and assist at the exhumation of the treasure, and when they
had got the treasure to act according to circumstances.

This being agreed upon, his Excellency went out,
giving the notary orders to watch for Antifer's return to
the hotel.   This return did not take place until late in the
evening.   Tregomain and Juhel went for a stroll in the
streets of Muscat, while Antifer—in imagination—went
for a walk a hundred miles or so away, to the east of
Sohar, on the shore of his island.   It would have been
useless to have asked him for his impressions of Muscat ;
he noticed nothing, while Juhel and the bargeman were
interested in everything they saw in this very Oriental
town.   They stopped in front of the shops and gazed at
the heaps of merchandise of all sorts, the turbans, the belts,
the woollen cloaks, the cotton cloths, and the mertaban
jars resplendent with coloured enamel.   At the sight of
these fine things, Juhel thought of the pleasure his beloved

Enogate would have in possessing them. What a reminder it would be of this inconvenient voyage! And these jewels, curiously worked, these articles of artistic value, would she not be all the more pleased at receiving them from the hands of her betrothed? Yes, far more so than with the diamonds promised her by her uncle.

This was Tregomain's idea, and he said to his young friend,—

"We will buy that necklace for the little one, and you can give it to her when you get back."

"When we get back!" said Juhel, sighing.

"And that pretty ring, let us have ten rings; one for each of her fingers."

"Of what is my Enogate thinking?" murmured Juhel.

"Thinking?" said the bargeman, "why, thinking of you, of course!"

"And we are separated by hundreds and hundreds of leagues."

"Ah!" interrupted the bargeman, "don't forget to buy a pot of those sweets the agent boasted about."

"Had we better not try them before we buy?"

"No, my boy, no," replied Tregomain. "I intend Enogate to have first taste."

"And if she does not like them?"

"She will think them delicious, because it is you who have brought them from such a distance."

How well the excellent man knew a girl's heart, although no girl, either at St. Malo or St. Servan or Dinard, had ever thought of becoming Madame Tregomain!

In short, neither of them regretted their walk through the capital of the Sultanate, the appearance and cleanliness of which many a European city might envy—with the exception, of course, of the birthplace of Antifer, which he considered one of the first cities of the world.

Juhel noticed, however, that there were a large number of police about who seemed to be very suspicious, and that they carefully watched these new arrivals at Muscat, who had given no account of what brought them there.

Unlike the meddlesome police of certain European states, who require passports, and require answers to untimely questions, these police confined themselves to following the strangers at a distance ; and the strangers would never be allowed to leave the Sultan's territory without the Sultan knowing why they had come there.

Fortunately, Captain Antifer had no suspicions of what was going on, for he would have been in a terrible state of fear for the success of his adventure. To take several millions away from an island in the Gulf of Oman was what his Highness would never permit. In Europe the State takes half of all treasure trove ; in Asia, the sovereign, who is the State, does not hesitate to take the whole.

When Antifer returned to the hotel he was visited by Ben Omar. Opening the door just a little way, the notary put in his head, and in his most insinuating tone asked,—

"May I know ? "

"What ? "

"May I know, Mr. Antifer, in what direction we are going ? "

" First to the right, second to the left, and then straight on."

And thereupon Captain Antifer shut the door with a bang.

CHAPTER XIII.

At dawn on the 23rd of March a caravan left the capital of the Sultanate along the road by the shore.

It was a regular caravan, such as the bargeman had never seen across the landes of Ille-et-Vilaine. So he told Juhel, and Juhel was in no way surprised at it. In the caravan were a hundred Arabs and Hindoos, and about as many beasts of burden. With numbers such as these the perils of the journey were reduced to a minimum ; no cause remaining for anxiety regarding land pirates, which under any circumstances would have been less dangerous than pirates of the sea.

Among the natives were two or three financiers or merchants mentioned by the French agent. There was no ostentation about them, and they had no thought for anything but the business which took them to Sohar.

The foreign element was represented by the three Frenchmen and the two Egyptians. The Egyptians had taken good care not to miss the departure of the caravan. Antifer had let them know that he was going to start in the morning, and they had made their preparations accordingly. Antifer, it need scarcely be said, did not trouble himself about Ben Omar and his clerk ; it was their business to follow him and not his to take care of them. He had made up his mind to appear as though he did not know them. When he saw them in the caravan he did not even honour them with a salute, and under his menacing look the bargeman dared not turn his head towards them.

The baggage animals were camels, mules, and asses. No vehicle was possible over this rough ground, where there was no definite road, and which was here and there a stretch of marsh.

Two sturdy mules carried the uncle and his nephew. These had been obtained from the Muscat Jews, at a good price, of course; but for no price had it been found possible to find a mule that would carry such a weight as Gildas Tregomain, and an animal of more strength and resistance had to be provided.

"Do you know that you are rather a nuisance?" said Captain Antifer, politely, as mule after mule was tried in vain.

"What would you have, my friend? I am not obliged to accompany you. Leave me at Muscat, where I will wait—"

"Never!"

"I cannot let myself be carried in several pieces!"

"Have you any objection to try a camel?" asked Juhel.

"None at all, if you can find a camel that will carry me."

"That is an idea," said Antifer. "He would do very well on one of those camels."

"So justly called ships of the desert!" added Juhel.

"Then let me have a ship of the desert," said the accommodating bargeman.

And thus it came about that Tregomain appeared on this occasion perched on the top of a colossal specimen of one of these ruminants. This in no way displeased him. In his place anybody else would have been as proud. If he had any feeling of this sort he did not show it, keeping himself busy in guiding his ship aright and saving himself from as many useless lurches as possible. When the speed of the caravan increased the animal's gait would probably become rather trying, but the bargeman was so well developed in the critical points as to be proof against discomfort of this nature.

In the rear of the caravan rode Saouk on a quiet mule.

Near him, and doing his best to keep up with him, was
Ben Omar on a donkey so small that his feet almost
touched the ground. Never would the notary have consented to bestride a mule. There was such a risk of his
falling too far. Besides, these Arab mules are high-
spirited and capricious, and require a strong hand to keep
them under control.

The caravan would accomplish its thirty-six miles a day,
with a rest of a couple of hours at noon ; in four days it
would reach Sohar if nothing occurred to delay it.

A journey of four days appeared interminable to
Captain Antifer, spurred on with the desire to reach his
island. But there his adventurous journey would be at an
end. And yet why did he become more nervous and
more anxious as he approached the decisive moment. His
companions could not get a word out of him and were
reduced to talking between themselves.

From the top of his camel, swaying from one hump to
the other, the bargeman remarked to Juhel,—

" Between you and me, do you believe in this treasure of
Kamylk Pasha ? "

" Hum ! " replied Juhel, " it certainly seems to me rather
fantastic."

" Suppose there isn't an island ? "

" If there isn't an island, there won't be a treasure, and
my uncle will be like that famous Marseillaise captain who
set out for Bourbon, and as he could not find Bourbon
returned to Marseilles.''

" It will be a terrible blow, Juhel, and I am not sure that
his brain will stand it."

But the bargeman and his young friend did not talk
like this in Antifer's hearing. What would have been the
use of it? Nothing would have shaken the convictions of
this obstinate man. Never did it enter his mind to
doubt that there were diamonds and other jewels of
enormous value buried by Kamylk Pasha in the island of
whose exact position he had been informed. All his
anxiety was with regard to the difficulties he might

meet with in bringing his campaign to a successful close.

The outward journey was relatively easy. Once at Sohar they would procure a boat, discover the island, and dig up the three casks. There was nothing in that to trouble a resolute man like Antifer. What could be easier than to travel in this caravan ; and what could be easier than to bring the treasure from the islet to Sohar ? But to return to Muscat, these barrels of gold and precious stones would have to be carried on camel-back like all the other goods along the coast. And how was this to be done without attracting the attention of the custom-house, without having to pay enormous duties ? Who could say but what the Sultan might seize upon them and declare himself absolute proprietor of all the treasures discovered on his territories ? Captain Antifer called it his island, but the island did not belong to him. Kamylk had not given it to him, and undoubtedly the island belonged to the Sultanate of Muscat.

Here were reasons enough for perplexity, to say nothing of the difficulties of transport on the return, the shipping of the goods on the mail-boat for Suez. What an absurd idea for the rich Egyptian to have buried his riches in an island in the Gulf of Oman ! Were there not hundreds more, thousands more, scattered over the seas, amid, for instance, the innumerable islands of the Pacific, which were quite away from observation, which belonged to no one, where the legatee could have entered into possession without awaking any suspicion ?

But so it was, and it was impossible to change it. There was the island in the Gulf of Oman ; what a pity it was they could not tow it to St. Malo ! That would have simplified matters considerably.

Captain Antifer, then, was naturally anxious, and his anxiety showed itself by paroxysms of internal rage ; and a deplorable travelling companion he was, always muttering to himself, riding apart and giving his mule many an unmerited cut with his whip. To speak the truth it was a

K

wonder that the too-patient animal did not kick and throw his rider.

Juhel guessed what was troubling his uncle but dared not say anything. Tregomain, from the height of his two-humped camel, was also aware of what was passing in his friend's mind. To reason with him was out of the question; all that could be done was to look at him and nod at each other significantly.

The first day's journey was not productive of extreme fatigue. The temperature was, however, high. The climate of Southern Arabia, just on the Tropic of Cancer, is very trying to Europeans. A burning wind, generally from the mountains, blew across a fiery sky. The sea-breeze is powerless to overcome it. The heights of Ghebel Achdan rise in the west like a screen, and appear to reflect the solar rays as if they were an immense receiver. And when the hot season is at its height the nights are suffocating and sleep impossible.

But the chief reason why there was not so much to endure in the first two days was that the caravan journeyed across the wooded plains that border the coast. There is nothing of the aridity of the desert about the environs of Muscat. Vegetation exists there in abundance. Fields of millet are under cultivation when the ground is dry, and fields of rice when the water-pools ramify their liquid veins over the surface. And there is no lack of shade under the forest of banyans, and among the mimosas which produce gum-arabic, the exportation of which is on a large scale.

In the evening the camp was pitched on the bank of a small river, fed by the mountains to the westward. The animals were unharnessed and left to graze as they pleased, without even being hobbled, so accustomed are they to these regular halts. To mention only the personages in this story, the uncle and nephew left their mules grazing on the common pasture, where Saouk left his as soon as he arrived. The bargeman's camel knelt like a Mussulman at the hour of prayer, and Tregomain alighted, giving his mount a caress on the muzzle as he did so. Ben

Omar's donkey pulled up suddenly, and, as the notary did not move as quickly as he might, it gave a jump and a kick and sent him flying off over its tail. The notary fell full length with his face towards Mecca, but probably thought more of cursing his donkey than praying to Allah and his prophet.

An uneventful night was passed on the usual halting-ground of the caravans. A start was made as soon as it was light in the morning, and the advance towards Sohar resumed. The country became more open. Away to the horizon stretched vast plains, where sand began to replace the herbage. It seemed like the Sahara, with all its inconveniences, scarcity of water, absence of shade, fatiguing travelling. For the Arabs, accustomed to these caravan marches, it was but an ordinary journey. They accomplish long distances in the very height of the summer, during the most overwhelming temperatures, but how would the Europeans support this trial ?

We hasten to say that they did so without damage ; even the bargeman, whose mass would have melted a few weeks later in the heat of the tropical sun. Rocked by the regular swing and elastic step of his camel, he slept in peace between the humps. Firmly seated, he seemed to be so like an integral part of the animal that there was no fear of his falling. He had now discovered that his obliging mount knew the difficulties of the road better than he did, and had given up attempting to guide it. The *Charmante Amélie* did not travel more safely at the end of a tow-rope along the Rance.

Although Juhel was on the road from Muscat to Sohar, his thoughts were far away in the Breton town, in the house where Enogate was expecting him. The famous princess his uncle wished him to marry did not trouble him in the least. Never would he have another woman than his pretty cousin. Was there in all the world a duchess who could compare with her ; even of the blood royal ? No, and Kamylk's millions could not alter this, even supposing that this adventure was not an Arabian Night's dream.

Antifer was more anxious on the second day than on the first, and probably would be worse on the morrow. He was thinking all the time how he could get the casks away, and the more he thought of it the less he liked it. And what would have been his apprehensions if he had known that in this very caravan he was being watched ? Yes, there was a native there, aged about forty, with a handsome face, who without awaking his suspicions was keeping him under close scrutiny.

The Suez steamer did not call once a fortnight at Muscat without the police taking a special interest in the event. Besides the tax he took on foreigners landing in his dominions, the Sultan indulged in quite an Oriental curiosity with regard to Europeans who came to visit him. Nothing could be more natural than for him to find out the object of their presence in the country, and if they intended to stay. When therefore the three Frenchmen appeared on the quay, and took up their quarters in the English hotel, the chief of the police did not hesitate to take them under his wise protection. The Muscat police are admirably organized as regards the safety of the streets, and none the less so with regard to the surveillance of travellers by sea or land. They never ask if their papers are in order, for every scoundrel is sure to have them all right. Nor do they ask questions to which answers would be easy. But they never lose sight of the new-comers ; they keep them under observation, they shadow them with a discretion, a reserve, and a tact which do justice to the intelligence of these Orientals.

Hence it came about that Antifer was under the eye of an emissary of the police, whose order was to follow him wherever he went. Without ever asking a question this policeman would succeed in finding out what these Europeans were doing in the Sultanate. If they found themselves in difficulties among a people whose language they did not know he would offer his services. And furnished with the information he obtained, the Sultan would prevent the departure of the

Amélie until nothing could be gained by keeping them any longer.

This arrangement would seriously interfere with Captain Antifer's plan. To unearth a treasure of such value, to bring it to Muscat, to ship it for Suez, was difficult enough, but if his Highness was to know all about it the difficulty would be insurmountable.

Fortunately Antifer did not know of this complication ahead. The present burden of his cares was almost too much for him. Never did he suspect that a policeman had his eye on him ; neither had his companions noticed among the caravan this quiet, discreet Arab who watched them without saying a word to them.

But if this manœuvre had escaped them it had not escaped Saouk. The so-called clerk of Ben Omar spoke Arabic, and had entered into conversation with several of the merchants going to Sohar. These people to whom the policeman was not unknown, made no mystery about him. Saouk suspected that the man was watching Antifer, and this made him uneasy. If he did not want Kamylk's millions to go to Antifer, he certainly did not want them to fall into the hands of the Sultan of Muscat. It is worth noting that the detective had no suspicion of the two Egyptians, and never supposed that they were bound on the same errand as the three Europeans. Travellers of their nationality often came to Muscat ; and there was nothing to be feared from them, which shows that the police are not perfect, even in the Sultanate of his Highness.

After a fatiguing day, broken by the midday halt, the caravan encamped a little before sunset by the side of a half-dry lagoon, one of the natural curiosities of these parts. Here was a tree under which the whole caravan could take shelter, a shelter that would have been much appreciated during the rest at noon. The rays of the sun could not have pierced the dome of these immense masses of foliage, extending like a veil, fifteen feet above the ground.

" A tree such as I have never seen before," said Juhel, when his mule stopped of itself under the first branches.

" And such as you will probably never see again ! " said the bargeman, rising between the humps of his camel, which had just knelt down.

"What do you say, uncle ? " asked Juhel.

The uncle said nothing, for the reason that he had seen nothing of that which had excited his nephew's surprise.

" I fancy," said Tregomain, "that at Saint Pol de Léon, in a corner of Brittany, we have a phenomenal vine which has some celebrity "

" Quite so; but it cannot be compared with this tree."

No! and the vine of Saint Pol de Léon, extraordinary as it might be, would have been a mere shrub by the side of this vegetable giant.

It was a banyan—a fig-tree if you would rather call it so —with a trunk that was at least a hundred feet in circumference. From this trunk, like a tower, rose an enormous tenfold ramification, the branches of which crossed and intercrossed, and forked and developed, until they covered more than an acre. An immense parasol against the solar rays, an immense umbrella against the showers, impenetrable to the fires as to the waters of the sky.

If the bargeman had had the time—for he had the patience—he would have given himself the satisfaction of counting the branches of this banyan. How many were there ? This could not but pique his curiosity. It was satisfied, and in this way.

As he was examining the lower branches of the banyan, and counting on his fingers, he heard behind him,—

" Ten thousand."

The words were pronounced with a strong Oriental accent.

Juhel knew English, and entered into conversation with the Arab who had given the information. The Arab was no other than the detective.

Finding a good opportunity for entering into communication with them he had taken advantage of it. In the course of conversation he informed Juhel that he was employed as interpreter to the British Legation at Muscat, and obligingly offered his services to the three Europeans.

Juhel thanked the native, and informed his uncle of this fortunate circumstance for their negotiations at Sohar.

"Good, good," said Antifer. "Arrange with the man, and tell him we will pay him handsomely."

"On condition, that we find something to pay him with!" murmured the incredulous Tregomain.

But if Juhel congratulated himself on this meeting, Saouk probably thought otherwise. To see the detective in communication with the Frenchmen was to inspire him with a surfeit of anxiety, and he decided to watch the proceedings of this native very closely. And then if Ben Omar could find out whither they were going—if the voyage was near its end? Was the island in the Gulf of Oman, the Straits of Ormuz, or the Persian Gulf? Were they to seek for it along the Arabian coast, or on the Persian side? How were they to begin operations, and how long would these last? Was Antifer going to embark again at Sohar? As he had not done so at Muscat, it seemed as though the island must be beyond the Straits of Ormuz? Unless, by caravan, the journey was to be continued towards Chardja, towards El Kalif, perhaps to Korenc at the top of the Persian Gulf? Cruel uncertainties, bewildering hypotheses which ceaselessly excited Saouk, and invariably reacted on the notary.

"Is it my fault," he would repeat, "if Mr. Antifer is so obstinate as to treat me like a stranger?"

Like a stranger? No! worse than that, like an intruder whose presence had been imposed on him by the testator! Ah! without that one per cent.! But was that one per cent. worth all these experiences? And when were they to end?

Next day the caravan crossed an interminable plain, a sort of desert without an oasis. The fatigue was extreme during this day, and the two that followed—fatigue due mainly to heat. The bargeman thought he was going to dissolve like one of those icebergs that drift from the northern seas to southerly latitudes. Without exaggeration he lost a tenth of his weight, to the evident satisfaction of his two-humped mount.

During these days the Arab, whose name was Selik, became more closely acquainted with Juhel ; but we may be sure that the young captain maintained a prudent reserve, and did not betray any of the secrets of his uncle. The search for a town on the coast favourable for the establishment of a branch business—that is to say, the fable already imagined for the benefit of the French agent at Muscat—did duty again for the pretended interpreter.

The caravan entered Sohar during the afternoon of the 27th of March, after a journey of four days and a half.

CHAPTER XIV.

It was fortunate that our three Europeans had come to Sohar on business and not on pleasure. The town is not worth a tourist's attention, and the visit is not worth the voyage. The streets are clean enough; the squares are sunny enough; there is a watercourse that just about supplies the wants of the few thousand inhabitants when their throats are parched by the ardour of the dog-days; there are a few houses scattered about, which are lighted from an interior court in the Oriental way; and there is a good-sized building of no particular style with which the Sultan has to content himself when he takes his two or three weeks' holiday in the north of his kingdom.

However unimportant it may be, Sohar none the less exists on the shore of the Gulf of Oman, and the best proof that can be given of this is that its geographical position has been determined with all the desirable precision. It is in longitude 54° 29′ E., and in latitude 24° 37′ N. Hence, according to the information given by Kamylk Pasha, the island had to be sought for in twenty-eight minutes of arc to the east and twenty-two to the north of Sohar.

Hotels are not numerous at Sohar. There is only a sort of caravanserai in which a few rooms, or rather cells, arranged in a circle are each furnished with a bed; and there it was that the interpreter Selik, always so useful took Captain Antifer and his two companions.

It need hardly be said that, fatigued by their day's journey, Juhel and Tregomain's only wish was for a good supper and twelve hours' sleep to follow ; but it was not easy to get Antifer to join them, reasonable as the suggestion might be. More and more excited by his near approach to his island, he would hear of no delay, but wished to charter a boat at once. To rest when he had but a stride to take—a stride of a dozen leagues it is true—to put his foot on this corner of the globe where Kamylk had buried his barrels !

There was an exciting scene before he calmed down sufficiently to agree to take a few precautions. Too much haste would make the Sohar police suspicious. The treasure was not likely to be stolen during the next twenty-four hours.

" Would it were ! " said Tregomain. " My poor friend will go mad if it is not there, and if it is there ! "

And these fears were in a certain measure justified.

But if Captain Antifer, deceived in his hopes, was in danger of going mad, a similar deception might affect Saouk so as to produce no less terrible consequences. The false Nazim might indulge in excesses of violence from which Ben Omar would not escape without damage. His impatience was as feverish as that of Antifer, and it may be safely affirmed that there were at least two travellers that night who knew no sleep in the cells of the caravanserai. They were advancing towards the same object by different roads. One was waiting for daylight to find a boat ; the other was thinking of securing a score of resolute scoundrels, who, for a good price, could be hired to carry off the treasure during the return from Sohar.

Day came at last, this memorable day, the 28th of March.

To take advantage of Selik's offers was evidently the best thing to do, and to Juhel it fell to make the best terms he could with this obliging Arab, who, more suspicious than ever, had passed the night in the court of the caravanserai.

Juhel was in some difficulty in explaining his wants to Selik. Here were three strangers, three Europeans, who had arrived the night before, and were in a hurry to obtain a boat. What they wanted was a sail—what other pretext could be given ?—a sail on the Gulf of Oman, which would last at least twenty-four hours ! Was not that a curious arrangement, and even more than curious ! Perhaps Juhel was mistaken in his surmises as to what the interpreter would think of it.

Anyhow the difficulty had to be faced ; and as soon as he met the Arab, Juhel asked him to find them a boat that could remain at sea for a couple of days.

" Are you going to cross the Gulf," asked Selik, " and land on the Persian coast ? "

An idea occurred to Juhel to elude this question by a very natural reply, which might allay any suspicion, even on the part of the authorities of Sohar.

" No," he said, " it is a geographical exploration. We want to determine the position of the principal islands in the Gulf. There are a few off Sohar, are there not ? "

" Yes, there are a few," said Selik, " but they are none of any importance."

" It does not matter," said Juhel ; " before we establish ourselves on the coast, we wish to visit the Gulf."

" As you please."

Selik said no more, although the young captain's reply seemed suspicious. He was aware of what had been told the French agent with regard to the establishment of a branch office in one of the coast towns, and he might well think that this hardly agreed with an exploration of the Gulf of Oman. And consequently Antifer and his companions were more seriously suspected than ever, and were more strictly watched.

A regrettable complication this, which rendered the success of the operation very problematical. If the treasure were found on the island, his Highness would probably be immediately informed of it. And his Highness, who was as unscrupulous as he was powerful, might make away with Kamylk's legatee, to save any future claim.

Selik undertook to find the boat required for the

exploration of the Gulf, and promised that it should be manned by a crew who could be thoroughly trusted. Provisions would have to be taken for two or three days. During the uncertain equinoctial weather, preparations were necessary for delays which if not probable were at least possible.

Juhel thanked the interpreter, and assured him that his services would be handsomely rewarded. Selik appeared most grateful for the promise, and added,—

"Perhaps it would be better for me to accompany you during this excursion? In your ignorance of Arabic you might have some difficulty in dealing with the captain of the boat and his men."

"You are right," replied Juhel; "remain in our service while we are at Sohar, and, I repeat, you will not waste your time."

They separated. Juhel went to rejoin his uncle, who was walking on the beach with Tregomain, and reported what he had done. The bargeman was delighted to have as guide and interpreter the young Arab, whom he considered not without reason to have such a very intelligent face.

Captain Antifer signified his approval by a mere nod of the head. Then he suddenly observed,—

"And this vessel?"

"Our interpreter is seeing about it, and also about the provisions."

"It seems to me that one of these boats in the harbour might be got ready in an hour or two. We are not going for a trip round the world."

"No, my friend," replied the bargeman, "but we must give the people a little time. Do not be so impatient, pray."

"And if I choose to be impatient, what then?" retorted Antifer, with a furious look at Tregomain.

"Then be impatient!" said the worthy bargeman, with a deferential bow.

However, the day was getting on, and Juhel had heard

no more of the Arab. It can easily be imagined how Captain Antifer's irritation increased. Already he began to talk of sending Selik to the bottom of the Gulf. In vain Juhel tried to defend him. As to Tregomain, he was told to shut up as soon as he began to praise Selik's intelligence.

"A beggar," shouted Antifer, "a rascal, your interpreter; a scoundrel in whom I have no confidence, and who has only one idea, to rob us of our money."

"I have given him none, uncle."

"Then you ought to have done so. If you had given him something good on account—"

"You would have said he wanted to rob us."

"It does not matter."

Neither Juhel nor Tregomain attempted to combat these contradictory ideas. The best thing to do was to keep Antifer quiet, and prevent him from committing some imprudence which would give rise to suspicions. Would they succeed with a man who would listen to nothing? Were there no fishing-boats in the harbour? Would it not be enough to take one, to agree with the crew, to go on board, to set sail, to steer to the north-east?

"But how could we understand these people?" said Juhel, "seeing that we do not understand a word of Arabic?"

"And that they do not know a word of French!" added the bargeman.

"Why don't they know it?" retorted Antifer furiously.

"They are in the wrong, quite in the wrong!" replied Tregomain, anxious to appease his friend by this concession.

"It is all your fault, Juhel!"

"No, uncle. I have acted for the best; and our interpreter will soon come back. After all, if you don't trust him, why not make use of Ben Omar and his clerk, who speak Arabic. There they are on the quay—"

"Never! That would be too much, it is already too much to have them always in tow."

"Ben Omar seems to wish to speak to us," said Tregomain.

"Let him do it, and I will give him a broadside that will sink him."

In fact Saouk and the notary were manœuvring in Antifer's wake. When he left the caravanserai they had followed him. Their duty was to keep him in sight, their right was to be present at the conclusion of this financial enterprise, which threatened to develop into a drama.

Saouk was urging Ben Omar to enter into conversation with the terrible Antifer. But the notary did not care to face him in his present state of fury. Saouk would have willingly assumed the place of this cowardly notary, and was sorry to have feigned ignorance of the language, which prevented his intervening directly in the matter.

Juhel could not but see that his uncle's treatment of Ben Omar made things worse. Once more he tried to make him understand this. The occasion seemed to be favourable, as the notary had evidently come to say something to him.

"Listen to me, uncle, whether you are angry or not. Let us reason a little, as we are reasonable beings——"

"It remains to be seen, Juhel, if what you understand by reason is not unreason. What is it you want?"

"To ask if, now we are nearing the end, you still persist in not recognizing Ben Omar."

"Certainly I persist. The scoundrel tried to steal my secret when his duty was to hand me over his. He is a rascal."

"I know that, and I do not wish to defend him. But whether or no, his presence is imposed on you by a clause in the will of Kamylk Pasha."

"Yes."

"Has he not to be on the island when you dig up the three casks?"

"Yes."

"And has he not the right to value them, by the very fact that he is entitled to a commission of so much per cent. on their value?"

"Yes."

"Well, if he has to be present at the operation, ought he

not to know where you are going and what you are going to do ? "

" Yes."

" And if by your fault or any other circumstance he is not able to assist as executor, might not the succession be contested, and would not that be a matter for a law-suit which you would certainly lose ? "

" Yes."

" Then have you to submit to the company of Ben Omar during your excursion in the Gulf ? "

" Yes."

" Will you, then, tell him that he is to get ready to go with you ? "

" No," replied Antifer.

And the " no " was uttered in so formidable a voice that it struck the notary full in the chest like a bullet.

" You see," said Tregomain ; " you will not listen to reason, and you are wrong. Why do you struggle against wind and tide ? Nothing could be more sensible than to listen to Juhel ; nothing more reasonable than to follow his advice. Ben Omar is no more to me than he is to you ; but do not lose your head about him."

It was rare for Tregomain to indulge in so long a monologue, and still rarer for his friend to let him finish.

" Have you finished ? " asked Captain Antifer.

" Yes," replied Tregomain, giving a glance of triumph at Juhel.

" And you too, Juhel ? "

" Yes, uncle."

" Well, then, you can both go to Jericho ! You can talk to the notary if you like. As for me, I will not have a word to say to the rascal. You can do just as you please."

And thereupon he swore a terrible oath, put up his helm, and ran off before the wind.

Nevertheless, Juhel had got what he wanted. His uncle, seeing that he was compelled to do so, had not forbidden him to let the notary know his intentions.

And as Ben Omar, urged on by Saouk, approached

with more courage now that Antifer had gone, only a few words were required.

"Sir," said Ben Omar, bowing low to atone by the humility of his attitude for the audacity of his proceedings, "will you pardon me if I permit myself—"

"Come to the point," said Juhel. "What do you want?"

"To know if we are at the end of our journey."

"Almost."

"Where is the island we are in search of?"

"About twelve leagues off Sohar."

"What!" exclaimed Ben Omar; "must we go on the sea again?"

"Apparently."

"And that does not seem to suit you," said the bargeman, taking pity on the poor man, who was almost fainting, as if his heart was already failing him.

Saouk looked on, affecting the most complete indifference—the indifference of one who did not understand a word of the language.

"Cheer up," said Tregomain; "two or three days at sea will soon be over. You may get your sea-legs at last —with a little practice."

The notary shook his head, and wiped his forehead, which was wet with cold perspiration. Then, in a mournful voice, he said,—

"And where do you start from?"

"From here."

"When?"

"As soon as our boat is ready."

"And when will that be?"

"This evening perhaps, or certainly to-morrow morning. You had better be ready to start, with your clerk Nazim, if you cannot do without him."

"I will—I will," replied Ben Omar.

"And may Allah help you!" added the bargeman, giving free vent to his natural kindness in the absence of Captain Antifer.

Ben Omar and Saouk had nothing more to learn except the position of the famous island. But as the young captain had not given it them, they retired.

When Juhel said that the boat would be ready that evening or next morning, was he not rather premature? So Tregomain remarked. In fact, it was three o'clock in the afternoon, and there was no sign of the interpreter. Juhel and Tregomain were getting anxious. If they had to dispense with his services, what difficulty there would be in dealing with the Sohar fishermen and having to make themselves understood by gestures. How could they manage in such a manner with regard to the cargo, the object of the expedition, the direction in which they were to go! As a last resource, it is true, Ben Omar and Nazim knew Arabic, but to call in their assistance was hardly desirable.

Fortunately Selik kept his promise. About five o'clock, as the bargeman and Juhel were returning to the caravanserai, he appeared on the scene.

" At last ! " exclaimed Juhel.

Selik apologized for the delay. It was not without difficulty that he had found a boat, and he had to promise high terms for it.

" It does not matter," said Juhel. " Can we go to sea this evening ? "

" No," said Selik, " the crew will not be complete until too late."

" Then we start—"

" At daybreak."

" Agreed."

" I will come for you to the caravanserai," added Selik and we will go out with the tide."

" And if the breeze lasts, we shall make a good course of it," said Tregomain.

A good course, indeed, for the wind was blowing from the west, and it was in the east that Captain Antifer had to look for his island.

L

CHAPTER XV.

IN the morning, before the Gulf had been gilded by the sun's first rays, Selik knocked at the door of the rooms in the caravanserai. Captain Antifer, who had not slept an hour, was on foot in a moment, and Juhel was with him almost immediately.

" The boat is ready ! " announced Selik.

" We follow you," said Juhel.

" And the bargeman ? " exclaimed Antifer. " You see he sleeps like a porpoise between two waters ! I will go and give him a shake that will wake him ! "

And off he went to the resting-place of the said porpoise, who was snoring, with both hands closed. But the shake from that vigorous arm soon opened his hands and his eyes also.

Meanwhile Juhel, as had been agreed, went to inform the notary and Nazim. They were both ready ; Nazim having some difficulty in restraining his impatience, Ben Omar very pale and very unsteady on his feet.

When Selik saw the two Egyptians appear on the scene, he could not restrain a movement of surprise, which did not escape the young captain. And was not this astonishment justified ? Here were these people, of such different nationalities, not only knowing each other, but going to embark together for an exploration of the Gulf ? Surely that was enough to provoke the detective's surprise !

" Do these two strangers intend to come with you ? " he asked Juhel.

" Yes," replied Juhel, with some embarrassment, " they

are travelling companions. We were on the same steamer
from Suez to Muscat."

"And you are acquainted with them?"

"Certainly. That they have kept apart from us is
due to my uncle being in such a bad temper."

Evidently Juhel was making matters worse by his
explanations. After all, he was not obliged to say
anything to Selik. The Egyptians came because he
chose they should come.

Selik said no more, although the matter seemed more
mysterious than ever, but he decided to keep as close a
watch on the Egyptians as on the Frenchmen.

Captain Antifer now appeared, towing along the
bargeman, like a tug bringing out a merchantman. And
we might continue the metaphor by describing him as a
merchantman just beginning to set sail, for he was still
half asleep. We need scarcely say that Antifer would
take no notice of Ben Omar or Nazim. He hurried
along, with Selik at his side, the others following him,
towards the harbour.

At the end of the jetty lay a "perm," a two-masted
vessel, moored bow and stern, her mainsail in the brails—all
that was wanted was to set it, ease away the sheet and the
mizen sheet, and be off to sea.

This perm, the _Berbera_, had a crew of twenty men—a
much more numerous crew than was required to handle a
vessel of fifty tons. Juhel noticed this, but took care to say
nothing: and he soon noticed that of these twenty men
only half appeared to be sailors. In fact these were Sohar
police, embarked under Selik's orders. Under such circumstances no man of sense would have given half-a-crown
for the four millions of Kamylk's legatee—that is, if he
found them on the island.

Three of the passengers jumped on board the _Berbera_
with the agility of sailors; but to tell the truth the perm
gave a sensible list to port under the weight of the
bargeman. There would have been some difficulty in
getting the notary on board, for his heart failed him, and

Nazim had to catch him round the body and hoist him in. As soon as the rolling began Ben Omar fled to the house in the stern, and there began to weep and groan. The instruments were embarked, with many precautions; particularly the chronometer, which Tregomain carried in a handkerchief, of which he held the four corners.

The captain of the perm, an old, rough-looking Arab, slackened off the hawsers, set sail, and at Juhel's orders, interpreted by Selik, headed off to the north-east.

They were now on the direct road to the island. With the wind in the west they ought to be there in twenty-four hours. But nature delights in troubling men. The breeze was favourable, but overhead the clouds were driving across the sky. Something else was required than to run to the north-eastward; the island had to be reached; and to do this two observations of latitude and longitude were necessary, the first in the forenoon, the second when the sun passed the meridian. To take the altitude the solar disk must deign to show itself, and on this occasion the capricious luminary obstinately refused to appear.

Captain Antifer strode up and down the deck of the *Berbera* in a desperate state of feverish agitation, watching the sky much more than he did the sea. It was not an island he was looking for on the horizon, but the sun amid the mists of the east.

Seated near the taffrail, the bargeman shook his head in token of disappointment. Juhel, leaning on the right of him, betrayed his disgust by a significant pout. Delays, still delays! Would this journey never end? And hundreds and hundreds of leagues away in the little house at St. Malo he thought he could see his dear Enogate, expecting a letter which could not yet have reached her.

"But suppose the sun does not appear?" asked the bargeman.

"It will be impossible for me to do anything," said Juhel.

"But if there is no sun, cannot you calculate our position by the moon and stars?"

"Of course ; but the moon is new, and as to the stars, I am afraid that the night will be as cloudy as the day. And besides, they are rather complicated observations, and not easily made on a lively vessel like this perm."

The wind began to freshen. Large wreaths of cloud accumulated in the west, as if the mists had been vomited forth from some inexhaustible volcano.

The bargeman found matters rather dull. He clasped on his knees the chronometer confided to his charge, while Juhel waited in vain to use the sextant he held in his hand. And in the bow of the perm were heard inarticulate cries and incessant objurgations. These were due to Captain Antifer, who varied the proceedings by actually shaking his fist at the sun, as if that could do any good.

The sun, however, did appear. Now and then a ray would shoot between, through a rift in the clouds ; but the rift closed almost instantly, and there was no means of keeping the sun long enough in view to obtain its altitude. Juhel tried again and again, but the sextant fell back without being used.

The Arabs are not very familiar with the use of nautical instruments. The men in the perm could not make out what the young captain was trying at. Selik, who was rather better educated than the others, did not trouble himself as much as he might about the importance Juhel evidently attached to this observation of the sun. Everyone could see that the passengers were much disturbed. Antifer strode about like the maniac he threatened to become, and when Tregomain and Juhel invited him to breakfast, he abruptly refused, and, contenting himself with a piece of bread, went to the mainmast, and forbade anybody to speak to him.

The afternoon brought no change in the state of the atmosphere. To leeward the clouds remained banked up. The sea was rough, and seemed "to smell something," as sailors say. What it smelt was a storm ; one of those south-west storms which so often devastate the Gulf of Oman.

The storm swooped fiercely down on the *Berbera*. With her sails reefed down, she could not keep her course; her freeboard was low, and the huge waves threatened to swamp her every minute. There was only one thing to do : run to the north-east. Juhel noticed, as Antifer might have done had he been paying attention to what went on, that the captain of the perm handled her carefully and skilfully. His crew displayed the coolness and courage of tried sailors. It was not for the first time that these brave fellows were struggling against a storm in the Gulf. But it was only part of the crew who seemed to be accustomed to these furious tempests; the rest were extended on the deck, and showed themselves very uncomfortable at the behaviour of the perm. Evidently these men had never been to sea before; and the idea occurred to Juhel that the police were following his uncle; that Selik perhaps—decidedly matters looked bad for the legatee of Kamylk Pasha.

Saouk could not be otherwise than furious with this bad weather. If the storm lasted some days, no observation would be possible, and how could they determine the position of the island ? Finding it useless to remain on deck, he took refuge in the cabin, where Ben Omar was being rolled from side to side like a cask which had broken its seizings.

After a refusal from Captain Antifer, whom they had asked to come with them, Juhel and the bargeman resolved to abandon the foot of the mast, where they were sheltered by a tarpaulin, and went to lie down on the crew's benches.

"Our expedition seems to be turning out badly," murmured Tregomain.

"That is my opinion," said Juhel.

"Let us hope that the weather will improve to-morrow, and that you can get an altitude."

"Let us hope so."

And he did not add that it was not only the state of the atmosphere he was anxious about. The sun would shine some day, even on the Gulf of Oman. They would find the island if it existed. But how about these suspicious fellows on board the *Berbera?*

The night was dark and misty, and the little vessel was in great danger; not so much from her buoyancy, which kept her rising to the waves, and escaping their foaming crests, as from the sudden bursts of wind, which would often have capsized her had it not been for the seamanlike ability of her old captain.

After midnight the wind began to moderate, owing to a persistent fall of rain. Perhaps a change of weather was preparing for the morning? No; and when the day returned, although the clouds were not so stormy as before, and the atmosphere was not disturbed by violent squalls, the sky was none the less veiled with vapour. To the abundant showers of the night succeeded the fine rain of low clouds, which, having no time to form itself into large drops, pours down in sheets of mist.

When Juhel arrived on deck he could not restrain a gesture of disappointment. With the sky in this state, an observation was hopeless. Where could the perm be now, after the changes of course, and the uncertainties as to direction to which they had been subjected during the night? The captain knew the Gulf of Oman well, but where he was he could not tell. There was no land in sight. Had they passed the island? Not unlikely; and it might be that the *Berbera* had been driven eastwards much further than was desirable.

Antifer had left his tarpaulin, and posted himself in the bow. How he fumed again and gesticulated when he had looked round the horizon! But he said not a word to his nephew, and remained standing near the starboard cathead.

But if Juhel took care to say nothing to his uncle, he had to submit to several questions from Selik, to which he could only reply evasively.

The interpreter approaching him, said,—

" The day promises badly, sir."

" Very badly."

" You cannot use your instrument for looking at the sun ? "

" I am afraid not."

" What will you do, then ? "

" I will wait."

" I would remind you that the perm only carries provisions for three days, and if the bad weather continues we shall have to return to Sohar."

" Exactly."

" In that case, will you give up your project of exploring the Gulf of Oman ? "

" Probably—or at least we will put it off till a better season."

" Will you wait at Sohar ? "

" At Sohar or at Muscat, it does not matter which."

The young captain maintained a well-justified reserve now that he suspected Selik, who failed to obtain the information he wanted.

The bargeman appeared on deck, almost at the same time as Saouk. One made a pout of disappointment, the other a gesture of anger, at seeing the mists that formed the horizon two or three cable-lengths from the *Berbera*.

" Nothing moving ? " asked Tregomain, shaking Juhel's hand.

" Nothing."

" And our friend ? "

" He is over there ; forward."

" If he has not taken a header overboard ! " murmured Tregomain. And it was always his fear that Antifer would end in this way.

The morning passed under such conditions as these. The sextant remained in its box as useless as if it had been a lady's necklace in its case. Not a solar ray pierced the thick curtain of mist. At noon the chronometer, which Tregomain had brought up, for conscience sake, could not fix the longitude by showing the difference of time. The afternoon was just as unfavourable, and although an account was kept of the course, the whereabouts of the *Berbera* were but imperfectly known. That this was so, appeared from a remark made by the captain of the perm to Selik, that if the weather did not change in the morning he would steer westward for the land. Where would he meet with it? At Sohar, at Muscat, or further to the north, towards the Straits of Ormuz, or further south, near Raz-el-Had?

Selik thought it his duty to let Juhel know the captain's intentions.

" Be it so," said Juhel.

And that was his only reply.

Nothing occurred up to nightfall. When the sun sank below the mists in the west not a ray pierced them. But the rain gradually became lighter until it was as fine as spindrift. This was probably an indication of some change in the weather. The wind went down, until it became but gentle, intermittent puffs. During these intermittences the bargeman, wetting his hand and exposing it to the air, thought he felt a light breeze rising in the east.

" Ah," said he, " if I was only on the *Charmante Amélie* between the delightful banks of the Rance, I should know what to do."

But the *Charmante Amélie* had been sold as firewood years before, and it was not between the delightful banks of the Rance that the perm was sailing.

Juhel made the same observation as Tregomain. Besides it seemed to him as though when the sun sunk below the horizon it shot up one ray through the clouds, as it through a crack in a door. Probably Antifer had noticed this ray, for his eye brightened, and replied to the solar ray by a ray of fury.

The night came, and at supper the provisions were served sparingly. It was reported that only enough remained for twenty-four hours. Hence the necessity of regaining the land next day, or at least making sure that the *Berbera* was not very far away from it.

The night was calm. The sea rapidly grew smoother, as generally happens in narrow gulfs. Gradually the wind hauled to the east, and the perm had to be put on the starboard tack ; but owing to the uncertainty as to the vessel's position, the captain, at Juhel's advice, decided to lay to until daylight.

About three o'clock in the morning the sky, completely cleared of the mist overhead, became brilliant with its last constellations. Everything promised a good observation. The sun rose from the horizon in full splendour, and Tregomain politely took off his hat to it by way of salute.

It can easily be imagined what a pleasant change this meant for all. With what impatience all, passengers and sailors, waited for the hour when the observation would be made. The Arabs now knew that the Europeans had the means of determining the ship's position exactly, although no land was in sight; and they were anxious to know if the *Berbera* was still in the Gulf, or had been driven past Cape Raz-el-Had.

The sun rose on a sky of admirable clearness. Nothing to fear, not a cloud to veil it, when the young captain judged the moment had come to obtain the meridianal height.

A little before noon Juhel made his preparations.

Antifer placed himself by his side, his lips closed, his eyes burning, without saying a word. The bargeman stood on the right, nodding his big red head. Saouk was behind, Selik was to the left, ready to follow the details of the operation.

Juhel, quite equal to the occasion, with his legs firmly apart, seized the sextant in his left hand, and directed the glass towards the horizon.

The perm rose gently to the undulations of a gentle swell.

As soon as the altitude was taken,—

" It is done," said Juhel.

And reading the figures on the graduated limb, he descended to the cabin to make his calculations.

Twenty minutes afterwards he returned to the deck and reported the result of his observation.

The perm was in latitude 25° 2' north.

She was consequently three minutes further to the south than the latitude of the island.

To complete the operation, it was necessary to measure the horary angle. Never had the hours appeared longer to Captain Antifer, to Juhel, to the bargeman, to Saouk. It seemed as though the much-desired moment would never come.

Meanwhile the *Berbera* was given a more southerly course, at Juhel's request.

At half-past two the young sailor took a series of altitudes, while the bargeman noted the time of the chronometer. The calculations gave the longitude as 54° 28'.

The perm was a minute too far to the east for the long-sought island.

Almost immediately there was a shout. One of the Arabs pointed to a blackish mound about two miles to the west.

"My islet!" exclaimed Antifer.

And it could only be the islet, for there was no other land in sight.

And Antifer began to twitch and jump as if he had St. Vitus's dance, so that Tregomain had to interfere and hold him in his powerful arms.

Immediately the perm was steered straight for the island. The slight breeze from the east took her there in half an hour. Reckoning the distance run since the observation, Juhel satisfied himself that the island agreed with the position given by Kamylk Pasha. The latitude bequeathed by Thomas Antifer to his son was 24° 59' north, the longitude brought to St. Malo by Ben Omar was 54° 57' east.

And as far as the eye could range there was no other land in sight.

CHAPTER XVI.

THERE it was then, this island, which Antifer valued at four millions or more. And he would not have taken sixpence off, even if the Rothschilds had proposed to buy it of him.

To look at it was but a naked, barren mass, without verdure, without culture. A rocky heap, oblong in form, and about two thousand yards in circumference. Its shore was capriciously indented. Here capes, there creeks, of no great depth. Nevertheless the perm found shelter in one of the creeks, which opened to the west, and was sheltered from the wind. The water was very clear. The bottom could be seen twenty feet down; a floor of sand, strewn with submarine plants. When the *Berbera* was moored, the very gentle undulation of the surge hardly moved her. But little as it was, it was too much for the notary to wish to remain a minute more on board. He had dragged himself along the deck, he had gained the bulwarks, and was just about to jump ashore when Captain Antifer seized him by the shoulder, and roared in a voice of thunder,—

"Stop there, Mr. Ben Omar! I go first, if you please."

And, whether he liked it or not, he had to wait until the intractable captain had taken possession of his island, which he did by forcibly impressing on the sand the sole of his sea-boots.

Ben Omar was then allowed to join him; and what a long sigh of satisfaction he gave when he felt the ground

firm once more !   Tregomain, Juhel and Saouk were soon
at his side.

All this time Selik was looking about him, wondering
what the strangers were going to do on this islet.   Why
such a long voyage, why so much expense and fatigue?
To make out the position of this h· ap of rocks could
hardly be the reason, unless these people were fools.
And although Antifer seemed somewhat of a madman,
Juhel and the bargeman were evidently in the full enjoy-
ment of their reason !   And yet they were assisting in this
exploration !   And then the two Egyptians mixed up in
such an adventure !

Selik had more reason than ever for suspecting the proceedings of these strangers, and he was preparing to leave
the vessel and follow them on to the island, when Antifer
made a sign that was understood by Juhel, who said to
Selik—

" There is no need for you to come with us.   We have
no need of an interpreter here.   Ben Omar speaks French
as if he were a native of France."

" It is well," was Selik's reply.

Annoyed though he was, the detective did not enter
into any discussion on the point.   He had entered Captain
Antifer's service, and it was his business to obey orders.
And this he resigned himself to, resolving to intervene
with his men if, on their return from their exploration, the
strangers brought anything on board the perm with them.

It was about half-past three in the afternoon.   There
was plenty of time to take possession of the three casks, if
they were in the indicated place, which Antifer did not
doubt.

It was agreed that the *Berbera* should remain in the
creek.   At the same time the captain, through Selik,
informed Juhel that he could not stay more than six hours.
The provisions were nearly exhausted.   It was urgent to
take advantage of the easterly wind, so as to reach Sohar at
daybreak.   Antifer made no objection ; a few hours would
be sufficient for him to bring his operations to a close.

What had he to do ?   Not even to search over this very
small island, yard by yard.   According to the letter, the
precise spot where the treasure was deposited was on one
of the southern promontories, at the base of a rock,
recognizable by the monogram of the double K.   The
pickaxe would soon reveal the three barrels, that he could
roll on board the perm.   He had arranged to work with
out witnesses, save the indispensable Ben Omar, whose
presence was imposed upon him, and his clerk Nazim.   As
the crew of the *Berbera* would have nothing to be anxious
about as to what the barrels contained, the return to
Muscat by caravan was the only thing that presented any
difficulty.   But that could be dealt with later on.

Captain Antifer, Tregomain and Juhel in one group,
and Ben Omar and Nazim in another, began to climb the
slopes of the island, whose mean altitude measured a
hundred and fifty feet above the level of the sea.   A few
flocks of sea-ducks flew off at their approach, quacking out
their protests against the intruders who were violating
their home.   Probably no human being had set foot on the
island since the visit of Kamylk Pasha.   Antifer carried
his pickaxe on his shoulder ; he would not give it up to
anyone.   The bargeman carried the mattock ; Juhel indicated the course, compass in hand.

The notary had some difficulty in keeping in front of
Saouk.   His legs still shook, although he no longer had
the perm's deck under his feet.   But we need not be
astonished at finding that he had recovered his intelligence, forgotten the trials of the voyage, and thought not
of those of the return.

The ground was pebbly ; its surface was not easy walking.   In working round some of the hillocks that were
difficult to cross, the centre of the islet was reached.   When
the group had attained this culminating point, they sighted
the perm, with her flag fluttering in the breeze.

From this point the outline of the island was easily
visible.   Here and there were a few promontories, and
among them was the cape with the millions in it.   There

could be no mistake, for the will indicated that it ran southwards.

Juhel recognized it immediately by the aid of the compass.

It was a long, barren tongue, beaten by the light foam of the surf.

And once more the thought occurred to the young captain, that the riches buried under the rocks were about to rise as an insurmountable obstacle between his betrothed and himself. Never would they triumph over their uncle's obstinacy! And envy—a cruel envy, which however he overcame—tempted him to send his companions astray.

The bargeman was in agony between two opposing feelings—the fear that Juhel and Enogate would never be married, and the fear that his friend Antifer would go mad if he did not lay hands on the legacy of Kamylk Pasha. And in a sort of frenzy he struck the ground so violently with his mattock, that splinters of rock began to fly around him.

"Hallo, bargeman," exclaimed Antifer, "what fly is biting you?"

"None, none!" replied Tregomain.

"Then keep your pickings for the right place, if you please."

"I will keep them, my friend."

Then the group went southwards towards the promontory, which was not six hundred yards away.

Antifer, Ben Omar and Saouk, now in front, hurried along attracted as by a magnet—the magnet of gold, all-powerful among men. They panted as they went. They seemed to smell the treasure at a distance—they breathed it in, and breathed it out; they were filled with an atmosphere of millions, and would fall asphyxiated if that atmosphere left them.

In ten minutes they had reached the point which ran out into the sea; and it was at its end that Kamylk had marked the rock with a double K.

Antifer's excitement was such that he fainted. If Tregomain had not caught him in his arms, he would have fallen in a heap. The only signs of life were a few spasmodic starts.

"Uncle! uncle!" cried Juhel.

"My friend!" cried the bargeman.

Saouk's expression no one could mistake. It said as clearly as possible,—

"May this Christian dog die, and I shall again become the sole heir of Kamylk Pasha!"

Ben Omar's physiognomy appeared to say just the contrary,—

"If this man dies, and he alone knows where the treasure is, away goes my commission!"

But the accident had no such sorrowful result. By the bargeman's vigorous rubbings, Antifer regained consciousness, and seized hold of the pickaxe he had dropped. And then the exploration began at the beginning of the promontory.

There was a narrow causeway, sufficiently raised for the high tide not to cover it, even during south-west winds. It would have been difficult to have found a better place in which to bury the millions. To recognize the place was not difficult, providing that the storms of the Gulf of Oman had not in a quarter of a century weathered away the monogram.

Antifer would have searched all over this promontory if necessary. He would throw over the rocks one after the other, and spend weeks, even months, at his task. He would let the perm go back to Sohar for provisions. He would not abandon the islet until he had torn from it the riches of which he was the legitimate possessor.

And Saouk was of the same opinion.

And now they were all at work, searching, foraging under the clumps of algæ, between the interstices of the rocks coated with seaweed. Antifer tapped about with his pickaxe on the loose stones. The bargeman attacked them with his mattock. Ben Omar crawled on all-fours

like a crab among the shingle. The others, Juhel and
Saouk, were quite as busy. Not a word was spoken.
The operation was conducted in silence. It could not
have been more silent if it had been a funeral ceremony.

And was it not a cemetery, this islet lost in the gulf;
and was it not a tomb they were seeking—a tomb from
which they longed to disinter the millions of the Egyptian?

In half an hour they had found nothing. But they did
not despair. That they were on Kamylk's island, and that
his barrels were buried on this promontory, they had no
doubt.

The sun blazed down on them. Sweat poured down
their faces. They knew no feeling of fatigue. They
worked with the ardour of ants in an ant-hill—all, even the
bargeman in the grip of the demon of greed, all but
Juhel.

At last a shout of joy—or rather the roar of a wild
beast—suddenly resounded.

It was Captain Antifer who had uttered it. Upright,
with his hat off, his hand stretched out, he pointed to a
rock rising like a stela.

"There! there!" he shouted.

And if he had prostrated himself before the stela like a
Transteverin before the niche of a madonna, not one of his
companions would have been surprised. He was soon
joined by them in common adoration.

Juhel and the bargeman, Saouk and Ben Omar, gathered
round Antifer, who had just knelt down. They knelt near
him.

What was there on this rock?

There was what the eye could see and the hands could
touch. There was the famous monogram of Kamylk
Pasha, the double K, rather eaten away at its edges, but
still visible.

"There! there!" repeated Captain Antifer.

And he pointed to the base of the rock—to the place
where the treasure buried thirty-two years ago slept in its
coffer of stone.

M

Immediately the pick came down on the rock and the splinters flew. Then Tregomain's mattock knocked off chips of rock and chips of concrete. The hole began to get bigger, to deepen. Chests panted, hearts beat ready to break, in expectation of the last blow, which would cause the millions to burst like a spring from the entrails of the ground.

And still they dug, but the barrels did not appear. Evidently Kamylk had dug a very deep trench. He was not wrong, after all, and what did it matter if it took a little time and a little fatigue to unearth them?

Suddenly a metallic sound was heard. Doubtless the pickaxe had encountered some sonorous object.

Antifer knelt over the hole. His head disappeared in it, while his hands dug into it greedily.

He rose.

He held in his hand a metal box, not above four inches in cube.

They all looked at him, unable to hide their feeling that they had been deceived. And doubtless Tregomain expressed the thoughts of all when he exclaimed,—

"If there are four millions in that, may the—"

"Silence!" vociferated Captain Antifer.

And again he felt about in the excavation, picking out the last fragments of rock, seeking to meet with the casks.

Labour in vain! There was nothing here—nothing but the iron box, on the side of which there stood in relief the double K of the Egyptian.

Had then Captain Antifer undergone such fatigues for nothing? Had they come all this way to be the sport of a mystificator?

Juhel would have smiled, if his uncle's face had not frightened him. His eyes were as those of a madman, his mouth was contracted in a horrible grin; inarticulate sounds escaped from his throat.

Tregomain declared afterwards that at this moment he had expected to see him fall stone-dead.

Suddenly Antifer rose : he seized his pickaxe, brandished it, and in a frightful access of rage, struck a violent blow which shattered the box. A paper fell out of it.

It was a piece of parchment, yellow with age, on which were a few lines written in French, and still legible.

Antifer seized this paper. Forgetting that Ben Omar and Saouk might hear and learn from him a secret it was his interest to keep, he began to read in a trembling voice the first lines :—

"This document contains the longitude of a second island which Thomas Antifer, or, in default, his direct heir, is to bring to the knowledge of the banker Zambuco, residing at—"

Antifer stopped his mouth by putting his fist into it.

Saouk was sufficiently master of himself to let nothing appear of what he had just ascertained. A few words more, and he would have learnt what was the longitude of the second island, of which Zambuco had the latitude, and at the same time where the banker lived.

The notary, no less disappointed, stood there, his lips open, his tongue hanging out, like a dog dying of thirst just dragged from his saucer.

But a moment after that sentence had been cut off short by the fist in the mouth, Ben Omar, who had a right to know Kamylk's intentions, rose, and asked,—

"Well—this banker, Zambuco—where does he live ? "

"At home !" replied Captain Antifer.

And folding the paper, he thrust it into his pocket, leaving Ben Omar to stretch his despairing hands to the sky.

The treasure was not on this island in the Gulf of Oman.

The only object of the journey was to invite Captain Antifer to put himself in communication with a fresh personage, the banker Zambuco ! Was this personage a second legatee whom Kamylk desired to reward for services rendered ? Was he going to share the treasure with Captain Antifer ? It looked like it. Whence the logical consequence that instead of four millions, only two would go into the pocket of Captain Antifer.

Juhel bowed his head at the thought that this was still too much to make his uncle modify his opinion relative to his marriage with his dear Enogate.

And, in fact, Juhel had divined what was passing in Antifer's mind. For what Antifer remarked by way of conclusion was, " Well, Enogate will have to marry a duke instead of a prince, and Juhel will have to marry a duchess instead of a princess."

CHAPTER XVII.

DREARY had been the house at St. Malo since Captain Antifer had left it, and the days and nights had been spent in anxiety by mother and daughter. Juhel's empty room made all the house empty, at least so thought Enogate. And then her uncle was not there, nor was his friend Tregomain !

It was the 29th of April. Two months had elapsed since the *Steersman* had left with three travellers on their adventurous campaign in quest of the treasure. How had the voyage ended ? Where were they then ? Had they attained their object ?

"Mother, mother," said the girl, "they will never come back again."

"Yes, my child, they will ; have confidence, they will come back," the old Breton would answer. "But all the same they would have done better not to have left us."

"Yes," murmured Enogate, "and just as I was going to be his wife."

Captain Antifer's departure had created an immense sensation in the town. People had been so accustomed to see him strolling, pipe in mouth, along the streets and on the ramparts ! And then there was Gildas Tregomain walking at his side, but just a little behind him, his legs bowed, his loose coat always in creases at the armpits, his face always placid and beaming with kindness ! And Juhel, the young captain, whose native town was as proud of him as he was of Enogate ! Where had the three gone to ? No one had any idea. They all knew that the *Steersman* had taken them to Port Said, but only Enogate and Nanon were aware that they were going down the Red

Sea to venture into the northern boundaries of the Indian Ocean. Antifer had wisely kept his secret, for he did not want Ben Omar to get wind of the position of the famous island.

But if he had not let them know where he had gone, he had been too loquacious, too exuberant, too communicative with regard to his plans. At St. Malo, as at Saint Servan and Dinard, everybody knew the story of Kamylk Pasha, and how Thomas Antifer had received a letter, and how the messenger had arrived, and how the longitude and latitude had given the position of an island containing millions of treasure—millions of millions, according to those who knew best. With what impatience then did they await the news of the discovery, and the return of the captain, transformed into a nabob, bringing into the port a cargo of diamonds and precious stones !

Enogate did not ask for so much as this. If her betrothed, her uncle, her friend, returned even with empty pockets she would be satisfied, she would give thanks to God, and her deep distress would change into gladness. She had not been without hearing from Juhel. A first letter, dated from Suez, had informed her of the details of the voyage since their separation, and mentioned how nervous her uncle was becoming and how Ben Omar and his clerk had been welcomed. A second letter, dated from Muscat, narrated the incidents of the voyage across the Indian Ocean to the capital of the Sultanate, and told her in what a state of excitement, bordering on madness, Captain Antifer then was, and how they had decided to push on to Sohar.

And again and again did she read these letters, which did not confine themselves to relating the impressions of the voyage, or reporting her uncle's excited state, but expressed all the annoyance of her betrothed at being separated from her on the eve of their marriage, at being so far away from her, and told of his hope of an early return, to gain her uncle's consent, even if he came back with his hands full of millions ! Over and over again did Nanon and Enogate read these letters, to which they could not reply—that consolation being denied them—and indulged in all the comments they suggested. They counted on their fingers the days during which the absent ones would have to remain in those distant seas. They crossed out day after day on the almanac hanging on the wall; and after the receipt of the second letter they abandoned themselves to the hope that the second half of the voyage would be devoted to the return.

A third letter arrived on the 29th of April, about two months after Juhel's departure. Seeing that it bore the post-mark of Tunis, Enogate felt her heart beat with happiness. The travellers, then, had left Muscat; they had returned to European seas; they were nearing France. In three days they might be at Marseilles. Three days at the outside; and to reach St. Malo by express—twenty-six hours!

Mother and daughter were seated in one of the rooms on the ground floor, after shutting the door on the postman. No one could disturb them. They could give free vent to their feelings. As soon as they had wiped away the tears that rose in their eyes, Enogate opened the envelope, drew forth the letter, and read in a loud voice, pausing between each sentence for it to be understood, as follows :—

> " La Goulette, Regency of Tunis,
> " 22nd April, 1862.

" MY DEAR ENOGATE,—

" I embrace you for your mother first of all, then for yourself, and then for myself. But we are far away from one another, and when this interminable voyage will end I know not. I have already written twice to you, and you should have had my letters. This is the third, more important than the others; in the first place, because it will tell you that the treasure business has had an unexpected change come over it, much to my uncle's annoyance—."

Enogate uttered a little cry of joy, and clapping her hands, exclaimed,—

"They have found nothing, mother, and I shall not have to marry a prince."

"Go on!" replied Nanon.

Enogate finished the sentence which she had interrupted:—

"And also because I am sorry to have to tell you that we are obliged to continue our search much farther away."

The letter shook between Enogate's fingers.

"Search farther away!" she murmured. "They are not coming back, mother, they are not coming back!"

"Courage, my daughter, and go on," said Nanon.

Enogate, with her lovely eyes full of tears, resumed the reading of the letter. Juhel briefly related what had happened on the island in the Gulf of Oman; how, instead of the treasure, they had found a document, and in this document the mention of a new longitude. Then Juhel added:—

"Judge, my dear Enogate, of my uncle's disappointment, of the rage he was in, and also of my disgust—not that we had not taken possession of the treasure, but that our departure for St. Malo was further delayed. I thought my heart would have broken—"

Enogate had much trouble in restraining the beatings of her own, and by her own feelings understood what Juhel had had to suffer.

"Poor Juhel!" she murmured.

"And poor you!" murmured Nanon. "Go on."

Enogate continued, in a voice changed by emotion,—

"In fact, this confounded longitude Kamylk Pasha requested us to bring to the knowledge of a certain Zambuco, a banker at Tunis, who was in possession of a certain latitude. Evidently it is in another island that the treasure has been buried. Probably the Pasha had also contracted a debt of gratitude towards this personage, who had formerly helped him, as had grandfather Antifer.

The legacy has to be shared between two legatees, which reduces the share of each to a half, and on this account arose the extravagant anger, you may imagine. Not four millions, but two! Well, I shall be only too pleased if those to whom the generous Egyptian owed debts of gratitude become so numerous, that so little comes to uncle that he will have nothing to say against our marriage."

Enogate continued,—

"When our uncle read the document he was so astounded that the figures of the new longitude and the address of him with whom he had to communicate for discovering the position of the island, almost escaped him. Fortunately, he restrained himself in time. Our friend, Tregomain, with whom I often talk about you, my dear Enogate, accomplished a most remarkable grimace when he learnt that he had to go in search of a second island. 'My poor Juhel,' he said, 'is this pasho-pashee-pasha having a lark with us? Is he going to send us to the world's end?' Will it be at the world's end? That is what we want to know at the moment of writing.

"In fact, if our uncle has kept from us the information contained in the document, it is because he mistrusts Ben Omar. Ever since this rascal endeavoured to get the secret out of him at St. Malo, he has held him in suspicion. Perhaps he has not been wrong, and as far as I am concerned, his clerk, Nazim, seems to be as doubtful. I do not like this Nazim, neither does Tregomain. I can assure you that our notary, Calloch, would not have him in his office. I am convinced that if he or Ben Omar knew the address of this Zambuco, they would endeavour to be before us. But uncle has not breathed a word. Ben Omar and Nazim do not even know that we are going to Tunis, and in leaving Muscat we are asking where the Pasha's humour is going to send us next."

Enogate stopped for a moment.

Juhel then related the incidents which had **marked** the return—the departure from the island, the obvious disappointment of the interpreter, Selik, at finding the strangers return with empty hands, confirming him in his opinion that there was something more in the wind than a mere tourists' trip; then the wearisome return by caravan to Muscat, and the waiting there during two days for the mail-boat from Bombay.

"And," continued Juhel, "if I did not write to you a second time from Muscat, it was because I hoped to have something to tell you. But all I can say even now is that we are returning to Suez, and thence going on to Tunis."

Enogate stopped reading, and looked at Nanon, who shook her head, and muttered,—

"It is to be hoped they are not going to the end of the world. There is everything to be afraid of amongst these Infidels."

The excellent woman spoke of these Orientals as they spoke of them in the days of the Crusades. And with the scruples of the pious Breton, the millions coming from such a source had an evil odour. But let her express such ideas before Captain Antifer!

Juhel then gave an account of the voyage from Muscat to Suez, the crossing of the Indian Ocean and the Red Sea—Ben Omar sick beyond all recognition.

"So much the better," said Nanon.

And during the whole voyage Antifer had not said a word.

"I do not know, dear Enogate, what will happen if uncle is deceived in his hopes; or rather I know too well, he will go mad. Who would have believed that of a man so wise in his conduct, so modest in his tastes? The prospect of being a millionaire—but how many heads would be able to resist it? Yes, we two, of course, but that is because our life is centred in our hearts.

"From Suez we reached Port Said, where we had to wait for the departure of a trading steamer for Tunis, where lives this banker Zambuco, to whom uncle has to communicate this exasperating document. But when the latitude of the one and the longitude of the other have

determined the position of the new island, where are we
to look for it? That is the question, and in my opinion it
is a serious one, for on it depends our return to France—
and you—"

Enogate let fall the letter, which her mother picked up.
She could read no more. She saw the absent ones carried
thousands of leagues away, exposed to great perils in
terrible countries, perhaps never returning at all, and this
cry escaped her,—

"Oh! uncle, uncle, what misery you bring to those who
love you so much!"

"Forgive him, my daughter," replied Nanon, "and pray
God to protect him."

There were a few minutes of silence, during which the
women united in the same prayer.

Then Enogate resumed :—

"We left Port Said on the 16th of April. We were
bound direct for Tunis. At first we kept near the
Egyptian coast, and what a look Ben Omar gave as we
sighted the harbour of Alexandria. I thought he would
have gone ashore, and resigned all claim to his commission.
But his clerk intervened, and in their language, of which we
did not understand a word, he made him listen to reason
—somewhat roughly it seemed to me. It is clear that
Ben Omar is in fear of this Nazim, and I am wondering
if this Egyptian is really the man he says he is ; he is so
much like a bandit. Whoever he may be, I am going to
keep a good watch on him.

"Leaving Alexandria behind, we made for Cape Bon,
leaving to the south the gulfs of Tripoli and Gabes. Then
the wild slopes of the Tunisian mountains appeared on the
horizon, with the abandoned fortresses on their crests, and
one or two marabouts between the curtains of verdure. In
the evening of the 21st of April, we reached the roadstead
of Tunis, and next day our vessel anchored before the
moles of La Goulette.

"My dear Enogate, if at Tunis I am nearer you than I
was in the Gulf of Oman, I am still far away, and who

knows what ill-fortune may not take us further ?   It is true that it is quite as miserable whether we are five leagues away or five thousand.   But do not despair, and remember that whatever may be the end of the voyage, it cannot be very long.

"I have written this letter as we came along, so as to be able to post it as soon as we land at La Goulette.   It will reach you in a few days.   It will not tell you what I do not know, and what is so important for us to know—namely, where we are going to.   But uncle himself does not know that, and it can only be determined by an interchange of communications with the banker, whose rest we have probably come to trouble ; for when he learns of this enormous legacy, the half of which belongs to him, Zambuco will certainly form one of the party, and become probably as excited as uncle is.

"As soon as I ascertain the situation of island number two I will let you know.   It is then probable that a fourth letter will succeed the third at a few days' interval.

"As for the present it carries with it, for both you and your mother, Tregomain's kind regards and my love, and also uncle's, although he seems to have lost all remembrance of St. Malo, and of the old house, and of those who live in it.   Dearest Enogate, I send you all my love, as I know you send me yours, although I cannot have a letter from you.   Believe me, for life,

"Your faithful and affectionate

"JUHEL ANTIFER."

CHAPTER XVIII.

WHEN you arrive in the roadstead of Tunis, you are not at Tunis. To get there you have to avail yourself of one of the local boats called "" mahonnes," and land at La Goulette. The port, in fact, is not a port at all in the sense that vessels of ordinary tonnage can come alongside the wharves, for only small coasters and fishing-boats can do that. Other ships, sailing and steam, have to remain outside at anchor, and though the hills may shelter them from the easterly winds, they are at the mercy of the squalls that come from the east and north. A harbour there is absolutely necessary, accessible for all ships, even ships of war, and this can be made either by enlarging that of Bizerta, on the northern coast of the Regency, or by making a channel through Lake Bahira.

And when Captain Antifer and his companions had reached La Goulette they were still not at Tunis. They had to go by the Rubattino railway, belonging to an Italian company, which runs by the side of Lake Bahira, passing at the foot of the little hill of Carthage, on which rises the chapel of St. Louis.

When our travellers had left the quay, they found a sort of town, through which ran a wide road, with governor's house, Catholic church, cafés, private houses—in fact everything European in character ; and they had to go as far as the palace on the shore, which the bey formerly occupied during the bathing season, to discover the first indication of Oriental colour.

But the Oriental colour did not trouble Captain Antifer nor did the legends of Regulus, Scipio, Cæsar, Cato, Marius or Hannibal! Did he even know the names of these great personages? He had heard of them, probably, as the good Tregomain had heard of the glories of his native town, and that was enough for his self-esteem. Juhel alone could have abandoned himself to these historic souvenirs if he had not had quite enough to think about in the present. It was with him as they say in the Levant it was of the absent-minded man—" He is looking for his son, whom he is carrying on his shoulders." What he was looking for was Enogate, from whom he was, to his annoyance, going farther away.

After passing through La Goulette, Captain Antifer, the bargeman, and Juhel, bag in hand—they expected to renew the contents at Tunis—went to catch the first train at the station. Ben Omar and Nazim followed them at a distance. As Antifer had not opened his mouth they knew nothing of this banker Zambuco, whom the caprice of Kamylk Pasha wished them to become acquainted with, much to the disgust—not so much of the notary, who would have the same commission providing he did not retire from the search—as of Saouk, who now had to deal with two legatees instead of one.

After waiting half an hour the travellers took their seats in the train. They waited a few minutes at the station, whence they could see the slope of the Carthage hill, and the monastery, renowned for its archæological museum, and in forty minutes they reached Tunis. They went to the Hôtel de France, in the European quarter, and took three rooms, rather bare of furniture, very lofty, and with mosquito-curtains round the beds. The restaurant on the ground floor would provide them with breakfast and dinner at whatever hour might be convenient to them, in a very comfortable room. But, after all, it did not matter, as they were not going to stay there long.

Captain Antifer did not even give himself time to go up to his room.

" I will find you here when I come back," he said to his companions.

" Go, friend," said Tregomain, " and carry your ship by boarding "

It was this very boarding that Juhel's uncle was anxious about. He had no intention of trying to cheat his co-legatee, as Ben Omar had tried to cheat him. He was an honest man, and perfectly straightforward, notwithstanding his originality, and he had decided not to beat about the bush at all. He would go straight to the banker and say to him,—

" Here is what I bring you. Let us have what you have to offer in exchange, and off we go together."

According to the document found on the island this Zambuco must have been informed that a certain Antifer was going to bring him the longitude necessary for him to fix the position of an island in which the treasure was buried, and the banker would not be surprised at this visit.

But Antifer had one fear, the fear that Zambuco did not speak French. If he knew English, Juhel could act as interpreter. But if he knew neither of these languages they would have to call in another interpreter ; and then they would be at the mercy of a third party with regard to this secret worth four millions—

On leaving the hotel, Captain Antifer, without saying where he was going, had asked for a guide. And he and his guide disappeared at the turning of one of the streets which open on to the Place de la Marine.

" As he does not want us—" said the bargeman, as he moved off.

" Let us go for a walk, and begin by posting my letter," said Juhel.

And these two, after leaving the post-office, which is next to the hotel, went down towards Bab-el-Bahar, so as to walk round the city by the crenellated wall, which is two good leagues in length.

A hundred yards from the hotel, Captain Antifer said to his guide and interpreter,—

" You know Zambuco, the banker ? "

" Everybody knows him here."

" And he lives—"

" In the lower town ; in the Maltese quarter."

" That is where I want you to take me."

" As you wish, Excellency ! "

In these Oriental countries they call you Excellency as if it were " Sir."

Antifer hurried towards the lower town. Rest assured that he took not the slightest notice of the curiosities of the road ; here one of those mosques that are in hundreds at Tunis, which is dominated by their elegant minarets ; there some Roman or Saracen ruin ; there a picturesque square sheltered by the foliage of fig-trees or palms ; then narrow streets with the houses looking into each other, rising, falling, bordered by gloomy shops where laces, and drapery, and odds and ends are heaped together anyhow. No ! Antifer only thought of this visit imposed on him by Kamylk Pasha, and the reception he was about to have, he had little doubt of that. When you bring a man two millions of money you need have but little fear that you will not be well received.

After half an hour's walk the Maltese quarter was reached. It was not the cleanest part of this town of a hundred and fifty thousand souls, which does not shine by excess of cleanliness, particularly in its old portions.

At the end of a street or rather a lane of this commercial quarter the guide stopped before a house of mediocre appearance. Built on the model of all Tunisian habitations, it was a big square block, with a terrace, without external windows, and a courtyard—one of those " patios " in Arab fashion from which the rooms were lighted.

The aspect of this house did not give Captain Antifer the idea that its owner was swimming—as he expressed it—in opulence. And he thought that this was all the better for the success of his plans.

" Is this where Zambuco the banker lives ? "

" This is his house."

"And is this his banking-house ? "

" It is."

" Has he any other house ? "

" No, Excellency."

" Is he supposed to be rich ? "

" He is worth many millions."

" Pheugh ! " went Captain Antifer.

" And as greedy as he is rich ! " added the guide.

" Pheugh—Pheugh ! " went Captain Antifer.

And thereupon he sent back the guide to the hotel.

We need hardly say that Saouk had followed them, taking care not to be seen. Now he knew where Zambuco lived. Could he get any advantage out of this banker ? Was there an opportunity for arriving at an understanding with him in order to oust Captain Antifer ? If he could bring about a disagreement between the co-legatees or Kamylk Pasha could he not use him for his own purposes ? It was certainly unlucky that when they were on island number one Antifer had not let slip the figures of the new longitude. If Saouk had known them he might have got to Tunis first and gained over the banker—at a price—if not got the secret out of him for nothing. But then he remembered that it must be Antifer and no other who according to the document must take the longitude. Well ! Saouk would stick to his programme—he would execute it pitilessly, and when the Maltese and the Malouin were in possession of the legacy he would rob them both.

Antifer entered the banker's house, and Saouk waited outside.

The buildings on the left of the entrance served as the office. In the courtyard there was no one ; it seemed as abandoned as if the bank had closed that morning through cessation of payments. But rest assured that Zambuco was not the sort of banker to fail.

He was a man of middle height, about sixty years old, thin and nervous ; bright, keen eyes with a shifty look in them, close shaven face, complexion like parchment, hair

N

grizzly and matted like a cap stuck on to his head, back slightly bowed, hands wrinkled, fingers long and hooked. Although he was not much of an observer, Antifer felt that this Zambuco was not an attractive man, and said to himself that he would never have much pleasure in his acquaintance. In fact, the banker was merely a sort of usurer, lending on pledges, who ought to have been born a Jew, and who was of Maltese origin. Of these Maltese there are from five to six thousand in Tunis.

Zambuco was reported to have amassed a large fortune in all the devious ways of banking—those which are practised with birdlime on the fingers. Rich he was, and he was proud of it. But be it understood you are never rich when you get no advantage from it. He was said to be many times a millionaire, and he was, notwithstanding the humble and miserable appearance of his house—which had misled Captain Antifer—showing a prodigious parsimony in all that concerned the necessities of existence. Was it then that he had no wants? Very few, and he took care not to increase them, thanks to his hoarding instincts. To fill up bags upon bags of money, and put his hand upon everything that represented any value whatever, he had made the sole business of his life. Hence the many millions in his coffers, lying there without his thinking it worth while to render them productive.

It seemed unlikely, contradictory even, that such a man should have remained a bachelor. But if there must be old bachelors, is it not as well that they should be of this type? Zambuco had never thought of marrying, "and so much the better for his wife,' as the wits of the Maltese quarter used to say. Brothers, cousins, relatives of all sorts he had none, except one sister. The preceding generations of his family were united in him. He lived alone in his house, talking of his office, talking of his money-chests ; having in his service but an old Tunisian woman, who cost little in food or wages.

This was the rival Antifer had to deal with, and it may well be asked what kind of service this unsympathetic personage had rendered Kamylk Pasha to deserve such a token of gratitude. It can be explained in a few words.

When he was but twenty-seven years old, he was living in Alexandria. There he carried on with indefatigable sagacity and perseverance the varied occupations of a broker—securing his commissions from buyer and seller, acting for the would-be buyer before he sold to him, and dealing in money, the most profitable of all trades known to human intelligence.

It was in 1829, it will be remembered, that the idea occurred to Kamylk Pasha, who was then anxious for the safety of his fortune—coveted by his cousin Mourad, and by the imperious Mehemet Ali—to realize his riches and take them to Syria, where they would be safer than in any town of Egypt.

To carry out this operation several agents were necessary. Those he applied to were all foreigners worthy of his confidence. They risked much, and at least their liberty in supporting the rich Egyptian against the Viceroy. Young Zambuco was of the number. He did his work zealously, and was rewarded handsomely ; he made several voyages to Aleppo, and in fact contributed largely towards the realization of his client's fortune and its transport to a safe place.

This was not without difficulties or perils, and after the departure of Kamylk Pasha, some of the agents he had employed, among them this Zambuco, discovered by the suspicious police of Mehemet Ali, were imprisoned. For want of sufficient proof they were released, but they had none the less been punished for their devotion And as Thomas Antifer had rendered Kamylk a service in 1799, when he picked him up half dead on the rocks of Jaffa, so thirty years afterwards, Zambuco had also acquired a right to the Pasha's gratitude. Kamylk did not forget. And this brief survey explains why, in 1842, Thomas Antifer and Zambuco, one at St. Malo and the other at Tunis, had each received a letter informing them that they

would one day have a share in a treasure worth four
millions of pounds, deposited in an island, each of them
having the latitu le, while the longitude was to be sent
them in due time.

If this information had produced the effect we know on
Thomas Antifer, on his son after him, it may be imagined
that the effect was no less powerful on a personage like
Zambuco. Of course, he said not a word about the letter
to anyone. He shut up the figures of his latitude in one
of the most secret drawers of his strong-box, and ever
afterwards expected every minute to behold the appearance of the Antifer announced in Kamylk Pasha's letter.
In vain he endeavoured to learn the fate of the Egyptian.
He had heard nothing of the captain of the brigantine in
1834, nor of the taking to Cairo, nor of the imprisonment
in the fortiess for eighteen years, nor of the death in
1852.

It was now 1862. Twenty years had elapsed since 1842.
Antifer had not appeared, and the longitude had not been
added to the latitude. The position of the island remained
unknown. Zambuco, however, had not lost confidence.
That Kamylk Pasha's intention would be realized sooner
or later he did not doubt. In his opinion the said Antifer
was as safe to appear on the horizon of the Maltese
quarter, as a comet announced by the observatories
appears in the sky. His only regret—a regret very natural
with such a man—was that he had to share the legacy
with another. But he could not alter any of the disposi-
tions made by the grateful Egyptian. But to share four
millions appeared to him to be monstrous. That is why
for years he had been heaping reflections on reflections,
and imagining thousands of combinations, having for
their object the placing of the whole sum in his hands.
Would he succeed? All that we can say is that he was
well prepared to receive Antifer when he came with the
promised longitude.

It is needless to add that Zambuco, although he knew
little about navigation, had ascertained why it was that

|

the union of a latitude and a longitude would give the position of a point on the earth's surface ; and that he also fully understood that the two legatees must be united, and that if he could do nothing without Antifer, Antifer could do nothing without him.

CHAPTER XIX.

" CAN I see Zambuco the banker ? "
    " Yes, if it is on business."
    " It is on business."
    " What name ? "
    " Say a stranger, that will be enough."

It was Captain Antifer who asked, and the replies were from a peevish old native, seated at the bottom of a narrow office divided into two parts by a partition with a barred window.

Antifer had thought it better not to give his name, as he was anxious to see the effect produced on the banker, when he said to him point-blank,—

" I am Antifer, son of Thomas Antifer, of St. Malo."

A minute afterwards he was introduced to the interior of a room without any curtains, the walls whitewashed, the ceiling black with lamp-smoke, the only furniture a safe in one corner, a writing-table in another, and a table and two stools.

Before this table was seated the banker. The two legatees of Kamylk Pasha were face to face.

Without rising, Zambuco adjusted with his finger and thumb the large round spectacles resting on his nose, and only just lifting his head, said, with an accent that would have done credit to any native of Languedoc or Provençe,—

" To whom have I the honour of speaking ? "

" To Captain Antifer," replied that personage, expecting that these three words would provoke a shout from Zambuco, a leap from the chair, and the brief reply,—

" You—at last ! "

But the banker did not leap, nor did he shout. The expected reply did not come from his lips. But an attentive observer would have noticed a sudden gleam in his eyes which instantly were hid by the falling eyelids.

"I tell you that I am Captain Antifer."

"I heard you."

"Pierre Servan Malo Antifer, son of Thomas Antifer, of St. Malo, Ille-et-Vilaine, Brittany, France."

"You have a letter of credit on me?" asked the banker, without the slightest alteration in his voice.

"A letter of credit? Yes," replied Antifer, quite disconcerted at the coolness of his reception, "a letter of credit for the amount of four millions."

"All right. Hand it over," replied Zambuco, as indifferently as if it related to only a shilling or so.

Antifer simply collapsed. What! For twenty years this phlegmatic banker had known that he was to have a share of this enormous treasure the day a certain Antifer came to bring it him, so to speak, and he did not even flinch before this messenger of Kamylk Pasha. Not a sign of surprise, not a gleam of satisfaction. Was there a mistake in this document from island number one? Was it somebody else that was meant? Was this the man who had the latitude of island number two, or was it somebody else?

The disappointed co-legatee shuddered from head to foot. The blood rushed to his heart, and he had barely time to sink on to one of the stools.

The banker, without the slightest effort to help him, looked at him through his spectacles with just the slightest suspicion of a smile at the corners of his mouth. And it seemed as though these words would have escaped him, if he had not been careful to restrain them,—

"That sailor is not strong."

Meaning "not difficult to manage."

Antifer recovered himself. Wiping his face with his pocket-handkerchief, he rose.

"You are really Zambuco the banker?" he asked, slapping his big hand on the table.

"Yes ; the only one of the name in Tunis."

"And you were not expecting me?"

"No."

"My arrival has not been announced to you?"

"And how should it have been?"

"By the letter of a certain pasha."

"A pasha? But I receive hundreds of letters from pashas."

"Kamylk Pasha, of Cairo?"

"I don't remember him."

Zambuco's object was to get Antifer to give himself away completely, so that he would offer to sell the longitude without being told the latitude.

At the name of Kamylk, he looked as though the name was not quite unknown to him. He seemed to be trying to remember.

"Let me see," he said, adjusting his spectacles. "Kamylk Pasha, of Cairo?"

"Yes," replied Antifer, "A sort of Egyptian Rothschild, who possessed an enormous fortune in gold, diamonds, and precious stones."

"Ah, I remember."

"And who informed you that the half of his fortune would come to you."

"You are right, Mr. Antifer, and I ought to have the letter somewhere."

"What? Somewhere! Do you not know where it is?"

"Oh, nothing is lost here. I will find it."

And at this reply, the attitude of Captain Antifer, the gesture of his two hands stretched out like claws, indicated pretty clearly that he would twist the banker's neck if the letter could not be found.

"You see, Mr. Zambuco," he continued, endeavouring to control himself. "Your coolness is embarrassing. You speak of this matter with an indifference."

" Pheugh ! " said the banker.

" Why—why pheugh ? when it is about four millions of money."

Zambuco's lips gave a disdainful pout. He seemed to think of a million as he might of an orange-skin.

"Ah ! the brute ! He must be a hundred times a millionaire !" thought Captain Antifer.

But here the banker turned the conversation on another track, with the object of learning what he did not yet know, the chain of events which had led to this visit, and so, in a doubting sort of way, he wiped his spectacles with the corner of his handkerchief, and said,—

" Do you really believe in this story of the treasure ? "

" Do I believe in it ! I should think I did ! "

And then he related how in 1799 his father had saved the Pasha's life, how in 1842 a mysterious letter had arrived at St. Malo announcing the deposit of the treasure on an island that had to be searched for ; how he, Antifer, had received from his dying father the secret known to him alone ; how for twenty years he had waited for the messenger with the longitude ; how Ben Omar had brought him the will which enabled him to discover the island in the Gulf of Oman ; how he and his nephew Juhel and his friend Tregomain, with Ben Omar and his clerk, had found the island off Sohar ; and how instead of the treasure they had there found a box in which was a document giving the longitude of a second island which Antifer was to communicate to Zambuco the banker of Tunis, who possessed the latitude which would enable them to determine the position of this new island.

However indifferent he might seem, the banker had listened to this recital with extreme attention. A slight trembling of his long fingers indicated his excitement. When Antifer, who was breathing with great gulps, had finished, the banker simply remarked,—

"Yes, quite so, there seems to be no doubt as to the existence of this treasure. But what object had Kamylk Pasha in acting in this way ? "

And indeed the object was not very clear.

"You might imagine," said Antifer, "that—but first, Mr. Zambuco, did you have any dealings with the Pasha? Did you ever render him any service?"

"Certainly; a very great service."

"And when?"

"When he thought of realizing his fortune. He then lived at Cairo, where I then resided."

"Well then, it is clear. He wished to associate in the discovery of the treasure the two persons to whom he desired to show his gratitude—you, and me in the place of my father."

"And why no others?" suggested the banker.

"Ah! Do not say that!" exclaimed Antifer, bringing his fist down on to the table. "There are enough already; two are too many."

"Just so," replied Zambuco. "But one more explanation. Why does this Alexandrian notary accompany you on your search?"

"A clause in the will gives him a commission on condition that he assists in person at the handing over of the legacy when it is taken out of the ground."

"And what is this commission?"

"One per cent."

"One per cent! Ah! the rascal!"

"The rascal, that is exactly the word for him!" exclaimed Antifer. "And, believe me, I have let him know it."

On this point the co-legatees were quite agreed.

"Now," said Antifer, "that you know the whole story, there is no reason, I suppose, why we should not be frank with one another."

The banker remained impassible.

"I have got the new longitude found on island number one," continued Antifer; "and you ought to have the latitude of island number two."

"Yes," replied Zambuco, with a certain hesitation.

"Then why did you pretend, when I told you my name, that you knew nothing about this story?"

" Because I did not wish to give myself away to the
first who came. You might be an intruder, Mr. Antifer,
and I wished to be sure you were not. As you have the
document which instructs you to put yourself in communication with me—"

" I have it."

" Let me see it."

" One moment, Mr. Zambuco. Give and take. You
have Kamylk Pasha's letter ? "

" I have."

" Well—the letter for the document. Let the exchange
be made in order and reciprocally."

" Quite so ! " replied the banker. And rising, he
walked to the safe, and turned over the papers in the
drawers, with a deliberation that made Antifer furious.

Why these inexplicable proceedings ? Did Zambuco
wish to imitate Ben Omar at St. Malo and endeavour
to get Antifer's secret out of him ?

Not so, for that was impossible with a man so resolved
not to part with the goods without cash down. But the
banker had a plan, a plan long and carefully thought out,
which, in the event of success, would retain Kamylk's
millions in his family, a plan that required as an indispensable condition that his co-legatee was a widower or a
bachelor.

Clicking the lock of his safe he turned round for a
moment and asked in a voice that trembled a little,—

" Are you a married man ? "

" No, Mr. Zambuco, and that is a social condition on
which I congratulate myself morning and evening."

The last part of the reply provoked a frown from the
banker, who resumed the search among the papers.

Had Zambuco a family, then ? No, his only relative
was the sister we have mentioned. Talisma Zambuco
lived very quietly at Malta on an allowance from her
brother. She was then forty-seven years of age, and had
never had an opportunity of being married, first because
her beauty, intelligence and fortune left something to

be desired, and secondly, because her brother had not·found a husband for her in default of any suitor putting in an appearance on his own account.

But Zambuco had made up his mind that his sister should marry some day. And whom? Why, this very Antifer whom he had been expecting for twenty years, and who would do very well for a husband, provided that he was a widower or a bachelor. Once the marriage had taken place the millions would remain in the family, and Talisma Zambuco would lose nothing by having waited. She was entirely dependent upon her brother, and any husband offered by him would be received by her with closed eyes.

But would Antifer consent to close his and marry this ancient Maltese? The banker did not doubt that he would, for he thought he was in a position to impose any conditions he pleased on his co-legatee. Besides, sailors are not very difficult to manage—at least, he thought so.

Ah! unhappy Antifer, in what a galley you have embarked, and how much better would be a trip on the Rance, even on board the *Charmante Amélie*, if she still existed.

We now know the banker's game. Nothing could be simpler or better devised. He would only give up his latitude in exchange for Antifer's life—that is, his life in chains by indissoluble marriage with Talisma Zambuco.

Before taking Kamylk Pasha's letter out of the drawer, he seemed to think of something, and returned to sit down at the table.

Antifer's eyes flashed as if in a thunderstorm.

" What are you waiting for ? " he asked.

" I was thinking about something," replied the banker.

" About what, if you please ? "

" Are you of opinion that in this matter our rights are absolutely equal ? "

" Certainly they are ! "

" Well, I don't think so."

" And why ? "

" Because it was your father who rendered this service to the Pasha and not you, while it was I who—"

Antifer burst out,—

" What! Mr. Zambuco, are you trying to play the fool with an old sailor? Are not my father's rights mine, when I am his sole heir? Yes or no, will you obey the wishes of the testator ? "

" I will do as I choose ! " replied the banker, sharply and drily.

Antifer clutched the table to prevent himself jumping up.

" You know you can do nothing without me ? " said the Maltese.

" Nor you without me," said Antifer. The discussion became heated. One was scarlet with fury, the other paler than usual, but quite collected.

" Will you give me your latitude ? " asked Antifer furiously.

" Begin by giving me your longitude," replied the banker.

" Never."

" Very well."

" Here is my document," roared Antifer, taking out his pocket-book.

" Keep it. I don't want it."

" You do not want it ! Do you forget that it means four millions ? "

" Four millions, yes."

" And that they will be lost if we don't find out the island where they are buried ? "

" Pheugh ! " whistled the banker. And he made a disdainful grimace which drove Antifer so mad that he tucked up his sleeves preparatory to clutching at the banker's throat. But the banker, seeing he had gone too far for his personal comfort, suddenly toned down and remarked,—

" But I think we can arrange this."

Antifer dug his hands into his pockets so as to be less tempted to use them.

"Sir," continued the banker, "I am rich, I have very simple tastes, and neither two millions nor four would change my mode of life.   But I have a passion for accumulating money, and I admit that Kamylk Pasha's treasure would look well in my coffers.   Well, ever since I knew of the existence of this treasure, I have had no other thought than to obtain entire possession of it—"

"Indeed!"

"Wait a little."

"And my share?"

"Your share!   You can have it only in such a way that it will remain in my family."

"Then it would be no longer mine."

"You can take it or leave it."

"Explain yourself."

"I have a sister, Talisma."

"My compliments!"

"She lives in Malta."

"So much the better for her if the climate suits her."

"She is forty-seven years old and by no means bad-looking for her age."

"That I am not astonished at if she is like you."

"Well, as you are a bachelor, will you marry my sister?"

"Marry your sister?" yelled Antifer, his face a vivid scarlet with congestion.

"Yes, marry her," continued the banker, in a decided tone that admitted of no reply.   "By that union your two millions on one side, and my two millions on the other would remain in my family."

"Mr. Zambuco!" answered Antifer.

"Mr. Antifer."

"Is this proposal serious?"

"Nothing could be more serious, and if you decline to marry my sister, everything is at an end between us and you can return to France."

A dull rattling was heard.   Antifer was choking.   He tore off his cravat, he clutched his hat, he rushed across the courtyard, he ran down the street, gesticulating and behaving himself like a madman.

Saouk, who had been waiting all this time, followed him, very much disturbed at his proceedings.

Antifer reached the hotel and flung himself into the vestibule. Seeing his friend and his nephew in the little room adjoining the dining-room he rushed up to them and roared,—

"The wretch! Do you know what he wants?"

"To kill you?" asked Tregomain.

"Worse! To marry me to his sister!"

CHAPTER XX.

ACCUSTOMED as they were to complications, it may be safely affirmed that neither the bargeman nor Juhel expected this one. Captain Antifer, the hardened bachelor, to be thus left at the foot of the wall—and what wall? The wall of marriage, which he was obliged to cross unless he was prepared to lose his share in this enormous legacy.

Juhel begged his uncle to give them the details of what had occurred. And he told the story amid broadsides of explosive exclamations, which unfortunately could not reach Zambuco, under shelter of his house in the Maltese quarter.

Here was this old boy of forty-six to be married to a girl of forty-seven, and become a species of Oriental, a sort of Antifer Pasha !

Tregomain and Juhel were absolutely dumbfounded, and looked at each other in silence; but the same thought, doubtless, occurred to both.

"Away with the millions !" said the bargeman to himself.

"Away with the obstacle to my marriage with Enogate !" said Juhel to himself.

That Captain Antifer would agree to Zambuco's demands, that he would consent to become the banker's brother-in-law was quite inadmissible. He would never submit to this absurdity even for a million millions.

Nevertheless Antifer strode backwards and forwards from one end of the room to the other. Then he stopped, sat down, looked at his nephew and his friend in the face, and then turned his eyes away. It was painful to see him ; and if ever Tregomain thought he was going out of his mind it was then. He and Juhel tacitly resolved to do nothing to irritate him, whatever he might say.

At length he spoke, furiously and jerkily :

"Four millions—lost by this rascal's obstinacy—he deserves to be guillotined—hanged—shot—stabbed—poisoned—impaled, all at the same time. He refuses to give me his latitude if I don't marry—marry this monkey-faced Maltese. Would you see me the husband of this Talisma !"

Certainly not ! His friends would not see him—and the introduction of such a sister-in-law and aunt into the bosom of the honourable family of Antifer would be one of the most unlikely events any one could imagine.

"Tell me, bargeman ?"

"My friend."

"Has any one the right to leave four millions hidden in a hole when he has only to take one step to pick them out ?"

"I am not prepared to answer that question," replied Tregomain evasively.

"Ah! You are not prepared !" shouted Antifer, throwing his hat into a corner. "Well, are you prepared to answer this one ?"

"What ?"

"If an individual loads a boat—say a barge—a *Charmante Amélie* if you will—"

Tregomain felt that the *Charmante Amélie* was going to have a bad time of it.

"If he loads that old carcase with four millions in gold, and if he publicly announces that he is going to scuttle her in the open sea, so as to sink those millions, do you think the Government would let him do so? Come now ! Speak !"

"I do not think so."

"Yet that is what this master Zambuco has got into

O

his head. He has but to say one word to save his millions and mine, and he is obstinately silent."

"Never heard of a more abominable rascal!" said Tregomain, in a tone of anger.

"Look here—Juhel?"

"Uncle?"

"If we report him to the authorities—"

"We might do that as a last resource."

"Yes, for the authorities can do what a private individual cannot do. They might torture him—put him on the rack—roast his feet at the fire—and that would bring him to reason—"

"That is not a bad idea, uncle."

"Excellent, Juhel, and to pay this fellow out, I would give up my share, and hand it over to the public."

"That," said the bargeman, "would be fine, noble, generous! worthy of a Frenchman! worthy of a real Antifer—"

In making the proposal, Juhel's uncle had probably gone further than he intended, for he gave Tregomain such a terrible look that the bargeman stopped short in his outburst of admiration.

"Four millions! Four millions!" repeated Captain Antifer. "I will kill this Zambuco."

"Uncle!"

"My friend!"

And really in his state of exasperation, it was to be feared that Antifer would attempt some unfortunate violence—for which he would not be responsible owing to an attack of mental alienation.

But when Tregomain and Juhel tried to calm him, he repulsed them fiercely, accusing them of conspiring with his enemies, of helping Zambuco, of not wishing to "smash him, like a sneak of a steward."

"Leave me alone!" he growled, "leave me alone."

And picking up his hat, he jerked open the door, and rushed out of the room.

The others, thinking he was off to the banker's, ran after

him to prevent a disaster, but were much relieved to see him hurrying up the grand staircase, to his bedroom, where he locked himself in.

"That is the best thing he could do," said Tregomain, nodding his head.

" Yes, poor uncle !" replied Juhel.

After such a scene they had very little appetite for dinner.

When it was over, they left the hotel, to breathe a little fresh air on the banks of the Bahira. As they went out they met Ben Omar, accompanied by Nazim. Was there any objection to their telling the notary what had happened? Certainly not. And when he heard of the conditions the banker required, Ben Omar's remark was,—

" He ought to marry Miss Zambuco. He has no right to refuse. No! He has no right to !"

This was also the opinion of Saouk, who would not have hesitated to contract any marriage whatever, if the marriage would bring him such a dowry.

Tregomain and Juhel turned their backs on them, and went down the nearest street.

A fine evening, with a fresh sea-breeze, had brought the people of Tunis out to take the air.

Juhel and his companion walked towards the wall, went through the gate, and along the lake for a hundred yards or so, and sat down at a table at the Café Wina, where they discussed a flask of Manouba and talked matters over. Nothing could be simpler as far as they were concerned. Captain Antifer would never consent to Zambuco's terms. Consequently he would have to give up all thoughts of discovering island number two. Consequently they would leave Tunis by the next mail-steamer. Consequently, immense satisfaction at returning to France by the shortest road.

This was evidently the only possible solution. They would be none the worse for returning to St. Malo without Kamylk Pasha's big bag. Then what was the good of his Excellency's ingenuities !

About nine o'clock, Tregomain and Juhel returned to

the hotel. As they went to their rooms, they stopped for
a moment before Antifer's room. He was not asleep.
He had not even gone to bed. He was walking about
talking to himself, and could be heard gasping,—

"Millions—millions—millions."

Tregomain made a sign, to show that he must have gone
wrong in his head. And then wishing one another good-
night, they separated, very uneasy.

In the morning they were up early. It was only their
duty to go and see how Antifer was, to ask him what he
intended to do. Surely he could only intend to pack his
portmanteau and clear out from Tunis? Juhel had ascertained that the steamer which had put in at La Goulette
was going to start that evening for Marseilles. What
would Juhel have given to have had his uncle safe on
board shut up in his cabin, and twenty miles away from
the African coast!

He and Tregomain went along the passage to Antifer's
room.

They knocked at the door.

There was no reply.

Juhel knocked more loudly.

The same silence.

Was his uncle sleeping the sleep of a sailor whom not
even the reports of twenty-four pounders can waken? Or
rather had he in a moment of despair—?

Juhel ran downstairs to the porter's lodge four steps at
a time. Tregomain clung to the rail to save himself from
rolling to the bottom.

"Captain Antifer?"

"He went out early," replied the porter to Juhel's
question.

"And he did not say where he was going?"

"He did not."

"Has he gone to that scoundrel Zambuco?" asked
Juhel, dragging Tregomain out.

"But if he has—it is because he consents—" murmured
the bargeman, raising his hands to the sky.

" It is not possible ! " said Juhel.

" No, it is not possible !   Fancy him returning to St. Malo, to his house in the Rue des Hautes-Salles, with Talisma Zambuco on his arm !   Bringing little Enogate a Maltese aunt ! "

" A monkey, as my uncle called her ! "   And, as anxious as they could be, they sat down at a café facing the hotel, where they could watch for his return.

It is said that the night brings counsel, but it is not said that the counsel is   necessarily good.   It was only too true that Antifer had gone out very early in the morning, hurried to the Maltese quarter, and reached the banker's house as quickly as if he had a pack of hounds at his heels.

Zambuco was accustomed to rise with the sun, and go to bed when it set.   Consequently he was in his armchair, with the table in front of him and the safe behind him, when Antifer was introduced to his presence.

" Good-morning ! " he said, adjusting his spectacles, so as to get his visitor well in the middle of the glasses.

" Is that your last word ? " asked Antifer, by way of beginning the interview.

" My last."

" You refuse to give me Kamylk Pasha's letter unless I marry your sister ? "

" I refuse."

" Then I will marry her."

" I knew that !   A woman who brings you two millions as a dowry !   Why, a Rothschild's son would be only too happy to become the husband of Talisma."

" Well, I shall be only too happy," said Antifer, with a grimace he took no pains to hide.

" Come then, brother-in-law," said Zambuco.   And he rose as if he were going to fetch her.

" Is she here ? " asked Antifer.

His face was like that of a condemned man on the morning of his execution when the jailor says to him, " Now then, courage, please.   To-day is the day."

" Calm your impatience," replied the banker.   " Do you
forget that Talisma is at Malta ? "

" Where are we going then ? " asked Antifer, with a sigh
of relief.

" To the telegraph-office."

" So as to send her the news."

" Yes.   And to receive her reply."

" Send her the news if you like, but I may as well tell
you that I have no intention of awaiting my intended at
Tunis."

" And why not ? "

" Because you and I have no time to lose.   The first
thing for us to do is to go in search of the island, when we
know where it is."

" What does it matter whether we are a week early or
late ? "

" But it does matter, and you ought to be quite as eager
as I am to enter into possession of Kamylk Pasha's legacy."

Yes, quite as eager, for the banker—avaricious and
rapacious, although he tried to hide his impatience under
affected indifference—was burning with desire to get hold
of his share of the millions.

" Be it so," he said, " I agree with you.   I will not send
for my sister until our return.   But I must let her know
the happiness which awaits her."

" Yes, which awaits her ! " replied Antifer, without thinking of the kind of happiness that was reserved for her who
had waited so many years for the husband of her dreams.

" Only," continued Zambuco, " we must have a regular
engagement."

" Write it out, and I will sign it."

" With a forfeit for non-completion ? "

" Agreed.   How much the forfeit ? "

" Let us say the two millions which will be your share."

" All right, be quick with it ! " replied Antifer, resigned
to becoming Talisma's husband, as he could not escape that
happiness.

The banker took a sheet of white paper, and in his large

handwriting drew out a contract to marry in all due form.
It was stipulated that the share received by Captain Antifer
as legatee of Kamylk Pasha should be handed over in its
entirety to Talisma Zambuco in the event of his refusing
to marry her within a fortnight of the discovery of the
treasure.

And with a furious flourish Antifer signed this contract,
which the banker placed in one of the drawers of his safe.

At the same time he took out a faded yellow paper—
the letter he had received from Kamylk twenty years
before.

Antifer had taken out of his pocket-book another
paper quite as faded and yellow.   This was the document
found on island number one.

What a scene for a painter !   The two legatees looking
at each other, like duellists about to cross swords, their
arms stretched out just a little, their fingers trembling
at the contact of these papers they turned to hand over
with regret.

"Your letter ? " said Antifer.

"Your document ? " said Zambuco.

The exchange was made.   It was time.   The two men's
hearts were beating so violently that they had nearly
broken.

The document indicating that it was to be taken by a
certain Antifer of St. Malo to a certain Zambuco of Tunis
bore the longitude of 7° 23' east.

The letter announcing that the said Zambuco, of Tunis,
would one day receive a visit from the said Antifer, of St.
Malo, bore the latitude of 3° 17' south.

All that was wanted was to cross these two lines on a
map to discover the position of island number two.

"You have, doubtless, an atlas ? " asked the banker.

"An atlas and a nephew," replied Antifer.

"A nephew ? "

"Yes, a sea-captain, who will take charge of this matter
for us."

"Where is this nephew ? "

"At the Hôtel de France."

"Come along then, brother-in-law," said Zambuco, putting on a broad-brimmed hat.

"Come along," said Antifer.

Off they went to the hotel. As they passed the post-office, Zambuco said he would go in and send a telegram to Malta.

Antifer made no objection. The least he could do was to let the lady know that her hand had been solicited by an "officer of the French marine," and with her brother's consent, under most acceptable conditions as to fortune and family.

The telegram having been paid for, the two legatees came out into the street, when Tregomain and Juhel caught sight of them, and hurried to meet them.

When he noticed them, Antifer's first movement was to turn away his head. But mastering this inopportune weakness, he introduced his companion in an imperious voice :

"The banker, Zambuco."

The banker gave his future brother-in-law's companions anything but an agreeable look.

Then Antifer added,—

"Juhel, my nephew ; Tregomain, my friend."

Then, at a sign, they all moved towards the hotel, avoiding as they passed Ben Omar and Nazim, whom they did not seem to know, mounted the stairs, and entered Antifer's room, and locked the door.

Antifer took out of his bag the atlas he had brought from St. Malo. He opened it at the map of the world, and handing it to Juhel, said,—

"Seven degrees twenty-three minutes east, and three degrees seventeen minutes south."

Juhel could not help a gesture of annoyance. Latitude south ! Kamylk Pasha was going to send them across the line ? Ah ! his poor little Enogate ! Tregomain hardly dared to look at him.

"Well, what are you waiting for ?" asked his uncle, in a tone which the young captain could only obey.

He took the compasses, and following the seventh meridian, with the twenty-three minutes added on, he ran down to the Equator.

Running along the parallel of 3° 17′, he stopped where it intersected the meridian.

" Well," said Antifer, " whereabouts are we ? "

" In the Gulf of Guinea."

" And more exactly ? "

" In Ma-Yumba bay."

" To-morrow morning," said Antifer, " we will take the diligence for Bône, and at Bône we will take the train to Oran."

This was said in the tone of a man-o'-war captain, ordering to beat to quarters, when the enemy is in sight.

Turning to the banker, he said,—

" You will accompany us, of course ? "

" Of course."

" To the Gulf of Guinea ? "

" To the end of the world, if necessary."

" Well, be ready to start."

" I shall be ready, brother-in-law."

Tregomain uttered an involuntary " Ah ! " At this qualification, so new to his ears, he was so astounded that he was unable to reply to the ironical salute with which the banker honoured him as he retired.

When the three were alone,—

" And so, you have consented ? " said Tregomain.

" Yes, bargeman. What then ? "

What then ? No one could say anything, and that was why Tregomain and Juhel thought it best to keep silent.

Two hours later the banker received a telegram from Malta.

Talisma Zambuco informed him that she was the happiest of sisters, and expected to be the happiest of wives !

CHAPTER XXI.

ANTIFER and his companions left Tunis at break of day. The banker was with them, and so was Ben Omar and his clerk—a veritable caravan of six persons, knowing now where this irresistible appetite for millions was taking them. There was no need now to make any mystery of the matter with Ben Omar, and consequently Saouk was not unaware that island number two was in the Gulf of Guinea.

"A long way this time," said Juhel to Ben Omar, "and if you are afraid of the fatigues of the voyage, you are quite at liberty to give it up."

And really it is a good many hundreds of miles by sea from Algiers to Loango.

Ben Omar, however, had no hesitation about going, for Saouk would have permitted none. And besides, there was the magnificent commission glittering before his eyes.

Thus on this 24th of April, Antifer dragging with him Tregomain and Juhel, and Saouk dragging with him Ben Omar, and Zambuco dragging himself, occupied their places in the coach or diligence which runs between Tunis and Bône. Perhaps they might not exchange a word, but at least they would travel together.

Let it not be forgotten that the evening before Juhel had written another letter to Enogate. In a few days the girl and her mother would know for what part of the globe Antifer was bound in search of his famous legacy, now reduced by fifty per cent. It was not too much to reckon

that this second voyage would last a month, and that
Enogate would see her lover again in the middle of May.
How Enogate would despair when she received this letter !
If she could only have hoped that at Juhel's return all the
difficulties would be smoothed over, and her wedding take
place without delay ! But what could she expect with
such an uncle !

Tregomain, then, was destined to cross the line. He,
the bargeman of the Rance, was to sail in the southern
hemisphere ! What would you have ? Life is made up
of such unlikely things that the excellent man would be
astonished at nothing, not even at being at the indicated
spot and digging out of island number two the three
famous barrels of Kamylk Pasha !

These considerations did not, however, hinder him from
casting a look of curiosity over the country through which
the diligence was passing, which only slightly resembled
the plains of Brittany, even those that are hilly. But probably he was the only traveller of the six who thought of re-
taining some remembrance of the appearance of the country.

The vehicle was not comfortable, and did not travel fast.
From one stage to another the three horses trotted along
up hill and down hill, with many a sudden turn, amid the
Alpine scenery—especially in this wonderful Medjerdah
valley—dashing over torrents, which had no bridges, with
the water often up to the axle-trees.

The weather was beautiful, the sky of a deep blue, or
rather a ripe blue, as if browned slightly by the intense
heat of the sun.

The Bardo, the Bey's palace, which they saw on the left
shore—so brilliantly white, that it would have been prudent
to look at only through smoked glasses. So it was with
the other palaces embowered in thick fig-trees and pear-
trees, like weeping willows, with their branches drooping to
the ground. Here and there were groups of tents of
striped cloth, under which appeared the heads of Arab
women of serious countenance, and the brown faces of
children no less grave than their mothers. Afar in the

fields, on the slopes, amid the rocky steeps, were herds of sheep, and goats as black as crows.

Now and then birds would fly around the diligence, and then the whip would crack in the air. Among these birds parrots were numerous, and distinguishable by their vivid colours. They were in thousands, and if nature had taught them to sing, man had not yet taught them to talk. And so the diligence travelled.

The horses were changed frequently. Tregomain and Juhel never omitted to get out and stretch their legs. Zambuco alighted occasionally, but never spoke to his companions.

"There is a man," said the bargeman, "who seems as greedy of the Pasha's millions as our friend Antifer."

"Quite so, Tregomain, and the two legatees are worthy of each other."

Whenever he alighted Saouk tried to overhear what was being said. Ben Omar remained quietly in his corner, engrossed in the thought that he would soon have to go to sea again, and that after the choppy waves of the Mediterranean he would have to brave the long rollers of the Atlantic.

Antifer also never moved; he sat with his thoughts concentrated on this island number two—this rock lost amid the burning African waters!

Before sunset there appeared a group of mosques, marabouts, white domes, slender minarets; this was Tabourka, encircled by a frame of verdure, and which retains intact its aspect as a Tunisian town.

The diligence stopped here for some hours. The travellers alighted at a hotel, or rather an inn, where they were served with a not particularly appetizing repast. As to visiting the town it was not to be thought of. Of the six, there was only the bargeman—and perhaps Juhel, if he asked him—who would have had such an idea. Besides, Captain Antifer ordered them, once for all, not to go far away, for fear of occasioning delay—and they took care to do as they were told.

At nine o'clock the journey was resumed ; the night fine and starlight. But it is not without danger that vehicles venture across these deserted districts between sunset and sunrise—for there are dangers from the bad state of the roads, dangers from robbers, Kroumirs and others, dangers from attack by wild beasts. Occasionally, from amid the tranquil gloom along the edge of the thick woods skirted by the diligence could be heard the roaring of lions and the growling of leopards. At this the horses shied, and it took all the driver's skill to master them. The cries of the hyænas were heard unheeded.

The zenith grew paler towards four o'clock in the morning, and the diffused light grew strong enough for the details of the landscape to be gradually visible. But the horizon was not extensive, only the grey hills in long undulations thrown on the ground like an Arab cloak. The valley of the Medjerdah lay curving at their feet, with its yellow river, sometimes a smooth stream, sometimes a troubled torrent, flowing among the oleanders and flower-ing eucalyptus.

The country is varied and mountainous in this part of the Regency bordering on Kroumiria. If the bargeman had travelled in the Tyrol, he might have thought him-self among the wilder portions of the Alps, if it had not been for the lesser height of the hills. But he was not in the Tyrol nor in Europe, from which he was daily going farther. And then the corners of his mouth would rise— which rendered his physiognomy more pensive—and his thick eyebrows would fall, which made him look more uneasy.

Now and then he and Juhel would look at each other, and these looks were quite a silent conversation.

In the morning Antifer asked his nephew,—

" Where shall we get to before night ? "

" Gardimaou."

" And when shall we be at Bône ? "

" To-morrow evening."

The gloomy Antifer resumed his habitual silence, or

rather his thoughts were lost in that uninterrupted **dream** which led him from the Gulf of Oman to the Gulf of Guinea; and rested on the only point of the terrestrial spheroid which could interest him. And then he thought to himself that other eyes besides his own were fixed on this point, those of the banker Zambuco. In truth, these two beings, of races so different, of habits so opposite, who ought never to have met in this world, seemed to have become of one mind, as if they had been linked together like galley-slaves with the same chain; only the chain was of gold.

The forests of fig-trees became thicker and thicker. Now and then Arab villages emerged from the glaucous greenery with which the castor-oil trees tint their flowers and leaves. Sometimes there appeared a "dreche" or two on the sloping sides of the mountains. Here tents arose, and sheep fed on the banks of a torrent. Then the station for changing horses would appear—generally some miserable stable where men and beasts lived together promiscuously.

In the evening they reached Gardimaou, or rather the wooden cabin surrounded by a few others which twenty years afterwards was to form one of the stations on the railway from Bône to Tunis. After a halt of two hours—too long for the rudimentary dinner furnished by the inn—the diligence resumed its journey along the windings of the valley, sometimes skirting the Medjerdah, sometimes crossing the brooks, of which the waters often rose over the travellers' feet as they sat in the coach, toiling up hills so steep that the horses could hardly draw the load, dashing down slopes with a rapidity that the brake could hardly check.

The country was magnificent, particularly in the environs of Moughtars. But no one could see anything in the very dark, misty night. And everyone was being overcome by the longing for sleep, after forty-three hours of such jolting.

The dawn had appeared when Antifer and his companions arrived at Soukharas, at the end of a tiresome winding on the flank of the hill, which united the town to the road along the valley.

A comfortable hotel welcomed the weary travellers. This time the three hours they rested did not appear too long, and certainly would have appeared too short if they had wanted to visit the picturesque town. Antifer and Zambuco, of course, protested against the time lost at this halting-place ; but the coach was not due to start until six o'clock in the morning.

" Calm yourself," said Tregomain to his irritable companion. " We shall be at Bône in time to catch the train to-morrow morning—"

" And why not, with a little more haste, catch it to-night ? " retorted Antifer.

" There is not one," said Juhel.

" Suppose there is not, is that any reason for us remaining in this hole ? "

" Here, my friend," said the bargeman, " here is a pebble I picked up for you. Yours ought to be nearly worn out by this time."

And Tregomain handed him a charming specimen of Medjerdah gravel, the size of a green-pea, which was soon being ground between the Malouin's teeth.

The bargeman then asked him to accompany them only to the principal square. He refused point-blank ; and drawing the atlas out of his bag, he opened it at the map of Africa, and plunged into the waters of the Gulf of Guinea at the risk of drowning his reason.

Tregomain and Juhel went for a stroll on the Place Thagaste, a vast quadrilateral planted with a few trees, bordered with houses of very Oriental aspect, with cafés, already open at that early hour, and which were crowded with natives. At the first rays of the sun the mists dispersed, and a fine day, warm and bright, announced itself.

As he walked, the bargeman was all eyes and ears. He tried to hear all that was going on, although he understood nothing ; he strove to see what was happening in the interior of the cafés, and in the shops, although he bought nothing and drank nothing. As wayward fortune had sent him on this unlooked-for voyage, the least he could do was to bring away a few lasting impressions.

And thus he spoke:

"No, Juhel, we cannot keep on travelling as we are doing. We stop nowhere. Three hours at Soukharas; one night at Bône; two days on the railway, with short stoppages at the stations! What have I seen of Tunis; what shall I see of Algeria?"

"I admit it It is only common sense. But say that to my uncle, and see what he will say to you. This is not a pleasure journey, but a business one; and who knows how it will end?"

"In a hoax, I think."

"Yes," continued Juhel, "why should not island number two contain a document referring us to island number three?"

"And so on to island four, and island five, and all the islands in the sea!" said Tregomain, nodding his big head.

"And you will follow my uncle—"

"I?"

"Yes, you; you cannot refuse him anything."

"That is true. The poor man troubles me much, and I am afraid his head—"

"Well, Tregomain, as far as I am concerned, I draw the line at island number two. Does Enogate want to marry a prince; do I want to marry a princess?"

"Certainly not! Besides, now we have to share the treasure with this crocodile of a Zambuco, it is only a question of a duke for her, and a duchess for you—"

"Do not laugh, Tregomain!"

"I was wrong, my boy; it is no laughing matter. And if we have to prolong this search—"

"Prolong?" asked Juhel. "No! We go to the Gulf of Loango—but beyond—never! I shall know how to make my uncle return to St. Malo!"

"And if he refuses?"

"If he refuse. I will leave him there and then. I will

return to Enogate, and, as she will be of age in a few months, I shall marry her in spite of wind and tide."

"Do not be obstinate, my dear boy, and have patience. All will come right, I hope. It will end with your marrying my little Enogate, and I will dance at your wedding. But do not let us miss the diligence. Let us return to the hotel. If it is not asking too much I would rather reach Bône before night, so as to see a little of the town. As to Constantine, Philippeville and all those other queer places, what shall we see of them? If it is not possible, I shall have to be contented with Algiers, where we shall stay a few days, I suppose."

"He is not likely to find a vessel ready to start immediately for the West Coast of Africa, and he will have to wait for one."

"We will wait!" replied the bargeman, smiling at the thought of visiting the marvels of the Algerian capital. "You know Algiers, Juhel?"

"Yes, Tregomain."

"I have heard sailors say that it is very fine—the town in a semicircle, its wharves, squares, arsenal, garden, its Moustapha, its Casbah—its Casbah particularly."

"Very fine, Tregomain," interrupted Juhel; "but I know something finer. There is St. Malo—"

"And the house in the Rue des Hautes Salles—and the little room on the first floor—and the little girl who lives therein! eh? I am of your opinion, my boy! But as we have to pass by Algiers let me hope that I may visit Algiers."

And abandoning himself to this hope, the bargeman, followed by his young friend, turned towards the hotel. It was time. The horses were being put to. Captain Antifer was striding to and fro growling at all late comers, although they were not late.

Tregomain bowed his head beneath the stormy look his friend launched at him. In a few minutes they were all seated, and the diligence was descending the rugged slopes of Soukharas.

P

It was really a pity that the bargeman was not allowed to explore this Tunisian territory. Nothing could be more picturesque—hills which are almost mountains, wooded ravines, which forced the future railway to take many a roundabout route across the opulent verdure, large rocks rising from the ground, here and there douars swarming with natives and with big fires round them at night, as a defence against wild beasts.

Tregomain would relate what the driver had told him, for he talked with him whenever he had an opportunity.

In a year forty lions at least are killed among the brushwood, and the leopards killed amount to several hundreds, to say nothing of the crowds of howling jackals. Antifer cared nothing for Tunisian leopards and lions. If there had been millions of them on island number two he would not retreat an inch from his purpose. But the banker on one side, and the notary on the other, listened to Tregomain's tales with interest. Zambuco would often take a sly glance out of the window, and Ben Omar would lean back in his corner, and start and turn pale whenever a growl was heard from the thickets along the road.

" I have heard," said Tregomain, " that the diligence has been attacked before now, and firearms had to be used to drive the beasts off. Last night even, the coach had to be burnt to drive off a lot of leopards by the glare of the flames."

" And the travellers? " asked Ben Omar.

" The travellers had to journey on foot to one of the places where they change horses."

" On foot ! " exclaimed the notary, in a trembling voice ; " I could never—"

" Well, you could have remained behind, Mr. Omar ; we should not have waited for you, you may be sure."

It can be guessed that this observation came from Captain Antifer. He did not again join in the conversation, and Ben Omar had to recognize that he was not born to be a traveller either on land or sea.

The day went by without the wild beasts manifesting

their presence except by distant growls. But, to his great disgust, Tregomain had to make up his mind that it would be night before the diligence reached Bône.

It was seven o'clock in the evening when they passed Hippo, a locality that is famous as being linked with the imperishable name of St. Augustine, and curious on account of its deep reservoir, where the old Arabs indulge in their incantations and sorceries. Twenty years later they would have seen the founding of the basilica and the hospital—which have risen from the ground under the powerful hand of Cardinal de Lavigerie.

As they entered Bône a deep darkness enveloped its promenade along the shore, its harbour terminating in the sandy point to the westward, the clumps of trees which shade the quay, the modern city with its large square, its Casbah, which might have given the bargeman a foretaste of the Casbah of Algiers.

The travellers chose a hotel in the chief square, had their supper, and went to bed at ten o'clock, ready for the journey next morning. And that night (thoroughly tired out by sixty hours in the diligence) they all slept—even the terrible Antifer.

CHAPTER XXII.

CAPTAIN ANTIFER thought he would find a railway between Bône and Algiers, but he had arrived twenty years too soon. The reply he received early next morning when he asked the hotel-keeper, proved a puzzler to him.

"What!" he said with a start, "is there no railway from Bône to Algiers?"

"No, sir," said the facetious hotel-keeper, "but there will be one in a few years' time if you like to wait."

Doubtless Ben Omar would have asked nothing better, for it would probably become necessary to go by sea to avoid delay.

But Antifer had no intention of waiting.

"Is there no boat announced to sail?" he asked in an imperious voice.

"Yes; this morning."

"Let us go on board."

And at six o'clock Antifer left Bone on a steamer with the two companions of his choice and the three necessity had imposed on him.

We need not dwell on the incidents of this short voyage of a few hundred miles.

Tregomain would have preferred to have performed this navigation in a carriage, so as to have been able to see these territories which the remarkable railway was to traverse a few years later. But he reckoned on making up for his disappointment at Algiers. If Antifer imagined that as soon as he arrived he would find a vessel starting for the West Coast of Africa, he would be deceived, and

would have to exercise a little patience. Meanwhile what
delightful walks Tregomain would have in the environs,
perhaps even to Blidah or the Monkey Brook! That the
bargeman would gain nothing by the discovery of the
treasure might be true, but at least he would gather a rich
collection of memories of the journey to the Algerian
capital.

It was eight o'clock in the evening when the steamer
which made a quick passage, dropped anchor in the harbour
of Algiers. The night in these latitudes was then dark, even
in the last week of March, although the sky was glittering
with stars. The confused mass of the town rose gloomily
towards the north, rounded by the Casbah—this Casbah
so greatly desired. All that Tregomain could see in leaving
the landing-place was that he had to climb a lot of steps
abutting on a quay supported by monumental arcades, and
that he had to go along this quay, leaving to the left a
square brilliant with lights, in which he would not have been
displeased to stop, then a block of high houses comprising
the Hôtel de l'Europe, in which Captain Antifer and his
party were hospitably received.

They were shown to their rooms—Tregomain's adjoining Juhel's—they had their luggage brought up, and they
went down to dine. That occupied them until nine o'clock,
and as there was plenty of time to wait for the departure
of the steamer, the best thing for them to do was to go to
bed and rest, so as to be in a fit condition next morning
to begin a series of walks through the town.

But before taking the rest justified by this long journey
Juhel wrote to Enogate. He did this as soon as he regained his room. The letter would go in the morning,
and in three days it would reach her. There was nothing
very interesting in the letter, except that Juhel was almost
mad at the delay, and that he loved her with all his heart
—in which there was nothing new.

But while Ben Omar and Saouk went to their room
and Tregomain and Juhel went to theirs, Antifer and
Zambuco, the two brothers-in-law—as it is surely per-

missible to describe them after the signing and sealing of
their contract—disappeared from the hotel after dinner,
without assigning any reason. This rather surprised the
bargeman and the young captain, and perhaps made Saouk
and Ben Omar uneasy; but it was not likely that Antifer
would have answered any questions on this subject.

Where did the legatees go? To stroll along the picturesque quarters of Algiers? Probably not.

It was noticed that during the latter part of the journey
Antifer had occasionally conversed in a low tone with the
banker, and that Zambuco had appeared to approve of his
companion's suggestions. What had they been talking
about? Was this going out late part of a pre-arranged
plan? What plan? What strange combinations were
possible with two men of this kind!

After shaking hands with Juhel the bargeman went
into his room. Before undressing, he opened the window
wide to breathe a little of this delightful Algerian air. In
the pale starlight he looked over the wide expanse, all
the roadstead up to Cape Matifou, over which glittered the
lights of the vessels, many of them at anchor, many of them
coming in with the night breeze, while the coast was
aglow with the torches used by the fishermen. Closer in
were the steamers getting under weigh, their large funnels
belching forth showers of sparks. Beyond Cape Matifou
was the open sea, bounded by a horizon on which the
splendid constellations were rising like displays of fire-
works.

The next day would be magnificent, if it fulfilled the
promises of the night. The sun would rise radiantly and
outshine the last stars of the morning.

"How pleasant," thought Tregomain, "will it be to
visit this noble town of Algiers, to have a few days' rest
after this diabolical rush from Muscat, and before being
hoaxed again at island number two! I have heard of
Moise's restaurant at Pointe Pescade? Why should we
not go to-morrow and have a good dinner at this
Moise's?"

At this moment came a loud knock at the door, just as ten o'clock was about to strike.

" Is that you, Juhel ? " asked Tregomain.

" No, it is Antifer."

" I will open the door, my friend."

" Useless. Dress and pack up."

" My portmanteau ? "

" We start in forty minutes."

" In forty minutes ? "

" And mind you are not late, for the steamers don't wait as a rule. I am going to tell Juhel."

Overwhelmed with surprise, the bargeman thought he must be dreaming. No! He heard the knock on Juhel's door, and Antifer's voice telling him to get up. Then he heard the departing footsteps descending the stairs.

Juhel, who was writing, added a line to his letter, telling Enogate that they were all going to leave Algiers that very evening. That, then, was why Zambuco and Antifer had gone out : it was to inquire if any ship was sailing for the coast of Africa. By unhoped-for good fortune they had found the said steamer preparing to start, they had secured the berths, and then, without troubling himself about ceremony, Antifer had returned to tell Tregomain and Juhel, while the banker warned Ben Omar and Nazim.

The bargeman was inexpressibly disappointed as he packed up. But nothing was to be said. The chief had spoken ; he must obey. Almost immediately Juhel came into the room.

" You are not going to stop ? " he said.

" No, my boy, although I ought to do so for your uncle's sake ! And I who promised myself at least two days in Algiers. And the harbour. And the gardens. And the Casbah ! "

" But what could you expect, Tregomain ? It is most unfortunate that my uncle has found a ship ready for sea."

" Yes, but I shall strike before it is over ! " said the bargeman with a gesture of anger.

" No, Tregomain, you will never strike. If you were to attempt such a thing, my uncle would only have to look at you in a certain way and you would have to give in."

" You are right, Juhel," replied Tregomain, lowering his head ; " I would obey. You know me well. It is a nuisance all the same, and this fine dinner I was thinking of giving you at Moise's at Pointe Pescade ! "

Vain regrets ! The poor man heaved a sigh and completed his preparations. Ten minutes afterwards Juhel and he had found Antifer, Zambuco, and the others in the vestibule of the hotel.

If they had been welcomed on their arrival they were not allowed to depart so cheerfully. They had to pay for their rooms as if they had occupied them for a day. Juhel put his letter in the box, and then they all descended the stairs leading to the harbour, while Tregomain took a last look at Government Square.

Half a cable's length away a steamer was moored with her steam up. Black smoke rose from her funnel to the sky. Her whistle was already announcing that she would soon be off.

A boat at the quay steps was waiting to bring the passengers on board. Antifer and his companions took their places in her. In a few strokes of the oars they were alongside. Before even Tregomain could make out where he was, he was conducted to the cabin he was to share with Juhel ; Antifer and Zambuco occupied a second ; the notary and Saouk a third.

The steamer was the *Catalan,* belonging to a Marseilles company. Employed in the regular service of the West Coast of Africa to St. Louis and Dakar, she called in at intermediate ports when necessary to receive or discharge passengers or goods.

A quarter of an hour after Antifer had arrived, a final scream of the whistle rent the air. Then her hawsers were slackened off and the *Catalan* began to tremble, her screw spun round violently, beating up a streak of foam on the surface of the sea, and she glided round the vessels at anchor, took the channel between the arsenal and the jetty, and headed to the westward.

A vague mass of white houses greeted the bargeman's eyes: this was the Casbah, of which he could only make out the general outline. A cape jutted out from the coast; this was Pointe Pescade, the point on which was the restaurant of Moise who made those succulent *bouillabaisses*. And that was all Tregomain brought away with him to remind him of his stay in Algiers.

We need hardly mention that as soon as the harbour was left, Ben Omar, extended on the couch in his cabin, began again to taste the delights of sea-sickness. And when he thought of his voyage to the Gulf of Guinea he also thought of his return. Fortunately that would be his last passage. On this island number two he was certain of getting his promised commission! But if some of the others had also been ill, it would have been more soothing to him. And not one of them felt the slightest nausea. He was the only one to suffer. He did not even have the very natural consolation of seeing one of his kind share his sufferings.

The passengers on the *Catalan* were mostly sailors returning to the ports on the coast, a few Senegalese, and a certain number of soldiers of the marine infantry, accustomed to the eventualities of navigation. They were all bound for Dakar, where the steamer was to land her cargo. She was not going to stop anywhere on the road, and Antifer could but congratulate himself on having precipitated himself on board. It is true that when he got to Dakar he would not be at the end of his journey: and to this Zambuco called his attention.

"Agreed," he said; "but I never expected to find a steamer going from Algiers to Loango, and when we are at Dakar we will see about matters."

In fact it would have been difficult to have done otherwise. The difficulty would be with the last part of the voyage, and therein was a subject for serious anxiety on the part of the expectant brothers-in-law.

During the night the *Catalan* kept along at some two or three miles from the coast. The lights of Tenez were observed, and the sombre mass of Cape Blanc could just be distinguished. In the morning the heights of Oran were sighted, and an hour afterwards the steamer doubled the promontory, on the other side of which is the roadstead of Mers-el-Kebir.

Further on, the coast of Morocco developed on the port side, with its distant profile of mountains dominating the Riff country, where game is so plentiful. On the horizon appeared Tetuan, quite striking under the solar rays; then at a few miles to the west, Ceuta planted on its rock, between two creeks, like a fort commanding one of the swing-doors of the Mediterranean, the key of the other swing-door being kept by Great Britain. And beyond in the offing through the Straits appeared the immense Atlantic. The wooded slopes of the coast of Morocco could be plainly made out Tangiers was passed hidden in the curve of its gulf, its villas amid the green trees, many marabouts here and there gleaming white in the sun. The sea was dotted with numerous sailing vessels waiting for a wind to take them through the Straits of Gibraltar.

The *Catalan* had no delays to fear. Neither the breeze nor the current, recognizable by a peculiar rippling in the vicinity of the Straits, could contend against her powerful screw, and towards nine o'clock in the evening she was beating with its triple blade the wide Atlantic.

The bargeman and Juhel were talking on the poop before retiring for a few hours' rest. Naturally the same thought occurred to them as the *Catalan*, steering southwest, doubled the extreme point of Africa—a thought of regret.

"Yes, my boy," said Tregomain, "it would have been preferable if, on coming out of the Straits, we had gone to starboard instead of port. At least we should not have turned our heels on France."

"And to go, whither?"

"To the devil, I am afraid! But you must endure evil

with patience, Juhel. You can return from everywhere, even from the devil. In a few days we shall be at Dakar, and from Dakar to the Gulf of Guinea—"

" Who knows if we shall find any means of transport from Dakar? There is no regular service beyond. We may be kept there for weeks, and if my uncle imagines—"

" He does imagine, never doubt it."

" That it will be easy for him to reach island number two, he is mistaken. Do you know what I think, Tregomain ? "

" No, my boy ; but if you like to tell me—"

" Well, I think that my grandfather, Thomas Antifer, ought to have left this confounded Kamylk on the rocks of Jaffa—"

" But, Juhel, the poor man—"

" If he had left him there, this Egyptian could not have left his millions to his rescuer, and if he had not left his millions, my uncle could not have run after them, and Enogate would be my wife."

" That is all very true. But if you had been there, Juhel, you would have saved the life of this unfortunate Pasha as your grandfather did ! What is that ? " he added, to turn the conversation. " What is that light? " showing a bright light on the port bow.

" That is the lighthouse at Cape Spartel," replied Juhel.

In fact it was the lighthouse placed at the western extremity of the African continent and maintained at the expense of the States of Europe, the most advanced of those that project their rays over the surface of the African seas.

The voyage of the *Catalan* need not be related in detail. The steamer was favoured. She picked up the land breeze in these parts and could keep at a short distance from the coast. The sea was agitated merely by the long, rolling swell coming in from the westward ; and it required the most susceptible of Omars to be ill in such weather.

The shore remained in view : the heights of Mekinez, of Mogador ; Mount Thesat, which dominates this region from a height of about 3000 feet ; Tarudant and Cape Juby, where the frontier of Morocco ends.

Tregomain did not have the satisfaction of seeing the Canary Isles, as the *Catalan* passed some fifty miles to the eastward of Fuerteventura, the nearest of the group ; but he was able to salute Cape Bojador before crossing the Tropic of Cancer. Cape Blanco was passed in the afternoon of the 2nd of May ; next morning they were off Portendik, and then the country of the Senegal lay spread before the travellers' eyes.

As all the passengers were bound to Dakar, the *Catalan* had no occasion to put in at St. Louis, which is the capital of this French colony. Dakar seems to be of more maritime importance than St. Louis, and Antifer would probably find it easier there to obtain some means of transport to the Loango.

At length, on the 5th, about four in the morning, the *Catalan* doubled the famous Cape Verde, situated in the same latitude as the islands of this name. She rounded the triangular peninsula which hangs like a flag on the edge of the African continent, and the port of Dakar appeared on the lower angle of the peninsula, after a voyage of eight hundred leagues from Algiers.

CHAPTER XXIII.

NEVER had Tregomain imagined that a day would come when he would be walking with Juhel on the quays of Dakar, the ancient capital of the Gorean Republic. And yet that is what he did on this particular day, visiting the port, protected by its double jetty of granite rocks, while Antifer and Zambuco, as inseparable as Ben Omar and Saouk, went up to the French agency.

A day is amply sufficient for seeing the town. There is nothing very interesting about it—a rather good public garden, a citadel affording quarters for the garrison, and Bel-Air Point, on which is an establishment to which are sent those suffering from yellow fever. If our travellers were to remain many days in this country, which has Goree for its capital and Dakar for its chief town, the lapse of time would appear interminable.

But it is as well to keep a good heart against ill-fortune, as Tregomain and Juhel said to one another ; and meanwhile they strolled along the wharves, and up and down the sunny streets, which are kept in good order by convicts, under the supervision of a few warders.

The only things that interested them were the ships— these bits of herself which France sent from Bordeaux to Rio de Janeiro—these steamers of the Messageries Imperiales, as the line was called in 1862. Dakar was not then the important station it has become to-day. It possessed but nine thousand inhabitants, with a tendency to increase its population, owing to the important works in progress for the improvement of the port.

If the bargeman had never made acquaintance with the M'Bambaras negroes, he had now an easy opportunity of doing so, as these natives swarmed in Dakar. Thanks to their dry, nervous temperament, their thick skulls, their woolly hair, they were able to support with impunity the fierceness of the Senegalian sun. Tregomain had hung his square handkerchief behind his head as the best substitute he could find for a sunshade.

"Good gracious, it is hot!" he exclaimed. "I really was not made to live in the tropics."

"This is nothing, Tregomain," replied Juhel. "When we are in the Gulf of Guinea a few degrees below the Equator—"

"I shall melt, for a certainty," replied the bargeman; "and I shall take nothing back to my country but skin and bones. And," said he with the sweetest of smiles, as he mopped his face, "it would be difficult to take home less."

"You are much thinner than you were."

"Think so? Bah! I have a margin yet before I am reduced to a skeleton. In my opinion it is better to be thin in countries where the people feed on human flesh. Are there any cannibals on the Guinea Coast?"

"Not many; at least I hope not."

"Well, my boy, do not tempt the natives by being too fat. Who knows if after island number two, we have to be off to number three, in countries where people feed on each other,"—

"As in the islands of the Pacific?"

"Yes! There the inhabitants are anthropophagous!"

He meant to say philanthropophagous, if he had been capable of inventing the word, for in these countries it is out of pure gourmandizing that the natives eat their kind.

But to think that Captain Antifer would be so obstinate as to let his madness for the millions drive him to such distant spots, was not admissible. Certainly his nephew and his friend would never follow him there, and would prevent him from entering on such a campaign, even if it meant having him shut up in a lunatic asylum.

When Tregomain and Juhel returned to the hotel they found Antifer and the banker.

The French agent had received them cordially, but when they asked for a vessel bound for a Loango port, his answer was not encouraging. The steamers engaged in this trade are very irregular, and under any circumstances do not call at Dakar more than once a month. There was a weekly service between Sierra Leone and Grand Bassam, but from there to Loango was a long way farther. The first steamer was not due at Dakar for a week. How unfortunate! A whole week for him to spend in this town chafing at his bit! And it would have to be of well-tempered steel, this bit, to resist the teeth of Captain Antifer, who was now chewing down a pebble a day. It is true that there is no want of pebbles on the African beach, so that Antifer would have no difficulty in supplying his wants.

We cannot avoid remarking that the week at Dakar was long, very long. The walks about the harbour, the excursions to the brook at the east of the town, had very soon exhausted their charms. Such patience was required as only an easy philosophy could give. But with the exception of Tregomain, who was remarkably gifted in this respect, Antifer and his companions were neither patient nor philosophical. If they blessed Kamylk Pasha for having chosen them for his heirs, they cursed him for the caprice by which he had buried the heritage so far away. It was really too much, to send them to the Gulf of Oman, and now they had to go to the Gulf of Guinea. Why could not the Egyptian have found a quiet little island in European seas? Was there not one in the Mediterranean, in the Baltic, in the Black Sea, in the North Sea, with every convenience for the stowage of three casks? Really the Pasha had indulged in quite a plethora of precautions! But so it was, and if you liked to abandon this treasure quest— Abandon it? See what a reception you would have had from Antifer and Zambuco and even the notary held in the grip of the violent Saouk.

The bonds which attached these companions to each other were being visibly relaxed. There were three distinct groups, Antifer and Zambuco, Omar and Saouk, Juhel and Tregomain. They lived apart, meeting each other only at meal-times; avoiding each other during their walks, they sorted themselves out into twos, and seemed as though they never would combine in the final sextette, which could only result in abominable cacophony.

As regards the Juhel and Tregomain group. We know the usual subject of their conversation ; the indefinite prolongation of the voyage, the gradual widening of the separation between the lovers, the fear that so many researches and fatigues could only end in a hoax, the state of Antifer's sanity—all of them causes of regret for the bargeman and Juhel, who had made up their minds not to withstand him, and to follow him to the end.

As regards the Antifer and Zambuco group. What a curious study these two future brothers-in-law would have made for a moralist ! One, up to then of simple tastes, living a quiet life in a quiet town with that philosophy natural to a retired sailor, now a prey to the lust for gold, his mind deranged by this mirage of millions gleaming under his eyes. The other, already so rich, but having no other care than to heap riches on riches, exposing himself to so many fatigues, to so many dangers even, in the endeavour to increase the heap.

" A week to get rusty at the bottom of this hole," said Captain Antifer, "and who knows if this wretched steamer will not be late ? "

" And then," said the banker, " our ill-fortune makes us land at Loango, and thence go up fifty leagues to Ma-Yumba Bay ! "

" I am uneasy about the end of this road," said the irascible Antifer.

" Enough to make you uneasy," observed the banker.

" It is no good anchoring till we reach the roadsteads. Let us get to Loango and then we will see."

" We might persuade the captain of the steamer to put in at Ma-Yumba. It would not take him far out of his way."

" I do not suppose he would consent, as he is not likely to be allowed to do so."

" If we were to offer him an indemnity, he might," suggested the banker.

" We will see, Zambuco, but you are always thinking of what never occurs to me. The essential is to arrive at Loango, and from there we can get to Ma-Yumba. At least we have legs, and if necessary, and there is no other way of leaving Dakar, I should not hesitate at going round by the coast."

" On foot ? "

" Yes, on foot."

He spoke quite airily. But the dangers, the obstacles the impossibilities of such a journey ! He might think himself lucky to be able to find a steamer, and thus avoid the perils of the journey ! Not one of those who accompanied him on such an expedition would have returned. And Talisma Zambuco would have waited in vain at home in Malta for the return of her too audacious husband that was to be.

And so they had to resign themselves to the steamboat, which could not arrive for a week. But how long seemed the hours spent at Dakar !

Quite different was the conversation of Saouk and Ben Omar. Not that the son of Mourad was less impatient to reach the island and carry off the treasure of Kamylk Pasha. His thoughts were concentrated on the way in which he could best rob the legatees. He had intended to carry this out on the return from Sohar to Muscat, now he would attempt it on the return from Ma-Yumba to Loango. Certainly his chances had improved. Among the natives and interlopers he ought to find a few fellows capable of anything, even of shedding blood, if necessary who would

O

manage this matter for him. And the prospect of this terrified the pusillanimous Ben Omar, less from delicacy of feeling than from fear, at being mixed up in such an affair.

He made a few timid suggestions. He remarked that Captain Antifer and his companions were men who would sell their lives dearly. He insisted on the point that no matter how much Saouk paid them, the scoundrels he employed would talk about it sooner or later, and that the truth is always found out at last regarding the massacre of explorers in any part of Africa. His arguments were directed, in fact, not against the criminality of the attempt, but arose from fear of being found out—the only reason which could stop such a man as Saouk.

But they had no effect on him. Giving the notary one of those looks which chilled the very marrow in his bones, he said,—

" I only know of one imbecile who is capable of betraying me ! "

" And who is that ? "

" You, Ben Omar ! "

" Me ? "

" Yes, and take care, for I know how to make people hold their tongues."

Ben Omar, trembling in all his limbs, bowed his head. One corpse more or less on the road from Ma-Yumba to Loango would not embarrass Saouk, as he well knew.

The expected steamer dropped anchor at Dakar in the morning of the 12th of May. This was the *Cintra*, a Portuguese vessel, bound with passengers and goods to San Paul de Loanda, the important Lusitanian colony of tropical Africa. She regularly stopped at Loango and as she started early next morning, Antifer and his companions at once booked their berths. As her speed was only from nine to ten knots, the voyage would last a week during which Ben Omar would suffer as usual.

Having dropped a few passengers at Dakar, the *Cintra* started next morning in fine weather, with the breeze blowing off the land. Antifer and the banker heaved an immense sigh of satisfaction, as if their lungs had not been working for a week. This was the last stage before setting foot on island number two, and putting their hand on the treasure it was guarding so carefully. The attraction the island exercised on them seemed to become more powerful as they approached it, conformably to natural laws, increasing inversely as the square of the distance. And at every turn of the screw of the *Cintra* the distance decreased.

And for Juhel it increased. He went farther and farther away from France, from Brittany, where Enogate sat in sorrow. He had written to her from Dakar as soon as he arrived, and the poor girl would soon learn that her lover was farther away from her than ever, and could fix no date as to his probable return.

Saouk tried to find out what passengers were to be landed at Loango. Among these adventurers, with consciences untroubled by scruples or remorse, who were in search of fortune in these distant lands, were there any who knew the country, and were likely to become his accomplices? His Excellency could not find any. He would have to choose his rascals when he reached Loango. Unfortunately he could not speak Portuguese, neither could Ben Omar. This was embarrassing, as he had to treat of delicate matters, and express himself quite clearly. Antifer, Zambuco, Tregomain, and Juhel were reduced to talking among themselves, for no one on board spoke French.

There was one whose surprise was equal to his satisfaction, Ben Omar to wit. To say that he felt no discomfort during this voyage of the *Cintra* would be untrue. But at the same time the intense suffering he had formerly experienced was now spared him. The *Cintra* kept within two or three miles of the coast : the sea was calm, and she felt very little of the swell of the open sea. This continued after she had doubled Cape Palmas, the extreme point of the Gulf of Guinea. As often happens, the breeze followed the line of Coast and the Gulf was as smooth as the ocean. But the *Cintra* had to lose sight of the land when her course was laid for Loango. The travellers saw nothing of Ashanti Land, nor of Dahomey, nor even of the summit of Mount Cameroon, which rises for some twelve thousand feet, beyond Fernando Po, on the confines of Upper Guinea.

In the afternoon of the 19th of May, Tregomain became somewhat excited. Juhel told him he was about to cross the Equator. For the first time, for the last no doubt, the bargeman was about to enter the southern hemisphere. What an adventure for him, the mariner of the Rance! And it was without regret that, following the example of the other passengers, he gave the crew of the *Cintra* his piastre in recognition of the honour of crossing the line.

At sunrise next morning the *Cintra* was in the latitude of Ma-Yumba, but about a hundred miles to the west of it. If the captain of the steamer had agreed to put in at the port which belongs to the State of Loango what fatigues, what dangers perhaps, might have been spared Captain Antifer! Such a call would have saved him an extremely difficult journey along the coast.

Urged by his uncle, Juhel tried to argue the matter with the captain of the *Cintra*. The Portuguese knew a few words of English—as what sailor does not?—and Juhel, as we know, spoke this language fluently. He introduced the proposal to stop at Ma-Yumba. It would take the steamer only two days out of her way, the expenses would be paid for the delay, the coal, the provisions, the indemnity to the owners of the *Cintra*, etc.

Did the captain understand Juhel's proposal? Certainly, when it was explained on a chart of the Gulf of Guinea. Sailors soon understand each other in such matters. Nothing was easier than to steer eastwards so as to land this half-dozen passengers at Ma-Yumba, provided the passengers were willing to pay.

But the Captain refused. He was freighted for Loango—he would go to Loango. From Loango he was bound to San Paul de Loanda, and to San Paul de Loanda he would go, and nowhere else, even if they bought the ship for her weight in gold. Such were the expressions he used, which Juhel clearly understood, and translated to his uncle.

Terrible was Antifer's anger, and fearful the broadside of oaths he let fly at the captain. If it had not been for the intervention of Tregomain and Juhel, Antifer, in a state of mutiny, would have been sent as a prisoner to the hold for the rest of the voyage.

Two days afterwards, in the evening of the 21st of May, the *Cintra* stopped before the long sand-bank which defends the coast of Loango, and landed with her launch the passengers in question. A few hours afterwards she was off again on her way to San Paul, the capital of the Portuguese colony.

CHAPTER XXIV.

NEXT day, beneath a baobab-tree, which sheltered them from the fiery rays of the sun, two men were in conversation. As they had come up the principal street of Loango, where they had met by the greatest chance, they had recognized each other, with many gestures of surprise.

One had said,—

" You—here ? "

Yes—here ! " the other had replied. And at a sign from the first, who was Saouk, the second, a Portuguese named Barroso, had followed him out of the town.

Although Saouk did not speak the language of Barroso, Barroso spoke the language of his Excellency, for he had lived for some time in Egypt. Two old acquaintances these. Barroso was one of the band of adventurers under Saouk when he was engaged in every kind of depredation, without being troubled by the agents of the Viceroy, thanks to the influence of Mourad, his father, the cousin of Kamylk Pasha. When the band had been broken up, after two or three outrages too bad to be overlooked, Barroso had disappeared. Returning to Portugal, where there was no scope for his peculiar abilities he had left Lisbon to work in a factory at Loango. At this period the trade of the colony, almost ruined by the abolition of the slave trade, was reduced to the export of ivory, palm-oil, ground-nuts and mahogany.

At the moment this Portuguese, who had been a sailor, and was then about fifty, commanded a small vessel named the *Portalegre*, engaged in the coasting trade.

Barroso was possessed of a conscience so utterly devoid of scruples, and an audacity acquired in his old trade that made him just the man Saouk wanted for his criminal machinations. When they reached the foot of this baobab—which the arms of twenty men could not have encircled, though it was nothing compared with the banyan at Muscat—they could talk without fear of being overheard, of anything they pleased that threatened the safety of Antifer and his companions.

To begin with, they told each other how they had spent their lives since the Portuguese had left Egypt, and then Saouk came to business without beating about the bush. Although he took good care not to let Barroso know the immense amount of treasure he was anxious to get hold of, he did not fail to tempt his cupidity with the bait of a considerable sum to be gained.

"But," added he, "to help me, I want a man, resolute, courageous—"

"You know me, Excellency," replied the Portuguese, "and you know that I will stop at nothing."

"If you have not changed."

"I have not changed."

"Know then that there are four men we must get rid of, and perhaps a fifth, if I find it necessary to disembarrass myself of a certain Ben Omar, whose clerk I am supposed to be, under the name of Nazim."

"One more makes little difference."

"In this case certainly, as he will give you no trouble."

"What are you going to do?"

"This is my plan," replied Saouk, after looking about to see that he would not be overheard; "three of these men are Frenchmen, a certain Captain Antifer, his friend, and his nephew, and a Tunisian banker named Zambuco, just landed at Loango, to take possession of a treasure deposited on one of the islands in the Gulf of Guinea."

"Whereabouts?"

"Near Ma-Yumba Bay," replied the Egyptian. "Their intention is to travel up the coast to that town, and I think it will be easy to attack them as they are returning with their treasure to wait for the steamer from San Paul to Dakar."

"Nothing easier," said Barroso, "I can find a dozen trusty fellows, always ready for business, who would be glad to assist you for an agreed sum."

"I was sure of it, Barroso, and in these desert places, we would be certain to succeed."

"Of course. But I have a better plan to propose."

"What is that?"

"I am in command of a vessel of a hundred and fifty tons, taking goods from one port to another along the coast. My ship is going to start in a couple of days for Baracka, on the Gaboon, a little to the north of Ma-Yumba."

"Ah! we might take advantage of that. Antifer would be only too pleased to take passage in her to avoid the fatigues and dangers of a land journey. You can land us at Ma-Yumba, deliver your goods at the Gaboon, and return to pick us up. And while we are on the passage to Loango—"

"That is understood."

"How many men have you on board?"

"Twelve."

"You can trust them?"

"As myself."

"And what are you taking to the Gaboon?"

"A cargo of ground-nuts, and six elephants bought by a house at Baracka, which are to be sent on to a menagerie in Holland."

"You do not speak French?"

"No."

"Do not forget that I am not supposed to speak it or to understand it. I will tell Ben Omar to make the proposal to you, and Antifer will not hesitate to accept it."

There could be no doubt of this, and there was every reason to fear that the two legatees would disappear with their companions during the return voyage across the Gulf

of Guinea.   And who could hinder the crime ?   And who
would find out the authors ?

Loango is not under Portuguese rule, like Angola and
Benguela.   It is one of the independent kingdoms of the
Congo, bounded by the Gaboon on the north, and the
Zaire on the south.   But at this period, from Cape Lopez
to the Zaire, the native kings recognized the sovereign of
Loango, and Paid him tribute, generally in slaves ; such
were Cassange, Tomba Libolo, and other vassals reign-
ing over the much-divided smaller territories.   Society is
regularly constituted among these negroes ; at the head
the king and his family, then the princes—that is the
sons of a princess, who alone can transmit nobility—then
the husbands of the princesses, who are suzerains, then the
priests, the fetishes, or "yangas," of whom the chief is
Chitome, by divine right ; then the courtiers, the merchants,
the retainers, that is to say the people.   As to slaves,
there are many, there are too many.   They are no longer
sold to foreigners it is true, owing to the consequences of
European intervention in abolishing the trade.

But although the king of Loango is the monarch of a
country that rejoices in independence, it does not follow
that its roads are sufficiently guarded, and that travellers
are free from peril ; and so it would have been difficult to
find a territory more favourable, or a sea more suitable for
a foul action.

This it was that made Juhel so anxious—at least with
regard to the land journey.   If his uncle thought little
about it, upset as he was, the young captain could not con-
template without serious alarm this land journey of a
hundred and twenty miles along the coast to Ma-Yumba
Bay.   He thought it his duty to tell the bargeman of
this.

"What would you do, my boy ? " replied Tregomain ;
" the cork is drawn, and we must drink the wine."

"In fact," continued Juhel, "it was only a promenade
between Muscat and Sohar, and then we were in good
company."

"Could we not make up a caravan of natives at Loango?"

"I would no more trust these niggers than I would the hyænas and leopards and lions of the district."

"Ah! are there plenty of those beasts?"

"Plenty of them, to say nothing of lentas, which are venomous vipers, of cobras which spit their foam at your face, of pythons thirty feet long."

"A nice place, my boy! Really this excellent Pasha could not have chosen a more convenient one! And you think that these natives——"

"Are not particularly intelligent, being like all the Congoese; but they are intelligent enough to rob and massacre the fools who venture in this abominable country."

This fragment of dialogue gives a fair sample of the anxieties that Juhel shared with Tregomain. And consequently they were both greatly relieved when Saouk, by means of Ben Omar, introduced the Portuguese Barroso to Captain Antifer and the Tunisian banker. No long stages across these dangerous countries, no fatigues in this excessive climate during so long a journey. As Saouk had said nothing of his previous connection with Barroso, and as Juhel could have no suspicion that these two scoundrels had formerly known one another his suspicions were not aroused. The voyage was to be by sea to Ma-Yumba Bay. The weather was fine. They would be there in two days. The vessel would land the passengers, go on to Baracka, embark them on her return, and they would all get back to Loango for the next steamer to take them to Marseilles. Never had chance declared itself so clearly in favour of Captain Antifer. Of course, he would have to pay well for his passage. But what mattered the cost?

There were two days to wait at Loango, until the halfdozen elephants sent up from the interior were shipped on board the *Portalegre*. And so Tregomain and Juhel— the former always anxious to learn—amused themselves by strolling through the town, the "banza" as it is called in Congoese.

Loango, or Bouala, the old city, measuring about two miles and a half in circumference, is built in the midst of a palm forest. It is composed of a collection of factories, surrounded by huts built of raphia twigs, and covered with papyrus leaves. The traders are Portuguese, Spanish, French, English, Dutch, and German ; quite a mixture, as you see. But how new everything seemed to the bargeman ! The Bretons on the banks of the Rance are not in the least like these half-naked natives, armed with bows and wooden swords and rounded axes. The King of Loango, dressed up in a ridiculous old uniform, was not in the least like the Préfect of Ille-et-Vilaine ; the villages between St. Malo and Dinan had no such huts sheltered by huge cocoanut trees. And the people of St. Malo are not polygamous, like the idle Congoese, who leave all the heavy work to their wives, and go to bed when their wives are ill. But the land in Brittany is not as fertile as the land in Loango. Here it is only necessary to scratch the ground to obtain superb crops—of " manfiigo," or millet, with ears weighing half a pound, of " holcus " which grows without culture, of " luco " which is used for bread, of maize giving three crops a year, of rice, yams, manioc, tamba, lentils, tobacco, sugar-cane in the marshy districts, vines in the neighbourhocd of the Zaire, imported from Canary and Madeira, figs, bananas, oranges, called " mambrochas," lemons, pomegranates, " coudes "—fruit in the shape of pine-cones, containing a floury melting substance—" neubanzams," a kind of nut much liked by the negroes, and pine-apples, that grow naturally on the desert spots.

And then what huge trees—mangroves, sandalwoods, cedars, tamarinds, palms, and a number of those baobabs, from which is extracted a vegetable soap, and a residuum much appreciated by the natives.

And what a crowd of animals—pigs, boars, zebras, buffaloes, deer, gazelles, antelopes, elephants, jackals, porcupines, flying squirrels, wild cats, to say nothing of the innumerable varieties of monkeys, chimpanzees, ostriches, peacocks, thrushes, partridges, red and grey, edible locusts, bees, mosquitoes, canzos, satoles, and cousins more numerous than desirable! A wonderful country, whose wonders Tregomain would have exhausted if he had had time to study its natural history.

Neither Antifer nor Zambuco could have told you if Loango was peopled by whites or blacks. No! their eyes looked elsewhere. They were searching far away more to the north, for an imperceptible point, a point unique in this world, a sort of enormous diamond with fascinating scintillations, weighing thousands of carats, and worth millions of pounds. Ah! How impatient they were to set foot on island number two, and reach the end of their adventurous campaign.

On the 22nd of May, at sunrise, the vessel was ready to sail. The six elephants had arrived the night before, and been embarked, with the necessary precautions. They were magnificent animals that would not have disgraced Sam Lockhart's circus. It need scarcely be said that they were stowed in the hold. Maybe it was not very prudent to load a vessel of a hundred and fifty tons with such masses, which might interfere with its equilibrium. Juhel mentioned this to the bargeman. The vessel was, however, rather beamy and drew very little water, so as to enable her to come close in over the shallows. She had two masts, rather far apart, and was of square rig; for a vessel of this kind only sails well before the wind, and if she is not very speedy she can at least be safely worked within sight of the coast.

Besides, the wind was favourable. At Loango, as in all the countries of the Gulf, the rainy season, which begins in September, ends in May, under the influence of winds coming from the north-west. On the other hand, though it may be fine from May to September, how insupportable is the heat, which is only tempered a little by the abundant dew of the nights. Since they had landed, our travellers had melted and grown thinner visibly. More than ninety-three degrees in the shade! In this country—if we are to believe certain explorers, little worthy of faith, who ought to have been born in Bouches-du-Rhone or Gascony—the dogs are obliged to be continually on the move to prevent them from burning their paws on the incandescent soil, and wild boars are found actually cooked in their skins ! Tregomain was almost inclined to believe these stories.

The *Portalegre* set sail at eight o'clock in the morning. The passengers were all on board, men and elephants. The groups were as usual. Captain Antifer and Zambuco, more hypnotised than ever by this island number two— and what a weight would be lifted from them when the look-out sighted it on the horizon ! Tregomain and Juhel, one forgetting the seas of Africa for the channel and the harbour of St. Malo, the other thinking of nothing but breathing the refreshing breeze. Saouk and Barroso, talking together—and what was there to be astonished at, as they spoke the same language, and it was owing to their meeting that Antifer had obtained a passage on the vessel ?

The crew consisted of a dozen sturdy fellows, mostly Portuguese, and of very unprepossessing appearance. The uncle was absorbed in his thoughts, and did not notice this ; but the nephew remarked it, and communicated his impressions to the bargeman, who replied that in such temperatures it is hazardous to judge of people by their looks, and that one must not be too particular with regard to the crew of an African vessel.

With the prevailing wind, the voyage up the coast promised to be delightful. *Portentosa Africa !* Tregomain would have said if he had known the pompous epithet with which the Romans greeted this continent. In truth, if their thoughts had not been elsewhere, Captain Antifer and his companions, in passing the factory of Chillu, would have abandoned themselves to the just admiration which the natural beauties of the coast deserved. Alone among them the bargeman gazed at it all like a man who wished to carry away with him some remembrance of his journey. And what could he have more splendid than this succession of green forests covering the hill sides, dominated here and there by the heights of the Strauch mountains, bathed with hot mists in their deep ravines. From mile to mile the beach ran back to give passage to the water-courses coming from the thick woods, which the tropical heats could not dry up. It is true that all this water did not reach the sea. Flocks of birds were gathered to drink of it—peacocks, ostriches, pelicans, divers, animated the landscape with the beatings of their wings. Herds of graceful antelopes, troops of "empolangas," or elands of the Cape—huge mammals capable of drinking a ton of this limpid water as easily as the bargeman would have tossed off a glass—herds of hippopotamuses, looking at a distance like pink pigs, whose flesh, it seems, is not despised by the natives.

Tregomain, finding himself near Antifer, in the bows, took occasion to remark,—

" Eh! my friend. Hippopotamus feet, à la Ste. Mene-hould—will that do for you?"

Antifer merely shrugged his shoulders, and gave the bargeman one of those weary, vague looks which look at nothing.

" He no longer understands what is said to him!" murmured Tregomain, using his handkerchief as a fan

On the edge of the shore were troops of monkeys, leaping from one tree to another, howling and grimacing when, by a movement of the rudder, the *Portalegre* approached the beach.

The birds, the hippopotamuses and monkeys would have done no harm to our travellers if they had had to walk from Loango to Ma-Yumba. No, what would have been a more serious danger was the presence of leopards and lions, which were seen bounding about the underwood, wonderfully supple brutes, anything but safe to meet with. When the night came, there were gruff howlings and lugubrious bayings to break the impressive silence which followed the fall of night. This concert reached the vessel like the moaning that precedes a storm. Troubled and excited, the elephants became restive in the hold,

replying by savage grunts, and shaking so as to make the
vessel's timbers groan. Decidedly the cargo was likely to
cause uneasiness to the passengers.

Four days elapsed. Nothing occurred to break the
monotony of the voyage. The fine weather continued.
The sea was a deal calm, and Ben Omar felt no discomfort. There was no pitching, no rolling ; and, although
the *Portalegre* was heavily laden, she was almost insensible
to the long undulations of the surge, which died out in a
light surf on the beach.

For his part, the bargeman never imagined that a
voyage at sea could be so quiet.

"One would think we were on the *Charmante Amélie*,
between the banks of the Rance," he said to his young
friend.

"Yes," objected Juhel ; "with this difference—that there
was not on the *Charmante Amélie* a captain like this
Barroso, and a passenger like this Nazim, whose intimacy
with the Portuguese seems to me more and more
suspicious."

"And what do you think they are meditating, my
boy?" replied Tregomain. "It will be too late, for we
ought to be near our goal."

In fact, at sunrise on the 27th of May, after doubling
Cape Banda, the *Portalegre* was within twenty miles of
Ma-Yumba. This Juhel ascertained from Ben Omar, who
at his request asked Saouk, who asked Barroso.

They would arrive, then, that very evening at this little
port of the Loango country. Already the coast began to
curve in behind Point Matooti, describing a large bay, at
the end of which the town was hidden. If island number
two existed, if it occupied the place indicated in the
document, it ought to be somewhere in this bay ; and
consequently Antifer and Zambuco kept their eyes at the
telescope, the glass of which they rubbed again and again.

Unfortunately the wind was light, the breeze almost
gone. The *Portalegre* was hardly making two knots an
hour.

About one o'clock she rounded Point Matooti. There was a shout of joy on board. The future brothers-in-law had simultaneously sighted a series of islets in the bay. Assuredly the one they were in search of was one of the series? But which? That they would find out next day, when they observed the sun.

Five or six miles to the east, Ma-Yumba appeared on a spit of sand between the sea and the Banya brook, with its factories, its houses luminous among the trees. In front of the beach were a few fishing-boats, like large white birds.

How calm was the surface of the bay! A canoe could not have been more tranquil on the surface of a lake— what shall we say—on the surface of a pond, or even on a large bowl of oil. The rays of the sun poured vertically down; Tregomain streamed like a fountain in a park on a festival day.

The *Portalegre* drew nearer, thanks to a few inter- mittent puffs from the west. The islands in the bay became more distinct. There were six or seven of them, like baskets of verdure.

At six o'clock in the evening the vessel was abreast of this archipelago. Antifer and Zambuco remained standing in the bows. Saouk, forgetting himself a little, could not hide his impatience, and justified by his manner the suspicions of Juhel. These three men devoured with their eyes the first of these islands. Did they expect to see it spout up a shower of millions from its flanks as from a crater of gold?

If they had known that the island in which Kamylk Pasha had buried his treasure was composed only of sterile rocks and bare stones, without a tree, without a shrub, no doubt they would have cried in despair,—

"No! It is not that one yet!"

But since 1831 there had been thirty-one years in which Nature had had time to cover the island with masses of verdure.

The *Portalegre* approached it slowly, so as to round its

northern point, her sails barely filled with the dying
evening breeze. If the wind fell altogether, they would
have to anchor and wait for the daylight.

But, suddenly, a lamentable groaning was heard at the
bargeman's side. He turned to see what it was.

It was Ben Omar. The notary was pale, he was livid ;
his heart was in his lips ; he was sea-sick.

What ! In such calm weather, in this sleepy bay, without a furrow on its surface ?

Yes ! And there was nothing surprising in the poor
man being fearfully sick, for the vessel had begun to roll
in a most absurd and inexplicable manner. She rolled
to port, then to starboard, in a most violent fashion. The
crew rushed forward and rushed aft. Captain Barroso
also ran.

" What is it ? " asked Juhel.

" What is the matter ? " asked Tregomain.

Was it some submarine eruption, the shocks of which
threatened to sink the *Portalegre ?*

Neither Antifer, nor Zambuco, nor Saouk, seemed to
notice what was happening.

" Ah ! " exclaimed Juhel. " The elephants ! "

Yes, it was the elephants who were making the ship
roll. Under the influence of some inexplicable caprice,
the idea had occurred to them to bear all together
alternately on their hind feet and their fore feet. They
made the vessel rock, and it seemed to please them,
as it pleases the squirrel in his gyratory course in his
revolving cage. But what squirrels, these huge pachy-
derms !

The rolling increased, the taffrails nearly touched the
water ; the vessel was in danger of filling first on one side
then on the other.

Barroso and a few of the crew hurried down into the
hold. They tried to calm the monstrous animals. There
were shouts and blows, but no result. The elephants,
brandishing their trunks, raising their ears, wagging their
tails, got more excited ; and more and more the *Portalegre*

R

rolled, rolled, rolled, until the water came pouring into her.

It did not take long. In ten seconds the sea had reached the hold, and down she went, while the screams of the foolish elephants were drowned in the abyss.

CHAPTER XXV.

" AT last I have been shipwrecked!" said Tregomain, next morning.

When the *Portalegre* had gone down, in fifteen or twenty fathoms, the islet in Ma-Yumba Bay, towards which she was nearest, became the refuge of those she carried. Nobody had perished in this extraordinary catastrophe. No one was missing from the roll-call among her passengers or her crew. They had all helped each other; Antifer had held up Zambuco, Saouk had held up Ben Omar. They had only a few strokes to make to reach the rocks of the islet. Only the elephants had disappeared amid the element for which Nature had not created them. They were drowned. After all, it was their fault. It does not do to make a boat into a seesaw.

Antifer's first remark on landing had been,—

" And our instruments ? And our charts ? "

Unfortunately—and the loss was irreparable—neither the sextant, nor the atlas, nor the nautical almanac had been saved, the disaster taking place in a few seconds.

Fortunately, the banker and the notary and the bargeman carried in their belts the money required for the voyage, and there would be no difficulty in this respect.

Neither had Tregomain had any difficulty in supporting himself in the water, the weight of the liquid displaced by his volume being greater than that of his body, and he had tranquilly drifted ashore on the surge like a cetacean.

It was easy to get dry. The clothes had only to be laid out in the sun for half-an-hour to become as dry as a bone. But there was rather a disagreeable night to be passed under the trees, every man abandoning himself to his own reflections. That they had arrived in the neighbourhood of island number two there could be no doubt. But how were they to determine the exact spot where 3° 17′ south latitude crossed 7° 23′ east longitude, now that Juhel had no sextant or chronometer, and could not take an altitude?

And so each of them according to his character and aspirations remarked to himself,—

Zambuco—" This is sinking in sight of port."

Antifer—" I shall not go away till I have ransacked every island in this bay, if it takes me ten years to do it."

Saouk—" My well-laid scheme has failed, owing to this absurd shipwreck."

Barroso—" And those elephants were not insured."

Ben Omar—" Allah protect us, my commission will have cost me dear, if I ever get it ! "

Juhel—" There is nothing now to prevent me going back to Europe, to Enogate."

Tregomain—" Moral ! Never go to sea on a ship with a cargo of facetious elephants."

Nobody slept very much that night. The shipwrecked ones might not suffer from cold, in what way would they next morning at breakfast time reply to the cravings of their hungry stomachs ? At least unless the trees were cocoanut trees laden with fruit, with which, for want of something better, they might support themselves until they reached Ma-Yumba. But how were they to reach this town, which was five or six miles off ? Make signals ? Would they be seen ? Swim five or six miles ? Was there one of the crew who could do that ? Anyhow, when daylight came the matter would have to be considered.

There was no appearance that this island was inhabited —by human creatures, be it understood. But there was no want of other living things—noisy, inconvenient, dangerous perhaps by their numbers. Tregomain had a notion that all the monkeys in creation had met on the island. Perhaps he had landed in the capital of the kingdom of Jocko—or Jockolia?

And though the atmosphere was calm, and the surf hardly rippling on the beach, there was not an hour of peace to be enjoyed on the island. The silence was continuously troubled, and it had been impossible to sleep.

There was a curious uproar among the trees. It seemed as though a troop of Congoese were playing on tom-toms. There was much running backwards and forwards under the branches and among the branches, with guttural cries from husky sentinels; the darkness of the night preventing anything being seen.

When daylight came, the mystery was revealed. The island served as a refuge for a tribe of chimpanzees; and although they had troubled his sleep, Tregomain could not but admire these magnificent specimens of the anthropoid family. These were the very Jockos of Buffon, able to do many things ordinarily reserved for human hands and intelligence, tall, strong, vigorous, the prognathism of the face little marked, the ridges of the eyebrows almost normal. It was by distending their stomachs, and rubbing them vigorously that they produced the drumming noise.

There were about fifty of these chimpanzees who had taken up their abode on the island, but how they had got there from the mainland, how they found sufficient food there, we leave to others to explain. Juhel was not slow to discover that the island—measuring about two miles long and a mile wide—was covered with trees of the different kinds common in tropical latitudes. No doubt these trees produced edible fruit, which gave the chimpanzees their means of existence. But the fruits, the roots, the vegetables, on which the chimpanzees fed, man could feed on also. Of this Juhel, the bargeman, and the sailors at once took advantage. After a shipwreck, after a night without food, it is pardonable to be hungry and to seek for something to eat.

The ground produced, in their wild state, a quantity of these fruits and roots. To eat them raw, however, is not very satisfying, unless you have the stomach of a chimpanzee; but you are not forbidden to cook them if you have the means of doing so. When you have a few matches that is possible, if not easy. Fortunately, Nazim had renewed his supplies at Loango, and the brass box in which he kept them had not got wet inside; and consequently almost as soon as the day broke, a wood fire was crackling under the trees of the encampment.

The company were gathered round this fire. Antifer and Zambuco were as angry as ever. Doubtless anger is nourishing, for they refused to share in the rudimentary breakfast, to which were added a few handfuls of the nuts the Guineans think so much of.

The chimpanzees also regaled themselves, and probably did not look kindly on these invaders of their island, these strangers who were attacking their reserves. Soon they began to draw in, and some of them capering about, the others at rest, but all grimacing violently, formed a circle round Captain Antifer and his companions.

"We must be on our guard," said Juhel to his uncle. "These chimpanzees are powerful fellows, ten times more numerous than we are, and we are without arms—"

Antifer was not likely to care much about chimpanzees!

"You are right, my boy," said the bargeman. "These fellows do not seem to be acquainted with the laws of hospitality, and their attitude is threatening—"

"Is there any danger?" asked Ben Omar.

"The danger of being knocked to pieces," replied Juhel seriously.

At this reply the notary would have fled—but it was impossible.

Barroso, however, placed his men so as to repel any attack. Then Saouk and he began to talk privately, while Juhel watched them.

The subject of their conversation may be guessed. Saouk could not disguise his irritation at the thought of this unexpected shipwreck having wrecked his plan. Another must be devised. As they had arrived in the vicinity of island number two, no doubt the treasure of Kamylk Pasha would be found on one of the islands in Ma-Yumba Bay, either this or another one. But nothing could be done as yet. This was clear enough to the two scoundrels, so worthy of understanding each other. Of course Barroso would be well paid by his accomplice for the losses he had undergone, and the value of the vessel, her cargo, and the elephants would be restored to him.

The main point was to get to Ma-Yumba as soon as possible. A few fishing-boats had just come away from the coast. They could easily be distinguished. The nearest was being sailed within three miles of the island. The wind was light, and she would not be in sight of the encampment for three or four hours, when they could signal to her. Before the day was over they could all be installed in one of the factories of the town, where they could but receive a hearty welcome and liberal hospitality.

"Juhel! Juhel!"

This appeal suddenly interrupted the conversation between Saouk and the Portuguese.

It was Captain Antifer who had made it, and it was followed by another,—

"Gildas! Gildas!"

Juhel and the bargeman, who had gone to the beach to watch the manœuvres of the fishing-boats, returned in reply to Antifer.

Zambuco was with him, and Ben Omar at a sign approached.

Leaving Barroso to return to his men, Saouk came gradually nearer the group, so as to hear what was being said. As he had been careful to let it be supposed that he did not understand French, nobody took much notice of his presence.

" Juhel," said Captain Antifer, " listen ; for the time has
arrived to come to a decision."

He spoke in a harsh jerky voice, like a man in a paroxysm
of irritability.

" The last document tells us that island number two
is situated in Ma-Yumba Bay. Now, we are in Ma-Yumba
Bay, are we not ? "

" There is no doubt of it."

" But we have no longer our sextant and chronometer ;
for this clumsy Tregomain, to whom I was fool enough
to trust them, has lost them——"

" My friend——" said the bargeman.

" I would rather have got drowned than lost them ! "
replied Antifer, harshly.

" And so would I," added the banker.

" Indeed, Mr. Zambuco ! " retorted Tregomain, with a
gesture of indignation.

" Well, they are lost," continued Captain Antifer ; " and
for want of the instruments it will be impossible, Juhel,
to determine the position of island number two——"

" Impossible, uncle ; and in my opinion the only
wise thing to do, is to go to Ma-Yumba in one of those
boats, return to Loango by land, and embark on the first
steamer that puts in."

" That——" replied Antifer—" Never ! "

And the banker like a faithful echo repeated,—

" Never ! "

Ben Omar, looking from one to the other, shook his
head, as idiots do, and Saouk listened without seeming to
understand.

" Yes, Juhel, we will go to Ma-Yumba ; but we will stay
there instead of returning to Loango. We will stay there
as long as it is necessary—understand me well—to visit
the islands in the bay—every one of them."

" What ? "

" There are not many of them, five or six, and if there
were a hundred or a thousand I would search them one
after the other."

" Uncle, that is not reasonable."

" Most reasonable, Juhel; one of them contains the treasure. The document indicates the position of the point where it was buried by Kamylk Pasha—"

" Confound the fellow ! " murmured Tregomain.

" With the will and the patience," continued Antifer, " we shall end by discovering the spot marked by the double K."

" And if we do not find it ? " asked Juhel.

" Do not say that, Juhel ! " exclaimed Antifer; " for the sake of heaven do not say that ! "

And in a paroxysm of indescri. able fury his teeth ground the pebble between his jaws. Never had he been nearer an attack of congestion of the brain.

Juhel did not think it worth while to say any more, in face of such obstinacy. The search, which he thought would end in nothing, could not take much more than a fortnight. When Antifer had convinced himself that there was nothing to hope, he would, whether he liked it or not, have to return to Europe. So he replied,—

" Let us be ready to embark in that fishing-boat as soon as it comes ashore "

" Not without searching this island ! " replied Antifer. " Why should we not begin with this one ? "

The observation was logical. Who knew if the treasure-seekers had not reached their goal without the aid of sextant and chronometer ? Not very likely, you say ? Perhaps so ! But considering all the disappointments, and fatigues, and perils, why should not the goddess of Fortune have shown herself propitious to her adorers ?

Juhel did not venture an objection. The best thing to do was to lose no time. The island might be searched before the fishing-boat reached them. As soon as she came near the rocks, it was to be feared that the crew of the *Portalegre* would want to go on board, in their haste to get a substantial meal in the factories of Ma-Yumba. Why should they compel these men to submit to a delay, the cause of which could not be explained to them ? To inform them of the existence of the treasure would be to put them in possession of the secret of Kamylk Pasha!

Nothing could be more reasonable; but when Antifer and Zambuco, accompanied by Juhel and Tregomain, the notary and Nazim, were leaving the camp, would not Barroso and his men be rather surprised, and would they not be tempted to follow them?

This was a serious difficulty. In case the treasure was discovered, what would this crew do at the exhumation of the casks, containing millions in gold, diamonds and other precious stones? Might it not lead to scenes of violence and robbery, with this mob of adventurers, not one of whom was worth the rope to hang him? Double as numerous as Antifer and his companions, they could soon overpower them, knock them about and murder them. Certainly their captain would not try to restrain them. He would be more likely to lead them on, and claim the lion's share in the business.

But to oblige Captain Antifer to act only with extreme prudence, to make him understand it would be better to wait a few days, to first reach Ma-Yumba with the ship-wrecked crew, and to return next day with a boat specially engaged for the trip, after getting rid of these suspicious fellows, was anything but easy. Juhel's uncle would refuse to listen to reason. Never would they get him away until he had ransacked the island. No consideration would stop him.

The bargeman was promptly sent to the right-about when he offered these very just observations to his intractable friend, the only reception he got being a broadside in two words.

"Come on."

"I entreat you—"

"Remain, if you like. I can do without you."

"A little prudence—"

"Come, Juhel."

And he had to obey.

Antifer and Zambuco left the camp. Tregomain and

Juhel followed them.   The men made no attempt to move. Barroso did not seem to take any interest in the reason for the passengers walking off.

How was this?

It was because Saouk had heard all that passed, and having no wish to delay or hinder the search, had simply given the Portuguese the word.

Barroso turned to his crew, and ordered them to wait at the point for the fishing-boats, and not move away from the camp.   And when that was done, Ben Omar, at a sign from Saouk, started after Antifer, who was not surprised at seeing the notary flanked by his clerk Nazim.

CHAPTER XXVI.

IT was about eight o'clock in the morning, to judge by the height of the sun above the horizon—an "about" with which we must be contented, owing to the watches having stopped on account of the immersion.

If Barroso's men had not followed the explorers, it was not so with the chimpanzees. A dozen of them left the troop with the evident intention of escorting the intruders; the others remained around the encampment.

As he walked, the bargeman looked sideways at this savage bodyguard, who answered him with abominable grimaces and threatening gestures and gruff exclamations.

"Evidently," he thought, "these brutes are talking amongst themselves. I am sorry I cannot understand them. It would be a pleasure to converse in their language!"

An excellent opportunity this to make philological observations, and ascertain if, as Garner the American says, the higher apes have vocal sounds expressive of their different ideas—such as *whouw* for food, *cheny* for drink, *iegk* for take care, in fact, if in the Simian tongue *a* and *o* are missing, *i* is rare, *e* little used, and *u* and *ou* are the fundamental vowels.

It will not have been forgotten that the document found on the island in the Gulf of Oman gave the particulars of the island in Ma-Yumba Bay, and mentioned the position in which the sign of the double K marked the site of the treasure.

On the first island it was on a promontory to the south that the search had to be made and was made. On the second island, on the contrary, it was on one of the northern capes that one of the rocks bore the monogram.

It was on the southern side that the shipwreck had occurred; consequently the exploring party had to march northward a distance of about a couple of miles.

There was nothing surprising in the two legatees being in advance of the group. They walked quickly, without exchanging a word, and would have allowed none of their companions to get in front of them.

Every now and then the notary gave an uneasy look at Saouk. He had no doubt but that he had arranged some villainy with the Portuguese captain. There was one thought he could not get rid of, that if Antifer lost the treasure his commission would probably go the same way. Once or twice he tried to talk to Saouk; but Saouk, with gloomy eye and angry look, feeling himself perhaps watched by Juhel, did not reply.

In fact Juhel's mistrust was greatly increased when he noticed how Ben Omar treated Nazim. Even in an Alexandrian office it is not customary for the clerk to command and the notary obey, and there could be no doubt that it was so with these two personages.

The bargeman thought of nothing but the chimpanzees. Now and then his good-looking face would respond to their grimaces, his eye would close, his nose turn up, his lips protrude. Nanon and Enogate would certainly not have recognized him when he abandoned himself to these Simian distortions.

Enogate! Ah! poor child! Assuredly at this moment she was thinking of Juhel, for she was always thinking of him! But that this very day he had been shipwrecked, and was marching amid an escort of chimpanzees—never, no, never, could she have imagined that.

In this latitude at this time of year the sun describes a semicircle from east to west as it passes near the zenith. Consequently the rays it projects on these countries are not oblique but perpendicular. The Torrid Zone is well named, for the zone is literally torrefied from dawn to eve.

"And these jokers do not seem to be warm," said the bargeman looking at the chimpanzees; "it is enough to make you wish you were an ape."

To avoid the solar rays, it might have been worth while to advance under the trees. But their trunks began to branch so low down that the forest seemed impenetrable. Unless you were an ape—as Tregomain wished to be— and could travel among the branches, it would have been impossible to have found a passage. And so it was along the shore that Antifer went, skirting the creeks, avoiding the high rocks rising here and there like menhirs, and stumbling over the stones when he could not find any of the sandy beach clear of the rising tide. Is it not a difficult road, hard to the feet, and rough to travel, which leads to fortune? He might sweat blood and water if necessary, but it would not be too much if he was to be eventually paid at the rate of a thousand pounds for every step he took in approaching his goal.

An hour after they left the camp they had only gone a mile, that is half as far as they wanted. From this place the northern points of the island were visible. Three or four ran out from the rest. Which was the right one? Unless they were exceptionally fortunate they would probably have to search them all under the terrific meridian heat.

The bargeman was quite done up.

"Let us rest a moment!" he entreated.

"Not a moment!" replied Captain Antifer.

"But uncle," said Juhel, "Tregomain is visibly melting."

"Let him melt!"

"Thank you, my friend!"

And at this reply Tregomain, who did not want to remain behind, resumed his march.

It took another half-hour before they reached the place where the four points branched out. The difficulties of the road increased; some of the obstacles appeared insurmountable. What an indescribable chaos of shingle and ridges of quartz. Really the place had been well chosen, and Kamylk had had a happy knack of hiding treasure which might have been envied by the monarchs of Bassora, Bagdad and Samarkand!

Here ended the wooded part of the island. Evidently the chimpanzees had no intention of going further. They do not willingly leave the shelter of trees, and the sound of the roaring waves has no attraction for them.

When the escort stopped at the edge of the trees it was not without manifesting intentions that were anything but conciliatory with regard to the strangers who were pursuing their explorations towards the extremity of the island. What howls they uttered! One of them picked up some stones and threw at them, and as the others followed his example, there was some danger of Antifer and his companions being stoned to death. And this is probably what would have happened if they had been imprudent enough to reply, as they were not equal to their aggressors either in strength or number.

" Do not reply—do not reply!" shouted Juhel, seeing Tregomain and Saouk picking up some stones.

" Nevertheless—" said the bargeman, whose hat had been knocked off by a stone.

" No, Tregomain, no; come further away, and we shall be safe. They will not come any further after us."

This was the best thing to do. Fifty yards more and they would be out of range of the stones.

It was then half-past ten. To the north three points ran out into the sea for a hundred and fifty or two hundred yards. It was the longest one, to the north-west, that Antifer and Zambuco decided to visit first.

Nothing could be more barren than this mass of rocks, some of them firmly buried in the sand, others scattered and rolled about by the sea during the bad weather. No trace of vegetation; not even of lichens coating the humid blocks, not even a scrap of seaweed, so abundant on the shores of the temperate zones. There was nothing to fear with regard to the monogram of Kamylk Pasha. If it had been inscribed on one of these rocks thirty-one years before it would certainly be found intact.

Our explorers began their search exactly as they had done that on the island in the Gulf of Oman. It may hardly be believed but the two legatees were so possessed by their passion that they seemed to suffer no fatigue from their trying march under the burning sun. And Saouk, in the interest of his master—for who would have imagined it was for his own sake?—set to work with indefatigable zeal. The notary sat between two rocks, and neither moved nor spoke. If they discovered the treasure, there would be time enough for him to intervene and claim the commission to which, being present, he was entitled by the provisions of the will. And he certainly would not be overpaid considering the tribulations he had undergone during three long months.

We need hardly say that by Captain Antifer's orders Juhel remained near him, and began a methodical examination of every foot of the ground.

"It is not very likely," he said to himself, "that we shall find the millions here. First, it is necessary that the treasure is buried on this island and not on one of the other islands in the bay. Secondly, it must be buried on this point. Thirdly we have got to find among this mass of rocks one that bears the double K. But if all these circumstances combine, if it is not a hoax on the part of this abominable Pasha, if I put my hand on the monogram, would it not be better to say nothing about it? My uncle would then give up this deplorable idea of marrying me to a duchess, and Enogate to a duke? Well, no! my uncle would never recover from such a blow. He would go out of his mind. My conscience would tell me I had acted dishonourably. I must go on with this thing!"

And while Juhel was indulging in these reflections, the bargeman was seated on a piece of rock with his arms swaying, his legs hanging down, his cheeks streaming, puffing like a seal come to the surface after prolonged immersion.

The investigations proceeded without result. Antifer, Zambuco, Juhel and Saouk, hunted about, patting all the rocks which by their position might bear the precious monogram. In vain were two wearisome hours devoted to this operation, up to the very end of the point. Nothing—nothing! And, indeed, was it likely that a place would have been chosen exposed to the beating of the surf and the violence of the waves? No! After the search was over on this promontory, would they resume it on the others? Yes; they would resume them next day, and Antifer would recommence his work on another island if he failed on this one.

Having found no trace, the group returned from the point, examining the rocks on the sand as they came. But there was nothing.

At present the only thing to do was to get back to the camp, embark on one of the boats, and cross to Ma-Yumba.

As Antifer, Zambuco, Juhel and Saouk came back from their search, they saw the bargeman and the notary still where they had left them.

Antifer and Zambuco, without uttering a word, went towards the edge of the forest, where the chimpanzees were waiting for them.

Juhel rejoined Tregomain.

" Well ? " asked the bargeman.

" Not a sign of a double or even of a single K! "

" Then we must get back ? "

" Just so, get up, and let us be off to the camp."

"Get up? Yes, if I can! Come! give me a hand, my boy!"

And with a vigorous haul from Juhel, Tregomain rose to his feet.

Ben Omar was already upright near Saouk.

Antifer and Zambuco were twenty yards in front.

From gestures and clamours the chimpanzees took to

action. A number of stones were thrown, and it became necessary to stand on the defensive.

Evidently these wretched chimpanzees intended to prevent Antifer and his companions rejoining Barroso and his men at the camp.

Suddenly a shout was heard. It came from Ben Omar. Had the notary been hit by a stone in some sensitive part of his person?

No! It was not a cry of grief that had escaped him. It was a cry of surprise—almost a cry of joy.

They all stopped. The notary, with his mouth open and his eyes shut, stretched out his hand at Tregomain.

"There!" he said, "there!"

"What do you mean?" asked Juhel. "Have you gone mad, Ben Omar?"

"No! There! The K! The double K!" replied the notary, in a voice choked with emotion.

"The K; the double K?" they exclaimed.

"Yes!"

"Where?"

And they looked at the rock towards which Ben Omar seemed to be pointing. But they saw nothing.

"But where, you animal?" asked Antifer, in a voice of fury.

"There!" replied the notary.

And his hand pointed at the bargeman, who turned and shrugged his shoulders.

"See it," said Ben Omar—"on his back!"

In fact, on Tregomain's jacket, there was clearly enough an impression of a double K. Probably the rock against which he had been leaning bore the monogram, of which the worthy man had taken an impression on his back.

Antifer gave a great leap, seized the bargeman by his arm, and ordered him to return to the place where he had been sitting.

The rest followed, and in less than a minute they were in front of a block of stone, on which the much-sought-for monogram was perfectly legible.

Not only had Tregomain sat with his back up against
the rock, but he had sat right down on the place where
the treasure was hidden.

No one spoke a word. They set to work. For want of
tools the task would be difficult. Could they clear away
these rocks with their pocket-knives?

Fortunately the stones, eroded by the weather, could be
pulled asunder without much difficulty. In an hour they
might have the barrels in sight; then they would only
have to take them to the camp, and then to Ma-Yumba.
This transport might probably be difficult, and how could
it be carried out without awakening suspicion?

Bah! Who was going to think about that? The
treasure first; the treasure from the tomb where it had
been buried for the third of a century! They could see
about the other things afterwards.

Antifer worked till his hands bled. He would not
abandon to another the delirious joy of feeling, of patting
the precious casks.

"At last!" he cried, as his knife snapped against a
metallic surface.

And then, what a yell there was! Good heavens!
Not joy, but stupefaction, disappointment, did his white
face show.

Instead of the barrels mentioned in Kamylk Pasha's
will, there was an iron box—a box like that found on
island number one, with the monogram as usual.

"Again!" Juhel could not help exclaiming.

"It must be a hoax!" murmured Tregomain.

The box was pulled out of the hole, and Antifer opened
it savagely.

A document appeared, an old parchment, yellow with
age, on which were traced these lines, which Captain Antifer read in a loud voice:—

"Longitude of island number three, fifteen degrees
eleven minutes east. After being noted by the co-legatees
Antifer and Zambuco, this longitude is to be taken and
communicated, in the presence of the notary Ben Omar, to

Mr. Tyrcomel, of Edinburgh, Scotland, who possesses the latitude of the third island."

Then it was not in Ma-Yumba Bay that the treasure was buried! They would have to search elsewhere on the globe by combining this new longitude with the latitude of the said Tyrcomel of Edinburgh! And there were not two to share Kamylk Pasha's legacy but three!

"And why," exclaimed Juhel, "should we not be sent from this third island to twenty others, to a hundred others? Come uncle, are you so obstinate, so foolish as to run about all over the world?"

"Without reckoning," said Tregomain, "that if Kamylk Pasha has made legatees by the hundred, his legacy will not be worth troubling about!"

Antifer looked down on his friend and his nephew, gave his pebble a grind with his jaw, and replied,—

"Silence in the ranks. We have not got to the end yet."

And straightening out the document, he read as follows :—

"Up to the present, as some compensation for their trouble and expenses, the co-legatees are to each take one of the two diamonds deposited in this box, the value of which is insignificant compared with that of the other precious stones they are asked to search for."

Zambuco threw himself on the box, which he snatched from Antifer's hand.

"Diamonds!" he shouted.

And there were in fact, two magnificent diamonds, worth—so the banker said—four thousand pounds the pair.

"It is quite that," said he, taking one of the diamonds and handing the other to his co-legatee.

"A drop of water in the ocean!" said Antifer, slipping the diamond into one pocket and the document into another.

"Ahem!" said the bargeman, shaking his head, "this is becoming more serious thar I thought! We shall see! We shall see!"

But Juhel merely shrugged his shoulders. And Saouk clenched his hands at the thought that never again would he have such a favourable opportunity.

As to Ben Omar, who had not had the smallest brilliant for his share, in spite of the obligation laid on him by this third document, he stood there with his features drawn, his arms limp, his knees shaking just like a half empty sack about to flatten out on the ground.

It is true that Saouk and he were not in the same position as they were when they left St. Malo, ignorant that they were going to Muscat, or when they had left Muscat ignorant that they were going to Loango. Carried away by regrettable excitement, Antifer had let slip the secret he should have rigorously concealed. They had all heard the new longitude, fifteen degrees eleven minutes east; and they all had heard the name of Mr. Tyrcomel, residing at Edinburgh in Scotland.

We may be certain that if Ben Omar had not done so, Saouk had already engraven these figures and this address in his memory until he could write them in his pocket-book; and Antifer and the banker would have to be careful not to lose sight of the notary, or his clerk with the moustaches, if they did not want them to outstrip them on their journey to Edinburgh. There might be some reason for thinking that Nazim had not understood, as he did not understand French, but there was no doubt that Ben Omar would reveal the secret to him. And besides, Juhel had noticed that Nazim had not concealed a feeling of satisfied curiosity, when the figures of the longitude and the name of Tyrcomel had so imprudently escaped the lips of Captain Antifer.

After all, what did it matter ? In his opinion, it would be madness to submit again for the third time to the post-humous fancies of Kamylk Pasha. What ought to be done was to return to Loango, and take the first steamer on their way to the good town of St. Malo.

Such was the wise and logical proposition that Juhel made to his uncle.

"Never!" replied Captain Antifer. "The Pasha sends us to Scotland; we will go to Scotland, and if I devote the rest of my life to this search—"

"My sister Talisma," added the banker, "loves you too well not to wait for you, even for ten years!"

"Goodness!" thought Tregomain, "the young lady will then be nearly sixty!"

Observations were useless. Antifer had made up his mind. He would continue in pursuit of the treasure, although the legacy was reduced to a third by the participation of Mr. Tyrcomel.

Well, Enogate would have to be content to marry an earl, and Juhel a countess.

CHAPTER XXVII.

" THE possession of wealth leads almost inevitably to its abuse. It is the chief, if not the only cause of all the evils which desolate this world below. The thirst for gold is responsible for the most regrettable lapses into sin. Imagine a society in which there were neither rich nor poor. What evils, afflictions, sorrows, disorders, catastrophes, disasters, tribulations, misfortunes, agonies, calamities, despair, desolation and ruin would be unknown to man ! "

It was the 25th of June ; the church was in Edinburgh ; the preacher was the Reverend Mr. Tyrcomel. His eloquent address had lasted for an hour, and the attention of his congregation gave no signs of failing. " The Gospel tells us," he continued, " that blessed are the poor in spirit. A profound axiom that the ignorant and irreligious have in vain sought to misunderstand. It does not say those who are poor *of* spirit, imbeciles in a word, but those who are poor *in* spirit, and despise those abominable riches, which are the source of evil in modern society. The Gospel tells us to despise wealth, and if unfortunately we are afflicted with a superfluity of wealth, if silver is stored in your treasure-chests, if gold flows in unto you, if diamonds and precious stones cling to your necks, your arms, your fingers, like an unhealthy eruption, if you are among those whom men call happy in this world, although I think you are thereby unhappy—I say to you, that your malady requires instant and energetic treatment, if you wish to be saved."

And the preacher, continuing, told his hearers that their only chance of safety lay in giving their riches over to destruction. He did not say, " Distribute your wealth among the poor, give it to those who have none." No! what he preached was the destruction of this gold and these diamonds and title-deeds and bonds and shares, either by burning them in the fire, or casting them into the water. In short the Rev. Mr. Tyrcomel would have no compromise with the habits and customs of the world in which he lived.

In appearance he was a man of about fifty, tall, thin, smooth-faced, with piercing eyes and a voice as penetrating as that of a preaching friar. Throughout the city he was well known ; there were some who thought he was inspired. The people crowded to his sermons; hearers he had many, proselytes he had none ; they listened, but they acted not.

Among his listeners on this occasion were five strangers who knew nothing of English and would have known nothing of his discourse if a sixth stranger had not explained it to them. The six were of course, Captain Antifer and Zambuco, Ben Omar and Saouk, Tregomain and Juhel.

We left them on the island in Ma-Yumba Bay, on the 28th of May ; we meet with them again here at Edinburgh on the 25th of June.

What has happened between these dates ?

After the discovery of the second document, all that could be done was to abandon the island to the chimpanzees, to avail themselves of the boat which had been attracted by the signals of the shipwrecked crew. Captain Antifer and his companions had returned along the shore, escorted by the chimpanzees, more demonstrative than ever, howling, growling and grimacing, and every now and then assailing the explorers with volleys of stones.

The camp was reached at last. A word or two from Saouk to Barroso told him that the plot had failed. It was impossible to steal treasure from those who had no treasure to steal.

The boat moored in a little creek near the camp, took on board all the survivors of the *Portalegre*. Two hours later she dropped anchor off the sandy spit on which stands Ma-Yumba. Our travellers, without distinction of nationality, were hospitably received at a French factory. They at once set about arranging for their return to Loango. Joining a party of Europeans on their way thither, they had nothing to fear from the wild beasts or the natives; but the heat was almost unbearable! When they arrived, the bargeman said that he was reduced to a skeleton. It was an exaggeration, of course, but it was not far from the truth.

Luckily Captain Antifer and his companions did not have to remain at Loango very long. A Spanish steamer from San Paul de Loanda bound for Marseilles happened to put in two days afterwards for repairs, which were effected in a day. Berths were booked on this steamer, with some of the money saved from the wreck; and on the 15th of June Captain Antifer and his companions left the West Coast of Africa, where they had found two valuable diamonds, a new document and a new disappointment. As to Captain Barroso, Saouk undertook to pay him later on, when he had got hold of the Pasha's millions—and the Portuguese had to be content with the promise.

Juhel made no attempt to argue with his uncle, although he fully expected that the campaign would end in some gigantic mystification. A change, however, began to come over the bargeman's opinion. Those two diamonds, contained in the box on island number two, had given him something to think about.

"If the Pasha," he said to himself, "has made us a present of these two diamonds, why should we not find some more on island number three?"

And when he talked to Juhel in this way, Juhel would shrug his shoulders, and say,—

"Well, we shall see; we shall see."

This was Antifer's opinion. As the third legatee, the possessor of the latitude of the third island, lived in Edinburgh; to Edinburgh he would go; and he had no intention of letting himself be outstripped in the race thither by either Zambuco or Ben Omar, who knew the longitude (15° 11′ east) which was to be communicated to Mr. Tyrcomel. He would not part company with them; they would go together to Edinburgh by the quickest possible way, and Mr. Tyrcomel would be visited by the whole of them. Of course this resolve was not satisfactory to Saouk. He was now in possession of the secret, and he would much rather have acted alone, found the man mentioned in the document, obtained the position of the third island, gone there and dug up the riches of Kamylk Pasha. But he could not get away without awakening suspicion, and he knew that he was being watched by Juhel. Besides, the only way he could go was by Marseilles, and as Antifer was going to Edinburgh by the shortest way, and in the shortest time, by travelling on the railways of France and England, Saouk could not hope to get there before him. He had therefore to resign himself to the inevitable. Once matters had been cleared up with this Mr. Tyrcomel, perhaps the attempt, which had failed at Loango and Muscat, might succeed at Edinburgh.

The passage was fairly quick, as the steamer made no calls at the by-ports. It was rough certainly, and of course Ben Omar was landed like a package on the quay of La Joliette.

Juhel had written a long letter to Enogate. He told her all that had happened at Loango. He informed her of the new campaign on which their uncle's obstinacy was sending them, and who could say where the caprice of the Pasha might send them in the future! He added that as far as he could see, Captain Antifer was quite equal to running about the world like the wandering Jew, and that he would not stop until he was raving mad—which would assuredly happen before all was over.

Juhel had only just time to slip this letter into the post. Antifer was off in the fast train from Marseilles to Paris, then by the express from Paris to Calais, then by boat to Dover, then from Dover to London, and then by the Flying Scotchman from London to Edinburgh. As soon as they had secured their rooms at Gibb's Royal Hotel, they started out in search of Mr. Tyrcomel, and to their great surprise Mr. Tyrcomel turned out to be a minister. They found his address, and then found that he was at the church ; and to the church they went.

Their intention was to introduce themselves to him when the sermon was over, to tell him their story. A man to whom they were bringing a million or so was not likely to complain at being intruded upon.

At the same time it all seemed rather strange. What connection could have existed between Kamylk Pasha and this Scottish minister ? Antifer's father had saved the Egyptian's life—well. Zambuco had saved his riches— well. Hence the feeling of gratitude he had shown towards these two. Were they to conclude that Mr. Tyrcomel possessed a similar right to recognition ? Evidently. But under what peculiar circumstances could a minister have helped Kamylk Pasha in any way ? It must be so, however, for this minister was the depositary of the third latitude necessary for the discovery of the third island.

But when the treasure-seekers saw the minister in the pulpit it was evident that some other explanation would have to be sought for. He could not have been more than twenty-two when Kamylk was thrown into prison at Cairo, by order of Mehemet Ali, and it was not likely that he could have rendered him any service before that. Was it his father, or his grandfather, or uncle, who had put the Egyptian under an obligation ?

However, it was of no importance. The point was that this minister possessed the precious latitude, and that before the day was out they would know all about it.

The sermon continued. The same thesis. with the

same impassioned eloquence. An invitation to kings to throw their civil-lists into the sea, an invitation to queens to throw their diamonds into the flames, an invitation to the rich to destroy every scrap of their wealth.

Juhel sat astounded, muttering to himself.

"Here is another complication! Decidedly uncle will have no chance with this man! Can this be the sort of man the Pasha knew? Is it from this excited minister that we are to ask the means of discovering a treasure? This man would be only too eager to destroy it, if it ever fell into his hands! Here is an obstacle we never expected—an insurmountable obstacle, which will bring our proceedings to a close. We shall get a peremptory refusal, a refusal to which we cannot reply, a refusal which will bring the reverend gentleman immense popularity. That will settle my uncle, and his mind will give way. Zambuco and he, and perhaps this Nazim, will do all they dare to get the secret of the minister. They are capable of everything. But if he keeps the secret? I do not know if, as he says, millions do not bring happiness, but running after those of the Egyptian certainly delayed mine! And if Mr. Tyrcomel refuses to cross his latitude with our longitude, which we have conquered at so much trouble, we can do nothing else than retire tranquilly to France, and—"

"When God commands we must obey!" said the preacher at this moment.

"That is my opinion," thought Juhel, "and my uncle will have to submit."

But the sermon did not end, and there seemed no reason why it should not last until eternity. Antifer and the banker began to give visible marks of impatience. Saouk bit his moustache. The notary, so long as he was not on shipboard, did not worry himself about anything Tregomain with his mouth open, his head nodding, his ears pricked up, tried to catch a word here and there, which he vainly endeavoured to translate.

"If," said Antifer, "he only knew the news I am

bringing him, this preacher would soon get out of his pulpit—"

"Would he?" asked Juhel, in a tone so singular that Antifer frowned at him in a terrible way.

But all things must end in this world—even a Scottish sermon. It became evident that Mr. Tyrcomel had reached his peroration. His delivery became more laboured, his gestures more violent, his metaphors more audacious, his objurgations more menacing. One more blow against the fortune-holders, the possessors of the vile metal, with an injunction to throw it into the furnace of this world if they would avoid being hurled into that of the next; and then a supreme effort, to the effect that when they were weighed in the balance the weight of their gold would sink them to perdition—the sermon was over, and the preacher had suddenly disappeared.

Captain Antifer, Zambuco and Saouk had intended to interview him as he came out of church. Would they have to wait until the morning? Were they to pass the night in the tortures of curiosity? No! They would rush to the central porch.

Juhel and the notary, and Tregomain followed them. But their endeavour was in vain. Evidently Mr. Tyrcomel, to avoid an ovation, had escaped by a side door.

"To 17, North Bridge Street!" said Captain Antifer.

"But, uncle—"

"Before he goes to bed we must see him," said the banker.

"But Mr. Zambuco—"

"No remarks, if you please."

"There is only one thing—"

"What is that?" asked Antifer angrily.

"What he has been preaching about—"

"What has that to do with us?"

"A good deal."

"You are making fun of us."

"I am quite serious, and I say that nothing could be more unfortunate for you—"

"For me?"

"Yes! listen!"

And in a few words Juhel explained what had been the purport of the sermon, that all the millions in the world ought to be thrown into the sea.

The banker was aghast. And so was Saouk, although he pretended not to understand. As for Tregomain, he indulged in a huge grimace of disappointment.

Antifer alone remained unshaken. In a tone of bitter irony he remarked,—

"Fool! The only people who preach like that are those who have not a halfpenny to lose! We have only got to talk about the millions that are coming, and you will see if this Tyrcomel will throw them into the sea."

Evidently this reply betrayed a profound knowledge of human nature. But it was decided to give up the idea of visiting the reverend gentleman that evening, and the six travellers returned to Gibb's Royal Hotel.

CHAPTER XXVIII.

THE house in which Mr. Tyrcomel lodged was in the neighbourhood of the Canongate, the windows looking out on to the valley in which runs the railway. It was a gloomy, uncomfortable house up one of those sordid, insanitary alleys known as closes, running out of this historic thoroughfare, which, under different names, extends from the Palace of Holyrood to the Castle of Edinburgh—one of the four Scottish fortresses which by the articles of the treaty of Union have always to be kept in repair.

It was at the door of this house, that on the morning of the 26th of June, Captain Antifer and the banker Zambuco accompanied by Juhel, arrived, just as eight o'clock was striking from the neighbouring church. Ben Omar had not been asked to join them, his presence being useless at this first interview, and consequently, much to his disgust, Saouk was also absent. If the minister divulged the secret of the latitude he would not be there to hear it, and it would therefore be impossible for him to outstrip Antifer in the search for island number three.

As to the bargeman, he remained at the hotel, and, while awaiting the return of the visitors, amused himself by contemplating the marvels of Princes Street, and the pretentious elegancies of the Scott monument. As far as Juhel was concerned, it had not been possible to dispense with him, as his uncle required his services as interpreter. It can be imagined how eager they were to find where island number three was situated.

Saouk, it may be observed, was furious when he found

himself left behind, and as usual vented his anger on Ben Omar.

"Yes! It is your fault," he shouted, knocking over some of the furniture, "and I have a great mind to pay you out with a good thrashing!"

"Excellency, I did all I could—"

"No, you did not do all you could. You should have forced yourself on this rascally sailor, and told him that your presence was necessary, and that you would be there. You would then have found out and told me about this new island, and I might have perhaps got there before the others. My plans were spoilt at Muscat, they were spoilt again at Ma-Yumba; do you think they are going to fail again because you remain stuck there on your feet like an old ibis stuffed with straw?"

"I beg—"

"And I swear, that if I fail, it is your skin that will pay for it."

The scene continued in this way, and became so violent that the bargeman heard the noise. He went to the door of the room, and it was lucky for Saouk that he was speaking in Egyptian. If he had assailed Ben Omar in French, Tregomain would have discovered his abominable schemes, and learnt who the so-called Nazim really was, and treated that personage as he deserved.

But although this was not revealed to him, he was thoroughly surprised at the violence with which Ben Omar was treated by his clerk, and saw that the young captain's suspicions were fully justified.

Entering the minister's house, Captain Antifer, Zambuco and Juhel began to ascend a wooden staircase with the aid of the greasy rope hanging on the wall. Never would the bargeman, thin as he might have become, have been able to make his way up these dark, narrow stairs.

The visitors reached the landing on the third floor, the last on this side of the house. In front of them was a small door in a recess, on which was the name Tyrcomel. Antifer uttered a vigorous grunt of satisfaction, and knocked.

The reply was a long time coming. Was not the minister at home ? Why not ? A man to whom you are bringing a million or so—

A second knock, rather louder than the first.

This time there was a slight noise in the interior of the room. It was not the door that opened, but a little hole just above the name.

Through this hole appeared a head, that of the minister.

" What do you want ? " asked the minister, in a tone that showed he was not over-pleased at being disturbed.

" We wish to speak to you for a few minutes," said Juhel.

" What about ? "

" A matter of important business."

" I have no business—important or otherwise."

" Ah ! " exclaimed Antifer, annoyed at so much delay. " Is he going to let us in ? "

But as soon as the minister heard him speak in French, he answered as if it were his native tongue.

" Are you Frenchmen, then ? "

" Frenchmen," replied Juhel.

And imagining that it might facilitate their introduction into the minister's room, he added, " Frenchmen, who heard your sermon yesterday."

" And who think of becoming converts to my teaching ? " asked the minister.

" Perhaps."

" On the contrary," said Antifer, " he must be converted to ours, unless he chooses to give up his share—"

The door was opened, and the three visitors found themselves in the minister's presence.

It was one room, lighted at the end by the window looking out over the ravine. In one corner was an iron bedstead, with a straw mattress and a counterpane ; in another corner was a table with a few toilet utensils. There was a bench for a seat. There was a cupboard in which the minister kept his clothes. On a shelf were a

T

few books and writing materials. There were no curtains, and the walls were bare. There was a table with a reading lamp, the shade of which was very low. It was a bedroom and a study, in which there was nothing that was not strictly necessary.

The minister, who was all in black except his collar and tie, did not ask his visitors to sit down, as he had but one seat to offer them. In truth, if ever millions would be welcome anywhere, it ought to be in this cell, the whole contents of which were not worth thirty shillings.

Captain Antifer and Zambuco looked at one another. How were they to open fire? As soon as their co-legatee began to speak French, Juhel's intervention was unnecessary, and he became merely a spectator. He preferred to be so, and it was not without a certain feeling of curiosity that he awaited the encounter. Who would be the conqueror?

At the outset Captain Antifer felt more embarrassed than he ever expected to be. After what he knew of this revolutionary minister, of his opinions regarding this world's goods, he judged it advisable to proceed with caution, to feel his way, to break the news gently, so as to persuade the minister to hand over the letter of Kamylk Pasha, which ought to be in his possession, and which there could be no doubt contained the figures of the new and —let us hope—the last latitude.

But Antifer had no chance of beginning. While his three visitors were forming a group in the back of the room, the minister placed himself in front of them in the attitude of a preacher.

Persuaded that these men had come of their own free will to accept his teaching, his only thought was to enlarge on his principles with as much eloquence as he could muster.

"My brethren," he said, clasping his hands in an outburst of gratitude, "I thank the Author of all things for not having refused me that gift of persuasion, which has enabled me to instil into your hearts that contempt of wealth—"

Imagine the faces of the two legatees at this exordium !

"By destroying the wealth you possess—" continued the minister,—

"Which we do not yet possess "—Antifer could not help saying.

"You will give an admirable example, which will be followed by all those whose minds are capable of rising above the materialities of life."

Antifer, by a sudden movement of his jaw, jerked the pebble from one side of his mouth to the other, while Zambuco whispered,—

"Are you not going to explain the object of our visit ? "

An affirmative sign was Antifer's reply, while he muttered to himself, "I must not let him give us his yesterday's sermon over again."

The minister, opening his arms as if to receive repentant sinners, said in a voice full of unction,—

"Your names, my brethren, in order that—"

"Our names, Mr. Tyrcomel," interrupted Captain Antifer, "are these. I am Pierre Servan Malo Antifer, retired coasting captain ; this is Juhel Antifer, my nephew, master mariner ; this is Mr. Zambuco, banker of Tunis."

The clergyman stepped to the table in order to write down these names.

"And doubtless you bring me your worldly wealth, thousands perhaps ? "

"Well, Mr. Tyrcomel we have come about millions, and when you have got your share you can destroy it as you please. But as far as we are concerned, that is another matter."

Antifer was off on the wrong tack. Juhel and Zambuco saw this at once by the change which took place in the minister's face. His forehead wrinkled, his eyes half turned, his arms, which he had opened wide, fell on his chest as if they were shutting the door of a safe.

"What, then, is all this about, gentlemen ? " he asked, stepping back.

"What is it all about?" asked Antifer. "Come, Juhel,

unroll the thing, for I should not be able to measure my words."

And Juhel " unrolled " the thing without reticence. He related all that he knew about Kamylk Pasha, the services rendered by his great-uncle Thomas Antifer, the obligations contracted with the banker Zambuco, the visit to St. Malo of Ben Omar, notary of Alexandria, the voyage to the Gulf of Oman, where lay island number one, followed by the voyage to Ma-Yumba Bay, where lay island number two, the discovery of the second document which sent the two co-legatees to a third legatee, who was no other than the reverend gentleman to whom he was speaking.

While Juhel spoke, the clergyman listened, without making a movement, without permitting his eyes to brighten or his muscles to twitch. A statue of marble or bronze could not have been more motionless. And when the young captain finished his story, and asked him if he had ever had any business with Kamylk Pasha, the minister simply replied,—

" No."

" But your father ? "

" Maybe."

" Maybe is not an answer," observed Juhel, calming his uncle, who was turning about as if he had been stung by a tarantula.

" It is the only answer I think it necessary to give," replied the minister, drily.

" Insist, Mr. Juhel, insist," said the banker.

" In every possible way, Mr. Zambuco," replied Juhel.

And addressing the minister, who evidently intended to maintain extreme reserve,—

" May I ask you one question," he said—" only one ? "

" Yes, and I can answer it or not as I please."

" Is it within your knowledge that your father was ever in Egypt ? "

" No."

" But if it was not Egypt, it might be Syria, or to be more precise, Aleppo ? "

It will not be forgotten that it was in this town that Kamylk Pasha had resided for some years before he returned to Cairo.

After a moment of hesitation, Mr. Tyrcomel admitted that his father had lived at Aleppo, where he had met Kamylk Pasha. There, no doubt, he had been of service to the Pasha, as had Thomas Antifer and Zambuco.

"I will now ask you," continued Juhel, "if your father received a letter from Kamylk Pasha?"

"Yes."

"A letter in which there was some mention of the position of an island in which treasure was buried?"

"Yes."

"And did not this letter contain the latitude of this island?"

"Yes."

"And did it not say that one day a certain Antifer and a certain Zambuco would come and see you on this subject?"

"Yes."

Every "yes" fell like a hammer stroke, louder and louder.

"Well," continued Juhel, "Captain Antifer and the banker Zambuco are in your presence, and if you will show them the Pasha's letter, they will have only to make a note of its contents, and be off to fulfil the intentions of the testator, of whom you and they are the three legatees."

As Juhel spoke, Captain Antifer struggled in vain to keep still. The minister paused before he replied.

"And when you have reached the place where the treasure is, what are your intentions?"

"To unearth it, of course!" said Antifer.

"And when you have unearthed it?"

"To divide it into three shares."

"And what are you going to do with your shares?'

"Whatever we please."

"That is it, gentlemen!" replied the minister, while his eyes glowed like fire. "You intend to take advantage of these riches to satisfy your instincts, your appetites, your passions. That is to say, to contribute towards the increase of the iniquities of the world!"

"Allow me—" interrupted Zambuco.

"No, I will not allow you; and I ask you this simple question: If this treasure falls into your hands, will you undertake to destroy it?"

"Each will do with his legacy as he judges best," said the banker, evasively.

Antifer exploded.

"That is not it, at all!" he shouted. "Do you know what this treasure is worth?"

"It makes no difference."

"It is worth four million pounds, and there is a third of that for you."

The minister shrugged his shoulders.

"Are you aware that you are not allowed to refuse us the information the testator requires you to give?"

"Really?"

"Do you know that you have no more right to leave four millions unproductive than to steal them?"

"That is not my opinion."

"Do you know that if you persist in your refusal," yelled Captain Antifer in a fury, "we shall not hesitate to bring you to justice—to denounce you as a fraudulent legatee, as a criminal."

"As a criminal!" repeated the minister, angry but cool. "Really, gentlemen, your audacity equals your absurdity. Do you imagine that I shall agree to spreading four millions over the earth to become the cause of four million sins the more? To stultify all my teachings, and give my congregation the chance of flinging four millions in my face!"

Juhel could not help admiring the preacher, while his uncle, wild with anger, was ready to spring on him.

"Yes or no!" hissed Antifer, clenching his fists and stepping forward—"yes or no, will you give us the Pasha's letter?"

" No."

Antifer foamed at the mouth.

" No ? "

"No."

" Ah. I will make you give it to us ! "

Juhel interposed. His uncle pushed him aside. Antifer would have strangled the minister, searched the rooms, ransacked the cupboard, and it would not take him long to do so. But he was stopped dead by this simple and peremptory reply,—

" It is useless for you to search for the letter."

" And why ? " asked Zambuco.

" Because I have not got it."

" What have you done with it ? "

" I have burnt it."

" He has put it in the fire ! " gasped Antifer. " The wretch ! A letter containing the secret of four millions— a secret never to be discovered now ! "

And it was only too true. Doubtless for fear of being tempted to make use of it—a use contrary to all his principles—the reverend gentleman had burnt the letter several years before.

" And now you can go ! " said he, showing his visitors the door.

Antifer was overwhelmed at the blow. The document destroyed ! The finding of the island impossible !

And so it was with Zambuco, who burst into tears, like a child deprived of his plaything.

Juhel had to help the two legatees out on to the stairs, then into the road ; and then sorrowfully they went back to the hotel.

CHAPTER XXIX.

SUCH emotions, disasters, anxieties, troubles, shocks, and alternations of hope and despair, were too much for Captain Antifer. Even the constitution of a coasting captain has its limits. And as soon as Juhel's much-harassed uncle reached the hotel he took to his bed. He was attacked by fever, a violent fever, with delirium, the consequences of which might be serious. What deceptive illusions haunted him! This campaign interrupted just at the moment when it promised to end successfully; the uselessness of further search; this enormous treasure of which they would never know the position; this third island lost in some unknown sea; the only document that could give its exact position destroyed, burnt, by this abominable minister; this latitude, which not even torture would make him disclose, and which he had voluntarily and criminally forgotten. Yes! It was to be feared that Artifer's much-troubled mind would be unable to resist this last blow, and the doctor called in in haste gave it as his opinion that there was every likelihood of the patient going mad.

Every care was taken of him. His friend Tregomain and his nephew Juhel would not leave him for a moment, and, if he recovered, would be entitled to his warmest gratitude.

As soon as he returned to the hotel, Juhel had informed Ben Omar, and through him Saouk learnt all about Mr. Tyrcomel's refusal. The fury of the false Nazim can be imagined. But this time there was no outward manifestation of his anger. He kept it to himself, hoping that the secret which Antifer could not discover might be discovered by himself, and utilized for his sole advantage. This was the object on which he concentrated his attention, and during that day and the subsequent days he was not seen at the hotel.

When the bargeman heard what had happened, he remarked,—

"I think the matter is buried at last."

"I think so too," said Juhel. "It seems impossible to get anything out of this obstinate fanatic."

"It is rather funny though, to take millions to a minister, and find him refuse them."

"Take millions!" exclaimed the young captain shaking his head.

"You do not believe in them, Juhel? You may be wrong!"

"How you have changed!"

"Since the finding of those diamonds. I do not say that the millions are on the third island, but they may be there. Unfortunately, if this clergyman will not listen to anything, we shall never know."

"Well, no, Mr. Tregomain, and in spite of the two diamonds at Ma-Yumba, nothing will prevent my thinking that the Pasha has a huge hoax in store for us."

"In that case your poor uncle will suffer! What we have to do now is to get him well. Let us hope his head will stand it. When we have set him on his feet again and he is strong enough to travel, he will, I think, agree to return to France, and resume his former quiet life."

"Ah!" said Juhel, "would we were only in the house in the Rue des Hautes-Salles?"

"And you near our little Enogate, my boy! By the way, did you think of writing to her?"

"I wrote this morning, and said I thought we might now talk of coming home."

A few days elapsed. The patient had become no worse. The fever had decreased, but the doctor was uneasy as to the mental state of his patient. Antifer, though his head was weak, was able to recognize Tregomain and Juhel, and his future brother-in-law. Brother-in-law? Between ourselves, if any lady was in danger of remaining single, was it not Talisma Zambuco, now on the confines of fifty, and waiting, not without impatience, for the appearance of her promised husband? No treasure, no husband, for one was the complement of the other.

From all which it resulted that neither the bargeman nor Juhel could leave the hotel. Antifer was always asking for them. Day and night he kept them in his room, listening to his complaints, his recriminations, and above all his menaces against the horrible minister. He spoke of nothing else than going to law with him. The judges would know how to make him speak. He could not keep silent when it meant keeping four millions out of circulation. He would be punished most severely, most terribly, might even be hanged, etc., etc.

From morning to night Antifer continued in this tone. Tregomain and Juhel took it in turns to be with him, except when some violent crisis required them both to be present. The patient would have got up, rushed out of his room, run away to the minister and blown out his brains, if the bargeman's strong hand had not kept him down.

Although he greatly desired to visit this superb city of Edinburgh, Tregomain had to give up the idea. Later on, when his friend was on the road to recovery, he would make up for it. He would visit the palace of Holyrood, the ancient residence of the Scottish kings. He would stroll along the Canongate to the Castle firmly planted on its rock, and see the little room in which the child came into the world who was to become James the Sixth of Scotland and James the First of England. He would make the ascent of Arthur's Seat, and enjoy the view from its summit.

Soon a rumour arose calculated to greatly increase Mr. Tyrcomel's already considerable popularity. It was reputed that the celebrated preacher had, in conformity with his expressed opinions, just refused a very large legacy. Perhaps the minister had himself started the rumour, which was so much to his advantage ; at any rate there was an immense crowd to hear his next sermon.

This time, for a very good reason, Captain Antifer and his companions were not present. But behind one of the columns in the nave, there might have been recognized a foreigner whom nobody knew, of from thirty to thirty-five years of age, with black hair and beard, hard featured, and of any but prepossessing appearance. Did he understand the language in which the minister spoke ? We cannot say that he did. Standing hidden in the shade, he watched the preacher narrowly. His gleaming eyes never lost sight of him for a moment.

The man remained in this attitude until the close of the sermon, and, when the last words were spoken, made his way through the crowd towards the minister. Did he intend to follow him from the church to his house in the Canongate ? It would seem like it, from the vigour with which he used his elbows on the steps of the porch.

That evening Mr. Tyrcomel did not return alone. A small crowd accompanied him. The mysterious man was one of them, but did not join in their expressions of enthusiasm. On reaching his house, the popular orator ascended some of the outer steps and addressed the crowd ; and then retired, without noticing that an intruder was at his heels. The crowd slowly dispersed, and when the minister mounted the narrow staircase leading to the third floor, the unknown followed him as stealthily as a cat.

The minister reached the landing, entered his room and shut the door.

The other stopped on the landing, cowered down in a dark corner, and waited.

And then what happened ?

Next morning the people in the house were surprised at not seeing the minister go out early as usual. They did not see him all the morning. Several visitors called and knocked at the door in vain.

This appeared so suspicious that in the afternoon one of the lodgers gave information to the police. The police came to the house, mounted the staircase, knocked at the door, and as they received no reply, broke it in, with that push from the shoulder peculiar to the officers of the force.

What a spectacle! Some one had evidently picked the lock of the door, entered the room, and ransacked it from top to bottom. The cupboard was open, and emptied of the few clothes it contained, which had been thrown on the ground. The table was upset. The lamp lay in a corner. Books and papers were scattered all over the floor; and near the bed, half-stripped, pinioned and gagged, was Mr. Tyrcomel.

The police quickly set him free. He was only just breathing. He had quite lost consciousness. Since when? He alone could say, if he recovered.

He was rubbed energetically. There was no need to take his clothes off, for he was almost naked; his shirt was torn from his back, his chest and shoulders were bare.

The policeman who began to rub him could not restrain an exclamation of surprise. On Mr. Tyrcomel's left shoulder some figures and a letter had been tattooed.

The tattoo marks were legible enough, brown in colour, on the minister's white skin. And this was the inscription—77° 19' N.

As may be supposed, this was the much-sought-for latitude! The minister's father, to prevent it being lost, had evidently had it tattooed on his son's shoulder when he was young, as if he had inscribed it in a note-book. A note-book might be lost, but not a shoulder. Thus it was that, although he had really burnt the letter of Kamylk Pasha addressed to his father, the minister possessed this inscription so strangely placed, an inscription he had never had the curiosity to read with the aid of a looking-glass.

But undoubtedly the rascal who had entered the room

while the minister was asleep had read it. The minister
had found him ransacking his cupboard and looking over
his papers. In vain had he struggled. After binding him
and gagging him, the scoundrel had fled, leaving him half
suffocated.

Such were the details given by Mr. Tyrcomel as soon
as a doctor, summoned in haste, had restored him to consciousness. He related all that had passed. In his
opinion the sole object of the assault was to wrest from
him the secret of the island of the millions he refused to
disclose.

The scoundrel, then, had found it out while struggling
with him. And with regard to this he spoke of the visit
he had received from two Frenchmen and a Maltese, come
to Edinburgh to interrogate him regarding the legacy of
Kamylk Pasha.

Here was a clue for the police, who began their inquiries
immediately. Two hours afterwards they discovered that
the foreigners in question were at Gibb's Royal Hotel.

And it was fortunate for Captain Antifer, Zambuco,
Tregomain, Juhel and Ben Omar that they could prove
an incontestable alibi. Antifer had not left his bed ;
Juhel and the bargeman had not left his room ;
Zambuco and the notary had not been away from the
hotel. And none of them answered to the description
given by the minister.

But there was Saouk.

Saouk was the man. He it was who had gone to get
the secret from Mr. Tyrcomel. And now, thanks to the
figures he had found on that gentleman's back, he was
master of the situation. He knew the longitude mentioned in the document found on the island in Ma-Yumba
Bay, and thus possessed the necessary elements for
determining the position of the new island.

Unfortunate Antifer ! It needed but this last blow to
drive him mad. In fact, after the description given in the
newspapers, Captain Antifer, Zambuco, Tregomain and
Juhel, had no doubt but that it was Nazim, this clerk of

Ben Omar with whom Mr. Tyrcomel had had to do; and when they learned that he had disappeaied, they took it for granted that he had seen the figures that had been tattooed, and that he had started for the new island, to take possession of the treasure.

The least astonished of the party was Juhel, whose suspicions with regard to Nazim we know, and next to him Tregomain, to whom the young captain had communicated his suspicions. The rage of Antifer and Zambuco was extreme, and it found a victim in the person of Ben Omar.

We need scarcely say that Ben Omar was more certain than anybody of the guilt of Saouk. And how could it be otherwise, knowing as he did his intentions, and that he was the sort of man who would recoil at nothing, not even at crime?

What a scene it was to which the notary had to submit! Juhel fetched him to the sick room. Ill as he might have been, Antifer was not the man to remain ill under such circumstances. If, as the doctor said, he was suffering from bilious fever, here was a splendid opportunity for him to relieve himself of his bile, and bring about his own recovery.

We really cannot describe the way in which the unfortunate notary was treated. He was told, to begin with, that the assault on the minister and the robbery—"Yes, you miserable Omar! the robbery"—was the woi k of Nazim. "What, is that the way you choose the clerks in your office?—Is this the sort of man you bring to assist you as an executor?—A nice sort of rascal, scoundrel, villain, to thrust upon us!" And now this wretch, this unscrupulous wretch, had fled with the position of island number three, and he would get hold of Kamylk Pasha's millions, and it would be impossible to lay hands on him!

"Ah! Saouk! Saouk!"

The name escaped the overwhelmed notary. All Juhel's suspicions were confirmed. Nazim was not Nazim. He was Saouk, the son of Mourad, disinherited by Kamylk for the benefit of the legatees.

"What !" exclaimed Juhel. "It was Saouk !"

Ben Omar would have recalled the name if he could. His face, his terror, his dejection showed only too clearly that Juhel was not mistaken.

"Saouk !" roared Antifer, jumping out of bed with a bound.

And with a tremendous kick he laid the notary flat on his back.

This kick, with the broadside of abuse that followed it, was a real relief to Captain Antifer, and when Ben Omar, with his shoulders up and his stomach in, tottered out of the room, he felt considerably better. One thing more completed the cure, and that was the news that appeared in one of the newspapers a day or two afterwards.

We know of what reporters and interviewers are capable. Of everything, it must be admitted. At this period they had begun to intervene in public and private affairs, with a vigour and audacity that had made them a new power in the world. One of them had been clever enough to obtain an interview with regard to the tattoo marks with which Mr. Tyrcomel's father had illustrated his son's left shoulder. He made a drawing of it, and this drawing appeared next day in a journal the circulation of which on that occasion was so phenomenal that in a short time the whole world knew of the famous latitude—17° 19′ N.

The public were not much the wiser, for before they could solve " the treasure problem " as it was called, they required the other element of the position namely, the longitude.

But Antifer had this longitude—and so had Saouk for that matter—and when Juhel brought him the newspaper in question, and he saw the drawing, he jumped out of bed, he put on his clothes—he was cured as never a patient had been cured before.

" Juhel, have you bought another atlas ? "

" Yes, uncle."

" The longitude of the third island is 15° 11′ E., is it not ? "

" Yes, uncle."

"The latitude tattooed on the minister's shoulder is 17° 19′ N., is it not?"

"Yes, uncle."

"Well, see where island number three ought to be."

Juhel took the atlas, opened up the map of the Arctic regions, applied the compasses, and remarked,—

"Spitzbergen, the southern end of the large island."

Spitzbergen? What, was it in this northern region that Kamylk had chosen an island for his millions? Was this the last island?

"Let us go," said Antifer, "this very day, if we can find a ship ready."

"Uncle!" exclaimed Juhel.

"We must not let this miserable Saouk get there before us."

"You are right, my friend," said the bargeman.

"Let us go!" repeated Antifer imperiously. And he added,—

"Go and tell that fool of a notary, for Kamylk Pasha wanted him to be present at the discovery of the treasure."

They had to bow to his will, supported as it was by the will of Zambuco.

"Well," said Juhel, "at any rate, it is lucky that this joker of a Pasha did not send us to the Antipodes."

CHAPTER XXX.

CAPTAIN ANTIFER and his four companions—including Ben Omar—had to go first to Bergen, one of the chief ports of Norway.

No sooner resolved upon than done. Nazim, otherwise Saouk, had a start of four or five days, and not an hour was to be lost. The noonday ball had not fallen at the Edinburgh Observatory when the tram deposited our five friends at Leith, where they hoped to find a steamer on the point of sailing for Bergen. The distance from Edinburgh to this port is only about four hundred miles. From there it would be easy to reach Hammerfest, the northernmost Norwegian port, by means of the steamer which, in the summer season, takes tourists to the North Cape.

From Bergen to Hammerfest is about eight hundred miles, and it is about six hundred miles from Hammerfest to the south end of Spitzbergen. For this last stage a vessel would have to be chartered fit for the voyage, but at this period of the year there is no bad weather in that part of the Arctic Ocean.

There remained the question of money. This third voyage would evidently be very costly, particularly that part of it north of Hammerfest. Tregomain's funds had begun to run low, after so much expenditure since leaving St. Malo. Fortunately the banker's signature was as good as gold. There are people so favoured by fortune that they can dip their hands into any money-chest in Europe. Zambuco was one of these. He placed his credit at the disposal of his co-legatee. The brothers-in law could adjust their accounts afterwards. Tl e treasure, and in default of the treasure, the diamond, of the one would yield more than enough to pay what the other had advanced.

Before leaving Edinburgh, the banker had visited the Bank of Scotland, where he was cordially received. Thus laden, our travellers could go to the end of the world, and who knows if they would not have to go there if things went on as they had been doing?

At Leith, situated a mile and a half from Edinburgh, on the Firth of Forth, there are always a number of vessels. If there was one outward bound for the coast of Norway? There was one. This time fortune seemed to favour Antifer.

Though the said ship was not to start that day, she was due out next day. She was a trading steamer, the *Viking*. Here was a delay of thirty-six hours for Juhel's uncle to fret about. He would not even allow Juhel and Tregomain to take a stroll through Edinburgh—much to the disgust of the bargeman, notwithstanding the interest he had begun to take in the millions of the Pasha.

On the 7th of July the *Viking* left the docks, and two days afterwards sighted the heights of Norway, arriving at Bergen about three in the afternoon.

We need scarcely say that before leaving Edinburgh Juhel had bought a sextant, a chronometer, and a nautical almanac, to replace those lost in the *Portalegre*.

If they could have chartered a vessel at Leith direct for Spitzbergen they would have saved time, but the opportunity did not present itself. Antifer's impatience, however, was not tried over-much. The steamer for the North Cape was expected next day; but the few hours seemed as long to him as they did to Zambuco. Neither of them would hear of leaving their hotel. Besides, it rained, for it seems that it generally rains at Bergen, which occupies a sort of basin surrounded by mountains.

This did not prevent the bargeman and Juhel from taking a run through the town. Captain Antifer, quite recovered from his fever, did not insist on their remaining with him. But all that was worth seeing they had seen when in the early morning the steamer came into the harbour. At ten o'clock she was off with her cargo of tourists, anxious to see the midnight sun on the horizon of the North Cape.

This was a phenomenon of supreme indifference to Captain Antifer and Zambuco, and especially so to Ben Omar, who was in his usual state of collapse in his bunk.

What most annoyed Antifer was the steamer's continual stoppages to satisfy the curiosity of the tourists.

The thought that Saouk was several days in front of him kept him in a state of irritation that was anything but agreeable to his travelling companions. The remonstrances of Tregomain and Juhel were of no avail, and the captain of the steamer threatened to put him ashore if he persisted in making himself a nuisance to those on board.

Whether he liked it or not, Antifer had to put in at Drontheim, the old city of Saint Olaf, which is not as large as Bergen, but more interesting. We need not be surprised at Antifer and Zambuco refusing to go ashore. Tregomain and Juhel, however, took advantage of the delay to explore the town. If the eyes of the tourists were to a certain extent satisfied, their feet were not. The streets might as well be paved with broken bottles, so pointed are the stones.

"Cobblers ought to make fortunes in this country," said the bargeman, judiciously trying in vain to save his soles from damage The only acceptable pavement the two friends could find was under the arches of the cathedral, where the kings, after being crowned at Stockholm as Kings of Sweden, come to be crowned as Kings of Norway.

After conscientiously visiting the Cathedral, and the vast cemetery that surrounds it, after following the banks of the wide Nid whose waters, increased or decreased by the flood or ebb, flow through the town between long stockades of wood that serve as quays, after sampling the odours of the fish market, and visiting the vegetable market, almost entirely supplied from England, after venturing across the Nid to the suburb round an old citadel, Tregomain and Juhel returned on board quite tired out. A letter addressed to Enogate, containing a pleasant postscript in the heavy handwriting of the bargeman, was that evening put in the post for St. Malo.

Next m rning at daybreak the steamer left, with a few new passengers, and resumed her voyage to high latitudes. There were more stoppages, more delays—much to the disgust of Antifer. In crossing the Arctic Circle, represented by a thread stretched across the deck, he refused to jump over it, though Tregomain good-humouredly complied with the tradition. At last, in advancing northward, the steamer avoided the famous Maelstrom, whose roaring waters turn in a gigantic whirlpool. Then the Loffoden Islands, so much frequented by the Norwegian fishermen, appeared to the west, and on the 17th anchor was dropped in the port of Tromsö.

To say that during the voyage it had rained sixteen hours out of the twenty-four would be only just, according to the figures. But the verb " to rain " is quite insufficient to give an idea of such deluges. Anyhow, these cataracts were not displeasing to our travellers. They showed that the temperature was relatively high ; and what was to be feared by men bound for the seventy-seventh parallel was the prevalence of the Arctic cold, which would have rendered very difficult, and even impossible, the approaches to Spitzbergen. This period of the year, July, is late for navigation in these parts. The sea might suddenly close in at a change of wind ; and if Antifer were detained at Hammerfest until the early ice had drifted south, would it not be dangerous for him to venture further north in a fishing-boat ?

The thought of this made Juhel anxious.

" And if the sea does close in ? " asked Tregomain.

" My uncle will have to winter at the North Cape, and wait for next season ! "

" Well, my boy, we must not abandon the millions."

The old mariner of the Rance no longer growled. And why not? He could not get those diamonds found in Ma-Yumba Bay out of his head.

But having been roasted under the sun of Loango, was he to be frozen among the glaciers of Spitzbergen? Confound that Pasha! What possessed him to bury his treasure in such extraordinary places!

The steamer stayed but a few hours at Tromsö, where the passengers could for the first time make acquaintance with the natives of Lapland; and on the morning of the 21st of July she entered the narrow fiord of Hammerfest.

There Antifer and his party landed. Next day she would take the tourists on to the North Cape. Little did Antifer care for the North Cape. There was no North Cape worth comparing, as far as he was concerned, with island number three, somewhere in Spitzbergen. But as there happened to be a North Pole Hotel at Hammerfest, it was to the North Pole that he went.

As soon as they had engaged their rooms, they went out, in their anxiety not to lose a moment, to endeavour to charter a boat to take them to Spitzbergen. They walked towards the harbour, which is fed by the limpid waters of a lovely river bordered with stockades, on which were built houses and warehouses, the whole pervaded by the odours from the neighbouring fish-drying establishments.

Hammerfest is above all things the town of fish and every fishing product. The dogs eat it, the cattle eat it, the sheep and goats eat it, and the hundreds of boats which work in these wonderful regions bring more fish than can be eaten. A curious town is Hammerfest, rainy as it may be, lighted by the long summer days, darkened by the long winter nights, and often illuminated by sheaves of the aurora borealis of inexpressible magnificence.

At the entrance of the harbour Captain Antifer and his companions stopped at the foot of a granite column with a bronze capital bearing the arms of Norway, and surmounted by a terrestrial globe. This column was erected by Oscar the First, and is commemorative of the measurement of the meridian between Hammerfest and the mouths of the Danube. From this point our travellers directed their steps towards the stockades, at the foot of which were moored the vessels of all rigs and every tonnage employed in the major and minor fisheries of the Polar Sea.

But you may ask, how were they to make themselves understood? Did any of the party understand Norwegian? No, but Juhel understood English, and, with the aid of that cosmopolitan language, there was every chance of his making himself intelligible in Scandinavia.

In fact, before the day was over, they had on moderate terms chartered a fishing-boat, the *Kroon*, of about a hundred tons, commanded by Captain Olaf, and manned by a crew of eleven. This would take the passengers to Spitzbergen, wait there for them during their search, load up with any merchandise they might find, and bring them back to Hammerfest.

This was fortunate for Antifer. It seemed that everything was going in his favour. Juhel inquired if a foreigner had been seen at Hammerfest a few days before, if anybody had embarked for Spitzbergen—and received replies in the negative to both questions. It seemed that Saouk —"Oh! you miserable Omar!"—had not got in front of them, or that he had gone to island number three by a different route.

The rest of the day was spent in walking about the town. Antifer and Zambuco being persuaded to do so on this occasion, as they were so near their goal. When they retired to rest at eleven o'clock it was still day, and the twilight did not end before the dawn appeared.

At eight o'clock in the morning the *Kroon* was off northwards before a good south-easterly breeze. As there were some six hundred miles to traverse, she would be about five days on the voyage, if the weather continued favourable. There was no fear of their having to meet with ice drifting southwards, nor of their finding Spitzbergen surrounded by pack-ice. The temperature remained at normal, and the prevailing winds rendered a sudden cold blast unlikely. The sky, dappled with clouds, which occasionally dissolved in rain, not snow, had nothing disquieting in its appearance. Now and then the cloud broke, and the sun's rays shot through the rifts. Juhel had every reason to hope that the radiant disk would be visible when it became necessary to use the sextant for fixing the position of the third island.

Evidently their good fortune continued, and there was nothing to lead them to think that after bringing his legatees to the uttermost part of Europe, Kamylk Pasha would send them once more several thousand leagues away.

The *Kroon* went splendidly, the wind never failing her. Captain Olaf averred that he had never made a better passage. At four o'clock in the morning of the 26th of July, high land was reported to the northward, above a horizon quite clear of ice. This was Spitzbergen, which Olaf knew well, from having frequently fished in these regions.

Twenty years ago, Spitzbergen was not often visited by tourists, but nowadays it is gradually being embraced in their round. The time is not far distant when return tickets will be issued for the Norwegian possession, as they are now for the North Cape, and may eventually be for the Pole of the same name.

As far as was then known, Spitzbergen was an archipelago extending to the eightieth parallel. It is composed of three islands, Spitzbergen, properly so called, the South East Island and the North East Island. Does it belong to Europe or America? A question of purely scientific interest which we need not stop to answer. One thing is certain, that it is chiefly Englishmen, Danes and Russians who send their ships there for the whale and seal fisheries. It mattered little to the legatees of Kamylk Pasha to whom these islands belonged once they had safely removed from them the millions earned by their courage and tenacity.

Spitzbergen, as the name indicates, is a land of pointed rocks, difficult of access. The islands were discovered by the Englishman Willughby, in 1553, and their name was given them by the Dutchmen Barents and Cornelius. Not only does the archipelago consist of three principal islands, but these are surrounded by numerous islets.

After marking on the chart the longitude 15° 11' east, and the latitude 77° 19' north, Juhel gave Captain Olaf orders to make for the South East Island, the most southerly of the archipelago.

The *Kroon* scudded rapidly before a following wind and the four or five miles which separated them from the islands were accomplished in less than an hour.

The *Kroon* dropped anchor two cables off an islet which had a high abrupt promontory rising from its end.

It was then a quarter past twelve. Antifer, Zambuco, Ben Omar, Tregomain, and Juhel embarked in the boat and rowed towards the shore.

An immense number of gulls, guillemots, and other polar birds flew off with deafening cries. A herd of seals rapidly shuffled off, not without protesting with mournful wailings against the intrusion.

The treasure was evidently carefully guarded.

Antifer leapt ashore, and took possession. What curious good fortune after so many failures. He had not even to search amid the masses of rock ! He had landed on the very spot where the Egyptian had buried his millions.

The island was deserted, as need hardly be said. There was not a human creature on it. And there was not a ship in sight save the *Kroon*. Nothing but the immensity of the Arctic Sea.

Antifer and Zambuco could hardly restrain themselves, and even the fishy eyes of the notary lighted up. Tregomain, more excited than he had ever been before, his back rounded, his legs far apart, was hardly recognizable. And after all, why should he not be happy at his friend's happiness ?

And what added to their joy was that there was no mark of a footprint on the ground. Assuredly no one had recently landed there. The ground, softened by the rains,

would have retained any footprint. There was no doubt,
then, with regard to Saouk.   Mourad's terrible son had
not preceded the legitimate owners of the treasure.   Either
he had been stopped on the way, or he had met with
delays which would render his search useless if he arrived
after Captain Antifer.

When good fortune takes you by the hand, the best
thing is to be led as she wishes you to be.   Antifer was
brought before a rock, rising like one of the landmarks
set up by Arctic explorers.

"Here !   Here !" he exclaimed, in a voice choked with
emotion.

They ran up.   They looked.

On the outer face of this rock appeared the monogram
of Kamylk Pasha, the double K, so deeply incised that
the rigours of a polar climate had not worn away its lines.

All remained silent at first, as if they had arrived before
the tomb of some hero.   And then they set to work.
This time pick and mattock rapidly made the chips fly at
the foot of the rock.   At every blow, they expected the
tools would ring on the metal hoops of a barrel, or stick
into a stave.

Suddenly Antifer's pickaxe grated against something.

"At last!" he shouted, removing the piece of rock
which covered the hole in which the treasure lay.

But to this cry of joy succeeded a cry of despair, a cry
so loud that it might have been heard for half a mile
around.

In the hole was a box, a metal box, marked with the
double K, a box just like those that had been found in the
Gulf of Oman and in Ma-Yumba Bay.

"Again !" groaned the bargeman, lifting his arms on
high.

That was the word!   Yes—again ! and again it
would undoubtedly be necessary to go in search of another
island !

Antifer, in a furious passion, seized his pickaxe and
dealt the box such a violent blow that it flew into splinters.

From it escaped a parchment, spotted, stained, dilapidated—the damage due to the infiltration of rain and snow.

This time there was not even a diamond for Tyrcomel, who had not been subject to expenses like his co-legatees. That was fortunate. A diamond for him! Why, he would have reduced it to vapour!

But to our parchment. To pick it up, to unfold it carefully—for it might easily have torn—was what Juhel did, for he alone retained his coolness.

Antifer shaking his fist at the sky, Zambuco bowing his head, Ben Omar collapsing, Tregomain all eyes and ears, all were as silent as the grave.

The parchment consisted of one sheet, of which the upper part had not suffered from the damp. On this sheet several of the lines were still legible.

Juhel read them, almost without interruption, and this is how they ran :—

"There are three men to whom I am under an obligation, and to whom I wish to leave a token of my gratitude. If I have placed these three documents on three different islands, it is that these three men, made acquainted with each other during their voyages, might be united in an indissoluble bond of friendship. If they have had a certain amount of trouble and fatigue in arriving at the possession of this fortune, they have not experienced as much as I have in keeping it for them. These three men are the Frenchman Antifer, the Maltese Zambuco, the Scotsman Tyrcomel. In their default, if death has removed them from this world, their natural heirs will enjoy the same right to my legacy. In the presence, then, of the notary, Ben Omar, whom I have appointed my executor, this box having been opened and notice having been taken of this document, *which is the last*, the co-legatees can proceed to the fourth island, where the three casks, containing the gold and precious stones have been buried by my own hands—"

Notwithstanding the disappointment they felt at finding another voyage necessary, Antifer and the others could not help a sigh of relief. At least the fourth island was to be the last. But where was it ?

"To find this island," continued Juhel, "all that is necessary is to bring—"

Unfortunately the lower part of the parchment had rotted away. The sentences were illegible ; most of the words had disappeared.

The young captain tried in vain to decipher them.

" Island—situated—geometrical law—"

" Go on, go on ! " said Antifer. But Juhel could not go on. There were only a few doubtful words which he sought in vain to connect together. As to the figures of the latitude and longitude there was not left a trace.

Juhel began again,—

"Situated—geometrical law—" At last he made out another word, " Pole."

" Pole ? " he exclaimed, " what, is it at the North Pole ? "

" Unless it is at the South Pole ! " muttered the bargeman, in despair.

Evidently here was the expected hoax. The Pole, now, the Pole ! Had ever a human being set foot on the Pole ?

Antifer jumped at his nephew, snatched from him the document, tried to read it, stumbled over the few words that were only barely legible—

Nothing, nothing to give him any indication of the whereabouts of the fourth island. He would have to give up all hopes of discovering it.

And when he saw that the search was at an end, he was struck as if by lightning, and fell rigid on the ground.

CHAPTER XXXI.

On the 12th of August, the house in the Rue des Hautes Salles, at St. Malo, was in a state of rejoicing. There was a wedding that morning, and the happy couple had left about ten o'clock for the mairie and the church, amid a numerous gathering of friends and acquaintances.

Juhel had married neither a princess, nor a duchess, nor a baroness. Enogate had neither married a prince, nor a duke, nor a baron. For want of the millions their uncle's wishes had not been realized ; and we have every reason to think that they did not regret it.

Two other personages were radiant with joy : Nanon, who felt sure of her daughter's happiness, and Gildas Tregomain, in a lovely new coat and trousers, and a silk hat, and white gloves, who was acting as best man.

Quite so. But how about Captain Antifer ?

An hour after the discovery of the document on island number three, which ended in such disappointment and despair, the passengers of the *Kroon* had returned on board, Antifer being carried in the arms of the sailors, who had been called up to help. So shattered had he been by the blow, that he spoke not a word.

The return voyage was accomplished as quickly as possible by sea and land. The *Kroon* took her passengers to Hammerfest, the steamer from the North Cape landed them at Bergen. The railway from Drontheim to Christiania not then being opened, they had to travel by road to the Norwegian capital. A steamer took them to Copenhagen, and thence the railways of Denmark, Germany,

Holland, Belgium and France brought them to Paris, and so home to St. Malo.

At Paris, Antifer and Zambuco bade each other farewell. Both were dissatisfied. Talisma Zambuco would probably remain single for the rest of her life ; it was written above that it was not Antifer who was to save her from this undesirable position, against which she had struggled for so many years. It need scarcely be said that all the moneys advanced to Antifer for the expenses of the voyage were repaid to Zambuco, and they amounted to a good round sum. But the sale of the diamond realized enough for there to be a balance left, and Antifer had no cause of regret on this head. Ben Omar paid his own expenses, and departed for Alexandria by the shortest way, declaring that he would never again venture on a treasure-hunt.

The next morning, Antifer, and Tregomain, and Juhel returned to St. Malo. And what a welcome they had ! Nanon and Enogate had nothing but affectionate consolations for their brother, uncle, cousin, and friend. And then it was that Captain Antifer, finding it impossible to endow his niece and nephew with millions, gave his consent to their marriage. But he took no part in it, and would not even leave his room. In vain did Tregomain try to persuade him to be present at the wedding.

" You really ought to be there."

" Indeed ! "

" The young people do not like your being away. I beg—"

" And I beg that you will leave me in peace."

And so the young people were married. They stayed at home only to leave it occasionally to visit the best of men, their friend Tregomain. There they often talked about Antifer, and their sorrow at seeing him so irritated and cast down. He never went out ; he saw nobody. No more walks for him on the ramparts, no more saunters along the quays, pipe in mouth. It was said that he was ashamed to show himself after such a failure, and there was a good deal of truth in this.

"I am afraid his health will give way," said Enogate, the tears coming into her eyes when she spoke of her uncle.

"And so am I," said Nanon, "and every day I pray that Heaven may grant that my brother may recover from his disappointment."

"That horrid Pasha!" exclaimed Juhel. "What did he want to throw his millions at us for?"

"Particularly millions we could not find!" said Tregomain. "But yet they are somewhere, if we could only have made out that document to the end."

One day the bargeman said to Juhel,—

"Do you know what I think, my boy?"

"What do you think?"

"That your uncle would have been less upset if he had learnt where the treasure was, even if he could not have put his hand on it."

"Perhaps you are right, Tregomain. What makes him angry is, that he had in his hand the document indicating the position of island number four, and yet was unable to decipher the last lines."

"There would have been no mistake about it this time," replied Tregomain. "The document was explicit on that point."

"Uncle has got it; he has it always under his eyes; he spends his time in reading it, over and over again."

"A waste of time, my boy, a waste of time. We shall never find his Excellency's millions—never!"

A day or so after the wedding they learnt the news of what had happened to that rascal Saouk. The reason that he had not got to Spitzbergen before the others was that he had been arrested at Glasgow. The day of his attack on Tyrcomel he had started for Glasgow, where he hoped to find a vessel sailing for Drontheim or Bergen. Instead of starting from the east coast of Scotland, as Antifer had done, he would go from the west. The distance was much the same, and he hoped to reach the island before the legatees.

Unfortunately for him, he had to wait at Glasgow for a

week before a ship started, and fortunately for human
justice, he was recognized just as he was going on board.
He was immediately arrested, and being sent to prison,
was saved from a useless voyage to Spitzbergen.

The days rolled on. Juhel and Enogate would have
had nothing to mar their happiness had it not been for
the truly melancholy state of their uncle. On the other
hand, the young captain could not look forward without
sorrow to the time when he would have to leave his wife
and his friends. Le Baillif's three-master was nearly
finished building, and of her he was to be chief officer. It
was a splendid position for a man of his age. In six
months he would have to be at sea, on a voyage to
India.

Juhel often talked about these things with Enogate, who
was always sad at the thought of being separated from her
husband. But in seaport towns are not families accustomed to these separations? Enogate, not wishing to talk
about herself, preferred to look at the matter as affecting
only Captain Antifer. Would it not be a cause of regret to
his nephew to have to leave him in such a state, particularly as it was doubtful if he would find him alive when he
came back?

Juhel returned continually to the incomplete document,
to the almost illegible lines of the old parchment. Yes!
in these lines lay the beginning of a sentence which he
tried again and again to decipher.

"All that is necessary is to bring—"

Bring—what?

And then these words, "island—situated—law—
geometrical—pole—"

What geometrical law? What was there that brought
the three islands in connection? Had the Pasha chosen
them at haphazard? Was it a mere whim that had sent
the treasure-seekers successively to the Gulf of Oman,
Ma-Yumba Bay and Spitzbergen? If the rich Egyptian
had, as was reported, some knowledge of mathematics
had he been giving them some problem to solve?

As to the word " Pole," did it mean the extremities of the earth's axis ?   Certainly not.   But, then, what did it mean ?

Juhel racked his brain to obtain some answer to all this, but in vain.

" Pole, Pole "—he repeated to himself—" that is the key to the mystery."

Often would he talk about this to the bargeman, who approved of his endeavours, for he had no doubt as to the existence of the millions.

" But, my boy," he would say, " there is no need for you to make yourself ill in trying to find the solution."

" Well, Tregomain, it is not for my own sake, I assure you.   I do not care a fig for the treasure.   But my uncle—"

" Yes, for your uncle, Juhel.   It is hard lines, certainly. To have there under his eyes the document, and not be able to—but have you no clue ? "

" No, and yet there is the word ' geometrical ' in the sentence, and it would not be without some reason that it would be there , and then it says, ' All that is necessary is to bring '—what ? "

" That is it.   What ? "

" And there is that word ' Pole '—which I do not understand the sense of."

" Unfortunately I do not understand anything about it. I might help you if I did."

Two months went by.   There was no change with regard to Antifer, and none with regard to the solution of the problem.

One day—it was the 15th of October—before breakfast, Enogate and Juhel were in their room.   It was rather cold, and a good fire was blazing in the grate.

The young wife, with her hands in her husband's, was looking at him silently.   Seeing him so absorbed, she wished to give another turn to his thoughts.

" Juhel," said she, " you often wrote to me during this unfortunate voyage which has brought us so much trouble.

I read your letters over and over again and I kept them carefully—"

"They can only recall unpleasant remembrances now, my dearest."

"Yes—but yet I have kept them ; and I will always keep them. But these letters have not told me all that happened to you, and you have never told me all about it yourself. Will you tell me to-day ? "

"What good would that be ? "

"It would please me. I should like to be with you on the steamers, in the train, in the caravan—"

"My darling, we should have to have a map, so that I can show you our route from point to point."

"Well, here is a terrestrial globe. Will not that do as well? "

"Quite as well."

Enogate went and brought the globe, and set it on the table before the fire.

Juhel, seeing that it would please Enogate, sat down by her, turned the globe so as to bring Europe opposite to them, and pointed with his finger to the town of St. Malo.

"Let us start," he said.

And, to begin with, Juhel passed from France to Egypt, where Captain Antifer and his friends had stopped at Suez. Then his finger ran down the Red Sea and Indian Ocean, and stopped at Muscat.

"And so Muscat is there," said Enogate. "And island number one is close by."

"Yes, a little out in the Gulf."

Then, turning the globe, Juhel reached Tunis, where they met with the banker Zambuco. He traversed the Mediterranean, he stopped at Dakar, and he crossed the Equator, descended the African coast, and paused at Ma-Yumba Bay.

"That is island number two," said Enogate.

"Yes, wife."

Then he went north again, along Africa, and across

Europe to Edinburgh, where he had met Tyrcomel. Then his finger went further north until he reached the deserted rocks of Spitzbergen.

"That is island number three," said Enogate.

"Yes, island number three, where we had the greatest disappointment we met with during this stupid adventure."

Enogate said nothing, but kept her eyes fixed on the globe.

"Why did your Pasha choose these three islands, one after the other?"

"That is what we do not know, and what we shall probably never know."

"Never?"

"And yet these islands ought to be connected by some geometrical law, if we are to believe the last document. And then there is that word ' Pole' which bothers me."

As he spoke, Juhel seemed to fall into a kind of trance, as though his whole mind was concentrated on the solution of this obscure problem. And while he remained silent, Enogate amused herself by tracing with her finger the route he had travelled. Placing her finger on Muscat, she moved it along to Ma-Yumba, and then in the same curve ran up to Spitzbergen, and returned to the point of departure.

"That is a circle," she said, with a smile; "you have been travelling on a round."

"On a round?"

"Yes, a circumference, a circular voyage—"

"Circular!" exclaimed Juhel.

He jumped up, and took two or three turns across the room, repeating the word,—

"Circumference, circumference!"

Then he stepped towards the table, took the globe, ran his finger round it, and uttered a cry.

Enogate was frightened, and looked at him anxiously. Was he going mad, like his uncle? She looked, and trembled, the tears in her eyes.

Juhel uttered a second cry.

"I have found it! I have found it!"

"What?"

"Island number four."

Surely the young captain had gone out of his mind. Island number four? Impossible!

"Tregomain! Tregomain!" shouted Juhel, opening the window, and calling in his neighbour.

Then he returned to the globe.

A minute afterwards the bargeman was in the room, and Juhel greeted him with,—

"I have found it."

"What have you found, my boy?"

"I have found how these islands are geometrically connected, and the place that ought to be occupied by island number four."

"Can it be possible?" replied Tregomain. And looking at Juhel he wondered, like Enogate, if the young captain had gone mad.

"No," replied Juhel, who understood the look, "I have not gone out of my mind. Listen."

"I am listening."

"These three islands are situated on the circumference of the same circle. Join them, two and two, by straight lines, bring them together, as the document says, and raise a perpendicular from the middle of each line ; the perpendiculars will meet in the centre of the circle, and that is the central point, the 'Pole' where we shall find island number four."

A very simple problem of geometry, as we see, which Kamylk and Captain Zo had put into practice. The solution had not previously occurred to Juhel, because he had not noticed that the three islands occupied three points on the same circumference.

And it was Enogate's pretty finger which had traced this thrice blessed circumference, and solved the problem.

"It is not possible," said the bargeman.

"It is so. Look again, and convince yourself."

It did not take long to convince him. And the young captain ran to and fro, no longer able to restrain himself, and kissed the globe, and kissed Enogate's two cheeks, which were much fresher than the painted cardboard, and said,—

"She found it, Tregomain, she found it. Without her the idea would never have occurred to me."

And then Tregomain became attacked by a sort of *delirium jubilans*. He began to kick out his legs and round his arms with the grace of a sylphide of thirty stone, and rolling from port to starboard more than he had ever done on the *Charmante Amélie* between the banks of the Rance, or on the *Portalegre*, with her cargo of elephants, he roared out,—

> I have my lon-lon-la,
> I have my gi—lon gi,
> I have my lon, I have my gi—
> I have my longitude.

But at length he calmed down.

"We must tell uncle!" said Enogate.

"Tell him?" said Tregomain, a little surprised at the proposal—"is it wise for us to tell him?"

"That requires reflection!" replied Juhel.

They called Nanon. The old Breton was told how things stood in a few words, and when Juhel asked if they ought to tell her brother, she replied,—

"We ought not to hide anything from him."

"But if another disappointment awaits him," said Enogate, "he will not be able to bear it."

"A disappointment this time? Certainly not!"

"The last document said the treasure was buried on island number four," said Juhel, "and island number four is situated in the centre of the circle we have travelled. I am sure of it—"

"I will go and see my brother," said Nanon.

A moment afterwards Captain Antifer appeared in the room, his eyes haggard, his look gloomy, his brows knit.

"What is the matter?" he asked.

Juhel explained what had passed—how he had first discovered the geometrical line uniting the three islands and the reason why island number four must necessarily be in the centre of that circle.

To the surprise of everybody, Antifer took matters quite coolly. He seemed to have been waiting for the news, as though nothing was more natural than that he should hear it sooner or later.

" Where is this central point, Juhel ? " was all he asked.

Juhel placed the globe on the table. With a flexible rule in his hand he joined Muscat to Ma-Yumba, and Ma-Yumba to Spitzbergen. From the middle of each line he drew a perpendicular, and the perpendiculars crossed in the centre of the circle on which the islands were placed.

The centre was in the Mediterranean, between Sicily and Cape Bon, close to the island of Pantellaria.

" There it is ! " said Juhel, " there it is ! "

And carefully going over the position again, and noting the meridian and parallel, he said in a firm voice,—

" Thirty-seven degrees, twenty-six minutes north latitude, ten degrees, thirty-three minutes east longitude."

" But is there an island there ? " asked Tregomain.

"There ought to be," said Juhel.

"Is there one there ? That is it exactly, Tregomain," said Antifer, in a voice that made the windows rattle. "Exactly ! It wants but that ! "

And he rushed out, shut himself up in his own room, and did not appear again during the day.

CHAPTER XXXII.

WHAT did all this mean if Antifer had not gone mad? During the following days he resumed his walks on the ramparts and along the harbour, smoking his pipe and grinding away at his pebbles. He was no longer the same man. A sort of sardonic smile was stereotyped on his lips. He made no allusion to the treasure, nor to his travels, nor to the final expedition which would enable him to put his hands on the much-sought-for millions.

Tregomain and the others did not return to the subject. Every moment they expected Antifer to give them their marching orders, but he said not a word.

"What can it mean?" asked Nanon.

"A change has come over him," said Juhel.

"Perhaps he is afraid of having to marry Miss Zambuco!" suggested the bargeman. "But that does not matter. It will never do to leave all those millions there!"

If Antifer's opinions had changed, it was evident that Tregomain's had. He it was who was now seized with thirst for gold. And yet he was logical. When they did not know if they would find an island, they went in search of it; now that they knew where the island was, why should they not be off?

Tregomain was constantly talking to Juhel about it.

"What is the use?" asked the young captain.

He spoke about it to Nanon.

"Bah!" said she. "Leave the treasure where it is!"

He spoke to Enogate.

" Look here, my little one, there's more than a million to put in your pocket."

" Well, Mr. Tregomain, there is a kiss for you, and that is worth more."

At last he resolved to mention the matter to Antifer. And a fortnight after the last scene he did so.

" Ah ! There's that—er—that—er—island—er—"

" What island ? "

" That island in the Mediterranean. It exists, I suppose?"

" Exists ? I am more certain of its existence than I am of yours and mine."

" Then why do we not go there ? "

Antifer's reply was so oracular that Tregomain tried in vain to understand it. But he was not discouraged. After all, the millions were not for himself, but for the young people who were not thinking of the future. He would think of it for them !

And so he persisted, and one day Antifer said to him,—

" So it is you who want to go ? "

" Yes. I want to go."

" Your opinion is that we ought to go ? "

" We ought to go—and better to-day than to-morrow."

" Very well. Let us go."

But before starting it was necessary to come to some determination regarding Zambuco and Ben Omar. Their positions as co-legatee and executor required that they should be present at the discovery of island number four ; and they were invited to be at that island on a certain day, the one to take his share, the other to take his commission.

Antifer would have everything done in order. Two letters were sent—to Tunis and Alexandria—making an appointment for a meeting to take place on the 23rd of October at Girgenti in Sicily, the nearest town to the island. Tyrcomel's share could be sent to him in due course, and he could do what he liked with it—throw it into the Firth of Forth, perhaps, if he was afraid of its burning his fingers.

When the voyage was decided on, no one will be

astonished at Tregomain having to be one of the party. What is more surprising is that Enogate had also to go, Juhel had only been married two months, and he would not consent to leave his wife behind.

How long would this new exploration last? Not long. They had only to go and return. They had no fifth document to search for. It was certain that Kamylk Pasha had not added other links to the chain of islands, which was long enough already. No! the statement was definite, the treasure was under one of the rocks in island number four, and this island was mathematically placed between the coast of Sicily and the island of Pantellaria.

"Only it cannot be of much importance, for it is not marked on any of the maps!" said Juhel.

"Probably not!" replied Antifer, with a grin that would have done credit to Mephisto.

Really it was incomprehensible!

It was decided to go by the shortest road, which was the railway. There existed already an uninterrupted line of rails across France and Italy, from St. Malo to Naples. Expense was no object, considering the millions that were in view.

On the morning of the 16th of October, Nanon bade good-bye to the travellers, who started by the first train. At Paris, where they did not stop, they took the fast train to Lyons, crossed the Franco-Italian frontier, saw nothing of Milan, or Florence, or Rome, and reached Naples on the 20th of October. Tregomain was as confident of the result of this new expedition, as he was exhausted by a hundred hours of shaking in a railway-carriage.

Leaving the hotel in the morning, Captain Antifer and his companions took passage on a steamer sailing for Palermo, and after a fine day's crossing, landed in the Sicilian capital.

Do not imagine that there was any talk of visiting the local attractions. This time, not even Tregomain thought of bringing away a fugitive remembrance of this last voyage, nor of piously assisting at those Sicilian vespers he had heard of. As far as he was concerned, Palermo was not the famous city captured in turn by Normans, Frenchmen, Spaniards, Englishmen ; it was merely the point of departure of the public conveyances, which run twice a week to Corleone in nine hours, and from Corleone to Girgenti, also twice a week, in twelve hours.

It was at Girgenti that our travellers had business, and it was in this ancient Agrigentum, situated on the southern coast of the island, that they were to meet Zambuco and Ben Omar.

This means of locomotion might be subject to certain incidents or accidents. The post roads are not very safe. There are still brigands in Sicily ; there always are. They flourish there like olive-trees or aloes. But nevertheless the coach started next day, and the journey was accomplished without adventure. They reached Girgenti in the evening of the 24th of October, and if they had not reached their goal, they were at least very near it.

The banker and the notary were already there, one from Tunis, the other from Alexandria. O inextinguishable thirst for gold, of what art thou not capable ?

As they met, the co-legatees exchanged but these words :
" Sure of the island this time ? "
" Sure."

But in what a sarcastic tone was Antifer's reply, and what an ironical look he had in his eye !

To find a boat of some sort at Girgenti was not difficult. Fishing-boats there are many, and coasting vessels also— balancelles, tartanes, feluccas, speronares, and every other sort of Mediterranean rig.

Besides, all they wanted was a short excursion on the sea—a mere trip of forty miles or so to the westward. With a fair wind they could start that evening, and in the morning would be so near their island that they could land there before noon.

The boat was soon engaged. Her name was the *Providenza*. She was a felucca of about thirty tons, commanded by an old sea wolf, who in spite of his fifty years, still frequented these parts. And well he knew them. With his eyes shut he could take his ship from Sicily to Malta, and from Malta to the coast of Tunis.

"There is no need to tell him what our business is," said Tregomain, and Juhel thought it prudent not to do so.

The name of the captain of the felucca was Jacopo Grappa, and it was fortunate for the travellers that he knew enough French to understand it, and make himself understood.

And the travellers were fortunate in another respect. It was October; there were a thousand reasons for expecting bad weather, a heavy sea, a cloudy sky. But no! The cold was already perceptible, the air was dry, the breeze blew from the land, and when the *Providenza* set sail, a magnificent moon poured its rays on to the high Sicilian mountains.

Grappa's crew consisted but of five men, enough for handling the felucca. The light boat flew over the quiet sea, a sea so quiet that even Ben Omar suffered no disturbance. The night passed without incident, and the dawn announced a superb day.

Antifer's behaviour was astonishing. He walked about the deck, hands in pockets, pipe in mouth, affecting perfect indifference. Tregomain, in a great state of excitement, could hardly believe his eyes. The bargeman had taken up his position in the bow. Enogate and Juhel were side by side, Enogate enjoying the charm of the voyage. Ah! Why could she not follow her husband wherever the chances of his sailor's life would take him!

From time to time, Juhel would stroll up to the steersman to see that the *Providenza* was keeping on her course due west At the rate at which she appeared to be going he reckoned that she would be at the desired place about eleven o'clock. Then he would return to Enogate, a proceeding which once or twice brought him an admonition from Tregomain.

"Do not devote so much attention to your wife, Juhel; give a little to our business."

Notice that he said "our" business! Oh, how he had changed. But was it not in the interests of his young friends?

At ten o'clock there was no sign of land. And in fact in this part of the Mediterranean, between Sicily and Cape Bon, there is no island of importance except Pantellaria. But they were not seeking an island of importance, nothing but an islet, a simple little islet.

Grappa could not understand why the felucca was put on this course. Were his passengers bound for the coast of Tunis? But it did not matter to him. They had paid him well to go west, and he would go west as long as they asked him to.

"Are we to go west all the time?" he asked Juhel.

"Yes."

"Very well."

At a quarter past ten, Juhel, sextant in hand, took his first observation. He found that the felucca was in latitude 37° 30′ north, and longitude 10° 33′ east.

While he was at work, Antifer looked at him sideways, and winked.

"Well, Juhel?"

"We are in the right longitude, but we have to drop a few miles to the south."

"Then drop a few miles, nephew, drop! I fancy that we shall never drop enough!"

The felucca was put on the port tack, so as to approach Pantellaria.

Old Grappa, with his eyes screwed up and his lips pressed together, was lost in conjectures, and when Tregomain came near he could not help asking him, in a low voice, what they were looking for in these parts.

"A handkerchief we lost here!" replied the bargeman, as if he were getting out of temper—if so excellent a man could do so.

"Very well, signor!"

At a quarter to twelve there was still no mass of rocks in view; and yet the *Providenza* ought to be on the site of island number four.

Nothing, nothing, as far as the eye could reach.

Juhel went up the starboard shrouds of the masthead From there he could see for twelve or fifteen miles around him.

Nothing, always nothing.

When he returned to the deck, Zambuco, flanked by the notary, approached to him, and in an anxious voice asked,—

"Island number four?"

"It is not in sight."

"Are you sure of your position?" asked Antifer in a jeering tone.

"Sure."

"Then it would appear that you no longer know how to take an observation."

Juhel flushed with anger, but Enogate calmed him with a supplicating gesture.

Tregomain judged it wise to interfere.

"Grappa!" he said.

"Signor?"

"We are in search of an islet."

"Yes, signor."

"Is there an islet anywhere near here?"

"An islet?"

"Yes."

"Do you mean an island?"

"An island!" said Antifer, shrugging his shoulders. "Yes, an island! a pretty little island! an islet! an icky little isliekie of an islet! Do you not understand?"

"Excuse me, excellency; are you really looking for an island?"

"Yes," said Gildas Tregomain. "Does one exist?"

"No, signor."

"No?"

"No! But there used to be one, for I have seen it, and landed on its surface—"

"Its surface?" repeated the bargeman.

"But it has disappeared—"

"Disappeared ?" exclaimed Juhel.

"Yes, signor ; thirty-one years ago, come San Lucia."

"And what was this island ?" asked Tregomain, clasping his hands.

"Why," said Antifer, " it was Graham's Island."

Graham's Island ! What a revelation to Juhel !

Yes ! It was Julia Island, or Graham's Island, or Hotham's Island, or Ferdinandea, or Nerita—whichever name you please—which had appeared on this spot on the 28th of June, 1831. What doubt could there be as to its existence ? The Neapolitan Captain Corrao had been present at the very moment of the submarine eruption which had produced it. Prince Pignatelli had observed the column which burnt in the centre of the new-born island with a continuous light as if it were a firework. Captain Ireton and Doctor John Davy had been witnesses of this marvellous phenomenon. During two months the island, covered with ashes and hot sand, could be walked over. It was part of the sea bed which plutonic forces had raised above the water level.

In the month of December, 1831, the rocky mass had sunk, the island had disappeared, and this portion of the sea had retained no trace of it.

During this lapse of time—so short—ill luck had led Kamylk Pasha and Captain Zo into this part of the Mediterranean. They sought an unknown islet, and they found one, which appeared in June and vanished in December. And now it was fifty fathoms down that the precious treasure lay. The millions which Tyrcomel would have hurled into the sea, had gone down into the sea of themselves, and would never be spread over the world.

And Captain Antifer knew this. When Juhel, three weeks before, had given him the position of island number four, between Sicily and Pantellaria, he had at once recognized it as Graham's Island. When he was a youngster at sea, he had sailed in these parts, and knew all about the double phenomenon in 1831—the appearance and disappearance of an ephemeral island, now three hundred feet below the level of the waves. When he had satisfied himself of this, after a fit of anger the most terrible in his life, he had made up his mind to give up all hope of ever obtaining the treasure of Kamylk Pasha. And that is why he had not spoken of resuming the search. If he had consented, under Tregomain's insistence, if he had plunged into the expenses of another voyage, it was only for his own self-esteem, to show that he was not the greatest dupe in the matter. The appointment he had made with Zambuco and Ben Omar was to give them the lesson which their duplicity towards him so well deserved.

Turning towards the Maltese banker and the Egyptian notary, he said,—

"Yes, the millions are there, under our feet, and if you want your share you have only to dive for them. Come Zambuco ; to the water, Ben Omar."

And if ever these two regretted their acceptance of Antifer's invitation, it was when he overwhelmed them with sarcasms, forgetting that he had been as keen as they were in the search for the treasure.

"And now for the eastward," said Antifer, "and for home."

"Where we will live so happily," said Juhel.

"Even without the millions of the Pasha !" said Enogate.

"We shall have to do without them !" added Tregomain, in a tone of comic resignation.

But meanwhile the young captain—out of curiosity—asked for a sounding to be taken.

Grappa obeyed, with a shake of the head, and when the line had run out to a little over three hundred feet, the lead struck a resisting mass.

That was Graham's Island. That was island number four, lost at this depth.

At Juhel's orders, the felucca wore into the wind. The wind being ahead, she had to beat to windward all night, and the morning was well advanced when the *Providenza* moored alongside the quay at Girgenti, after this fruitless exploration.

But as the passengers were taking leave of old Grappa he said to Antifer,—

"Excellency?"

"What is it?"

"I have something to say."

"Speak, my friend, speak."

"Signor, all hope is not lost."

Antifer drew himself up, and it was as though a look of supreme covetousness illumined his glance.

"All hope?" he answered.

"Yes, excellency. The island disappeared towards the end of the year 1831, but—"

"But—"

"It has been rising ever since 1850—"

"Like the barometer, when fine weather is coming!" said Antifer, with a loud shout of laughter. "Unfortunately, when it appears with its millions—our millions!—we shall not be here, not even you, Tregomain, unless you die a centenarian many times over!"

"Which is hardly probable!" replied the bargeman.

But it is true, as the old sailor said. The island is gradually rising to the surface of the Mediterranean. And a few centuries later it may be possible to have quite another ending to these wonderful adventures of Captain Antifer.

THE END.